FRESH MEAT

DS JAMIE JOHANSSON BOOK 2

MORGAN GREENE

ALSO BY MORGAN GREENE

DS Jamie Johansson Prequels
Bare Skin
Fresh Meat
Idle Hands

The DS Johansson Prequel Trilogy Boxset

———

DI Jamie Johansson
Angel Maker
Rising Tide
Old Blood

Death Chorus
Quiet Wolf

FRESH MEAT

1

SHE SAT on a hard wooden chair, staring at the window. Her hands were across her stomach.

The air was cold and droplets of rain ran down the pane, a thin sheen of condensation clinging to the inside.

There was a knock at the door and she stiffened, her head twisting around, the skin around her eyes quivering as she stared at it.

Her throat constricted and she pulled the blanket tighter around her shoulders, feeling her heart beat against the inside of her ribcage.

After a few seconds, the knock came again.

Soft.

The chair squeaked as she rose and shuffled forward, conscious of her creaking footsteps on the boards under the ratty carpet.

She didn't dare call out.

Creeping up on the frame, she lifted her eye to the peephole, moving onto her toes to see, her shoulders like the points of a coat hanger under the thick woollen cloak.

She sighed and sagged backwards, exhaling, her pale hand reaching for the tarnished handle.

With her other, she pulled back the bolt and dragged the chain from the latch, pulling it open just a few inches at first.

She looked the visitor up and down and then stepped back, widening the gap just enough for them to squeeze through.

She glanced down the corridor to make sure they were alone, and then turned back to the shabby apartment.

It was a studio buried in the bowels of the city with a kitchenette that had peeling countertops, browned tiles, and a tap that dripped when it wasn't supposed to.

There was a single bed and a lonely wooden chair tucked under a tiny desk sticking out from the wall. But otherwise, the apartment was stark and depressing.

Her eyes drifted back to it, and she started forward, her feet throbbing. 'I'm surprised you're here,' she said quietly, 'but it's good to—'

She cut off, stumbling, a strange feeling of coldness running up her spine.

She blinked, tasted copper in her mouth, and then stepped sideways.

Her ears were roaring.

Pain lanced through her chest and she looked down, seeing blood on the carpet, her breath caught in her throat.

She smeared it backwards with her heels and felt a bolt of pain shoot down her left arm, curling her fingers into claws.

She dragged in a sharp, choked inhale and then let out a strange, mewling cry.

A sound like someone was tearing paper echoed around her and her vision strobed black.

She convulsed, hunching over, watching blood pour and run down over her stomach, pattering on the carpet.

It looked black in the light of the weak bulb overhead.

'I…' she began to say, feeling her jaw lock up and ache.

A deep twist of nausea exploded in her guts and she watched her thin knees begin to buckle.

The blood kept pouring, her vision closing to a pinhole.

Her heart hummed in her chest.

Distantly, she heard the door open behind her.

Footsteps faded away.

She sank to the floor, clutching her weak body, and then sagged onto her side, curling into a ball.

She felt her own blood warm against her cheek and then closed her eyes.

Her heart slowed, thudded softly in her ears for a moment.

And then stopped.

2

'NICE MORNING,' the postman said ironically, screwing up his face, his red coat pulled up over his head, still pinned around his shoulders. It made him look like a kite.

He'd detached the hood, and then been caught out by it.

'Mm,' Jamie said, trying to smile.

It was cold and had been raining for three days non-stop. Why the postman had decided that a frigid and wet Tuesday in January was the right time to ditch his hood and opt for shorts, she didn't know. But she had no intention of asking, either.

'You know you don't have to come out to meet me,' he said brightly, standing on the step. 'I could just put it in the box.' He laughed, not knowing what he was talking about. 'Unless there's another reason.' He arched a bushy eyebrow, his lined face expressing a mixture of emotions Jamie couldn't quite put her finger on. Something like pride, maybe.

'Uh,' she said, wishing he'd just hand the mail over and leave.

He lifted a wrinkled left hand and rolled a wedding band around his finger with his thumb. The nail was yellowed. 'I'm married, I'm afraid, darling.'

He wasn't her type for about a hundred reasons. 'Just my luck,' she said instead and offered her hand for the mail.

Between his exposed, bandy legs and the strands of white hair growing out of the end of his nose, she didn't think she'd ever been less disappointed in her life to find out someone was unavailable.

And that he was probably almost twice her age was just another reason to add to the already long list.

He grinned at her and handed over the letters, bound with an orange rubber band.

Jamie immediately pulled it off and began shuffling through them, stopping abruptly when the colourful card she was waiting for appeared on top.

She set her jaw and stared at it.

'Must be someone special,' the postman remarked lightly, lingering longer than he needed to.

Jamie stared at the postcard which displayed Christ the Redeemer behind a bold scrawl in neon pink that said, 'Greetings from Rio!'

She willed her hand not to close around it like a vice.

'What's that, third one this month?' he added.

Jamie looked up, fire in her eyes.

The mailman paled a little, forced a weak smile, and then took one step backwards, stumbling as he hit the pavement. 'Sorry, it's none of my business.' He held his hands up. 'Have a lovely day.'

Jamie's throat had all but closed up. She wanted to tell him that it was nothing, and not to worry about it, but she couldn't. It was like his hands were around her neck. Not the postman's.

His.

Elliot's.

She put the stack of letters under her arm and let herself back into her building, her ultra-light trail boots – kevlar capped – squeaking on the wooden stairs as she headed for her apartment.

It was a little before eight and she'd already been to and come back from the gym, showered, dressed, and headed down to wait for the mail. Despite drying her hair and plaiting it half an hour before, the rain had glued the few loose strands that had escaped the braid to her forehead.

She scraped them back with her free hand, kicked the door closed behind her, leaving a wet boot mark on the white paint, and then headed for her bedroom.

She could feel her pulse in her temple, her knuckles aching from the early workout. Cake, her trainer and probably closest friend, had told her to slow down.

She hadn't listened and now they were red and raw.

Though she could barely feel them just then.

Jamie reached out for her wardrobe door and slid it aside, the huge mirrored panel sliding smoothly on the runners. She'd spent a long time choosing the right company to install them. She never wanted to worry about them again, and she always appreciated how well put together they were whenever she opened them. But this morning, she didn't even think about it.

Her arm moved out in front of her and swept her clothes to the side – mostly shirts, long sleeve base-layers, and jumpers. She didn't go out for dresses much.

The metal hooks scraped along the rail, exposing what was behind.

Jamie swallowed and stared at it, her fingers moving automatically for the pull cord she'd installed.

She tugged on it and a lamp she'd screwed to the ceiling of her wardrobe came to life, throwing a harsh white light on the giant world map that took up the entirety of the rear panel.

The first pin she'd put in it was at Dover. The next was at Calais and a line of red yarn stretched between them.

Underneath the Calais pin was a photograph of a postcard she'd received, dated just four days after he'd escaped in late November. It had a picture of the white cliffs of Dover on it, the caption reading, 'The view is better from this side!' On the back he had simply written:

Jamie

I wish I could have been the one to tell you. Things could have been
different.
I'm sorry –
Elliot

Nine days after that, she'd received one with a medieval castle on the front, saying, 'Welcome to Luxembourg'. That one had said how beautiful the town was, and that Grace was safe and well.

That Jamie shouldn't worry about her.

The next came from Lichtenstein. Then Venice. From there, he'd caught a ferry to Croatia by the looks of it.

There were pictures of each pinned to the map.

The postcard he'd sent from Split said that he and Grace were doing well and that she felt bad about lying to Jamie, though he was sure she would forgive her.

Jamie didn't know if she could.

From the first one she'd received, she'd gone straight to Henley Smith, the DCI in charge of her department. Handed them over – after taking photos for her own board – and he'd passed them along to Interpol.

Five days after the Croatian card arrived – two weeks before Christmas – Smith had called her into the office to inform her that an Interpol agent had been found dead about ten miles outside the city, his throat opened with expert precision. A clean cut with a small blade, directly across the jugular.

A scalpel, they thought.

The agent had two children. Two children that would spend Christmas without their dad.

Jamie's blood had run cold.

Smith had said that the body had been dumped out of a car on the side of the road by the looks of it. That Elliot wanted it to be found.

'We have to catch this son of a bitch,' Smith had said gruffly, leaning on his elbows, the dark skin of his forearms showing through the strained cuffs of his shirt. 'And it seems he wants to keep in touch with you.' Smith sighed. 'So if you get another one of these things, you bring it to me. Immediately. Got it?'

Jamie nodded slowly. 'Got it.'

But she didn't.

That day when she'd got home, she found another postcard. This one from the tiny Greek island of Symni. She'd turned it over with shaking fingers. The words on the back had read:

Jamie,
I didn't want to do that, but you forced my hand. He was a good man,
but you left me no choice. I can be of more help to you than harm.
Ryan Cunningham. A life for a life.

The name meant nothing to her, but she knew Elliot did nothing without thinking about it first. She'd told Smith about the cards and a man had ended up dead. *A life for a life.*

Jamie hadn't slept that night. Thinking about it. Thinking about him.

She looked into Ryan Cunningham the day after. He'd been arrested for a few things – drunk and disorderly behaviour, assault, aggravated assault, and inciting hate speech. A real charmer.

His sheet had been quiet for a year or so now so Jamie did nothing.

Two days after that, he walked into a Mosque in South London and tried to stab someone. He was tackled to the ground before that could happen, but Jamie still understood the gravity of what was going on.

She got the next card the week before Christmas from Tripoli, Libya. It simply said, *Merry Christmas. I'm working on your gift.*

The follow up came on Christmas Eve from Casablanca. It said, *Act quickly. Leslie Bowman.*

Jamie didn't hesitate this time.

Leslie Bowman was sixty-two years old. He'd been imprisoned

twice, once for assaulting a minor, and the second time for possession of child pornography. He was released in early November from his second incarceration.

It didn't take her long to find the connection.

There was a park a street away from the house that he had inherited from his mother. She'd died while he was in prison.

He was living there alone.

Two days earlier, an eleven-year-old girl had gone missing from that park.

Jamie had thought about going to Smith about it.

And then she'd rung the anonymous tip line that the Met maintained, saying she'd walked past a house a few minutes ago and thought she heard a child screaming for help.

Jamie parked her car nearly a kilometre away and walked over in a hoodie, the hood up, and stood at the corner of the street as the police cars roared in.

If it was anyone else, they would have needed a warrant – it would have taken days. But Bowman was a repeat offender and any judge would have granted an emergency warrant in a heartbeat.

In less than four minutes a rapid response officer carried the girl out in his arms, her bloodied wrists clasped around his neck.

She had been tied up in there.

Jamie had felt her fists tighten at her sides.

A life for a life.

Was this really the deal she was agreeing to? Let a murderer walk free to save the lives of others? Where did she stand on this morally, let alone professionally? Could she tell Smith? What would he say? No. She couldn't. Not now. Not after she'd acted on it. It was too late. And she couldn't tell Roper either. Sure, he was sober now and she trusted him with her life. But this? This was something else. This was a Detective Sergeant in the London Metropolitan Police who was in contact with a wanted serial killer, intentionally obfuscating it from her superiors. Any way she spun it, she'd have her warrant card taken the instant she opened her mouth.

But the postcards kept coming.

And she kept lying to Smith about them.

To everyone.

How Elliot knew these things, she couldn't say. But he did.

Another tip came in a week later. This one was the name of a known drug dealer who was living out of a hostel.

Jamie looked into it.

Two girls who had been travelling in the city had stayed there over Christmas and had both reported being robbed. Both stories were the same – they'd lost time, woke up in the morning with their belongings gone.

One had submitted to a rape test.

It came back positive.

The other declined.

Jamie nearly crushed the mouse in her hand.

Another call to the tip line let two officers search his room.

They arrested him for possession of ecstasy, GHB, and Rohypnol.

His DNA was matched to the sample collected from one of the girls.

Jamie hated this.

It wasn't how things were supposed to go. But it was effective.

Just after New Year's, she got another postcard, this one from Fortaleza in Brazil. It said, *I've been keeping up. You're doing well. But we're not done yet. We make a good team, don't you think?*

She was staring at that postcard now, pinned to the eastern tip of Brazil, a red line of yarn stretching from to the western tip of Africa. It was crumpled and spread flat again from when she'd balled it in her fist after reading his words.

She couldn't help herself that time.

Jamie had committed to not handing them to Smith. She wasn't about to have anyone else die on her account.

She'd hunt them down herself.

Elliot and Grace never stayed in the same place for more than a week. He was smart. He was careful. And he was obviously well connected.

He must have amassed a lot of contacts in London during his time as an illicit organ trafficker. And now he was calling in his chits.

It would never be a big fish. Jamie knew that. He wouldn't betray the ones he'd worked with. The ones running things. But a rapist here, a paedophile there… Those were the kind of scum that even criminals wanted to see pay. And that's what was happening. He was getting a name from whoever had their ear to the ground in the sleazy, torrid underworld that he was still jacked into, and then feeding it back to her.

And Jamie couldn't help but feel a little better with them off the street.

Until now.

She stood in front of the map staring at the postcard in her hand. Christ the Redeemer was facing the floor as she read the back, her free hand stopped halfway to the little pouch of pins hanging from the corner of the map.

It read:

Jamie,
I don't know more than this, but I trust your mind. Figure it out.
Jane Doe, Chinese, early 20s.

Jamie froze at the last word, her teeth digging into her tongue. She swallowed hard, rereading it.

Pregnant.

3

ROPER ARRIVED to pick her up for work fifteen minutes later.

Jamie and he had started carpooling.

She knew better than anyone that routine was one of the most important things for someone who was battling for sobriety. Dropping her off every night meant that a supportive face was the last thing he saw before going home. It also meant that if he'd had a shitty day they could talk about it. Talk about how he was going to go home and not think about it. Not drink about it.

And picking her up in the morning meant accountability. If he showed up with booze on his breath, she'd know. That feeling of responsibility, the sense that hiding things wasn't possible, and shouldn't be attempted. These were all things that Roper needed to stay on the straight and narrow.

She'd suggested he take up exercise as a way to fight the craving.

Instead, he'd upped his nicotine and caffeine intake.

If he wasn't smoking, he was chewing gum. And at any one time he had a coffee cup in his hand and at least six patches spread between his forearms.

Addicts had to turn it up to eleven. It was compulsion.

His beaten up Volvo saloon sidled around the corner, sagging on its wheels like a boat. The fan belt squeaked as it pulled up to the curb, the rain running in thick streams over the rusted paintwork.

Jamie came forward and opened the door, a mist of cold smoke billowing into the frigid air.

'Get in,' Roper said quickly. 'The seat's getting soaked.'

Jamie stood there in her raincoat, feeling the drops of rain pinging off the hood. It was made by the same brand that produced her shoes. She never would have paid what it cost retail, but she went through three pairs of boots last year alone – the first she wore through, the second got doused in human excrement when she and Roper had looked into a satchel full of pills that got caught in a sewer grating that let out into the Thames, and the third were soaked in Simon 'Sippy' Paxton's blood.

As a loyal customer, they'd offered her the coat for half price.

She couldn't say no.

Jamie stood stoically, watching the air clear in the car. 'If you wanted me to get straight in you should have cracked the window,' she said flatly. She wasn't in the mood today.

'It's pissing down,' Roper protested. 'I'm not going to drive around with the bloody windows open.'

'You know,' Jamie said airily, looking up over the car and pulling the door wider so Roper's awkward grab and lunge across the centre console came up short. 'They say the air in Beijing is so bad that it's the equivalent of smoking ten a day.'

Roper flopped across the passenger seat and swore as rain dripped off the roof and down the back of his neck. 'Bloody hell,' he said, pushing himself back upright. 'Will you just get in? It's not bloody China!'

'No, it's worse.' She fanned the door for a few seconds and when she felt Roper was right on the edge of putting the car in first and planting his foot, she slid in and closed the door, smirking to herself.

He was fragile, sure, but not above taking some well-deserved shit.

The wet seat was a small price to pay.

He'd been torturing her for years turning up hungover, skipping out on paperwork, generally being lacklustre at his job. Now that he'd stopped drinking, he'd definitely improved. But she wasn't letting him get off lightly. He had a lot of making up to do.

His finger drummed on the steering wheel and the wiper blades flapped madly, the ancient rubber doing little to move the torrent of rain splashing against the glass.

The world looked blurry outside.

'How are you?' Jamie asked. Loaded question.

'I'm…' Roper drifted off, pulling to a halt in front of a red light. 'I'm okay.' He sighed heavily. 'Same shit every day, you know?'

He looked at her wearily.

She nodded. 'I know. But that's all life is. Days. One after another.'

'Save it,' he said, not scornfully. 'I get enough of that crap at the meetings.'

Jamie nodded. 'Of course. Just know that I'm proud—'

'You watch anything good on TV last night?' He cut in before she could finish.

She pulled her hood back and let it sit for a few seconds. It was always good to let tension dispel. It was a Tuesday, which meant that he had a meeting the night before. Which meant he wasn't up for any of the self-help stuff this morning. She should have remembered. 'Not really,' Jamie said. She wasn't lying.

She'd fallen asleep reading a book on psychopaths and how to spot them.

Fool me once and all that.

'Me neither,' Roper grumbled. 'TV is shitty when you're sober.'

'Not that I've got anything to compare it to,' Jamie said, watching the city go by in a grey muddle. 'But I'm inclined to agree.' She didn't like TV much.

'Any news on the Raymond case?'

'Uh-uh,' she said, not looking around. Carl Raymond had been missing for three days. His mother was worried, but he was seventeen and the statement taken from the mother had said that he'd run away before and that he mixed with a crowd she didn't really like.

Kids from that part of the city went missing all the time. And it was the second time she'd reported Carl missing. The first time he'd come back after five days. His mum had come home to find him rummaging in the fridge for food, stoned out of his mind.

She'd already found out that two of his friends were also 'missing'. Though the parents of those kids didn't seem concerned at all. They were probably crashing with friends, and the other kids she'd spoken to had told her where to shove her warrant card, called her and Roper pigs, and used the word *blood* excessively. Some people just didn't want to be helped.

It was a slow month. January usually was.

Until this morning.

Until the postcard. Jamie couldn't get it out of her head.

'Jamie?'

'Huh?' Jamie turned to look at him.

'You hear what I said?'

'About the Raymond case?'

'No, about coffee.'

'What?'

'You want a coffee?'

She looked around and realised they were at a drive-through window. She'd completely zoned out, her mind tracing Elliot's route through Europe, Africa, and now South America. She cleared her throat. 'Sure.'

Roper wound down the window and stuck his head out. 'Two large coffees. One with skimmed milk.'

The kid in an apron raised his eyebrow. 'Is that grande or vente?'

Roper sighed. 'It's two larges, one with skimmed milk. One black.'

The kid rolled his eyes and turned around, cupping a hand to his pimpled mouth. 'Two grande Americanos, one with skinny.' He turned back, his straightened hair sticking out from under the brim of his peaked cap at an odd angle. 'Eight-eighty.'

'Jesus,' Roper practically scoffed, turning to Jamie. 'I think coffee is more expensive when you're sober, too.'

'I think you just care more.'

Roper flashed his card on the machine hanging off the counter and drove on to the next window. 'That's a distinct possibility. But four-forty for a coffee is still ridiculous. It's just beans and water.'

She didn't have the energy or focus to debate the rising cost of coffee farming with him. She was thinking about the girl on the postcard. Jane Doe. Chinese. Pregnant.

The other names had been perpetrators.

If she was a Jane Doe that meant she was a victim.

And that she was dead.

Jamie kept her hands around the coffee all the way to the station, letting the warmth seep into her fingers.

Elliot said that he trusted her mind.

The question was, did she?

Jamie swiped herself into headquarters with her coffee still warm and full in her hand, and stepped into the lift next to Roper.

'You feeling okay?' he asked.

She looked around absently, the image of Elliot sitting in front of a cafe in Rio with a coffee, reading the paper without a care in the world burning in her mind. 'Huh? Yeah, I'm fine, why?'

They stood there with the door open, Roper with a dumbfounded look on his face. 'I don't think I've ever seen you take the lift.' He narrowed his eyes and drained the last of his coffee. 'I'm okay, really, Jamie. You don't need to watch me.' He shook the empty cup. 'No Irish, I swear.'

Jamie smiled at him, snapping out of her head. 'You're right.' She clapped him on the back and stepped back into the foyer. 'Being stuck in a metal box with you doesn't sound so fun after all.'

She turned to see him raise his middle finger as the doors closed.

Exercising always cleared her mind. Maybe the stairs would give her some perspective.

When she landed on the fourth floor and stepped out, she took a sip of her now-cold coffee. A skin had formed on top and she sucked it into her mouth, then coughed, swallowing it reluctantly. 'Shit,' she muttered, dropping the whole thing into the trash. She needed to shake this off.

'Johansson,' Smith called out to her as he strode across the floor, the detectives and officers in his path parting like the red sea. 'Where are we on the Raymond case? His mother called again last night.'

'We're working on it,' she said diligently.

'You and Roper rehearse that?' he asked loudly, stopping six feet short of her, his voice carrying around the room. He wanted people to hear. 'Because he just gave me the same bullshit answer.'

She studied his face. He looked tired. She didn't know if he'd slept much. There were some high-profile cases going on – nothing she and Roper had a hand in – but DCI Smith was in charge of them all, and it didn't look like they were going too well.

'No, sir,' she said, standing straighter.

'Well, if you spent as much time doing actual police work as you did running lines, maybe you'd find him.'

That needed no answer, and giving one would probably only anger him further. He was hunting murderers – the last thing he needed was a hysterical mother clogging up his phone lines.

'She's coming in at ten.' Henley Smith checked his watch. 'That gives you fifty-six minutes to find something tangible. I want her off my back, Johansson.'

'Yes, sir.'

'Oh, and Johansson?' Smith said, turning his watch outwards towards her. 'You're four minutes late. Stop for coffee on your own time, not mine.' He sucked air through his teeth and then walked away, shoulders swinging.

In the background, Roper stuck out his bottom lip and shrugged.

Jamie sighed and screwed up her eyes. It was going to be a long day.

Leanne Raymond was sitting in front of her desk before ten to ten, and Jamie had little to tell her.

'We're working on it,' she said quietly. She could see Smith watching through the glass walls of his office.

'What does that even mean?' Leanne was a little over a year younger than her. Just thirty-two years old. She'd had Carl at fifteen.

Jamie wasn't even thinking about children – and she couldn't imagine having a seventeen-year-old son. Sometimes she still felt like a kid herself. Though Carl's friends didn't see her that way. She'd spent the first forty minutes at her desk calling all of the contact numbers she had on file, as well as the local places that Carl could have been. She'd got little out of the friends, and the bowling alley, corner shop, cinema, and youth centre all within half a mile of his address couldn't pick him out of the dozens of local kids that came through every day. All she'd ascertained so far was that on the day that Carl Raymond left home, his mother had found about a hundred pounds worth of cannabis under his bed and flushed it down the toilet. She'd come clean about it after the attending officer had found bits of it stuck to the toilet bowl and all over the floor, along with a sizeable ziplock bag dusted with cannabis pollen in the kitchen bin.

Carl had come in as she was doing it, they'd grappled. It had spilled. She couldn't hide it, but there was nothing to charge for – a few leaves and stems scattered on the floor? You could find that in most footwells of the cars rolling around the city.

The shit was prolific.

Leanne had said that he'd run out right after she flushed it.

But witness reports said otherwise.

The neighbours said they'd argued.

The neighbours said *madly*.

And then he'd left, after the screaming was done.

Jamie knew that anyone who was buying that much weed knew someone selling it in bulk, and going by the fact that Carl didn't have a job, and neither did his mother, she guessed that he hadn't paid upfront. Tick, they called it. So Carl was either hiding from the dealer until he scraped together the cash – likely story – or he was with the dealer, running deliveries for him to work off the debt.

His mother was afraid for his life.

Jamie knew that people didn't get stabbed for a hundred quid's worth of weed.

No, a dumb kid who owed a dealer was more valuable alive than anything else. And by the sounds of that dumb kid, he was the sort to not give a damn about making his mother sweat. By all accounts, he was a true-blue little shit. The school he'd attended until last year were happy to expound on that. In detail.

But saying, *you're son's fine. He's probably just working for or hiding from a drug dealer,* probably wasn't going to reassure her. And of course, none of his friends were going to give him or the dealer up. She just had to wait for him to come home, and ride this out until then. Wasting any more time on it was just going to take her focus away from the real case here.

The Jane Doe.

'It means,' Jamie said, sitting back, 'that you didn't tell the truth when the officers asked you what happened.'

Leanne shrank a little, eyes narrowing. She was scared and Jamie was getting her back up. 'What?'

'Look, Leanne,' Jamie said, resting on her forearms. 'Can I call you Leanne?'

'Miss Raymond,' Leanne said defensively.

Jamie forced a smile. 'Sorry. Miss Raymond – witnesses say you argued with your son before he ran out.'

'Who? What witnesses?' Leanne shook her head, scoffed. 'I bet it was that bitch next door, always effin' lyin' about me and my son!' She censored herself for Jamie's sake as though swearing was a crime.

Jamie restrained a smirk at that. She doubted Leanne had ever stopped herself from saying the word *fuck* all her life before that second. 'Regardless,' Jamie said calmly, meeting Leanne's eye. 'Your son was in possession of a Class B controlled substance – enough to charge him with intent to—'

'My son ain't no—' She was shaking her head furiously, her knuckles white around the top of her knock-off bag.

'But we're not talking about that – Miss Raymond? Listen to me. Witnesses say you argued loudly. Aggressively.'

'We never—'

'I know. But look – I can't get his friends to talk. I don't know where he is. I can't pull them in and interrogate them – they're all underage and we have no proof that they know anything at all. And without their parents' consent...' Jamie clasped her hands together. 'What I'm saying is – they didn't seem concerned. I think Carl is out there, *trying* to make you worried. Disappearing like this? It happens. If he's into smoking—'

'He's not.'

'If he *is* or *isn't* isn't of concern here. But with no signs of violence, no threats made against him, and the lack of concern of his circle of friends... This all points to a simple case of familial distress.'

'What's that supposed to mean?'

Jamie was trying to put it nicely. 'I'm sure he's fine and that you don't have anything to worry about.'

It could have gone one of two ways. And it went the second, worse way.

'Well, what fucking good are you?' She didn't censor herself this time, and instead rose out of the chair like a cobra. 'You drag me all the way down here to tell me you don't know shit about shit and that you're *sure* he's okay.' She lifted her arms to illustrate the sarcasm. Jamie got it anyway.

'Miss Raymond—' she started, unsure whether to draw attention to the fact that it was her who had made the appointment, not Jamie.

'No, don't you *Miss Raymond* me! My son is out there – alone, scared!' She was almost shouting now and people were looking around. 'And all you have to say is that you're *working on it.*' She scoffed. 'You'll be hearing from me.'

She shoved her index finger in Jamie's face, almost poking her eye out with a two-inch long acrylic nail, and then stormed away, her hooped earrings flapping like wings.

Jamie sighed, rubbed her eyes, and leaned back. Roper was hanging over the back of his chair, looking bored. 'Now what?' he asked, his voice low.

Around them, people began to go back to work.

Jamie made an indistinct noise and looked up, her eyes drifting to Smith through the glass of his office.

He was sat awkwardly in his chair, like he'd been carved from a gnarled piece of driftwood. He had one elbow on the arm of the thing, and his other hand flat on the desk.

The lines on his forehead looked like they'd been chiselled in.

Jamie looked back at Roper. 'Now we get out of here.'

Roper sat up in his chair, seemingly piqued. He was bored by his desk now that he didn't need it to rest his aching head-on. 'Where we going?'

'Coroner's office.'

'Which one?'

Jamie got up and pulled her coat off the back of her chair. 'I don't know.'

'You don't know?' Roper got up too. 'Then why are we going?'

'Do you trust me?' Jamie watched as Smith pushed back from his chair in his office and got up, his eyes locked on her.

'Of course.'

'Then run.'

4

SHE DIDN'T LIKE LYING to Smith, but it was getting easier.

As far as he knew, they were out chasing down Carl Raymond.

Except they weren't. They were sat in the car park of a Subway. Roper was sinking his teeth into a meatball sub with extra cheese like he'd not eaten in a week, and Jamie was moving lettuce around her salad bowl with a bendy fork, the thumb of her left hand moving down the list to the next number. She pressed it and waited for it to ring, switching it to speaker.

If they were in her car, she would have had bluetooth. But they weren't – and not having it was a small price to pay for not having Roper spill marinara all over her seats.

It rang twice, gave her silence for a few seconds, and then stuck them in a queue.

Jamie sighed and shovelled a pile of lettuce into her mouth.

'You gonna tell me what this is about?' Roper asked, spitting crumbs.

'I don't know myself, yet.'

'What aren't you telling me? You're ringing every coroner's office in the city – asking about Jane Does.' He coughed, wiped his lips with the back of his hand, and then swallowed a mouthful far too large to gulp down in one. 'And then asking about ethnicity? And telling Smith we're chasing down Raymond? Come on, I'm all for bunking off school, but what gives?'

Thankfully, the line connected. 'West London Coroner's Office,' the female voice said flatly.

'This is Detective Sergeant Jamie Johansson,' Jamie said. 'With the Metropolitan Police.'

There was silence for a second. 'Yeah?'

'I'm checking out to see whether you've had any Jane Does come in during the last few days.'

There was an emphatic groan from the other end. 'Let me check.'

Before Jamie could thank her she was put on hold.

Roper eyed his partner, chewing his toasted bread.

The woman came back. 'Three.'

'Three Jane Does?'

'Well, two. One's a John. All unidentified, though.'

'Great,' Jamie said, a rush of excitement filling her for a second. She hoped she wouldn't have to make any more calls.

'Not for them.'

'No,' Jamie said, looking at Roper who was almost choking on a meatball as he tried not to laugh. 'I suppose not. Can you describe them for me?'

'Describe them?'

'Yeah – age, ethnicity…'

'Right…' The woman didn't seem very obliging. 'Would it be quicker if you just told me what you were looking for?'

Jamie was reluctant to be forthcoming about anything. 'Just tell me, and I'll know.'

'Oh right,' the woman said airily. 'Cryptic but okay. Who am I to stand in the way of an investigation I suppose.'

Jamie was quiet. She wanted to be as unmemorable as possible, leave as little trail as she could until she knew what she was looking at.

'Let's see.' She tutted for a few seconds. 'One is approximately ninety years old – Caucasian – she was discovered in a park on a bench. Looks like natural causes. That who you're looking for?'

Roper arched an eyebrow.

'No,' Jamie said stiffly, feeling her pulse rise.

'Second one… Uh…' Papers flipped in the background. 'Came in three days ago. Twenties, east-Asian. '

'Was she pregnant?' Jamie asked quickly.

Roper stopped chewing and looked grave.

'Hmm,' the woman hummed, reading the notes. 'Yes,' she said without any hint of remorse. Jamie figured they got used to it. They all did. 'Second trimester.'

'Okay,' Jamie said quietly.

'That the one you're looking for?'

'Yes.' Jamie exhaled, staring into her anaemic-looking salad. 'I'd like to see the body.'

'A case has been filed. Officers already came by, collected the examiner's report. I can email a copy to you if you—'

'No, no,' Jamie insisted. 'That's okay. I'd like to see the body for myself. Can you prepare a paper copy of the report for me? We'll be there in twenty minutes.'

'Sure,' the woman sighed. 'Why not.'

Jamie hung up and clipped the lid back onto her salad bowl. She'd lost her appetite.

'Jesus, Jamie,' Roper said, barely above a whisper. He'd put his sandwich down. 'What are we getting into here?'

Jamie stared solemnly out of the window, watching the rain run down it in streaks. 'You said you trusted me, right?'

'I do,' he said tentatively.

'Can I tell you something? Can I trust you?'

'Jamie…'

'Promise me, Roper. Because once I say it, you're in it, and there's nothing that can be done.'

'What the hell is going on, Jamie?'

She exhaled. 'Promise me, Roper. Or drop me at my car. I won't blame you.'

'We're partners, Jamie. Friends, right? You've got to tell me what the hell's going on here.'

'It's Elliot,' she said quickly.

'Day?'

She nodded.

'Jesus. Did he contact you, or?'

'Yeah.' It felt good to say it out loud. 'Remember that postcard? From Croatia? The dead Interpol agent?'

'Of course.'

'It wasn't the last.'

'Shit.' Roper ran a hand through his thinning hair. 'Does Smith know? Of course not.' He answered his own question. 'Otherwise, we wouldn't be out here behind his back.'

'Don't do that. Don't say that.'

'Well, we are, aren't we?'

'This is a legitimate case, Roper.'

'So what the hell does Day have to do with a dead pregnant Asian girl?' He sounded as baffled as Jamie felt.

'He's been giving me... leads.' She shook her head, not sure how to say it.

'Leads?' Roper's voice was strained. 'What do you mean, leads?'

'Names. Of people.'

'What people, Jamie? You're not making sense here.'

'The first was a young guy... I didn't do anything, and then a few days later he walked into a Mosque and tried to stab someone.'

'Christ.'

'The second was an older guy, just got out of prison. A girl had gone missing near to where he was living... I called in an anonymous tip on his house, and...'

'And what, Jamie?'

'They found her in there.' Jamie's throat tightened. 'She was eleven, Roper. He had her, tied up in there, and Elliot knew.'

Roper let out a long exhale and filled the car with onions. 'That's some heavy shit, Jamie. But how did he know?'

She shook her head. 'The messages aren't exactly heavy on detail. A life for a life.'

'What's that?'

Jamie bounced her head against the headrest. 'A life for a life. He said he didn't want to kill that Interpol agent – that I forced him. And then the names started coming. I think... I think it's a trade, you know?'

'His freedom for leads.' Roper shook his head a little, incredulous. 'Son of a bitch. You play dumb with Smith, don't tell him you're getting the cards, and in exchange... He what, talks to his scumbag friends, gets the word on the street, and...?'

'I guess.' She looked down at her hands. 'I don't like it any more than you do – but these guys, Roper. The third one was a dealer set up in a hostel, feeding girls pills. Ecstasy... Then slipping them GHB.'

Roper stayed quiet.

'He raped two of them.' The words were bitter on her tongue. 'And now, because of him, that guy is back in prison. So...'

'So?'

'I don't know. Cosmic justice?'

'Doesn't feel very cosmic. Feels like he's buying his freedom. But there's one thing that doesn't make sense.'

'What's that?'

'Why he's sending them at all. You only know where he is because he's sending them. If he didn't, you wouldn't know so couldn't tell Smith. So why not just disappear?'

Jamie could feel her cheeks hot. 'It's me.'

Roper processed.

'He wants me to know he's out there. To know that he's thinking of me.' She felt a little sick at the thought. She felt sicker not saying that he wanted to remind her that they were alike – that they both saw the world through the same eyes. That was the truth that cut the deepest of all.

'You could always move.'

'I could. But then...'

'The cards. The names.' He nodded. 'They stop coming.'

'And I don't mind putting pieces of shit behind bars.' She swallowed. 'God knows we need all the help we can get. If I move, how many get away with it? And what about the person that moves in after me, huh? What happens when postcards start turning up? How long before they tell someone who tells someone and it gets back to the Met, huh? And then Smith will know that—'

'I think you're getting ahead of yourself here. It's a pretty small chance that—'

'I can't risk it,' Jamie said definitively. 'I'm in this now and that's it. I have to see this through. Wherever it leads. Whether Smith finds out now or in ten years, my career is over the second he does – and probably my life. A good barrister would argue this is aiding and abetting.'

'A better barrister could argue that it's not.'

'It doesn't matter. If I stop, then that's one guy who's getting away with something every time he sends a name. And now? This? I don't know – it's different. It's not a name. But this is something that someone's going to get away with if I do nothing. And I can't let that happen. I just *can't,* Roper. I'm sorry. I just can't, okay? I let Oliver get... And the others... And I didn't know. I didn't see. And I should have. I should have known. And he got away. And I can't...' She could feel her voice cracking as she trailed off, her nails digging into her palms hard enough to leave purple welts that wouldn't fade for hours.

'Then... shit.' Roper sighed loudly, crumpled the paper around his meatball sub and rolled it up, stuffing it into the cupholder in the centre console. He cranked the ignition and slotted the car into gear.

'What are you doing?'

'Well, your pregnant east-Asian Jane Doe isn't going to catch her own fucking killer is she?'

They pulled up outside the coroner's office, Roper's fan belt announcing their arrival before they'd even turned the corner.

It wasn't exactly the sort of *low profile* entrance she was hoping for.

Jamie had her coat on and pulled the hood up tight around her head before she got out. Roper was wearing the battered brown leather jacket he'd been in since winter began, and had to borrow Jamie's plastic salad container to hold over his head.

She rolled her eyes behind the Gore-Tex storm-guard hood as Roper balanced a box of lettuce on his head and ran for the door.

Jamie's hands were shaking in her pockets as she shouldered through the front door, hoping to hell that there wasn't going to be any other officers there. When she had something tangible, she wanted to be the one to tell Smith she wanted the case. Until then it was a suspension waiting to happen.

The interior was cool and smelled faintly of chlorine.

The tired brown linoleum on the floor was scuffed and marked, and the ceiling was made entirely of flame-retardant tiles separated by grey strips.

Jamie unzipped her jacket and pulled her warrant card out, leading with it towards the front desk.

A mid-forties woman sat behind it with curled hair, thin glasses, and a piece of gum between her left molars. Her jaw moved in circles as she chewed it.

'Detective Sergeant Jamie Johansson,' Jamie said, conscious that she'd be overheard despite the entrance hall being empty. 'I called a little while ago. This is my partner,' she added, nodding to Roper, who was still holding the lettuce.

'DS Paul Roper. Do you have a bin?'

The woman looked at him, then at the salad – which was dripping onto the floor – and then pointed to the corner of the room.

Roper headed there and Jamie stepped closer. 'We're here to see the Jane Doe.'

'Sure.' She nodded, reaching for the phone. 'I'll get one of the assistants to take you down.'

'Thank you. Did you manage to print that report for me?'

The woman pinned the phone to her shoulder and turned, grabbing a stack of papers off the printer behind her. 'Yeah,' she said into the phone. 'It's Cheryl' — she handed the papers to Jamie — 'can you come up here and escort two detectives down to storage for me?' She flashed Jamie a smile as she began leafing through the report. 'Yeah, now. They're here. Great. Thanks.' She put the phone down and clasped her ringed hands in front of her. 'Won't be a moment.'

'Thanks,' Jamie said, turning back to the waiting room. Roper was hovering behind her, hands in his pockets.

'Okay?' he asked.

She nodded, looking at the report. The body had been discovered by a neighbour on Sunday evening. Three days ago. Paramedics had been called, and they pronounced her dead at the scene. She arrived at the coroner's office just before ten PM, and an examination was carried out Monday morning.

Yesterday.

Jamie processed, drawing the timeline.

After it was done, two detectives arrived to speak to the coroner about his findings. They were pretty definitive.

She didn't recognise the names of the two detectives. DI Amherst and DS Brock. Maybe Roper would. He'd been around a lot longer than her and had brushed shoulders with most of the detectives in the Met, for better or worse.

There was little else in the report regarding the case – the coroner's findings were strictly to do with the body. She'd need to get the full details from Amherst and Brock when she knew what she was looking at.

'Anything interesting?' Roper asked, folding his arms now, his wet leather jacket groaning.

Jamie stuck out her bottom lip. 'It's not pretty.'

He proffered his hand and she gave him the papers. At the same time, the security door next to the desk buzzed open and a young guy – late twenties, with dark hair – stuck his head out and looked at Jamie and Roper. 'Are you two the detectives?'

Jamie glanced around at the empty room. 'Yeah.'

'Okay, you can come through.'

Roper nodded for her to take the lead and she did, following the kid down a halogen-lit hallway. His Crocs squeaked on the linoleum, scrubs and apron rustling, but he didn't say anything.

They passed examination rooms one through six and then stopped at another security door. The sign on the front said 'Morgue'.

The assistant pulled a magnetic key card up from his waist where it was clipped, and held it against the scanner. It buzzed and the lock disengaged.

He pushed through wordlessly and held it open for Jamie and Roper.

Inside was cold.

The same brown linoleum persisted throughout, but the smell of chlorine got stronger. Or maybe it was bleach. Or both. Something industrial-strength that stung the nostrils. Jamie didn't know that it mattered what it was exactly.

The room was sizeable and two steel tables stood in the middle of it, bolted to the ground. A metal gurney sat on the far side, and occupying the entirety of the left-hand wall was a bank of refrigerated lockers. The doors were square, about fifty centimetres across and high, with polished handles.

On the front of each was an upright plastic tray that held a clipboard. Jamie could see the names of the occupants written on each of them.

'Right,' the young assistant said suddenly, making both Roper and Jamie jolt.

Neither had been aware of the utter silence in there until then.

'Which one was it? The Asian Jane Doe, eh?' He grinned at them, the thin hairs on his chin bristling.

'That's right,' Jamie said, trying not to read too much into his enthusiasm.

'Great.' He clapped once and then began looking through the clipboards, clicking his tongue as he searched for her. 'I wonder what they call Jane Does in China,' he said absently. 'Probably something like—' He turned around, ready to make some sort of insensitive quip, but cut off when he saw the look on Roper and Jamie's faces. Neither were impressed.

He cleared his throat. 'Ah, here we are.' He pressed his lips into a line, pulled the handle, and opened the door.

A quiet hiss filled the silence and he reached in, pulling the drawer out, exposing the ghostly figure of a woman hidden beneath a white cloth.

'Here she is,' the assistant said almost nervously. He lifted his arms awkwardly and gestured to the woman like a novice magician would to a rabbit he'd just pulled out of a hat.

Jamie studied him for a second. He was strange. Though you'd have to be to want to work at a coroner's office, she thought. Maybe his name would pop up in her mailbox one day.

She shivered at the thought and looked at the shape beneath the cloth.

Roper read the situation and stepped up next to Jamie. 'The room,' he said flatly to the assistant.

'What?' he asked, not computing it.

'Give us the room.' Roper wasn't intimidating by any stretch, but over his career he'd perfected that authorial tone that gave no hint of waver. I'm a police officer. My word is law. Get the fuck out of this room, now. I'm not asking.

The assistant opened his mouth, no doubt to say that he didn't think he was supposed to leave them alone, but then reconsidered, nodded quickly, and squeaked out in his rubber Crocs. 'I'll be right outside,' he said quietly, taking a wide circle around the examination tables.

He buzzed himself out and the door clacked shut.

Jamie and Roper both exhaled and relaxed a little.

'Weirdo,' Roper muttered, turning towards the examination tables. There was a box of blue latex gloves sat on the end of one.

'Mm,' Jamie said, taking a chemical-laced breath. 'No one who works in a morgue should be that upbeat.'

Roper blew air through his nose. Almost a laugh. 'Here,' he said, handing her a pair.

They pulled them on, rubber smacking at their wrists, and both stared down at the figure.

Jamie clenched and unclenched her hand a few times, forcing blood back into it and then raised it towards the sheet.

She knew that the second she pulled it back that was it, there was no backing out of this. As soon as she saw her face, saw what was done to her, she was all in. She couldn't let it go after that.

Jamie glanced at Roper for reassurance, and he nodded.

She was glad he was there. That she wasn't facing this alone any more.

'Well,' she said, her voice barely above a whisper. 'Here we go.'

5

JAMIE THREW BACK the cover and the milky, naked skin of the woman beneath glowed in the harsh white light.

She had a Y incision running from the points of her collar bones down to her sternum, and then the entire length of her body, finishing at her pubic mound. She'd been closed up and sutured, but Jamie couldn't help but look at the exit wound in her chest, a deep near-black welt. Her eyes lingered there for a second, and then travelled down to her stomach, to the purple lines running across it. The stretch marks in her rippled, loose skin.

The foetus had been removed during the post mortem it seemed.

There was nothing they could do.

Jamie wasn't maternal in the slightest, but the thought hit her deep in her guts like someone had driven their heel into it. And it didn't go away.

They'd no doubt test it for DNA, though whether they'd find the father, she didn't know. No one had come forward to identify or claim the body, and there was nothing listed under next of kin.

God, he probably didn't even know.

She cleared her throat and cracked her neck. 'Cause of death?' she asked, her voice strained.

Roper exhaled and then swallowed, lifting the top page. Single gunshot wound to the upper back.

Jamie looked down at her, at the serenity in her still face. She could have only been nineteen or twenty. Though maybe younger even. She was as thin as a rake, and both pregnancy and the light bearing down on her were doing her skin no favours.

'From behind,' Jamie muttered, visualising it, closing her eyes. 'Where in the room was she?'

Roper shook his head. 'There's nothing else in here.'

'Murder weapon?'

He sighed. 'Small calibre pistol. Nine-millimetre. Point-blank. No bullet recovered though.'

'Mm. Single shot? Well-placed?'

'What do you mean?'

'Through the heart?'

'Uh,' Roper said, scanning the notes. 'Nicked the right ventricle, severing the aorta – caused massive internal haemorrhaging. But it wasn't a straight-on hit. Though it's hard to not hit something important from that range.'

'Still target.'

'What's that?'

'One shot, right between the shoulders, flat trajectory.'

'Yeah?'

'She didn't move, wasn't running. She turned her back to her killer, not knowing what was coming' Jamie narrowed her eyes at the girl in front of her. She looked serene, but tired. She had dark circles under her almond shaped eyes, her eyelids taped to her cheeks to keep them closed. Her skin was almost alabaster in the halogens. 'Any signs of forced entry?' She knew the answer before she asked.

'It's not in here,' Roper said.

'Of course.' Jamie pursed her lips, knowing she couldn't prolong it any longer. 'Can you help me here? I want to get a look at the entry wound.'

Roper grimaced. 'Sure.' He moved around the far side of the

drawer, curling the report into a tube and pushing it into his jeans pocket.

Jamie put her right hand under the shoulder of the girl and her left under her jutting hip bone. She couldn't believe how cold her skin was.

Jamie had examined two other bodies in her career so far, but never touched them. Usually, they were already her cases and she was in the examination room with the coroner. But there was nothing usual about this. In any sense.

'On three?' she asked, looking up.

Roper twisted his lips, his hands reaching across her, one just above Jamie's at the hip, and the other on her upper arm. 'Just lift her,' he said quickly, pulling upwards.

Jamie followed his lead and turned the girl onto her side.

Roper held her there as Jamie stooped to look at the hole. It was tiny. The size of the nail on her little finger.

It had clean, sharp edges. It looked neat almost, harmless in the white light.

It was hard to imagine that it had killed her.

Jamie studied it for a few seconds, trying to see in her mind how it would have gone.

'Any time today,' Roper grumbled, turning his head away.

Jamie traced the length of her spine, looking for anything else.

She examined her neck – no sign of bruising or anything else. She wasn't manhandled. Not beaten before she was killed. Not harmed other than the bullet wound.

Jamie checked the ends of her hair. Well kept. No split ends. Though it looked like it needed to be cut. The shape of the fringe told her it was probably a few centimetres longer than it should have been. Though that didn't really tell her anything

'Okay,' she said to Roper, who laid her back down carefully.

His lips were still curled into an odd 'S' shape.

Jamie tilted the girl's head back straight as lightly as she could and pressed her thumb to the pale top lip, lifting it up. With her other hand she cupped her chin and pulled it down.

The lips smacked gently as Jamie opened the girl's mouth.

'What are you doing?' Roper asked, barely above a whisper.

'Something my dad taught me,' Jamie said, just as quietly. It seemed wrong to talk normally.

'Of course.' Roper scoffed a little.

Jamie ignored it. It wasn't strictly something her father had *taught* her, but she remembered one of his old cases – the murder of a guy who'd turned up in a river to the north, tortured to death. Her father had told her about the teeth. *You can tell a lot from teeth,* he'd said. Primarily whether the person had access to first-world dental care. It had put them onto a new path and her father had ultimately caught the killers. The victim turned out to be Russian, and the murder was related to organised crime. She didn't know much more than that. But once they stopped looking for a Swedish guy, the whole thing opened up. And she'd always kept it in her head.

'Look,' Jamie said, moving her head out of the way so Roper could look.

'She's got teeth,' Roper said.

'You don't say. What do you notice about them?'

'That she's not seen a professional dentist in her life?' he said glibly.

'Exactly.'

'I'm not following.'

'When are you ever?'

He made a frustrated noise. 'What's your point?'

'Children in the UK have access to free dental care – fill-ins, braces… Most adults keep up with a dentist, too.'

Roper raised an eyebrow.

'She's got at least two cavities – one black fill-in. Looks metal.' Jamie let go of her chin and it stayed where it was. After a second, she pushed it closed with her index finger and cleared her throat. 'Her teeth are white though – bleached by the looks of her gums.'

'Meaning?' Roper folded his arms, then unfolded them, looked at the hands he'd just put on his jacket, and then sniffed one. He grimaced and kept them at his sides.

'She wanted them to look good, despite not really taking care of them.'

'Meaning?' Roper said more emphatically this time.

Jamie sighed. 'I don't know.'

'Great.'

She ignored him and moved down the girl's body now. Despite being pregnant, she kept herself in good order. Her muscles were reasonably well defined – she wasn't overweight, but she also wasn't muscular. Just lean. She wanted her body to look good, too.

And it did. She did, in her entirety. The longer Jamie stared at her, the more she realised how beautiful the girl was.

She shook it off and kept going.

Her body was completely unmarked and clean. She was well-kempt, too. Her underarms were shaven, her legs too. The only thing that wasn't free of hair was her pubic mound. Though Jamie could see it had been until recently. There was perhaps three weeks growth? Four or five maybe? Did they give her any sort timeline for anything? She didn't know.

'Huh,' Jamie said aloud, pausing.

'What is it.'

She reached for the girl's left hand and turned it out to face Roper. 'Ever seen anything like this before?'

Roper leaned in and squinted. He did the same at menus and his computer screen. She wondered if he needed glasses but was just too proud or stupid to admit it.

On the inside of the girl's wrist, about an inch above her hand, was a tattoo.

It looked like a badly drawn dragon. Like a thick spiral with legs sticking out and a bulb-shaped head on the end. If it wasn't for the fins and curled whiskers, she would have mistaken it for something else.

'A dragon?' Roper asked.

'Looks like.' Jamie thought of the bad tattoos kids got when they were sixteen as an F-you to the world, and their parents. They were inherently terrible.

Was this that? Or something else. It didn't look like it was done by an artist. And nor did it look like it was done with any sort of care.

Jamie filed it away with the other details that didn't make sense. The white, cavity-filled teeth. The unshaven pubic mound.

Jamie put the hand down carefully and tucked it against the girl's hip.

What the hell had happened to her?

'We need to see the report,' Jamie said, not taking her eyes off the girl's serene face. 'From Brock and…'

'Amherst.' Roper gave her the name. 'One thing at a time, Jamie.'

'Who would do this, Roper?'

'I don't know.' He sounded grizzled. 'Some sick fuck, no doubt.'

'What does the coroner's report say about blood work?'

Roper pulled it from his pocket, unfolded it, and lifted the top few pages. 'Toxicology was clean. No alcohol. No drugs. Looks like she was taking care of herself.' He stepped closer. 'A little underweight maybe, but…'

'Who do you think she was?' Jamie turned to look at him.

'I don't know. There's no—'

'Roper,' she said stiffly. 'You've been around longer than I have. Take a guess. Who is she?'

He made a cycling motion with his arms. 'I don't know, Jamie.' With his free hand he went to rub the back of his neck, pausing only when he realised he was still wearing the latex glove. 'I wouldn't like to say, but…'

'Roper.'

'Young Chinese girl like this, no name, no ID, tattoo like that on her arm, found where she was…' He was scanning the pages.

'Where was she found?'

'Run-down shit hole bed-sit apartment block in the south of the city. The kind of place that takes cash and doesn't ask questions. The kind of place you pay by the week. The kind of place you go when you have nowhere else.'

She let him continue.

'I don't like to guess without seeing the whole report...' He was hedging.

He wasn't saying what he was thinking. But he could tell by the look on Jamie's face she wasn't going to stop asking.

'A prostitute. Illegal immigrant too.'

'Why?'

'The tattoo for starters. They're as good as brands. I've not seen that one before' — he pointed to the girl's wrist — 'but I've seen others.' He sighed. 'The story is never pretty. They're brought over, get their passports taken off them... Then they're put to work, trying to earn their freedom, pay back their passage. Except they never do.' Roper finally pulled his gloves off and scratched at the hairline on the nape of his neck. 'It's a story as old as time, and unfortunately, it still goes on. More than anyone would like to think.'

'And the baby?'

'Who wants to screw a pregnant prostitute?' he asked crassly.

'So she ran,' Jamie said.

'The alternative probably wasn't pretty.' Roper grimaced. 'And I can think of a dozen reasons that the guy managing her wouldn't want her running off. Sets a bad example to the other girls, for one – these girls, they need to be afraid for their lives. Otherwise the whole system breaks down.' Roper sounded as disgusted as Jamie felt about the whole thing.

'So you think he came after her, killed her? Her manager, or whatever – to set an example?' Jamie was watching him closely. For all his faults, Roper was sharp, and a good detective when he tried.

He made a sort of groaning noise. 'Hard to say. But it takes a special kind of evil to do this... If that's the story here, I don't know. But it doesn't feel right to me. You'd want that sort of thing to be public – brutal.'

'This not brutal enough for you?'

He sighed. 'It's maybe a little... Restrained? Gentle?' He was searching for the right word. He didn't find it.

They were silent for a while, looking at the girl.

Jamie didn't know what she expected. But she wanted to see. And now she had. 'What do you think?' she asked eventually.

'About what?'

'About her.'

'I said I don't know. Without—'

'No, not about how she died. About *her*. About the case.'

'I'm not following.'

'Do we do this?'

Roper measured her expression, seeing the surefooted detective he'd worked Oliver's case with just a shadow of her former self.

He nodded slowly.

'Can we catch the bastard?'

He nodded again. 'We can do this, Jamie.'

'Good.' She exhaled, blowing out a bleach-rich breath. 'Because I want to get him.'

'I know you do.'

'So where do we start? We've got the girl, but nothing else.'

He chuckled once. 'Would you kick me in the head if I said we needed to return to the scene of the crime?'

'Say it and see.'

'Actually, first, I think we need to tell Smith.'

Jamie grumbled and pulled the cloth back up over the girl's body. There wasn't a mark on it. She looked like a china doll. 'I was afraid you were going to say that. You think Amherst and Brock will trade the Raymond case for it?'

'Only one way to find out.'

They drove quickly back to HQ.

Jamie poured over the coroner's report as they did.

Roper wasn't lying – she was as clean as a whistle, and other than being a little on the thin side, she was in good health. The baby too.

They'd removed the foetus during the autopsy and taken a DNA sample. The writeup about the child was cursory, though it said that it was the coroner's belief that the father was Caucasian.

A john. One of her clients. Did he even know that he was going to be a father?

The bullet had nicked her lung on the way through, blown through the aorta before exiting. She'd bled out quickly. Quick enough that she didn't drown in her own blood from the punctured lung.

It was an act of evil.

But it didn't seem that the killer was going for the child. That much was a relief.

Roper knew Amherst, so that was a start. Though he didn't hold much confidence that they could take a first-degree murder from them and palm off a missing person who wasn't really missing.

Amherst was a little older than Roper, who had described him as a 'big son of a bitch' with the temperament of a bear. Brock he didn't know, but if he was partnered up with Amherst, he was probably just as mean.

With each set of traffic lights they passed, Jamie's stomach tied itself into another knot. Even if they convinced Amherst and Brock to give the case up, they'd have to get Smith to sign off. And even if he went for it – which he wouldn't, because she and Roper weren't high ranking enough to snag murders like this – how was she going to explain how she'd been put onto it?

She was racking her brain trying to figure out how she was going to lie her way into it. Or out of it if Smith cottoned on.

Telling the truth was out of the question. She knew that much for sure.

She breathed out hard, unable to get the stench of the chemicals out of her nose. Roper cast her a sideways glance and sped through an amber light.

She was going to take it one step at a time. Amherst and Brock were first. They'd get them on-board, and then deal with Smith when the time came. If it came at all.

'You good?' Roper asked, watching her.

Jamie stared out at the drizzle-drowned city. She sighed and closed her eyes, feeling the glass cool against her forehead. 'I don't even know.'

6

AMHERST AND BROCK had desks on third, but weren't at them when Jamie and Roper arrived.

A middle-aged detective on the next one over said they'd been out all morning following up on some leads but should be back soon.

Jamie didn't like lingering. There was no good reason for her to and she didn't want anyone asking questions.

She left a business card on Amherst's desk, asked the detective to ask him to call her when he got in.

The detective didn't seem thrilled with the responsibility, but he didn't look busy either and begrudgingly agreed.

She and Roper were back at their desks a few minutes later and though she knew digging into the Raymond boy was what she should have been doing, she just couldn't. Not when there was a killer out there.

It didn't take her long to find the case.

She didn't have clearance to access all of Amherst and Brock's files and could only see what was on the system so far.

It was what the attending officers uploaded, but that was about it.

No signs of forced entry. No signs of a struggle. No ID found at the scene. Nothing to suggest who she was or where she came from.

Jamie kept reading.

In terms of the personal effects recovered, there was a single plastic bag with new clothes in it – bought from a supermarket. No receipt. A couple of pairs of cotton underwear and socks, some jogging bottoms, a hoodie, some plain t-shirts. Two magazines – one copy of a women's health magazine dated three weeks prior – just after the new year. And the second was a teen magazine.

Jamie opened up the photos folder and started skipping through them. She found the magazines – the first had an ebullient looking woman on the front wearing a Barbour coat and throwing handfuls of snow at the camera. The words 'New Year, New You' were riding underneath her ten-grand smile. Jamie clicked to the next one, the teens magazine. The front was emblazoned with a brooding boyband who all looked like they'd just been told that they had to stop playing, come inside and have tea. It was dated a little under two weeks ago, and apart from having been read a dozen times, the only remotely interesting thing about it were the four Chinese characters scrawled across the top in biro.

She could see that there was an attachment to the file and opened it. Another photo filled the screen and showed a closeup of the characters. The words 'Sun Princess' had been placed underneath it and the text note read: 'No results found from initial search. Waiting on secondary results and analysis.'

Nickname, maybe? Something for the baby? She'd check out the Chinese calendar, any traditions to do with the sun and new babies. See if anything jumped out.

Jamie closed it and went back to the original file, re-reading the list of the effects. Seeing what she could glean from them.

Basically nothing.

All the file told Jamie was that wherever the girl had run away from, she'd left there with just the clothes on her back.

Jamie sat back and pulled out her phone. Before she and Roper had left the coroner's office she'd snapped a photo of the girl's tattoo.

She stared at it, remembering what Roper had said. It was as good as a brand. Jamie shuddered.

Jamie decided she needed to keep looking, and went back to the file.

The initial photos of the crime scene were bloody.

The girl was curled into a ball on her side, a deep puddle of near-black blood around her like paint. Her white shirt was soaked through.

Jamie skipped through the photos until she found a closeup of the wound. It was tiny.

The next was of her chest, of the exit wound. The edges were ragged, the hole angry, the tattered strips of her torn shirt stuck in the congealed blood.

The pressure of the impact had blown through her ribcage.

Roper said that the bullet had hit the lower right ventricle, severing the aorta.

She'd never stood a chance.

There was a single photo of the window, the glass barely holding. A spider's web of cracks ran outwards from a hole in the centre.

The bullet had gone right through the girl and out of the window. Beyond, there was the street, and an empty building site across the road. The area was being developed, but trying to find a bullet in that mess would be almost impossible.

Jamie sighed and clicked through to the next one.

Other than the photos though there was little else.

Where the hell was Amherst? She needed that file. Needed him to hand the case off. The Raymond thing was a dud in all senses of the word. This was what mattered. This was *all* that mattered.

The phone on Jamie's desk rang and she lurched forwards for it. 'Johansson,' she said quickly, hoping it was Amherst.

'Johansson,' came Smith's unmistakable voice. 'What's the latest on the Raymond case?'

Jamie shrunk behind her computer monitor to get further out of sight.

'I, uh…' She trailed off and cleared her throat.

'If you say you're working on it, I'm going to have to get out of my chair.' He paused for a second. 'And why is detective Amherst standing at your desk?'

Jamie jolted so hard she almost fell off her own chair. Amherst was standing behind her wearing the thickest, biggest parka she'd ever seen. He did look like a bear – Roper was right. Amherst was at least six-foot-three, and in the boots he was wearing he stood at least an inch taller.

His face was square, his strong chin hidden under a thick beard. With his shaggy hair on top it looked like he was staring out through a bushy porthole.

'Looking for me?' he grunted, not pulling his big hands out of his deep pockets.

Jamie's brain, for the first time that day, began firing on all cylinders. 'Let me call you back with an update,' she said confidently, the adrenaline surging through her system suddenly giving her clarity.

She hung up before Smith could say another word and spun on her chair. She caught Roper's eye as she did. 'Run interference,' she said out of the corner of her mouth.

He nodded once and pushed out of his chair to intercept Smith who was already heading for her desk. Roper had always had her back, but now, since he'd gotten sober, they'd grown closer, and besides Cake, her trainer, she didn't know that she was closer to anyone else.

Not that her life was awash with friends.

Jamie was on her feet now as well, dwarfed by the huge Amherst. 'Let's walk,' she said, taking him by the arm.

It was like trying to move a tree.

He let himself be guided towards the lift, where Jamie spotted another unfamiliar face. A woman in her late thirties with short, dark hair and tanned skin was leaning against the wall, one knee crooked, sole of her boot pressed to the paint. She had at least five years and four inches on Jamie, and looked like she could handle herself.

Beneath the leather jacket she was wearing, Jamie could see well-muscled shoulders. Above the arcing cut of the vest she had on, Jamie could make out the lines of her upper pectorals. Her skinny jeans contoured around the rugged quads and outlined defined calves. The woman was well-built and strong. And the way she looked up from picking her nails and focused on Amherst told Jamie that this had to be Brock.

When they reached her, Amherst pulled his arm away like he'd been humouring Jamie the whole time. 'I don't appreciate being led like a dog,' he said, his voice like sandpaper.

'Woof,' Brock added, chiming in.

Jamie cast a glance over her shoulder, shadowed by the two detectives. Roper was feeding Smith a line about the Raymond case, but she still needed to get out of there.

Without asking, she reached out and jabbed the call button for the lift. 'Going down?' she asked, looking from one to the other.

'We just came up.' Amherst looked at Brock. 'And we don't appreciate being summoned without a fucking explanation.'

The lift arrived.

'Please,' Jamie said, gesturing to it.

They exchanged a look again and Brock shrugged almost imperceptibly.

Amherst nodded and they stepped in.

As soon as the doors closed, he spoke again. 'So what is it that we can do for you that you don't want Smith to know about?' he asked airily as Jamie jabbed the button for the ground floor.

She knew there was no bullshitting this guy.

He stood next to her and Brock lingered behind, strong arms folded.

'Your case,' she said.

'Which one?'

'Jane Doe.'

Amherst stuck his bottom lip out but said nothing.

'The dead pregnant Chinese prostitute?' Jamie said, wondering what sort of test this was. She was already on the back foot and had no time to mess around.

Amherst raised an eyebrow. 'Oh? Been doing your homework. What about it?'

She had to just come right out and say it. 'I want it.'

He laughed and it sounded like someone hitting a whiskey barrel with a rubber mallet. 'Do you now? And why would that be?'

She gritted her teeth, having no other answer other than the fact that she trusted the judgement of a known serial killer to be able to spot another heinous villain who needed to be stopped. 'I just do. It's... It's important.'

'I'm sorry,' Amherst scoffed and turned to Brock, who Jamie could see shaking her head out of the corner of her eye. 'I thought first-degree murder was one of the fun, light cases. Silly me.'

Brock tutted behind her.

'I assure you the case is well taken care of,' Amherst said. 'Is that all?' He reached out to press the button for three and Jamie grabbed his hand.

'Look,' she said, sighing. 'If you don't want to give it up, then fine. But I want to help.'

Brock chimed in. 'Score yourself some points with *daddy?*'

Jamie knew she probably didn't know anything about her father, and she meant Smith. But it still got under her skin.

'Well, tough luck,' Brock snapped. 'You gotta *earn* these cases.' She snorted. 'And after the way you fucked up the Day case, well' — she drew breath and put her hands on her hips — 'I don't know a detective in this place who'd throw you a scrap.'

Jamie could feel her hands curling at her sides. Though Brock was at least a weight class above her – maybe two – she still thought she could snap her heel into the side of her temple before she knew what was what.

Amherst waved his partner down. 'I think the important question here is why this case is so important – and more so what detective Johansson here is willing to do for it. Is it the accolade she wants under her belt? Solving a Jane Doe like this is no easy feat... Or does she just want to nail the bastard who did this to the wall?' Amherst turned and leant forward, balancing his paws on his knees so that he was level with Jamie. 'So which is it, huh?'

She met his iron gaze with fire.

'What kind of detective are you, Jamie Johansson?' He narrowed his eyes. 'Do you want glory? Or do you want blood?'

Jamie showed her teeth. 'I want blood.'

Amherst stood up, amused, and then looked at Brock over Jamie's shoulder.

'Fine,' he said. 'If that's how it is, you can work it.' He pulled a pack of Skittles out of the pocket of his parka and slung one between his back teeth. 'But it's under me.'

Brock cleared her throat.

'Us,' Amherst said, correcting himself. He laughed a little. 'Whatever you find, you report to us. We get the collar. And you get—'

'Nothing,' Brock cut in from behind her. 'You get nothing. Just the knowledge that we got the guy.' She strode around Jamie and stood next to Amherst. 'But that's what you want, right?' She asked airily.

Jamie looked at Amherst, kept her mouth shut, and nodded.

The lift stopped a few seconds later, and the doors opened.

'It's settled then,' Amherst said. 'You work the case, and let us know when you find something.'

'And you're not going to tell Smith?' Jamie had to make sure.

'Why would we?' Amherst was grinning now with big square teeth that wouldn't have looked out of place in the mouth of a cart-horse. He extended a hand and buried Jamie's inside it, shaking hard. 'We'll be in touch.'

He'd backed out of the lift then, Brock ahead of him, and let it close.

As soon as it did Jamie balled her fist and slammed it into the wall of the elevator. She snorted, regretting saying the words as they came out of her mouth. She lifted her hand, felt it throb in the way that it did when she'd been working the bag for an hour straight, and then regretted hitting the wall, too.

'I want blood.' She grimaced at herself.

It sounded just as ridiculous then as it did the first time.

Luckily, she'd kept a straight face in front of Amherst.

It didn't stop him giving her a shit-eating grin though. Then again, why wouldn't he be grinning?

If Smith didn't know, then there was no reason not to let Jamie work it.

If she helped and found who did it, then it would make their lives a damn sight easier.

And if Jamie's investigation came to nothing, then it would make no difference to them.

It was the perfect arrangement.

For them.

And now Jamie was riding back up in the lift with nothing but a tentative agreement to do all of the leg-work and get none of the credit.

And of course she had to do it without Smith finding out.

And she still had to find the Raymond kid.

She wasn't sure if this was turning out to be a good day, or a really bad one.

By the time she got back to her desk, there was an email waiting for her from Brock. It contained nothing but a link to the in-progress file on the system. Inside were the crime scene photos, the full report from the attending officers, as well as the witness statements from the surrounding apartments, and both Amherst and Brock's initial reports on the body and the scene. She'd go over it in detail when she had time.

For now, she was flying through the pages, keeping one eye on the now open door to Smith's office. There was no sign of him, and Roper wasn't at his desk either.

She kept expecting them to come up behind her. Though she felt like she was being paranoid.

She wished she could have stayed there all afternoon to read through, but she couldn't. Not if she wanted to make any real headway. The trail was already going cold. And as Roper said, they needed to go back to the scene of the crime.

And now she knew exactly where it was and had the blessing of Amherst and Brock to go there and start kicking down doors.

Or at least turning over stones.

But the latter didn't quite seem serious enough for the murder of a pregnant runaway.

Jamie forwarded the link to her phone and logged out of her work-station. The day wasn't over yet, and she'd find Roper along the way. To think that it was important enough for Smith to be looking for her with everything on his plate was ridiculous. She was just being paranoid.

Guilty conscience, maybe.

No. She shook off the thought. She was doing a good thing.

Jamie took the stairs to clear her head, and pounded down them one at a time, bringing her knees up to raise her heart-rate.

By the time she landed on the ground floor, Roper had texted asking where she was.

'Meet me in parking,' she texted back, and headed there.

Less than four minutes later, he came panting into the lot.

Jamie was waiting next to his Volvo and had already Google-Mapped their route to the apartment, as well as got back into the file. She was looking at the photo of the tattoo on the girl's wrist again.

She held it up as Roper approached and he squinted, breathing hard.

'This is the key,' she said.

'To what?' He tried to catch his breath, his throat tight, the breath wheezing in and out of him.

'The case.'

'So you managed to convince them to swap for the Raymond kid?' he asked hopefully.

'Not exactly.'

He narrowed his eyes at her, curling the key he'd removed from his jacket pocket back towards his body. 'What do you mean not exactly?'

She exhaled. 'Can we just get in the car? I'll explain on the way.'

'Explain now, Jamie.' Roper pocketed the key again. 'I'm already out on a limb here for you. I'm not just going to barrel forward on blind faith.'

She couldn't not tell him. 'We haven't got the case. At least not officially.'

'Which means?'

'We work it, report to them, hand off the collar when we find the guy.' She said it quickly, the words blurring together in her mouth.

Roper laughed. 'You've got to be kidding me.' His key was firmly in his pocket now. 'We do all the shit-work and get none of the credit? Jamie, I'm all for catching bad guys here, but this is just stupid. And we're taking on the case without Smith's approval, I'm guessing?' He paused for a second, read the look on her face, and carried on, even more incredulous. 'Juggling one that we should be finishing, and what, hunting down traffickers and murderers in London's seedy criminal underbelly?' He scoffed. 'I'm sorry, Jamie, but don't you think this is biting off a little more than we can chew here?'

'What the hell's that supposed to mean?' She felt her fist ball, and then throb. It was still sore from where she'd socked the inside of the lift.

'Look, I know you went through the wringer with the Day case—'

'I—'

'No, Jamie, let me finish.'

She clammed up.

'But you need some perspective here.' He stared hard at her. There was no escaping his gaze. 'You got taken for a ride and then screwed over with the best of them. That hurts. Trust me, I've fucked up enough cases to know.'

'I didn't fuck anything up—'

'But what you're doing here?' He began to shake his head. 'Ducking an assigned case, taking on another one without the DCI knowing? And all off the back of a tip you got from the same killer that you let slip through your fingers?'

'Keep your voice down.'

'Jesus, Jamie? Don't you see how fucked this is? And now you want me to throw away what little is left of my own career so you can what, absolve your guilty conscience?'

There it was again.

She ground her teeth.

'I get that this is a bad one. And I know there's evil in the world –

too much for you or I to bear alone. But this case will lead nowhere good. And you're too raw over this, and going too fast. You're running blind, Jamie, and you need to open your bloody eyes.'

She was seething now. Angry because she knew he was right. 'I'm not,' she said stubbornly. Spitefully almost.

'Trust me, Jamie. You're off the fucking rails here, and I don't like it.'

'Trust goes both ways, Roper,' she said with scorn in her voice.

'I trust you with my life,' he said, his voice hard and sure. 'But you need some time to process. He's under your skin whether you like it or not, and that level-headed detective that I felt could shoulder the investigating for both of us while I got shit-faced every night, well, I don't see her standing in front of me right now.'

Fucking AA. Acceptance. Admittance. All part of the process, but she didn't like him throwing it in her face like this. She knew he wasn't doing it maliciously, but he was as good as saying that he was glad he was sober because she needed someone to look out for her just then. It felt like he was burying his fist in her stomach, not pleading with her to see reason.

And the worst part was that she could see it. Could hear it in his voice. But that it was falling on deaf ears. 'I'm still me,' she said. 'And pissed off or not about Day – and you can believe that I am – at him, at myself, at the fucking world right now – I'm a damn good detective, and credit or not, Smith or not, Amherst and Brock don't give a shit about this girl, and from the looks of their report, they've got shit-all to go on.' She exhaled hard. 'The trail is getting cold, and no one is coming to claim her body.'

Roper's expression was blank. He was like a waxwork of himself standing there.

'And in a week – in two weeks – they'll still have nothing. Because the witnesses didn't see shit, and if there's no family waiting in the wings, then who the hell cares if the killer walks, huh? Another case will come along, and push this one down, and then eventually, they'll forget all about it. But I won't.'

'Jamie…'

'Frankly,' she said, cutting the air with her hand, bile rising in her, 'it doesn't fucking matter where the lead came from. What matters is that the guy gets caught. That we get a killer off the street. That we nail his ass to the damn wall, because if we don't, then no one will.' She stepped forward. 'Amherst and Brock swagger around like they're hot shit, and they've palmed this off like it's some little joke to them, but I'll tell you what, if they thought they could solve it, they wouldn't want anyone else stomping all over their investigation. They've taken a punt – if it doesn't get solved, so what. If some jumped-up DS from upstairs takes a crack at it and gets somewhere, well hell, that's a big win for them, isn't it?'

Roper inhaled gently.

'I'm done letting guys walk, Roper. I'm done letting them get away with bad shit. And you may think I've changed, and that's probably because I have. I have changed, Roper. I used to want justice, but now I don't.'

'Jamie—'

'Now I want blood.'

'What?' he raised an eyebrow.

'I want fucking blood! Now get in the damn car.'

He blipped the button from his pocket and she stormed around to the passenger seat.

It sounded just as stupid the third and fourth time she said it. But if it wasn't the truth, then she didn't think she knew herself any more.

And as she caught a glimpse of herself in the wing-mirror as she slammed the door shut, she wasn't sure she did. The person staring back looked different to how she expected.

She wondered if that person would disappear, or if she'd just come to know her. To accept her. To be her.

As Roper got in and cranked the ignition wordlessly, she decided that right now, it didn't really matter.

And maybe more importantly, she didn't really care.

7

THREE DAYS.

That's what Roper had given her to make some serious headway. Otherwise, he was pulling the plug. And if she wouldn't drop it, then he'd go to Smith.

Jamie did not like being strong-armed. But she knew that it was more than she probably deserved. Whether Roper had thought she'd get shot down by Amherst and that would be the end of it she didn't know. Was he just humouring her at the coroner's office?

'This is the place.' Roper pulled in at the curb and lifted the hand-brake. It clacked upwards sharply and the car lurched to a stop.

Rain fell heavily on the windscreen.

Jamie lowered her head to look up at the obelisk in front of her.

The apartment block was grey-stained-black from the rain. Most of the windows were lit up, glowing orange in the darkening afternoon light. It was barely after two, but night was already closing in.

'Sure you want to do this?' Roper asked.

Jamie scrolled through the case notes on her phone. 'Come on, it's on the second floor.'

She zipped up her coat and pulled the hood tight to her head, and then slipped from the car and made across the street to the shelter of the entrance alcove.

There wasn't a buzzer system or anything listing names – this place wasn't that official as that it seemed.

Instead, there was a sign bolted to the wall that said. 'Rent Weekly. Call For All Inquiries.' Below it, a number was engraved into the metal.

Someone had scrawled the words 'fuck off' across the sign in big black letters with a Sharpie.

Roper came up beside her, water dripping from his ears, and looked at the sign. He made a little 'tsk' noise and Jamie pushed open one of the battered wooden double doors. It had been lockable at one stage, but someone had rammed what looked to be a crowbar into the gap between the two of them and levered it open.

The wood was splintered and rotting in the winter weather. It didn't look recent. But whether anyone had the money or inclination to see to it, Jamie guessed not.

Inside, the hallway smelt like wet carpet, even though the floor was tiled.

Above them, the ceiling was peeling down in lengths of paper, exposing the water-stained plasterboard above. That was where the smell was coming from, then.

All around the door, the yellowed paint was flaking and cracking, the plaster beneath bubbling. Jamie felt the compulsion to scratch at it with her nails, but resisted.

She cleared her throat, lifting her phone. 'The report says the land-lord's apartment is on the ground floor. Apartment one.'

'Original.'

She ignored the snide comment, accepting the fact that Roper was now going to be exactly no help at all for the next three days. The responsibility of making enough progress so that Smith wouldn't suspend the both of them for working on it was down to her.

He still probably would, even if they did make good progress. But if they were onto the killer before then, and Amherst and Brock still had nothing, they might have a fighting chance.

The door to apartment one was as Jamie expected. About as beaten up as everything else in the building.

She fished her warrant card from her pocket and knocked with her other hand, hard.

Music was droning on the other side of it, and she wanted to make sure the landlord heard her.

Somewhere above them, a baby was crying.

And it didn't sound like the person taking care of it was doing anything about it.

She shivered, throwing the beads of rain on her shoulders onto the already wet floor.

Bolts began to slide on the door. Jamie counted three, picking them out from the middle, top, and bottom.

It opened a few inches, and then stopped, hitting the limit of the chain.

A young face appeared in the gap.

A girl's face. She could only have been in her early twenties, and though she was pretty, she looked tired. Her nose was pierced twice – a bar through the left nostril, and then a purple ring through her septum. She also had a stud through her philtrum.

Her eyes were dark brown, her skin pale, her hair dyed black and tied back into a bun punctuated by long, shiny chopsticks.

She was wearing a tank top, showing off the matching wings tattooed across her upper chest, the tips reaching out to her collarbones.

It took all of two seconds for the smell of cannabis to hit Jamie's nose.

The girls' red eyes widened, seeing the warrant card, and instead of asking what they wanted – which was what Jamie could see forming on her pink lips, she said, 'Shit,' instead, and tried to close the door.

Jamie's hand shot forward and hit the wood, her foot following quickly, wedging itself into the gap.

The girl disappeared behind it, leaning into the thing. 'It's medicinal,' she called, like that was any sort of defence.

'I don't care about the weed,' Jamie said back. There were bigger fish to fry in every sense of the word. 'I'm looking for the landlord, and I really don't think you're him.'

The name on the file was Jonathan Grigoryan. Jamie hadn't looked it up, but she knew it to be Armenian or Georgian. And though she didn't like to assume anything, she very much doubted that the stoned twenty-something white girl behind the door was either the landlord of the apartment building, or the man she was looking for.

'He's not here,' she said quickly, still leaning against the door. 'You'll have to come back.'

'Listen, kid,' Jamie said, trying not to sound derisive. The girl was maybe ten years her junior. She didn't know what she was doing in the landlord's apartment, but she could guess. 'Open the door, alright? I just want to talk.'

Guys who owned buildings like this owned a lot of them. And there was no way he'd be spending any more time here than he absolutely had to.

The girl was pretty – probably a lot younger than him. It wasn't hard to put it together.

If Jamie looked into Grigoryan, she knew she'd probably find him to be a family man. No doubt the girl was half mistress, half house sitter. She lived here, probably for nothing, and Grigoryan dropped in whenever he felt like it to collect his *rent*. Sex for room and board agreements were rife in most cities. Though people liked to think society had moved on, sex was still a bartering tool, and it wasn't going anywhere.

'I can't let you in – Jonny will kill me.'

Kill her? It was hard to make the call on hyperbole when a girl had been murdered upstairs.

'I don't care,' Jamie said coldly. 'We're looking into the murder upstairs and I need the key.'

'I don't have it.'

Jamie ground her teeth, thinking quickly. The room was locked up, the key that they'd recovered from the apartment was in evidence, and Jamie hadn't wanted to check it out. She was still trying to stay under the radar. 'You know what obstruction of justice is?'

'What?' The girl's voice quaked.

'Obstruction of justice. When a person knowingly impedes an official investigation in order to intentionally affect the outcome of the case.' She paused for a second to let it sink in. 'You're about two seconds from being charged with it.'

'But I—'

'One,' Jamie cut in.

'Shit, shit – hold on, I – wait. Please. Okay, I'll open it. Just don't—'

Jamie pulled her foot out of the gap and let the door close.

She turned to look at Roper, who was staring at her unhappily. She ignored him.

The chain came off and the door opened slowly.

Jamie stared into the dim interior, past the scantily clad girl. She was wearing just a vest and shorts which barely made it onto her thighs. Though the tattoos and piercings weren't something that Jamie personally went for in a partner, she could see why Grigoryan liked her.

Roses and thorns snaked up over the girl's hands and onto her forearms. The right was completely covered up to the shoulder, and the left ended just around her elbow. She had a dreamcatcher on the outside of her bicep, a Mexican inspired Day of the Dead mask on her shoulder.

Her eyes were wide now and Jamie could see her heart hammering in her neck.

Inside the apartment was hazy with smoke, and Jamie waved through it, trying not to take in too deep a lungful.

Roper grumbled something behind her and walked in with his hands lodged in his pockets.

The apartment was clean and expensively decorated. Jamie's wet boots squeaked on the hardwood floor, and the walls had all been freshly plastered.

The living room was square and a huge wrap-around sofa made from leather and suede clung to three of the four walls, facing a wall-mounted television that was twice the size of the one she had at home.

In the centre of it all was a glass coffee table, and on It was a ziplock bag of cannabis the size of a fist. A glass water pipe filled with ice cubes sat eerily, smoke settled inside it, spilling over the lip and drifting down to the glass surface like a waterfall.

The ice cooled the smoke. Made for a smoother experience. Of course she'd never tried it herself, but when you're a DS you work a lot of drugs cases and you pick up a thing or two.

Next to it was all the necessaries to roll a joint. A pouch of tobacco, oversized skins. A business card with squares cut out of it to make the *roach* – an open-ended filter.

Jamie tilted her head to read what was on the card. Grigoryan Property Management.

She had to guess the last word as it had already been torn off in parts to craft the two joints sitting spent in the chrome ashtray.

Roper made a subtle clicking noise behind Jamie – their little call when they didn't want to alert a witness or suspect to something.

She turned half-on to look at him while the girl rushed in to try and clean the drugs up. Though there was nothing she could do and Jamie watched out of the corner of her eye as she picked up the pipe in one hand and the bag of cannabis in the other, and then spun in circles on her bright white legs.

Jamie caught sight of the bruising now – yellowed and reddened patches of skin on the inside of her thighs. Four purple welts in the shape of fingers on the flesh just below the curve of her bottom.

Grigoryan, when he came by, obviously wasn't gentle. But the girl seemed to be living in luxury, so the trade was even in her mind, Jamie guessed.

It wasn't like she was a prisoner here.

Roper clicked again, his tongue against the inside of his teeth.

Jamie focused on him now.

He was stopped about four feet behind her, next to what had to be a bedroom door.

It was half pulled too, and he was looking through the gap. Gently, with his knuckles, he pushed it open a little more, letting the light from the living room fall across satin sheets.

They were dark red, rumpled, and the smell of sex hung heavily in the air.

The iron-framed headboard had two silk ties attached to it. One around each corner, and there was a used condom lying on the thick cream carpet.

Grigoryan had been there recently. And he obviously wasn't taking chances.

Jamie made a mental note to look into him further. If he was married, then it meant he was into infidelity. And if he was hiding this girl here, then it meant he had something to lose.

It was hardly motive, but if he didn't have any qualms about being rough with the girl… No, it was too big a leap. But good to bear in mind. At the very least, Jamie could use the information to leverage—

No. She cut that thought off. Leverage was just a word that people used when they were trying to convince themselves they weren't blackmailing someone. That's what her father always said. You call a spade a spade and own up to what you're doing. If you catch the guy, it's all worth it.

She hated that his words stuck with her like that, especially because she didn't believe in them.

Roper pushed the door open further and the wall came into view. There were hooks hanging from it, and on them Jamie could see riding crops, paddles, handcuffs, and something made out of leather and chains that would have looked at home wrapped around a horse's head.

Grigoryan had some unconventional tastes – but how far did they extend? It was hardly gyroscopic swings and iron maiden coffins, but still. It wasn't vanilla.

'Hey,' the girl called out.

Jamie and Roper turned to face her now, still clutching the pipe and the cannabis.

'You can't look in there,' she said, moving the ziplock bag behind her back. 'You need a warrant.'

Jamie raised an eyebrow. 'We're already in the apartment – you invited us in, remember?'

'No, I— you—' She started, but then cut herself off and flopped down on the sofa. 'Shit.'

'What's your name?' Jamie asked, softening her voice. She moved her right hand out of sight towards her hip and made a sideways waving motion with her fingers.

Though she and Roper might not have been on the best of terms, they were still good detectives and well-practised at this. It was about teamwork. Two detectives sitting, grilling one witness never ended well. Jamie was taking the lead this time, and Roper would scout the apartment. That was how this worked the best. The click, the hand signal. All moves they'd perfected over the last few years. A code that only they knew.

If Roper transferred his cigarettes from one pocket to the other while looking around, that meant he thought Jamie should ease off on the witness.

If Jamie rubbed the toe of her boot on the back of her calf while she was on her feet, that meant that she'd found something of interest.

If Roper scratched the tip of his nose with his left hand, Jamie was onto something with her line of questioning. Press harder.

And if Jamie rubbed her earlobe, it meant that she'd found nothing out of the ordinary and that the search was a dud.

Jamie slid down onto the sofa next to the girl and reached out for the pipe. She tugged it from her grip and put it back on the coffee table. 'I really don't care,' she said. 'I'm trying to find a killer, not bust you for smoking some weed.'

The girl looked at her with tearful eyes. 'Really?'

Jamie nodded, her voice soft. 'Yeah, really.'

The girl exhaled hard. 'Then do you mind if I…' She pulled the bag from behind her back and held it up.

'I'm not going to bust you,' Jamie said, 'but don't take the piss.'

'Oh,' the girl said, lowering it. 'Yeah, I mean…' She nodded, her cheeks flushing.

Roper smirked from across the room as he moved through the door into the kitchen.

'Hey,' Jamie said, bringing the girl's attention back to her. 'What's your name?'

'Stephanie,' she said, almost timid. 'But my friends called me Effy.'

'Effy?' Jamie smiled now, as warmly as she could, and watched as the tension drained from the girl's shoulders.

Jamie shuffled back on the couch and leaned onto a fur-covered cushion, propping herself up on her elbow so that she was basically sprawled out comfortably. 'Do you mind if I...' she asked, already doing it.

'No, no,' Effy said, with a little more surety now. 'Please.'

'Thanks.' Jamie flashed her that smile again and felt the girl relax a little more. She took a more comfortable position as well, facing Jamie, sitting back, one heel tucked under her hamstring.

'So how long have you lived here?' Jamie asked.

'Nearly three months,' she said, nodding in confirmation to herself.

'And before that?' Jamie said, making what might have seemed like idle conversation.

'I was living with my boyfriend. But we, uh...' She pressed her mouth into a sad line. 'You know how it is.'

'Boys, huh?' Jamie said with a sigh. She'd only been in a relationship with one guy, and he was great. She was the one who ended it, and for no good reason, really. She had no idea what boys could be like. At least not first hand. But it seemed to comfort Effy.

'Yeah. Ain't they just.'

'So how'd you end up here? If you don't mind my asking,' she added, disarming her own question.

'You know how it is.'

'Yeah.'

'I was staying with friends, between jobs... My parents wouldn't take me back.' She laughed a little. 'I knew a guy who said that he'd stayed here for a few weeks – that it was cheap, you know? I could pay cash, crash here, get back on my feet.'

'Mmm.' Jamie nodded, not pressing.

'He gave me the number and I called – it was an automated thing, like an answering machine. Asked me to leave my name, age, number, why I wanted a room, and whether I was a guy or a girl. I remember thinking at the time that the voice sounded weird, had like a weird accent. Within five minutes, I got a call back. I had to give them a reference – someone to vouch for me, you know? And then they said they'd call back again.'

Jamie nodded, making a mental note of it. A reference was required. So that meant that someone had vouched for the Jane Doe. She'd called, or someone had on her behalf, and given their details presumably. That wasn't in Amherst and Brock's file. The notes on their conversation with Grigoryan were sparse. He'd pretty much stonewalled them straight away, referred them to his solicitor. A mean pit-bull son of a bitch that sent them round in circles, laying on the legal-shit thick. They hadn't followed up yet.

'And they did,' Effy went on. 'My friend was with me right then, and they called him straight away. He had a job, you know? Was renting properly, so they believed him.'

'Just like that?'

Effy nodded as if that seemed normal to her.

The process was pretty loose to Jamie's eyes, but then again, nothing about the building seemed official, least of all its rental process.

'They told me to come down that day at four, bring two weeks rent in advance – one for a bond and one for the week. Payment could be cash under the door,' she said, pointing back towards the front door to the apartment. 'Or a bank transfer every Sunday. If you were late, they'd throw your stuff into the corridor, and change the locks. Were serious about it, you know?'

Jamie nodded, taking it all in.

'So I came down with my friend, and met this guy—'

'Jonathan?'

She shook her head. 'No, this big guy – bald head, in a black suit. Not Jonny, but someone who works for him.'

'Did you get his name?' Jamie was dying to pull out her note-book and start making notes, but she didn't want to spook the girl. Right now they were just talking.

Effy shook her head. 'He told me when he introduced himself, but his accent was thick, and I forgot it straight away.' She shrugged. 'One of those things, right?' Her eyes went to the bag of cannabis on the table. It was after two now and the girl had been stoned all day. She probably got stoned every day. She was probably stoned when she moved in.

'Okay. And then what happened?'

'He showed me to my room – opened the door, let me look around. Then asked if I wanted it. He seemed impatient. I nodded, and then he showed me his phone – there was a contract on it that I signed. Had to click an accept button then do my signature with my finger. Like when you receive a parcel.' She shook her head and laughed a little bit, eyeing the water pipe again.

'Did you read it?' Jamie cleared her throat, feeling her eyes glaze a little. The room was smoky and she was getting a contact buzz. She pushed through it.

'No, I didn't really have time. He just stuck his hand out for the money, and then gave me the key. And that was it.'

Jamie smiled, processing.

Effy stared at her, waiting for her to say something else.

Her mind ticked over, choosing the next path. 'And when did you meet Jonathan?' she asked brightly, bringing one knee up onto the sofa, looping her other knee over her ankle. 'How did you get from there to here?' She was building up to the line of questioning she wanted to get at. The Jane Doe. The murder. If she'd been here when the girl moved in, they might have crossed paths.

Roper came out of the kitchen and pretended to brush lint from his chest. Kitchen was clean.

Effy sighed, leaned on her hand, pushing the skin on her cheek and temple into a little fold above the heel of it. 'Jeez, uh – must have been a week after that I first met Jonny.'

Jonny. Jamie noted it. Was he Jonny to his girls? Jonathan to his wife? Mr Grigoryan to his tenants and business associates? She needed to meet him. But that came after. Right now she needed to get everything she could from Effy.

Roper moved back towards the corridor leading to the bedroom. Opposite it was another door that Jamie presumed had to be the bathroom.

He paused and pulled out his phone, hooked his other thumb into his back pocket. That meant clear the room.

'So how did you two—' Jamie cut herself off, put her hand on her chest, and then coughed. 'Sorry, my throat's a little scratchy.' She paused and caught Effy's eye. 'Must be the smoke.'

Effy reddened a little and looked away.

'Can you get me a glass of water?'

Effy met her eyes now. 'Sure. Of course.' She jumped up and headed for the kitchen.

As she passed Roper she dipped her head and looked away. He must have been a little too cop-like for her liking.

As she did, Roper lifted his head and nodded after Effy. Follow her.

Jamie got up quickly, shaking off the slight wooziness from the air and followed the girl in there.

They crossed paths in silence, but Roper lifted his left hand to his face and scratched the tip of his nose.

Jamie nodded in understanding and went into the kitchen.

Behind her, Roper headed for the bedroom.

8

WHEN JAMIE GOT into the kitchen, she paused at the door, making a blockade. She leant against the frame as casually as she could and felt strangely like her arms were a lot longer than they used to be, and that they were tied in a knot more than folded.

She shook her head to try and get the feeling out, but the smoke really had crept in, and ploy or not, her throat and chest was tight.

Effy was running a glass under the tap. 'Here,' she said, turning it off and coming towards Jamie.

Jamie lifted her hand towards the window at the back of the modest kitchen. The countertops and cabinets were all gloss black, the floor and tiled splashbacks white. 'Do you mind cracking the window, get some fresh air in here?'

'Oh,' Effy said, putting the glass down. 'Sure.' She reached over the counter and Jamie's eyes went to the back of her thighs again. She had bows tattooed at the top of them, mimicking the top of stockings. Along with the fresh bruises, there were plenty that were taking their time to fade. He frequented the apartment then, *Jonny*.

'Can we stay in here?' Jamie asked, partially to give Roper more time, and partially to let her head clear. 'Don't want to head back to

HQ with a buzz, you know?' She laughed a little, trying to be disarming. It was the truth though.

Effy just sort of smiled politely, doubting that she could say no.

She nodded and looked around the room, settling on the kettle next to the stove. 'Tea?'

'Sure,' Jamie said, reaching out to grab her glass, careful not to come too far away from the door. 'So, Jonny? What's he like?'

Effy ran her tongue along her bottom lip and then bit it, unsure what she could or should say. 'He's nice.' She reached out for two cups hanging off a mug tree next to the kettle.

'Yeah? How'd you two meet?'

'He, uh,' she said, nervously grabbing her left bicep with her right hand. 'He came to my apartment about a week after I moved in.'

'Just showed up?'

'Yeah. Sugar?' Effy asked, taking a pot from the back of the counter.

Jamie shook her head. 'Thanks. What happened?'

'He, um, said he was there to do a surprise inspection?' She laughed nervously, leaning on the counter.

'You let him in?' Jamie asked casually, knowing that by law landlords had to provide twenty-four-hour's notice for any inspections.

She nodded. 'I guessed I had to.'

The kettle started to whistle.

Jamie let her go on.

'He came in, walked around, didn't really look around much though, you know? Not much to see up there.'

'What are the rooms like?' Jamie folded her arms again, ignored the same knotted, uncomfortable feeling.

'Small. Empty. Just studios, you know? Most of them not very clean.' She smiled to herself for a second. 'Not like my parents' house – they were always a *shoes off* family, you know?'

Jamie nodded.

'No shoes on mum's carpet, but upstairs I never took them off.' She chuckled like it was funny to look back on.

'And then he left? Thanks.' Jamie said, taking the tea from Effy.

She'd put milk in without asking – full cream – and the tea was practically white. But she didn't want to interrupt to ask for it strong and black if Effy didn't have skimmed. Which she didn't.

'No, he… *lingered.*'

Jamie raised an eyebrow. 'Oh?' She smirked a little bit and Effy returned it.

'Started asking things like where was I from, did I have a job, did I have a boyfriend… And then stuff like did I drink? Did I do drugs…' She trailed off a little and cleared her throat. 'I don't. I mean, not hard drugs, you know?'

Jamie nodded. 'Sure. And then?'

'I think he was trying to find out if I was suitable – if I was clean, just down on my luck, or if I was, you know…'

Jamie turned her head slightly, feigning ignorance. She had a fair idea of what Effy was going to say, but fair assumption and having a witness say it themselves were two vastly different things in a police investigation.

'An addict, or a prostitute,' Effy said quickly.

'Are there a lot of both here?'

'I try not to go out of the apartment if I can help it.'

Jamie nodded. So Jonny had the nod from the guy who checked Effy in that she was pretty, went to check it out for himself, did some due diligence, then made his move.

There was a process here.

She thought back to the Jane Doe. She was pretty. Did Jonny's man give him a nod for her as well? Jamie had to keep pushing.

'Is he handsome?' she asked, knowing where this was leading.

Here, to this moment, to his apartment. To the bruising on her thighs and the shit hanging on the wall in the bedroom.

Effy ran her tongue over her teeth. 'In a way. But he's older, you know? More sophisticated than the guys I messed around with. He had a suit, and a nice watch, clean shoes, and good skin. He smelled nice, held himself like a man, you know?'

Jamie noted that *you know.* The second in as many sentences. People did that when they wanted confirmation and reassurance. 'Of course,' Jamie said brightly. 'When you're young, the guys your age are like kids.' She sipped her tea. It felt thick on her tongue and tasted like cream and nothing else to her. 'Older guys are always more attractive. I don't blame you.'

'Right?' Effy seemed to relax a little. 'Finally. You get it.' She shook her head in relief. 'My friends think I'm crazy for doing this. For being here. For being his—' She stopped abruptly and swallowed. 'Sorry, I shouldn't say any more. Jonny wouldn't...'

'It's okay,' Jamie said. 'I know he's married.' That was a lie, but she was taking a punt.

'You do?' Effy looked up from under her thick, dark fringe.

'Yeah, of course.' Jamie put the cup down and pushed her hands into her jacket pockets. It felt less strange. 'And I don't think there's anything wrong with it – he knows what he's doing. He's a man, like you said.'

'Yeah. You don't think I'm a home-wrecker?' The words didn't sound like hers. She was quoting from a friend.

Jamie shook her head. 'Nah, he's the one who's doing it. You're not to blame. He's only getting what he's not getting at home, right?'

Effy sort of half-smiled, a little ashamed maybe, and Jamie didn't know if she'd gone too far. She didn't want to make her feel like an object. She had to tread carefully.

'Sorry, I didn't mean for it to come out like that. I'm sure you and Jonny are—'

'No, you're right.' Effy's voice sounded tight. 'It is what he's not getting at home. He comes around every day or two, we fuck, and then he leaves.' She looked sad, tired again. 'But what can I do?'

'You can always leave if you don't—'

'And go where?' She scoffed. 'Look at me. I'm not exactly *employable.*' She moved her hand around her face to gesture to the piercings, and then down her arms at the tattoos. It was a changing world but a lot of businesses still overlooked younger applicants because of their appearance. Even in the Met there were rules on that sort of thing.

'I don't have any qualifications, no degree,' Effy went on. 'No experience. Who would hire me? And without a job, how can I pay for my own place? I went from my parents' to my boyfriend's to here. In that order.' She was shaking her head now, clasping her cup with both hands. 'Jonny isn't in love with me – I'm not naive. But how long can this last, huh? That stuff in the bedroom was here when I got here. Lingerie, toys, dildos. You name it.'

Jamie kept a straight face and let Effy talk. She obviously didn't get many people lending a sympathetic ear.

'He's into this stuff, you know? And I don't mind, not really, but I gotta wonder how long he kept the last one around? How long until he gets tired of fucking me?' She looked up at Jamie, her eyes full and teary. 'I've got nowhere else to go.'

Jamie looked at her, picturing the Jane Doe where she was standing. That girl was pregnant though. Would that bother Jonny? Was that one of his kinks maybe? Did he push and things got ugly? No, she was leaping. She had to keep on track here.

But she didn't have an answer for the girl. It was a tough situation to be in. 'You can't think like that,' Jamie said. As much as she hated to, she had to steer Effy back to stability. While her prospects looked grim here, nothing illegal was going on. It was consensual. But she had said *Jonny would kill me.* Shit. Jamie needed to get what she could out of Effy, and then line Jonny up for an interrogation, his army of solicitors be damned.

'Look, Effy, I get it. I know what it's like to be in your shoes,' she lied. 'With a guy you rely on, but can't rely on…' That was a half-truth. Her and her mother had relied on her father to be there for them, and he was little more than a drunk and a cheat. 'But you can't think that you won't land on your feet. You're stronger than you know.'

Effy didn't say anything.

'You'll make it through this.' She was building. Roper would be done soon, and this conversation was meandering. She needed to close in on the goal here. 'But not everyone does.'

'What?'

'Some girls don't get out of things – they get in with bad guys, and bad shit happens to them.'

Effy was silent.

'You know there was a girl upstairs who got killed, right?'

'Oh.'

'Oh?'

'That's what this is about.'

Jamie narrowed her eyes a little. 'What else would it be about?'

'Nothing,' Effy said, looking up. 'I just thought that you were...' She waved her hand in front of her face. 'I'm just being stupid. Sorry.'

Jesus. She thought Jamie was there for her – that a detective had come over to what, investigate Jonny's infidelity? Or something else? The roads were diverging. She'd come back to Effy. There was more going on here, and she needed to dig into it. But she couldn't lose sight of the goal. She needed to get the key to the Jane Doe's room, and she needed to get up there.

Jonathan Grigoryan would come after.

'You're not,' Jamie said softly, walking closer to her. She put her cup down and touched the girl on the elbows. 'You're a young, beautiful girl who's in a difficult situation, and there's nothing to be sorry about.' She lowered her head so she caught Effy's eye. 'If there's something going on here – if he's hurting you, or you know that he's—'

'He's not,' she cut in, almost defensively. 'He's not like that. I didn't mean to make it sound like – shit – he's just... And I'm... It just feels wrong, you know?'

Jamie nodded. 'I know. But you have the power to do things right. Even now.'

'Like what?'

'The girl who died.'

Effy nodded. 'I heard... I mean, I saw the police. Jonny spoke to them – there were cars, ambulances, two other detectives I think. They argued with Jonny.'

That was Amherst and Brock.

'Yeah. It was terrible. Do you know what happened?'

'I didn't see anything.'

'I know – no one did. But that's okay. I meant do you know what happened to her?'

'She was shot, right?'

'That's right,' Jamie said, conscious of keeping her voice quiet and serious. 'She was shot in the back, right in her own apartment. Upstairs. And I'm trying to catch who did it.'

'Like I said, I didn't see anything.'

'That's okay. I just want to take a look around up there. Do you have a key?'

'I shouldn't – Jonny keeps them in a safe…'

'Do you know the combination?'

Effy looked scared suddenly. 'I, uh – I really shouldn't. Don't you need, like, a warrant, or?'

Jamie needed to tread carefully. 'Look, Effy – if you do want to go that route, kick us out now – and you can, because that's your right, then I will have to come back with a warrant. What you've told me today is enough for me to get one and be back here first thing.' She didn't know if it was, but she figured she could bluff Effy. She didn't like doing it, but she'd come too far already. 'Have this place searched, top to bottom. And the guys who come here aren't going to be as understanding as me about that pile of weed out there.'

Effy stiffened.

'Whether everyone smokes or not, cannabis is still class B and that's enough out there to convict on intent to supply.'

Effy paled.

'That's not to mention the other shit they're going to find when they turn this place inside out. And of course, Jonathan is going to find out—'

'No!' Effy almost yelled. 'If he finds out I let you in, he'll—'

'He'll what, Effy? Hurt you? Kill you?' Jamie gripped her elbows a little tighter and saw her own father step out from behind the girl, stand at the back of the kitchen, curling a wry smile. She ignored him.

'No! But—'

'You're not helping your case here, Effy. If you're in danger – if you say your life is in danger, then that's grounds to arrest Jonathan right now. The bruises on your thighs – that's all evidence that will—'

'No, you can't! It's not like that. We— he—' She began to sob.

'This goes one of two ways, Effy.' Jamie's voice hardened and she did everything she could not to meet her father's disgustingly approving eyes. 'You open that safe and give us that key willingly, or I'm going to come back with a warrant, and you and Jonathan Grigoryan are going to be at the centre of a giant hurricane of shit. You, him, his wife, you're all going to be pulled into a room and—'

'Stop!' she yelled. 'Just stop! Fine, fine! I'll do it.' Effy cried now and Jamie let go of her elbows, feeling sick to her stomach. Leverage. The word tasted sour even in her mind.

Tears hit the floor and Effy curled up around her mug of tea.

'I'll do it,' she muttered through the sobs. 'I'll do it...' She shouldered past Jamie and out of the kitchen door.

Her father stood there, smirking at her. *Good,* he said. *Now you're getting the hang of it.*

'Fuck you,' Jamie muttered, baring her teeth like a dog and turning away.

As she left the kitchen, she heard words echo behind her that sent a chill down her spine. *That's my girl.*

Jamie followed Effy through the living room, looking up at Roper who was standing next to the coffee table, his jacket zipped up. As Jamie entered, he unzipped it to the chest. That meant he'd found something. But so had Jamie – an exposed nerve – so it would have to wait.

Roper watched Effy storm past and into the bedroom, and cast a questioning eye at Jamie.

'Just go with it,' she said, wondering if this was how her father always felt. Or if he'd come to like it after all those years.

Would she?

'Okay,' Roper said, and followed them.

Inside the bedroom, things were a mess. But they were the same mess as they were when they arrived.

Jamie didn't doubt Roper's thoroughness, but everything looked untouched. That was the art of it.

They watched as Effy pushed the doors of the mirrored wardrobe aside. There were handprints and smears across the glass.

Jamie tried to breath as little as she could. The air was thick and there were no windows to let the stench out.

Effy knelt down in front of it and reached inside, pushing stiletto heels away from the inner wall.

Roper tapped her on the shoulder and pointed silently at the wall that Effy put her hands against. He wanted Jamie to know he'd found it already. She wasn't surprised. When Roper was sober, he was sharp.

Effy put pressure against the wall and it moved backwards, and then sprung out on a hidden hinge.

'You can see it's not butted up against the dividing wall,' Roper whispered proudly in Jamie's ear. 'That's just plasterboard with nothing behind it.' He pointed to the wall next to the wardrobe. 'Had to be something hidden.'

Jamie nodded reassuringly at him. 'Good work.'

They watched together as Effy pulled the hidden door open, exposing a safe with a keypad embedded in a thick concrete block, set right in the wall.

'Must be five hundred kilos,' Roper muttered. 'You'd need a bull-dozer to rip it out.'

'Someone doesn't want something found, that's for sure,' Jamie mumbled back.

'Or stolen,' Roper added.

'Mhm.'

Effy paused at the keypad, as pale as porcelain, and turned to Jamie, looking at her like she was holding a knife to her throat. 'You have to promise,' she choked out, tears still rolling down her cheeks.

'Promise what?' Jamie said.

'Promise that you won't… That you won't…' She couldn't get the words out.

Jamie felt tension in her spine, felt her hands clenching. 'Open the safe, Effy.'

'If I do, you have to… you… promise…' She was convulsing, half in the wardrobe, half out. 'If he finds out…'

'Open the safe. Now.'

With shuddering fingers, the girl reached out, her thighs all thin and bruised, and typed in the code.

Eight beeps punctuated the stale air and the safe buzzed, ejecting the door. Effy pulled it wide and then meekly crawled away as though a cloud of arsenic had flooded out.

She fell into a heap against the far wall and pulled her knees into her chest, bows pressed against her heels.

Jamie and Roper stepped forward slowly. Silently. Together. Leaning sideways to see inside.

'Shit,' Jamie muttered, stopping dead.

'Shit is right,' Roper growled.

There in the safe, atop a stack of rolled-up banknotes, the shelf below the box full of spare room keys, was a sleek black pistol.

It glinted ominously in the dim lighting, well oiled and ready to fire.

But there was only one question on Jamie's mind, and that wasn't whether it was ready to fire, but whether it already had been.

There was a girl lying dead in the coroner's office with a bullet hole between her shoulders, and in this city, guns weren't that common.

Effy sobbed quietly into her knees behind them as Jamie and Roper stared at it.

All around them, the air hung thick and pungent with the smell of sex.

The tang of steel coming off the pistol seemed to meld with it. Taint it even.

Jamie's nostrils stung now, the air tinged metallic.

It didn't smell like sex any more.

It only smelled like one thing to her, and that smell was unmistakable.

It smelt like blood.

9

IT WAS six-forty-three PM when they knocked on Jonathan Grigoryan's front door.

The pistol that had been recovered from his apartment was a Glock 17. Effy was inconsolable over it all, and demanded to be taken into custody. Begged Roper and Jamie to arrest her.

Though they weren't quite sure what for. Possession of an illegal firearm? Possession of a class B substance? Jamie opted for the second one. She'd known about the pistol, but it wasn't hers. Where the hell would she get a gun? London was getting worse, but gun crime was still low. It was damn hard to get hold of one. Sure, there was still nearly two and half thousand reported gun crimes in the last year, but in a city the size of London, that wasn't high. It was around a tenth of what LA was reporting. But figures didn't really mean or prove anything. The question was whether or not that gun had been fired recently. The coroner's report on the Jane Doe said that the bullet wound was congruent with a small calibre – likely a 9mm – round. Which was what the Glock 17 took, and subsequently fired.

Jamie hadn't wanted to call it in just then, but her hand had been forced. She'd taken Effy into custody for possession of cannabis, but nothing else. They'd not called Jonathan, but instead put a call into Smith.

The cat was out of the bag now, and Jamie would have to face whatever mood it was in. And she likened Smith more to a mountain lion than a tabby.

'London Metropolitan,' came the voice from the other end of the line as Jamie's phone connected. She put her left finger in her ear to drown out Effy's mewling and stepped out of the bedroom. 'This is Detective Johansson,' she said. 'I need to speak to Detective Amherst.'

'One moment,' the operator answered. 'I'll put you through to his desk.'

The line clicked, gave her static for a second, and then rang three times.

'Amherst,' came the gruff voice from the other end.

'It's Johansson,' Jamie said, her voice harder than she meant it to sound. An image of Amherst buckled over a desk in the dark, a cigarette in his hand, smoke curling lazily through the slatted shadows falling across his face, courtesy of the window blind across from him, flashed in her mind. In black and white, a fedora on his head, a look of consternation on his face. She shook it off.

This wasn't the movies, some gritty noir. No matter how much it felt like it sometimes.

'Johansson,' he said emphatically, no doubt alerting Brock to the caller. The squeak of a desk chair told her that Brock was scooting closer to listen. 'What can I do for you? Giving up the ghost already?' He chuckled heartily.

'Look, I'm going to cut right to it because I'm in the shit here,' Jamie said, sighing and turning back to Grigoryan's dungeon.

'Oh ho ho,' Amherst said. 'Screwed the pooch have we?'

Brock humphed with amusement in the background.

'Not exactly,' Jamie said, pinching the bridge of her nose. 'Let's call it being a victim of my own success.' She walked back into the room and dropped her voice a little.

Amherst was silent.

'I'm standing in Jonathan Grigoryan's bedroom right now staring at an open safe with a Glock 17 in it.'

More silence.

'It's a handgun.'

'I know what it is,' he said coldly.

Jamie waited for him to continue. She could hear him drawing a long breath.

'Okay.' He said, processing it. 'Is Grigoryan there?'

'No.'

'Shit. You didn't break-in, did you?'

'No, Amherst,' Jamie said, indignant.

'Well that's a fucking start,' he growled. 'The bastard hit us with a bloody legal avalanche.' He sounded sour about it. 'How the hell did you talk your way in there?'

'Grigoryan's not here,' Jamie said quickly.

Amherst sucked on his teeth. 'The girl.'

'You met her?'

'No, but Grigoryan ordered her back into the apartment like a damn dog when we questioned him at the door.'

'Sounds about right.' Jamie cast an eye at Effy, still curled up and crying.

'And she gave it up willingly? The safe? The gun?'

Jamie bit her lip.

'Johansson,' Amherst said, his voice like a hot iron in her ear. 'Tell me she gave it up willingly – if Grigoryan finds out that you muscled your way in or coerced her into crossing him, he'll—'

'She gave it up willingly,' Jamie said, cutting him off. She pulled her eyes from Effy. Grigoryan was a piece of work and Amherst was scared of him – not physically, but legally. There was nothing more dangerous to a cop than a rich guy with a vendetta and a team of solicitors.

Jamie could convince Effy of what *really* happened. She'd just have to get her out of Grigoryan's way to do it. She ground her teeth thinking about it. Coercing a witness, then coercing her into lying about the original coercion? She looked up and saw her father kicking back on the rumpled bed, big hands laced behind his head. He nodded approvingly at her and she turned away.

Amherst sighed with relief. 'That's good. Grigoryan would have our guts for garters if we went outside the law on this one.' He cupped the receiver and said something to Brock that Jamie couldn't make out.

'Amherst?' Jamie said, getting nervous. She didn't like just standing there and Roper was giving her that anxious look he seemed to be getting really good at these days. Now that he gave a shit about his life, there was a lot of pressure on Jamie not to screw anything up for him. She didn't like him better when he was drinking, that was for sure, but he'd definitely have been happier to be strung along for this whole mess. Or at least less resistant to it.

'Hold on,' Amherst said through his hand.

'What are we doing here?' Jamie turned her back to Effy and cupped her own hand around her phone to shield her voice. 'I've got a gun, a murder scene, and a girl blubbering that our prime suspect is going to kill her when he gets back. And if I call this into Smith he's going to eviscerate me.' She could hear the shake in her own voice.

'Goddammit, Johansson, I said hold on.' Brock and him were having what sounded like stern words.

The phone rustled as he wrestled it into his other hand, his voice muted as he crushed the receiver against his shoulder, scribbling something down with his now-free hand. 'Okay, listen to me carefully – because it's not just your ass on the line here.'

'Go.' Jamie's mind settled, her focus returning.

'Smith's on the warpath the last few days and if he finds out that I laid this off on you and you came up trumps, well, he'll put my balls in a vice – and that's a pleasure reserved solely for my wife.'

Jamie didn't laugh. 'So why did you?'

'Because honestly, I didn't think you'd come up with anything, and I could see it in your eyes that if I didn't say yes you would have been like a damn dog with a bone. And frankly, I didn't have the time nor the energy to deal with your nagging bullshit.'

Jamie swallowed hard, gripped her phone a little tighter, but kept her mouth shut.

He pressed on. 'But lo and behold, here we are. So shut up and do what I say, alright?'

'Okay,' she said, trying to keep her voice straight.

'Brock's on her way over there right now.'

'Okay.' Jamie didn't like this already.

'I assume Roper is with you?'

'Yeah.' She looked at him and he lifted his chin a little, questioningly.

'Okay, well get him out of there.' Amherst cleared his throat. 'In fact, he was never there, alright? You went there with Brock.'

'What, why?' Jamie wrinkled her brow. This would have to go in the report, and it meant lying in it. Something she didn't want to do.

'Because I said so, that's why,' Amherst grunted, his voice telling her that it wasn't anything short of an order. 'Send Roper outside – when Brock shows up, she'll tell him where to go. Then, you follow her lead. As far as you're concerned, you're her bitch, alright?'

Jamie looked at Roper, then to Effy.

'Johansson.'

'I heard you.'

'Good. Now listen closely – this is damn simple, but I wouldn't put it past you to screw it up.'

Jamie didn't get the sense that he liked her – but then again, why would he? She'd been on this for all of five minutes and had already shown him and Brock up, and now put them in the shit with Smith too.

He went on. 'That place has got a lot of hookers working out of it – lot a women with no place else to go, too. Like our Jane Doe. Brock wanted to go back there, re-canvas potential wits without me scaring them silent.'

'Okay.' Jamie was grinding her teeth.

'Don't interrupt me.'

She swallowed the bile in her throat.

'Kind of a shitty job though – bad place, no fun at all. Most detectives have got better things to do – better cases to work. Except you.'

Jamie stifled a groan.

'So Brock asked you along to watch her back. And I took Roper to chase down some other leads, see if we couldn't ruffle some feathers elsewhere.'

Jamie stayed silent.

'Johansson, you got that?'

'Yeah.'

'Good. Brock's already out the door. Should be with you soon.' He let out a long breath and pushed up out of his chair. 'You let me handle Smith, okay? If he comes at you, you tell him I said it was good. You got that?'

'I got it.'

'Say it again, Johansson, because if you don't, then we're all in the shit here.'

'I said I got it.'

'Good.' He pulled on his jacket with a loud rustle. 'And one more thing.'

'What is it?'

'Don't touch anything, don't say anything. You send Roper outside, and you sit on that girl until Brock arrives. Not a fucking word to her or anyone else.'

Jamie swallowed more than bile. 'Okay.' Her voice was small in her throat.

He put the phone down without another word and Jamie let the dull beeps ring in her head.

After a few seconds, she pulled the handset away and turned to Roper, who was looking at her expectantly. Her mouth was dry, her free hand balled into a fist at her side.

'We good?' Roper asked.

She nodded slowly, and then shook her head. 'I don't even know.'

Jamie was standing shoulder to shoulder with Brock, watching from across the street as Roper and Amherst knocked on the front door of a townhouse.

Trees lined the upmarket street and black saloon cars with big engines and lots of chrome trim all rocked gently on their tyres, the wind swirling through the avenue of houses. The leaves twisted and slapped each other, the trunks whining as the rain sheeted down, crackling against the hood pulled tight around Jamie's face.

Brock had gotten to the apartment in record time, Roper had disappeared wordlessly, and then quickly after, uniformed officers and investigators arrived to bag and tag the scene. Brock had been there from the start, of course – had searched the apartment while Jamie spoke to Effy – and if she thought Brock was a middle-aged guy, well, who was going to believe someone who's blood-work looked more like a horticulture than haematology? It took all of ten venomous words from Brock, all broad-shouldered and standing like a pit-bull to make Effy's knees buckle. And then she ordered Jamie to take her in – she didn't care what for, but she wanted her in custody and out of Grigoryan's reach.

With the pistol alone there was enough to bring Grigoryan in. Suspicion of first-degree murder and possession of an unlicensed firearm were the two that got the rush on the arrest warrant. All the housing laws he'd broken were just icing on the cake.

Brock had her hands buried in the pockets of her long black coat. It hung to her knees, and though Jamie didn't recognise the brand, she could see the quality in it. She respected that.

'So,' Brock said without looking at her. 'I hear you're a fighter.'

'What?' Jamie said, surprised by the statement.

Ahead of them, a light came on in Grigoryan's hallway, a crescent of yellow burning in the evening darkness.

Loose leaves tumbled down the street, pinning themselves against the two silent patrol cars parked at the curb-side, and against the legs of the four uniformed officers who were standing with their hands clasped in front of them, their yellow jackets alight in the dim orange glow of the streetlights.

'You fight.' Brock was unmoving in the wind.

The door opened ahead of them, a woman standing there in an expensive-looking pantsuit. She was maybe in her fifties, slim and smart, but not finely made up. Her dark hair was pulled back around her head in a shiny bun, and her high cheekbones and narrow eyes gave her away as Armenian – this must have been Jonathan Grigo-ryan's wife. Her name was Adya and Brock had already told Jamie that she worked in finance. She and Jonathan were both high flyers, both private-school kids who came from money, both second-generation. Their families were both Armenian and had their fingers in the banks, in commerce, in hospitality. Bars, restaurants, shops, you name it. When Jonathan and Adya got together, it was as much of a business merger as it was a relationship.

It sounded to Jamie from how Jonathan had been described that he was an asshole in all senses of the word. And by the way Adya was barring the door and demanding to see the warrant and to know what the hell this was about before she let Roper and Amherst in, she wasn't so sweet herself. Jamie didn't pretend to know the intimate details of their marriage, but she knew the intimate details of what Jonathan did outside it, and judging by Adya's resume, she wasn't dumb in any sense of that word. She knew. She had to. Maybe they just got on with it for the sake of the three kids. Maybe she had her own side piece. Either way, she wasn't the one on trial here... Or was she? Jamie looked at the fierce woman in front of her, at the way she was standing forward on the step to keep Roper and Amherst below her. At how she was holding her shoulders ramrod straight. How she was delivering her words like stiff punches.

Maybe she was capable of spilling blood.

Her husband starts another illicit affair with a young Chinese girl in one of his flats, she finds out, decides it's the last straw, goes to his apartment, finds his gun, shoots the girl, frames old dirty Jonny for the murder... It would score her the house, the kids, pretty much every-thing. Was it so much of a stretch? People had done more for love, and far more for hate.

'Johansson?' Brock asked her again.

'Hmm?' Jamie said, turning her head now. Amherst was holding the warrant up high, stepping forward as he did.

Adya stepped begrudgingly aside and proffered them the hallway complete with ceiling mouldings and hardwood floors. She stepped back into the doorway and sliced across the street with her eyes, measuring every body out there with surgical precision. The way that a lioness sizes up the herd.

'You fight,' Brock said again, facing her now. She rolled her shoulders smoothly, lifted her hands a little to illustrate. 'Punching, kicking, you know, the old one-two.' Her teeth flashed with a dangerous smile.

Jamie squared up, tentative, but not backing down. 'Who told you?'

She curled a smirk. 'A little birdie.'

'Roper?'

'Pshh,' she said. 'Don't insult me.'

'He's the only one who knows.'

'If you were trying to keep it a secret you weren't doing a very good job.'

Jamie narrowed her eyes.

'…Then I performed a rear hook kick,' Brock parroted. 'Twisting into my feet, I was able to execute the manoeuvre which used Donald McCarthy's own body weight and momentum against him. He swung his weapon in a flat arc, and it connected with my elbow, resulting in a fractured ulna. At the same moment, I was able to land the blow and incapacitate McCarthy until more officers were able to arrive at the scene and assist with subduing the assailant.'

Jamie ground her teeth a little.

'I get that about right? I didn't memorise it or anything.' She grinned a little. 'But it makes for good reading. Riveting, really.'

'You read the McCarthy incident report.' The Donnie Bats one. Jamie flexed her right arm instinctively, her elbow aching with the fresh heal. She'd come out of plaster just after the new year, and though she was back training it still hurt. Fractured and chipped, as well as a little bit of nerve damage. On cold mornings, the outside three fingers of her right hand would be numb. But she didn't tell anyone that.

'I did. I was curious – after you came grovelling to me and Amherst—'

'I wasn't grovelling.'

'Tomayto-tomahto.'

Jamie made a little growling noise, much to Brock's amusement.

'I looked you up – of course, everyone knows the story of how you let Elliot Day slip away, that much was headline news. But you also turned up to work with your arm in plaster and a rumour that you'd caved someone's head in with the heel of your boot. I can't say I was interested enough to make inquiries before…'

'But you are now,' Jamie said with a sigh, turning back to the house. 'Aren't I lucky?'

Roper appeared in the doorway and waved two of the uniformed officers in through the door. Adya made no effort to move, forcing them to squeeze against the frame. If they didn't, they'd have brushed against her and that would have been a misconduct or assault claim waiting to happen. No doubt she'd bill the Met for the scratches on her doorframe anyway. It would cost her ten times as much to have a solicitor draft a letter for that and run it down to HQ than it would to get the door fixed. But she wasn't short on cash and it was about the principle of the thing.

'So so,' Brock said airily. 'But if you know how to sling a hook kick into the side of someone like Bats McCarthy's face while he's swinging for you with his namesake, well, you must be a tough bitch. Or stupid.' She side-eyed Jamie. 'Haven't decided which yet.'

'Is there a point to this ramble?' The orange of the streetlights was starting to burn into Jamie's eyes, causing a dull ache behind them. 'Or do you just like the sound of your own voice?'

'Humph,' Brock laughed. 'I hope you're this mean in the ring.'

Jamie's mind put it together. 'I'm not going to fight you.' She had an inkling that Brock was a fighter too. She could tell by how she carried herself. Nothing quite so finessed as Tae Kwon Do or Karate she didn't think. By the curve of her shoulders and the way her quads were pressing through her jeans like stacked breeze blocks, she would guess mixed martial arts. MMA. Ground and pound. Jamie grimaced at the thought. Too much contact for her. Too many faces wedged in armpits and sweaty thighs clamped around ears.

'I'm not asking to fight you – but there's nothing wrong with a little friendly sparring is there?' It was as if they weren't standing at the side of the road watching someone get arrested for the murder of an innocent girl.

'I don't fight unless I have to.'

'Ah, so you'll lay into someone if they're holding a bag, is that it? But when it comes to actual flesh and bone…' She studied Jamie's face. 'What, afraid you might like it?'

Jamie tried not to let her know she struck a nerve. That was her biggest fear of all.

'Where do you train?' Brock pressed.

'We're not having this conversation.' She watched as Grigoryan was walked out of the house in handcuffs, sullen and silent, his face painted with a look of grim determination.

His wife stood stoically in the doorway watching. She didn't look shocked. Was this their first time? Or maybe she'd just been awaiting this day for a while. Jamie couldn't tell.

Jamie stepped forward off the curb towards Roper as he came down the steps. She needed to be out of Brock's orbit. She'd been ordered around by her for the last three hours and she couldn't stick the schoolgirl-headmistress dynamic any more.

'I'll find out,' Brock called after her. 'I'm a detective you know. A good one!'

Jamie ignored it and mounted the curb in front of Roper.

Amherst breezed past her without a second glance.

'You okay?' Roper asked. He wasn't happy about any of this, but he could see Jamie was strung out, and your partner's wellbeing came above everything else.

'Yeah, I'm okay,' she lied. 'Just ready to go home.'

Roper glanced at his watch. 'Seven o'clock. Still early yet. Sure you don't want to head back to HQ, get a jump on our paperwork?'

Jamie cracked a wry smile and listened to the rain patter on her hood. It was smacking Roper in the face and beading down his stubbled cheek. 'Not tonight. I could do with a hot bath.'

'I'm guessing that's not an invitation?'

'Shut up, Roper.'

'Come on,' he said, 'We'll grab a ride in one of the patrol cars.' He pointed to the one that remained at the curb, waiting for them. Neither of them had their own transport with them. 'I'm guessing you don't want to get a lift home with Brock.'

'Gee,' Jamie said, reaching for the handle of the patrol car. 'Anyone ever told you that you'd make a good detective?'

Roper laughed and slid into the back next to her. 'Funny you should say that.'

10

JAMIE DID SLIP into the bath, and stayed there for almost an hour.

Her elbow was aching and despite her top half being dry, her legs and feet were soaked through. It took her forever to get warm, and though by the time she got into bed she could barely stand, sleep came kicking and screaming for her.

She dreamt she was drowning. That the rain was falling as it had for the last few weeks, but now there was nowhere for it to drain. She was in her apartment and it was running down the walls, coming through the windows. She threw the door back and went down the stairs as it gushed around her in streams. Then she was sloshing in it, wading to the bottom step, flopping into the hall, up to her chest in it, fighting the current to get to the front door. She pulled it open and water came in, unrelenting, and crushed her against the wall. She was pinned there, hands pulling her down, tugging at her jacket, and no matter how hard she kicked, how much she clawed, she couldn't get back to the surface.

It was just after five when she opened her eyes, subdued and bathed in sweat. She'd fought the water for a while, then accepted it, felt it crush her chest to a paste, and closed her eyes. A single, slow blink under the water, the world a twisted, shimmering mess overhead. And when she'd opened them, she was aware that the weight was gone from her chest, but she still couldn't breathe.

A single tear rolled from the corner of her eye, cool against the heat on her skin, and wetted her hair.

Her throat folded over on itself as she tried to swallow the lump there, and then she pulled herself out of bed and dressed without turning the light on.

Lycra leggings, a padded sports bra, and a thick sweatshirt that said 'Go Broncos!' on the front. It wasn't hers, but she'd never gotten rid of it. The guy that she'd dated – almost, what was it, seven years ago now? Jesus – left it there and never came back for it.

She didn't know why she kept it, or why she'd reached for it that morning. Especially over all the other more weather-appropriate things she had in her drawers. But there was something about it that felt right when things got rough.

Maybe it was because their relationship had fallen apart expectedly. It was clichéd even. You work too much, I don't see you, blah-blah-fucking-blah. Trivial shit is what Jamie had called it.

Trivial, normal human bullshit that wasn't important when you had to deal with killers and rapists, their freedom riding on your ability to catch them.

He didn't like that definition of their relationship.

And she didn't have time for trivial shit.

And yet she kept the hoodie. And when things were rough, it reminded her of the trivial shit.

Of how simple life would be if that's all she had to deal with.

She'd worn it just the once with him. Somewhere she couldn't even remember. Some outdoor gig in a park he'd dragged her to, where the bass was too loud and the ground was wet, muddy, and covered in crushed plastic beer cups. She couldn't remember anything about that night except what she was doing that day in work, and that he'd pulled off that hoodie and given it to her because she was cold.

If she had to remember his name it would take her a few seconds, but she knew she was a uniform back then, and that she'd been called to a domestic. A guy had given his girlfriend a real going over. And he'd taken a swing for Jamie, too. That was before she knew how to handle herself.

And in comparison to that – the concert, the hoodie, the guy… trivial.

She pulled a beanie down over her head to keep her hair in place, laced up her waterproof running shoes, hiked the hood up high, and then bolted out of the front door, the night and the rain still in full swing.

Her feet hit the pavement and sent water flying everywhere. She ignored the cold stabs against her ankles.

She paused for shelter in a bus stop after the first ten kilometres, and then carried on once the stitch had abated. She hadn't drunk anything that morning.

At six, she was outside the gym, hands on her hips, breathing hard.

The door was already open – she'd text Cake on one of her breaks and let him know she was incoming. He was glad to receive her.

They'd not seen each other much over the last few weeks. With Jamie's arm, Roper's sobriety, the holidays – which saw Cake go north to spend some much needed time with his brother Sam and his nephew Trevor. They'd driven up to Manchester and then flown to France, took him to Disneyland for Christmas. Or at least that limbo time between Christmas and New Year's. Finding time to spend with Trevor was difficult for both his father and Cake – it had been tough.

But right now she needed stability and routine more than anything.

She had no intention of bringing Cake into this mess, making him implicit too, but he could help in other ways.

'Jamie,' he called brightly, sweeping some dust out of the raised ring in the middle of the gym. The place had that damp smell that old buildings did when it rained. The single-pane windows were foggy and wet on the inside and the lights buzzed like they were protesting about being operated with such a thin roof to protect them from the weather.

'Cake,' Jamie said, hearing the relief in her own voice. 'Thanks for opening up.'

'Don't mention it,' he said, flapping his big dark hand. 'Who needs sleep anyway.'

'Not me.'

'Me neither.' He leaned on the ropes. 'Jesus, you're soaked.'

'Just a bit of rain,' Jamie said, pulling off her sopping hoodie and hanging it on a squat rack. It dripped onto the concrete floor. 'Let's get to it, shall we?'

Cake shrugged, grinned, and then lifted the rope so she could climb in.

Jamie sank into her heels, danced from her right to her left foot, raised her right knee, counterbalancing with her body, and then snapped her foot forward.

It thwacked into the bag that Cake was holding against his body and left a foot-shaped imprint.

'Breathe,' he ordered her. 'Again.'

She hit the bag in the exact same spot – what would be the kidney of any normal-sized opponent. A hard shot to the flank would stun most and leave them open for a follow-up – usually a full counter-rotation into a roundhouse or overhead depending on their position. But this was training for the single move. Lift, swivel, snap, back. Repeat.

'Breathe,' he commanded again.

Jamie grunted, lashing out at the bag.

'Breathe, Jamie!' He nearly shouted this time.

She wound up, fists locked into exposed knuckles, and kicked again.

Cake came forward this time, pushed back against the strike, and shoved her off balance. He took another step, inside her guard and before she could break out of whatever trance she was in threw the bag forward into her chest. His forearms were locked through the padded loops on the back, and he didn't go easy on her either. He was six-two and practically twice her body weight.

It was like being hit by a truck.

Jamie was on one foot as it was, and the blow had no trouble throwing her clean off her feet.

Her brain slingshotted back to reality in mid-air and she dragged a sharp, ragged breath into her lungs, landing hard, flat on her back. She bounced and rolled over her shoulder, coming to settle on her side, her heart pounding, the wind knocked out of her.

She didn't even have a chance to pick herself up before he was on her.

Jamie felt the pad press into her back and then the weight of Cake's knee against her spine, pressing the air out of her.

She tried to squeeze out a word but nothing came. All she could do was slap her palm on the ground. I give, I give.

Cake released after a second and stood up, panting a little.

Jamie filled her lungs, rolled over, and then coughed violently, clutching her stomach. He might have been retired, but he still hit like champ. 'Shit,' she wheezed, pulling herself up. 'What's up your ass this morning?' She fired him a scornful look, massaging her ribs.

'My ass?' He raised an eyebrow. 'Get your head together, Jamie. Your technique is sloppy, your breathing is all over the place, and your awareness is shameful.'

She narrowed her eyes at him.

'Are you here to train or to hit a bag, huh?'

Jamie levered herself to her feet and beckoned him forward. 'Come on, get the bag up.'

'Uh-uh,' he answered, shaking his head. 'We're not doing anything else until you tell me what the hell's going on with you.'

'Nothing,' she said, limbering up. 'I'm fine. Bag.' She nodded to it, bouncing on her feet.

'You come at me, Jamie, and I'm going to knock you on your ass again.' He wasn't screwing around.

She stopped bouncing and filled her chest.

'We're not here to hit bags. We're not here to work off whatever anger you've got in you – tell me what's wrong or don't. But if you want to train, if you want to learn – that takes discipline. Right now you're just emotion, and there's no room for both in the ring.'

She put her hands on her hips, the wraps around her knuckles straining against her wrist. 'So what, you're a sophist now? Get the bag up.'

He threw it down on the ground. 'You've barely spoken to me since last year – and now that your arm has healed up, you're back training, and that's great.' He cut the air with a big hand. 'I didn't hear from you when you weren't, but hey, we're not friends, I get it – but I'm not a punching bag. Literally.'

She looked at him and felt guilty. She had meant to call over Christmas – she thought that they were becoming friends. But she'd been too caught up. In work. In Elliot. In everything. 'Cake…'

'It doesn't matter.' She couldn't tell if he really didn't care or whether he was just good at hiding it. 'But what does matter is whether something's changed in your head.' He pointed at her. 'Because if you're not in this for the right reasons any more – I'm not here for you to take out your frustrations on, or to teach you how to hurt people. There's a hundred gyms for that, but not this one. Okay?'

She swallowed and relaxed her shoulders a little. It was almost seven by the grubby clock on the wall above Cake's office. Jamie dropped her hands and shook her head. 'I'm sorry. You want to get some coffee?' She could talk. She should talk. Not about everything, but Cake was right, he wasn't a punching bag, and she was being unfair to use him as one.

He nodded after a few seconds. 'Sure.' She always admired how perceptive he was. Not learned or book smart, but he knew people and had his fair share of life experience.

The V60 – which looked to be new, maybe a present from his brother for Christmas – drained slowly into the pot underneath.

Cake had heated up a kettle on a hotplate he kept behind his desk, and poured it into the contraption on the low table in the middle of the floor. There was a leather sofa and chair facing inwards.

Cake took the latter, filling it completely with a hiss of escaping air.

Jamie perched on the sofa and rubbed her eyes.

'We going to talk about what's really going on or do you just want to make small talk?' There was a little bit of venom in his voice. Maybe he did care a little that she hadn't bothered to call.

'How were the holidays?' Jamie asked, meeting his eyes. 'Disneyland, right?'

Cake sighed and settled back a little more. He rested the side of his right foot on his left knee, his size fourteen running-shoes more like flippers than anything else. 'It was okay – Trevor would rather have been home with his friends, showing off his new bike. You know how kids are.' He shrugged sadly. 'We made the best of it. I think by the end he came around a little, but what can you do, huh?'

'Mm,' Jamie said. She didn't though. She had no idea how kids were.

'What about you? See your mum over the new year?'

Jamie laughed a little. 'No, she was on a cruise – a singles cruise. To the Caribbean. She sent me a postcard from Barbados saying Merry Christmas, the picture on the front was of a naked couple holding hands walking down the beach, facing away, thank God' — she shook her head at the thought — 'that said, *who needs clothes when life is this good?*'

Cake furrowed his brow, the coffee dripping into the pot the only sound in the room.

Jamie let out a long breath. 'Crystal Waterfall Five-Star Clothes-Optional Resort,' Jamie parroted off the front of the card. 'No thanks. Especially not if my mum is there.'

Cake burst out laughing. 'Christ, and I thought my family was bad.'

'Tell me about it.' Jamie relaxed a little more. Cake's laugh was booming, infectious. 'I've been dodging calls from her since she got back. Hearing about her visit to the isle of sunburnt testicles isn't exactly at the top of my priorities list right now.'

Cake slapped his knee and howled. It seemed over the top, but somehow Jamie didn't think it was faked.

She couldn't help but join in.

'Wow, that's…' He sucked air through his teeth and reached for the coffee pot, pouring out two steaming black cups. 'That's *something* alright. How old is your mother?'

'Don't get any big ideas,' Jamie laughed, taking the cup off him.

'Hey, I wasn't – but I might be interested to know what that resort was called again.'

'And risk you running into my mum there? Fat chance.'

'Everyone deserves to be happy, Jamie, even me.'

'Yeah, but not my mother.'

Cake spat coffee back into his cup – partially because it was too hot, and partially because he was laughing. 'Damn. She really did a number on you.'

'You have no idea.'

He settled backwards again but didn't ask about it. That was a conversation for another day – maybe even another year. Too much to go over in the short amount of time they had before Jamie would need to get back in time for Roper – and the mailman – to arrive. She pushed the thought out for now and focused on Cake.

'What's eating you, Jamie? We may not be close, but I can tell when you're not yourself.'

She couldn't tell if that was a dig or not. She probably deserved it if it was. 'It's…' She was going to say *nothing* but she knew he wouldn't buy it. 'It's work.'

'No shit.'

'Hah,' she said, sipping her coffee. 'Good coffee.'

'Right?'

'It's this case.'

'Bad one?'

'They all are.'

'What makes this one different?'

She had to choose what she said carefully. 'It's a young girl. Gunshot. Right through the back.'

'A kid?' He sounded reluctant to hear the answer.

She shook her head, swallowed the coffee in her mouth. 'No, but she can't be more than twenty or something.'

'Damn. Gunshot you said? In the back?'

'Yeah, point-blank.'

'Local girl, or?'

'Jane Doe. No ID. We think an illegal immigrant. Sex worker maybe.' Jamie was almost shocked by how casually it rolled off her tongue.

Cake processed for a while, nodding slowly. 'Why do you think she's a sex worker?'

Jamie shrugged. 'Just a working theory – but there's no shortage of girls being brought over from China, the Philippines, Thailand... They're put to work, and then...'

'So you think a disgruntled John – uh, client—' He cleared his throat, a little and carried on. 'Killed her?'

Jamie narrowed her eyes a little. John? He seemed familiar with the world. Or was she reading into it too much? 'Don't think so,' she said. 'But maybe. We've got a few leads. Hard to say right now. She was pregnant.'

Cake stiffened at the news, resting his coffee cup on his chest as he processed. 'It's a sick world out there.'

'Isn't it just. Looks like she got pregnant, then ran. Seems like someone caught up with her.'

'So you're trying to track down the guy running her? You think he did it, to send a message to the other girls?'

Jamie watched him closely. It had occurred to them, but she was surprised Cake went straight there, too. 'You seem to know a lot about this.'

He shifted uncomfortably. 'I watch a lot of TV.'

'Sure you do.' Jamie finished her coffee. 'You uh, ever... You know?' Jamie's lip curled a little. 'With a girl like that?'

It was hard to see his cheeks flush with his dark complexion, but they definitely reddened. 'Me?'

'I'm not judging.'

'And there's nothing wrong with it!' he almost yelled. Not angrily, just surprised that the conversation had steered so quickly towards an admittance that he'd slept with a sex worker.

She held her hands up. 'Hey, I'll take any help I can get here. This isn't even my case yet, and any information I can dig up right now is going to help my cause a lot.'

He folded his legs more tightly and sat a little straighter in the chair. 'Whatever I can do to help.'

Jamie weighed it up. Showing him photos of an active case was a big deal – the kind of offence that could get you suspended. But there was little she had done in the last month that wouldn't land her with one. If Cake could help, somehow, in any way, then it was worth another roll of the dice. 'Screw it,' she said, pulling her phone out and opening the file. She enlarged the photos on screen and handed it to him.

'What are these?' Cake asked, taking it tentatively.

'Photos. Just take a look – couldn't hurt.'

He looked at her questioningly – this was a big departure from the professional lines they'd crossed before.

'Who knows,' Jamie said, refilling her cup from the pot. It really was good coffee. 'Maybe you know her. Maybe you slept with her.' She shrugged and slumped backwards. 'Would sure as hell help my case.'

Cake made an *mmnngghh* noise of disapproval at the comment, but went through the photos anyway. 'My God,' he muttered, skipping through some quickly and pausing on others. 'Poor girl.'

'Yeah, takes a real sick fuck to do that.'

Cake paused suddenly and looked up at Jamie. 'You know what this is?' He turned the phone around and held it up to her.

It was the photo of the girl's wrist and the symbol there. The badly drawn spiral dragon.

'Yeah, it's a traffickers thing – right? Like a cattle brand.'

'Yeah, I guess,' he said grimacing. 'If you want to put it like that – but it's not a trafficking thing. They want the girls to come off the boat as clean as they can. No tattoos, scars, nothings like that.'

'Okay.' Jamie leaned forward. 'Then what is it, and how do you know?'

'Girls talk,' he said quickly, bashfully. He cleared his throat again. 'No, these tattoos are given when the girls get chosen.'

'Chosen?' She arched an eyebrow.

Cake rolled his head back and forth. 'Yeah, I mean, I don't know exactly – I was told by a guy who went there a lot more than I did. Was telling me all these stories – I thought they were bullshit, you know?'

'Who went *where, Cake?'*

'The casino.'

'What casino?' She was almost off the edge of the chair.

'The Jade Circle.'

'Tell me.'

'Well – these casinos, you know – they're not like normal casinos.' He was squirming. 'They're not exactly... Uh...'

'Spit it out, Cake,' Jamie demanded. 'I don't give a shit if they're legal or not.'

'If you spend money, they have these girls that, you know... If you win enough, or lose enough, they'll...' He sort of made a shuffling motion with his hands. 'They have these rooms upstairs. And the girls there have these tattoos on their wrists. This is the symbol for that casino. The Jade Circle. Every one has their own mark.'

'Jesus,' Jamie said, feeling a flood of relief and heat rear up inside her. 'You sure?'

Cake looked scared, like he'd just admitted to murder. 'Yeah,' he said quietly. 'I'm sure. That guy I mentioned, some businessman who goes there a lot, I guess – he said that there's a guy there that chooses the girls. New ones every few months. That's what he said. Chooses. And then marks them – so if they try and run, people will know who they belong to. But I swear I didn't know any of this before I went there. And I haven't been back since.'

Jamie was stunned. 'Shit.'

Cake was quiet for a few seconds. He seemed small all of a sudden, despite still dwarfing the chair. 'Jamie?'

'Yeah?' she said absently, ordering it in her head.

'You don't, uh, think worse of me or anything?'

Jamie thought for a second, and then and stood up. 'No, I don't. I know what these places can be like. They seem okay at first, like everything's above board, but dig deeper...' She forced a smile. 'I know you're a good guy, Cake.'

He nodded but didn't seem sold. Didn't quite believe her.

She stepped closer now and rested her hand on his shoulder. 'Look, Cake, if I can get over my mother sending me postcards from a swingers' clothes-optional resort in Barbados, then I think I can get over this.' She squeezed a little. 'I actually *like* you, remember?'

He sighed, reaching up and putting his big hand over hers. 'Thanks. Same time tomorrow?'

She smiled at him, feeling energised, in more ways than one. 'Yeah. Sounds good.'

'And bring your head, okay? None of that shit I saw out there this morning.' He patted her hand and then let it drop.

'Thank you, Cake. For everything.'

'Don't mention it.'

'I won't.'

'Seriously though,' he said, looking up at her. 'Don't mention it. If my brother finds out I've been anywhere near a casino again, he'll kill me.'

Jamie laughed. 'I won't mention the prostitutes either, then.'

'It's not funny, Jamie.'

She pulled her hand away and reached for her sodden Broncos hoodie. 'Come on,' she said, flashing him a final grin from the door. 'It's a little funny.'

11

JAMIE WAS at the curb waiting for Roper to pull up.

The rain had turned from heavy droplets to a light drizzle and a murky fog had descended on the city. The air was thick and heavy with smog, the moisture seeming to soak it up. It clung to her skin and made her feel dirty, despite the shower she'd taken a few minutes ago.

She was successfully ignoring the mailbox over her shoulder. Elliot had never sent two so close together, but she refused to look. Not when she had a break in the case like this.

Roper was already ten minutes late, but she'd heard nothing from him.

She pulled her phone out of her jeans and checked it again, nothing.

Her boots squeaked as she rocked back and forth on her heels, her free hand buried deep in the pocket of her waterproof coat.

The squeal of a wet fan belt cut through the fog and Jamie came down from the porch to meet the battered Volvo. It sidled out of the grey sea and rocked to a stop in front of her.

'Took your time,' she said, pulling the door open.

Roper was scowling. 'Grigoryan walked.'

'What?' Jamie climbed into the car and sniffed the air. Stale, but

not smoky. He'd not lit a cigarette in there that morning, and that was
something at least.

'Grigoryan walked. Around four a.m. this morning.' He was pissed
off about it.

'How? We had him with a gun in his apartment – in the same
building that a woman was shot in.' Jamie knew that despite it being
a slam dunk on almost anyone else, against someone with pull, there
was no such thing. 'We should have been able to hold him for
twenty-four-hours for questioning at the least, even without charging
him.'

Roper sped away from the curb, the old springs wallowing under
them. 'Except the gun wasn't his.'

Jamie's blood ran a little cold. 'You're kidding. Effy?'

Roper growled. 'That son of a bitch's pit-bulls got her to claim it
was hers.'

'Shit.' Jamie kicked the footwell. 'In a locked safe in his apartment? While she's screaming *no, no, he'll kill me, he'll kill me?*
You've got to be kidding.'

'His solicitor was in with her by nine last night, by ten she was
signing a fully drafted confession explaining in detail how she'd gotten
hold of the gun and stashed it there without Jonathan's knowledge.
And then swore in writing he'd not been in the apartment on the day of
the murder.' Roper smacked the steering wheel. 'And to top it all off,
she's saying she gave it up willingly to us in order to exonerate herself
from suspicion in the murder, knowing that it's not the murder
weapon.' He laughed. 'She's pleading guilty to possession of an unlicensed weapon and taking whatever is handed down.'

'That bastard,' Jamie muttered. 'Fucking Jonathan Grigoryan. We
can appeal though? Contest the story – say how terrified she was of
him, argue she's doing this under duress?'

Roper laughed. 'Well I can't be a part of that.'

'Jesus, Roper, grow a backbone will you?'

He side-eyed her. 'No, Jamie, I mean I can't be a part of that…
Because I wasn't there.'

'You were there, Roper. You saw—'

'No, Jamie, I *wasn't*. I was with Amherst, remember? It was Brock that was with you.'

Jamie's mouth opened a little as her brain stuttered. 'Crap.'

'Crap is right. And I don't think Brock's going to be attesting to anything that happened in there – especially not in court. Her memory's probably a little fuzzy on the details, you know?'

Jamie ground her teeth. 'You think they know?'

'The solicitors?' Roper rolled his head side to side. 'Probably. Even if they don't, it doesn't much matter. Because if Effy told them how it went down, they know there's an element of coercion in there – or at least they'll argue it.'

Jamie stayed quiet.

'But they know what they're doing – they're laying this on Effy, making Grigoryan out to be clean. The girl hasn't exactly got a lot of prospects, and doing this for Grigoryan will net her a fat pay-check when she gets out. Hell, with the story Grigoryan's solicitors have spun, she won't see any time behind bars anyway. She'll walk away with a suspended sentence, I'd bet, and a couple of extra zeroes in her bank account.' Roper was cynical, but Jamie knew he was dead on the money.

'We still should have been able to keep him for questioning,' Jamie said sullenly.

'Yep, and apparently Amherst told them where to shove it. He wanted first crack at Grigoryan in the morning, after he'd stewed a little.' Roper indicated and then swung a hard right through a changing orange light. 'But after they got that confession from Effy, they got on the phone and rang everyone they knew, including a former DCI, a couple of MPs, and some journos that they have on retainer apparently. All of which amounted to a couple of phone calls to Smith in the early hours – putting the screws to him, so I hear.'

'Shit. Bet he's in a good mood then.'

'Oh-ho-ho.' Roper laughed sardonically. 'You bet. But anyway, I wouldn't bank on it mattering a damn anyway.'

Jamie sighed. 'And why is that?'

'Because Grigoryan wouldn't throw Effy to the wolves on that possession charge if he knew that gun had put a bullet in someone.'

Jamie leaned her head back and drew in a stale breath.

'For a possession charge with a signed confession, they won't bat an eyelid sticking it to her. But on a first-degree murder charge? I don't buy them trying to lay that on a twenty-something kid with no motive. If that gun turns out to be the murder weapon, I'll quit smoking.'

Jamie sighed, shook her head, and wondered if there was anything in the world that would get Roper to quit smoking. 'I guess you're right.'

'Grigoryan didn't do this. He may be a grade-A asshole, but I don't think he killed that girl. Still was nice to put him in cuffs.' Roper smiled a little and turned to Jamie. 'Whether we can catch him for anything or not, there was something satisfying about seeing the look on his face as we walked into his living room and pulled him out of the chair. Whether it was guilt for this or something else, the way the colour drained from his face...' Roper smirked to himself. 'Makes the job worth it.'

Jamie scoffed a little. 'Every cloud I guess.'

'Yup. So what now? Amherst and Brock have taken the brunt of the shit from Smith, but you know what they say about it rolling downhill.' Roper clicked his tongue and weaved through traffic. Jamie found it easier not to look. 'So we'd better have a plan for when we get in there, otherwise we're going to get our asses kicked all up and down the corridor. They bet on our find, and it came up... hell, I don't even know the word for it. But it's not good.'

'It's a lucky thing we've got a lead then,' Jamie said quietly.

'What was that?'

'I said it's lucky we've got a lead.'

He narrowed his eyes. 'What lead?' He was tentative.

Jamie didn't blame him. 'The tattoo.'

'On the girl's wrist? Amherst and Brock have already run that down – it doesn't match any known trafficking rings operating in the UK. It looks like it's just a tattoo. There's nothing there.'

Jamie let a smile creep over her lips. 'Good.'

'Good?'

'Good that everyone thinks that, because they're wrong.'

'I'm not following.'

'When are you?'

'Don't mess around here, Jamie, our jobs are hanging by a thread.' Roper stood on the brakes and they crunched onto the front disks, threatening to lock the wheels in the rain. The car juddered to a halt in traffic, the lights around them like strands laced through the fog.

'Ever hear of the Jade Circle?'

'Should I have?' Roper raised an eyebrow.

'Depends if you like illegal Chinese casinos and illicit prostitution.'

Roper turned to look at her, his eyes like drills.

'Roper,' Jamie urged. 'We're moving.' Around them, the traffic began to sidle forward.

Roper was unphased. 'Don't fuck with me, Jamie.'

'I'm not.'

'If this is the part where you tell me you've been out skulking around underground casinos in the dead of night, I'm going to be even more pissed off than I already am.'

Jamie filled her chest, listening as the cars behind them began to lean on their horns. 'Don't worry, I didn't.'

'Jamie.'

'Jesus, Roper, just drive,' Jamie said, shaking her head. 'No, I didn't go out to any. Someone identified the marking for me.'

Roper pushed in the clutch and jammed the old Volvo into first, pulling off with a whine of the badly serviced engine. 'Who?' He practically demanded it.

'A source,' she said, immediately realising that protecting him was pointless and that Roper wouldn't drop it. 'Cake. My trainer. He… He's been there. Seen the tattoo on the girls. He said that the guy who runs them there marks them with it.'

'Do I even want to know why he was looking at a picture of it? Or are you just showing case photos to anyone these days?'

'Christ, Roper, lay off, alright,' Jamie said coldly. 'You're up to your ass in this the same as me. And we're supposed to be on the same side here.'

'Oh yeah?' He scoffed. 'Because from the tally I'm keeping you've implicated me in the aiding and abetting of a fugitive, obstruction of justice, concealing evidence in an ongoing investigation, and lying on an official document. So it doesn't exactly feel like we're on the same side.' The dim headlamps of the Volvo died ahead of them, the orange glow of the taillights of the car in front swimming distantly in the gloom. Jamie didn't know that she'd ever seen fog so thick.

'I get it, Roper. You're pissed.'

'I'm more than pissed.' His teeth were gritted. 'I don't know why we couldn't just find the Raymond kid, keep our heads down, have an easy couple of months. Leave the messy shit to the other detectives.'

'The Raymond kid is *fine*,' Jamie said emphatically. 'He's at a friend's house getting stoned, making his mother sweat. That's all.' She exhaled hard. 'And I understand you're going through some shit. I do. And you have my sympathies. But that doesn't change the fact that a poor girl is lying unclaimed on a slab in a coroner's office with a bullet hole in her heart while the evil son of a bitch that *bought* her, and then gave her away by the hour to whoever dropped money in a damn casino, is walking around *free* – knowing that nobody's going to fucking touch him.' Jamie turned to look out of the window, feeling her cheeks grow hot. 'So while I appreciate that getting your life together has been no walk in the park, Roper, you've got it easy in comparison to some. And before we came along, Amherst and Brock were ready to give up on this thing. So excuse me if I don't agree with you that getting chewed out by Smith is worth dropping this.' She inhaled hard and unzipped her jacket, feeling warm. 'We've got a new lead – the Jade Circle, and it's the first solid one we've had. And Smith's go ahead or not, Amherst's blessing or not, and with or without you, I'm headed there the first chance I get. So if you want to run down the Raymond kid and bust him for the joint in his pocket and arguing with his mother, then be my guest. But there're people dying out there, and I'll be damned if I'm going to let you talk me out of trying to stop that from happening.'

Roper didn't say another word all the way to the station.

And neither did Jamie.

There was no avoiding him this time.

Smith was standing at Jamie's desk as she walked out of the stair-well – even when things were this screwed up it still wasn't an excuse to skip your daily steps.

'Johansson,' he said flatly, arms folded across his broad chest. 'My office, now.' He looked tired.

Jamie nodded without a word and walked past him.

She heard the elevator open behind her and then Smith commanded Roper to follow her.

They both went in and sat down and Smith came in quickly, closed the door, and circled around to the far side of his desk.

Jamie straightened in her chair as he pressed his tie against his stomach and sat down with a sigh. He had the expression of someone who'd been woken up at four a.m. to be accused of wrongly arresting an upstanding member of society with no evidence.

Smith had round shoulders and a head that he fastidiously mani-cured so that the only hair on it was his eyebrows. He was always clean-shaven on both the bottom and the top. His eyes were dark and circled, his tanned skin, courtesy of what Jamie guessed might have been a little bit of Greek or Cypriot heritage, was lined. He'd aged so much in the last four years, since his promotion. But Jamie guessed that heading up a fleet of detectives working the worst cases in the city would do that to a guy.

But despite everything that had happened in the last four years, and the last four hours, he didn't look angry. At least no more than on a good day.

'What a mess,' he said after a full minute of silence. 'What a damn mess.'

'Sir—' Jamie started, but then stopped as he raised a hand and cut her off.

'This morning, I've had nothing but phone calls. From the press, from solicitors, from the damn IOPC...' He shook his head. 'Before I saw his name on the arrest warrant yesterday afternoon, I'd never heard of Jonathan Grigoryan, and now they're telling me that I'm responsible for racial profiling?' He sounded incredulous about it. 'That I've singled him out based on his background and tried to pin a murder charge on him.' He laughed. 'Can you believe that?'

Jamie swallowed. 'Sir, I—'

The hand came up again.

She coughed quietly and put her hands on her lap.

'It's bullshit, of course. And it will never stick, but still – you certainly pissed off the wrong person.' Smith shook his head. 'And to boot, he wants Amherst's head on a platter.'

'Sir?'

Roper sat in silence.

'Yep, supposedly he's demanding Amherst be pulled off this case and put under investigation. Apparently we're in cahoots.'

Jamie swallowed, unsure where he was going with it.

Smith waved his hand dismissively, suddenly. 'It's all bullshit, of course. But I looked into Grigoryan – he's a real piece of work. And slippery, too. Nothing will stick to the bastard.'

'We have a new lead to suggest that he's not involved with the murder anyway,' Jamie said quickly, determined to get it in before he could stop her.

He looked at her for a few seconds. 'I know that, Johansson.'

'Sorry, sir.'

He closed his eyes and shook his head lightly. 'But it's one hell of a show he put on. And if there's one thing I've learned in my years doing this, it's that anyone who's that determined to put on a display of strength like that wants to make sure he stays untouchable. And you only need to be untouchable...' Smith clapped his hand on the desk and made his keyboard jump. 'If you've got your hands in some dirty shit.'

'I don't understand, sir,' Jamie said as apologetically as she could.

'Why would you?' Smith said. It wasn't meant to be cutting, but it still was. 'Your name comes up far more than I'd like it to, Johansson.

And you've got a knack for bringing other people into the messes you create.'

She shrank a little.

'But I can't say that it's all your fault. You've got a nose for trouble, that much I'll give you. And a shit-load of enthusiasm, too.'

It didn't feel like a compliment.

'But what you lack is experience, and perspective.' He paused for effect. 'Which is where you come in, Roper.' He looked at Roper for the first time now and Jamie saw him stiffen in the chair next to her. 'We put younger detectives with older ones so that they can learn – but also so that they'll be reined in when they're getting too headstrong. Something you seem to be failing spectacularly at.'

Roper pressed his lips into a sharp line but said nothing. Jamie could see the pulse in his neck quicken.

'At no point during this whole thing did you think to offer any wisdom of your years?' Smith had a strange sort of calmness about him, like he didn't really give two shits about either of them.

Roper hung his head but didn't say a word. What could he say without explaining the situation?

Smith leaned back now and turned away slightly. 'When I threw you two the Hammond case, it was just to see. A homeless kid washing up in the river? Who the hell was going to be able to solve that? No one, I didn't think. It was a grimy, dirty case that would have you crawling through the depths of the city. To any other detectives it would be a punishment. But to you two? To the disgraced DI fresh off a demotion and the young DS with a chip on her shoulder so big I'm surprised she didn't walk with a hunch? I knew you wouldn't see it that way. And what did you do? Not only found the killer – who could have been one of a thousand people – you also managed to put away a piece of shit we've been trying to nail for the last year and a half, as well as uncovering a bloody organ-harvesting serial-killer.' He chuckled to himself and rubbed his tired eyes. Maybe he was so sleep deprived he was bordering on insanity.

Jamie couldn't figure out what was so amusing, but it was making her nervous.

Smith went on. 'You let him get away, of course. But hell – we'd never have even known about him if it wasn't for you, and now he's topping Interpol's most wanted.' DCI Henley Smith shrugged, and then smiled broadly. 'And now, you've got your nose into another one...'

He met their eyes now, looking from one to the other. He looked deadly serious and Jamie all but shuddered under his gaze.

'I don't presume to know why this one,' he continued, his voice low and cold. 'But what was a dud of a case, without a lead – completely dead in the water – is now... I don't even know what. You shouldered your way into it – which is no mean feat considering who the detective heading it up is. I've known Amherst for a long time, and he's no pushover.' He met Jamie's eye for a second and restrained what might have been a smile.

She flushed a little, not sure if Amherst had told Smith the circumstances of how she'd convinced him to let her in on it. She thought he probably had, which was what was so funny to him. Her nostrils flared as she relived saying that stupid thing. *I want blood.* She'd be paying for that one for a while.

'Grigoryan wasn't even on our radar, and we didn't give him a second look. A wall of barristers will do that to a detective. I don't blame Amherst for backing off. I would have too. But when you, fearless and bloody dogged as you are, managed to talk your way into his apartment, convinced that girl to open the safe – and then came up with a pistol?' He raised his trimmed eyebrows. 'And then the way Grigoryan threw his full legal weight at us, convinced that girl to take the rap for it... Threatened Amherst, threatened me, got on the phone to the IOCP?' He stuck out his bottom lip and then sat forward again. 'I pulled Amherst from the Jane Doe first thing this morning – at four a.m.'

'I'm sorry, sir,' Jamie said, her voice quiet. 'I never meant to—'

'Will you just shut up,' Smith said with a sigh.

Jamie buttoned it.

'I pulled him from the Jane Doe at four a.m., and put him straight to work on Grigoryan.'

Jamie and Roper both looked up at Smith.

'He and Brock are going to turn over some stones, find out what they can about him.' Smith nodded. 'But from what he's found in the last five hours alone… Well, let's just say Grigoryan's going to need an *army* of damn solicitors. He's about as dirty and connected as they come, and has ties to about a thousand known criminals in everything from drugs to stock tampering. Which means that once again, Johansson, you've managed to sniff out a piece of shit worth knowing about. Guess it's in your blood. Let's hope it's the only thing you inherited from him.'

Jamie wasn't sure whether to smile, thank him, or apologise. She nodded instead and kept her face straight. Smith rarely acknowledged her father, but when he did, it often came with a backhanded compliment like that.

'Which means,' Smith said, inflating himself, finally coming to the point of the meeting. 'That there's a murder case with no one working it.'

Jamie tried to manage her expectations of what was coming next. She still half-expected Smith to say that he was giving it to someone else and that she was suspended.

'And you two are the only ones who give a damn about the poor girl. Amherst and Brock found less in four days than you did in a single afternoon, so while I'm still inclined to put someone else with more experience on it, if you're going to do your dog with a bone act regardless, then it would be a waste of time, wouldn't it?' He looked at each of them in turn. 'That was a question.'

They both nodded quickly, Jamie more enthusiastically than Roper.

'So then take it and get out of my office.' Smith said, the amusement now spent.

They both made a move to stand up.

'But before you do,' Smith said, making them freeze, half stooped.

Jamie knew it wouldn't be that easy.

'Don't presume to ignore a mandate again.' He looked at Jamie, his eyes burning into her face. 'If I give you a case, or an order, I expect it to be worked on, and carried out. Detective Sergeants do not have the liberty of choosing their own cases, whether they feel strongly about them or not. Emotional involvement is not a quality I look for in my detectives, Johansson, and it's not a quality that gets rewarded in this job.' He paused to let it sink it. 'So if you presume to try and brush off a case I give you again and pursue something else without my express orders, then it will be the last case you *ever* work. Do you understand?'

Jamie's mouth opened, but no sound came out. She nodded in understanding.

'And Roper, if she goes down, you go with her.'

'Yes, sir,' Roper said, barely above a whisper.

'You've strong-armed me into giving you this, Johansson, so don't screw it up. It's above your pay grade. I know that going into this. But with Grigoryan out of the way – for you at least – I hope that you can make some progress on it. If not... Then I'll be sorry I staked this on you, and you can expect to ride a desk for a very long time. You got that?'

Jamie nodded again, keeping her jaw clamped shut. Her cheeks felt hot.

'I don't appreciate not getting to make my own decisions, and I know you won't make a habit of doing it for me.'

'No, sir,' Jamie squeezed out.

'This is your shot, Johansson. Don't waste it.'

'I won't, sir.' Jamie stood straight now and backed towards the door. Roper was right beside her.

'Oh, and before you go,' he added, glancing from one to the other.

They both stopped and looked at Smith, wishing that he'd just stop talking and let them leave.

'Find that Raymond kid. Because if I get one more phone call from downstairs telling me that the mother is on the phone and hysterical again, whether you're out catching a killer or not, you'll both be yanked back in here and assigned to digitising the archives so fast you'll have carpet burn on your ass. Good?'

They both nodded quickly.

'Then get out.'

12

THE JADE CIRCLE was just a door halfway down what could only be described as an alley.

Jamie and Roper stopped between two Chinese restaurants with rotisserie ducks in the window, and headed down the side street, out of the throng of people.

'I mean,' Roper said, flicking the butt of his spent cigarette into a drain with the accuracy of a professional darts player, 'It could have been worse.' It bounced on the grate in a shower of sparks and dropped between the bars, washed away by the rainwater filtering down into it.

'I think getting threatened with desk duty forever is pretty bad,' Jamie said. Though she did feel a little better about their situation now. At the end of the day, she had made progress on the case, and Amherst and Brock now had bigger fish to fry. It would have made no sense to bring anyone else into it when Jamie and Roper were already primed to take the reins. Whether Smith liked the idea or not.

'Could have been suspended. Or sacked.' Roper shrugged. 'Or be in Grigoryan's crosshairs. I don't envy Amherst.'

Jamie said nothing. She sort of did. If Grigoryan was as big a fish as Smith said, then taking him down would be a career-maker. But as Smith had said, a murder like this was above her pay grade as it was.

So maybe Grigoryan was out of her league, too. She'd have to work up to that. And she had no doubt she would. If she could keep her head down long enough.

They came up on the door slowly, the only indication that it was there at all a lamp hanging over the top of it. It was off.

The door itself had no handle. It was a flat slab of rusted steel that sat flush to the frame.

On one side was a pair of dumpsters that had been opened up. Bags of rubbish spilled out and flies circled in a swarm.

On the other was a puddle of brown water with skaters in it, and several pipes that shot out of the ground vertically and then hooked back into the wall at a right angle. Jamie guessed they were drainage pipes from the restaurant that the door was set behind. And the large, foiled ventilation fan that was blowing out hot, fish-scented air was confirmation of that.

A little way down, a young Chinese guy was leaning against the dirty brick wall of the building opposite, one heel tucked up under his thigh, smoking a cigarette. He was wearing jeans and heavy, food splattered boots. He had just a t-shirt on, but what looked like a chef's smock thrown over his shoulder. He was on his phone, and didn't even look up as they approached.

The door was well hidden and poorly signposted, and had they not flashed their warrant cards at the old man sweeping the frontage of one of the restaurants, they never would have spotted it. Google Maps had it somewhere around there, but hadn't pinpointed it.

It was, after all, a legitimate casino with a legal gambling license – it was above board in that sense. It was just everything else that was shady.

They stopped in front of the steel door, not noticing the green dragon painted on the rusted surface until they were right on top of it. Jamie pulled back her hood and felt the thin mist of drizzle wet her forehead and glue the few loose strands from her long plait to her skin.

The sign was roughly painted in one long, fluid swirl. It was the same design as on the girl's wrist.

Jamie turned to Roper and raised an eyebrow, smirking a little.

'Yeah, yeah,' he muttered, lifting his hand, the rain beading down his cheeks and dripping onto the shoulders of his leather jacket. His fist balled and he wound up to rap on the rough surface.

'What'chyou want?' came a voice from behind them.

They both turned to look at the young chef. He was staring at them.

'We're looking for the Jade Circle.'

'Closed,' he said flatly, taking a long drag on his cigarette.

Roper licked his lips on Jamie's right, immediately wanting one.

'We're not here to gamble,' she called back, pushing her hands into the pockets of her coat, her fingers closing around her warrant card. 'We're looking for the owner.'

'Not here,' he said, looking back at his phone. 'Closed.'

'I don't think you understand,' she said again, stepping towards him now, pulling her warrant card out. 'We're not here to gamble.'

He sighed, tapping on his screen. 'Opens at two,' he called back. 'Wait if you want.' The chef ground the cigarette out under his boot and headed back towards the main street.

Jamie and Roper watched him go.

'You want to knock anyway?' Roper asked.

Jamie let out a long breath and checked her watch. It was after midday already. 'Couldn't hurt.'

Roper thumped on the metal with the heel of his hand.

They stood in silence, getting wet for almost a minute before Jamie spoke. 'Let's come back. We'll ask around a little, grab some lunch.'

Roper pushed a soggy cigarette into his mouth and lit it. 'I could eat.'

No one wanted to talk about the Jade Circle. They chose a restaurant across from the alley and set up in the window with a clear line of sight to the door.

No one went in or out before two p.m., and when it rolled around, nothing seemed to change.

They paid their bill, leaving a bowl of rice and some slimy prawns on the plates in front of them. The restaurant hadn't appealed really, but if offered the best view. Turned out there was nothing worth seeing anyway.

Roper and Jamie approached more quickly than before, not wanting to waste any more time.

As they stepped into the stream of warm air billowing out of the vent next to the door, it opened in front of them.

A tall Chinese guy with a black suit, the sides of his head shaved, and a tattoo of a snake coming up behind his right ear, stepped out. He slipped from the door and let it close behind him. Jamie heard the tell-tale click of a magnetic lock latching.

He stopped in front of the entrance and held his hands up, the tail of the snake reaching his knuckles. They looked uneven. He was no stranger to fighting

He was well-kempt, clean-shaven, and his suit looked expensive. Jamie admired the cut of it.

'Can I help you?' he asked, his English natural. He was a Londoner through and through.

They stopped in front of him, both looking up to meet his expression – not confrontational, not friendly.

Jamie and Roper both produced their warrant cards in unison.

'We're looking for the owner,' Roper said. 'He here?'

The bouncer smiled slightly. 'I'm afraid not.'

'Manager?' Jamie asked.

He shook his head. 'Sorry. What's it regarding?'

'What about the guy who runs the girls?' Roper asked casually.

'Beg your pardon?' the bouncer asked politely.

'What's your name?' Jamie asked, trying to sound warm.

'Matt,' he said, not a hint of fluster in him.

'You seem like a smart guy, Matt.'

He didn't respond.

'So let's just handle this like a couple of smart people, shall we?' Jamie's smile was unwavering but he didn't return it. 'We're investigating a murder, and we've tracked the victim back to this establishment. We need to come inside, look around if we can, speak to the staff, find out who she was, who knew her, and who might have had cause to hurt her.'

He looked from her to Roper, who had his arms folded sternly, and then back. 'I suppose you have a warrant then?'

Jamie smiled a little more widely. 'This isn't the first time you've had police knocking on this door, is it?'

'I can pass your details on if you'd like, get someone to give you a call back.'

Jamie didn't break his stare, but she wasn't sure how to play this. If there was probable cause, they could come inside without a warrant. But at the moment, they had nothing. Just a tattoo on a girl's arm which vaguely resembled a painting on a door, which was one of the most common pieces of iconography in Eastern culture and decorated at least half of all of the Chinese establishments in the city. It was circumstantial at best, and without anyone prepared to corroborate her employment there, they couldn't really do anything. There was no real reason for them to come inside. And she knew that if she gave a card, that no one would call her back. And every time they came back, they'd get the same run around and wouldn't be allowed inside.

Jamie stood there, thinking. Matt didn't move, and clasped his hands in front of him. Roper was no use at all.

She could feel her father at her back, his big hand on her shoulder. *Kick him in the fucking teeth. That'll make the owner come out. Or at the very least get the door to open.*

Jamie ignored him. 'Okay,' she said after a few seconds. 'I understand. Thank you, Matt.'

'Our pleasure.' He flashed them a quick smile with well looked after teeth and then picked his head up and looked absently over their heads.

Roper fell in behind Jamie as she walked away and then caught up. 'Well, that was a bust,' he said, wiping the rain from his head. 'What now?'

Jamie inhaled deeply. 'Now we make a nuisance of ourselves.'

. . .

'Hi there, excuse me, sir,' Jamie said, stepping forward and holding her hand up, her warrant card between her fingers. 'Detective Sergeant Jamie Johansson with the London Metropolitan Police. Do you have a second?'

The guy stopped dead in his tracks, his cheap suit damp in the rain. He was in his fifties, with an unshaven beard and a large, aquiline nose. 'I, uh, don't,' he said quickly, clearing his throat and glancing over Jamie's shoulder. She'd acquired a large umbrella and the guy she'd stopped was unsure whether to let her hold it over him or not. 'I have to, uh—' He pointed limply down the alleyway that she and Roper were blocking, towards the door with the green dragon on it.

'Go to the Jade Circle. I understand.' Jamie gave him a broad grin, as close to charming as she could muster. She'd never been very good at using her feminine wiles on men. Probably because she disagreed so fundamentally with the idea that men could be manipulated by a sultry glance, a subtle biting of the bottom lip, or by a light touch on the arm. And she hated it even more that they could be. 'But I just need a second of your time.'

Jamie didn't know whether you could say that someone looked like they were the sort to pay for sex. She didn't like to assume, and she was fully aware that *anyone* might. Just that morning she'd found out that Cake did, and she'd never have guessed that. But by what she'd dug up on the Jade Circle so far, it seemed that as far as casinos went, there were far better ones. So people probably didn't go for the tables.

The guy danced from foot to foot, glancing at Roper, who was speaking to another guy just a few metres away. It was a little after eight, and the foot traffic to the casino was beginning to pick up.

'Look…' Jamie said, offering her hand, fishing for a name.

'Har— John,' the guy said, cutting himself off halfway through his real name and offering a fake one instead. Either that or he was the fifth stuttering John she'd met that evening.

'John,' Jamie said, flashing him another smile. 'Just tell me if you've seen this girl.' Jamie held her phone up, a photo of the face of the victim displayed.

She'd had the go ahead from Smith to use the photo for canvassing, and she felt good being on the right side of things for once.

The guy barely looked at it and then shook his head. 'No. Never seen her before. Now please, I really have to—' He looked to be getting upset.

'John,' Jamie said, touching his arm, hating that she was doing it.

He stiffened a little and looked at her, freezing like a rabbit.

'Someone killed her – and we know she worked here. We know lots of girls work here…'

John swallowed.

'We don't want to stop them, and we don't want to arrest anyone. Not for gambling, and not for… *that.*' She waited for a second, waiting for him to meet her eyes. 'But someone killed her. Shot her, right in the back.'

John's face was a mixture of looks. Sad, scared, tense. Jamie thought he was going to turn and bolt.

'We don't know who, and we need your help. She worked here, she got pregnant, and she ran away. And then someone killed her.' She tightened her grip on John's arm. 'Hunted her down, and killed her. She was alone, John, scared for her life. And we need to catch whoever did this.'

'I told you, I don't know her.'

'Look again.' Jamie held up the phone with her other hand, the screen casting a pale blue glare over his lined face. His eyes were watery in the light.

He studied it for a few seconds. 'I… I don't know. The girls are all young… pretty… It's dark in there and the drinks…' He shook his head. 'They can… all look the same, you know? It's not a race, thing, it's—'

'I know,' Jamie said, releasing him. 'It's okay, John. I understand.'

He sighed heavily. 'I'm sorry, I really am. About her. And I wish I could help, I do, but…' He looked past her down the alley. 'Please…'

Jamie nodded and stepped to the side. 'Sure. If you remember anything, we'll be here all night. And tomorrow night. And every night.'

John's brow furrowed and he stepped awkwardly around them, heading for the door. He looked back over his shoulder before he reached the Jade Circle.

Then he knocked, waited, and went in.

For a second, Matt's face appeared in the gap. He glared at them a little, and then closed it.

Jamie restrained a smile.

Roper let his own John go and walked over, their umbrellas bumping against each other. 'You think they'll bite?' Roper asked.

Jamie kept her back to the door and shrugged. 'Maybe not tonight, but eventually. Three guys I've spoken to have already turned and left instead of going in. At least half a dozen more have turned and walked away as soon as they clocked me. And the ones who have gone in are no doubt being asked what we talked about. And with some luck, hopefully they're communicating that we're not intending to go anywhere.'

Roper pushed a cigarette into his mouth. 'Here's to hoping,' he mumbled out of the corner of his lips. He lit it, the flame from his lighter carving his face in the night.

'I mean, how busy does it get mid-week? How many customers can they afford to lose?' Jamie scoffed and shook her head. 'Gambling's not illegal, but the guys don't go for the tables, do they?'

'Probably not,' Roper said, sucking on his cigarette.

'And no one wants to go into a brothel with two detectives standing outside. I'd say it won't be long before they invite us in.'

'Hope so,' Roper said. He was shivering, and soaked.

So was Jamie.

If they had to come back tomorrow, they'd both dress a little more appropriately for the weather. But she didn't think they would. The longer they were there the more damage they would do to the business. And it wasn't the only place like this in the city. The guys could, and would go elsewhere if getting to the Jade Circle meant crossing paths with two detectives with the Met.

'Detectives.'

They both turned.

'What did I tell you?' Jamie said quietly.

'Never doubted you,' Roper muttered back.

Matt was walking towards them, beaming, hands open like a priest. 'Detectives,' he said again. 'I've been asked to extend an invitation to you to come in, and meet with the manager.'

'What changed his mind?' Jamie asked dumbly.

Matt laughed a little. 'That's good.'

'I thought so,' Jamie replied, resting the umbrella shaft on her shoulder.

'Follow me,' Matt said, not wasting any time. He turned on his heel and walked quickly towards the casino.

On her right, her father was leaning against the wall, arms folded across his chest, his bright blue eyes burning in the gloom. *Still would have been quicker just to kick him in the teeth,* he called after them.

Jamie ignored it and slowed as Matt approached the door. It opened in front of him and Jamie scanned the wall for cameras, seeing none, but guessing there must be one tucked away somewhere, and that she'd very much like to see the footage from it.

He stood to the side, keeping it open with one hand, and then motioned them in with the other.

The air was warm and perfumed, smoky with incense and tinted red.

A low throb of bass-heavy music rose out of the stairwell beyond the threshold and the figure of another bouncer swam in the darkness.

Roper stopped to let Jamie pass. 'After you,' he said.

Jamie glanced from Matt to Roper, and then shook her head. 'Gentlemen, the pair of you.' And then she went in and the door closed behind them with a heavy metallic snap.

13

Ho Zhou was the manager of the Jade Circle, and had spent the last three hours watching Jamie and Roper intercepting his patrons at the mouth of the alley.

There were five cameras in all that covered the outside of the Jade Circle, none of which could be seen by anyone unless they were really looking for them.

The first was set about ten metres above the door itself, pointing straight down. It was zoomed in to provide a full bird's eye view of the doorway and the surrounding five metres. Though you could only see the tops of people's heads, it was more than enough to see when something was happening that shouldn't be. And besides, if he needed to see the faces of the people coming in or out, there were other cameras for that.

The second was directly across the alley from the door, pointing straight at it.

It was suspended above a dumpster, disguised as a small drainage pipe, and clocked the face of every single person coming out. Zhou had hundreds of high-resolution still-images of businessmen, politicians, and other powerful individuals leaving his casino with his girls. Images that were worth a lot.

Of course, none of them knew he had them. To them Zhou was an upstanding businessman, a gentleman, and the sort of person willing to write off some debts just because. But Zhou never did anything for free, and while they bartered small favours – a night with his girls, free of charge, a few hundred or a thousand or two in debts written off in exchange for a stock tip, the removal of a parking ticket, or a few freebies from whatever company that they were running – Zhou was banking the thing that had real value. The thing that would allow him to take the wrist of whoever he wanted to leverage and drive it up between their shoulder blades, bending them over a table with nothing to do but grit their teeth and say, *yes sir, of course, sir.*

Zhou was good at plying people. He was good at getting the people he wanted to come to his casino. And he would know when they were because the third camera covered the mouth of the alleyway itself.

This one faced out into the street, and never missed anyone turning off and heading down the alley. The other end was long and rutted with nasty potholes, puddles of rubbish-water, and a stench of urine so strong it would send rats scurrying. Zhou had seen to that himself.

He wanted people coming from one direction, and they certainly did. They even thought it was their idea.

The fourth and fifth cameras covered the two exits that ninety-nine percent of the clientele didn't know existed.

One was hidden inside a smoke detector right above a steel door that had no handle in the back of the Chinese restaurant in front of the casino.

If you headed towards the bathrooms, passed them on your left, and came to a dead-end, you'd find two doors. One was just a normal maintenance cupboard with mops, buckets, and a whole lot of bleach in it. The second was this door. On it was a sticker with a high voltage symbol, and above it was a smoke detector that stared right at whoever was standing in front of it.

Behind the door was a stairwell, which led to the Jade Circle's private games room. It was reserved only for those with money to burn, and who didn't want to be disturbed. Closed games could be attended and left without anyone on the main floor seeing the players.

They could be hosted out of regular hours and go on for days without anyone knowing. The players could throw money down, snort drugs, and have sex right there on the table if the mood took them. And during *these* games, it often did. Zhou made sure of it.

The last camera was above the staff entrance known only to those who already knew where it was.

Zhou kept that list short.

And if the time came, he wasn't shy about trimming it.

The casino operated underneath a commercial office building accessed from the opposite side of the block to the restaurant. The ground floor was vacant for 'construction work', while the three floors above were leased long-term by a charity that offered aid to Sumatra's rainforests and the indigenous peoples there, a catering company that offered traditional Chinese catering for large events, and an online-school that taught English to Nepali migrants settling in the city. And while all were more than legitimate businesses registered with the Companies House, all with real people in charge and real personal addresses, none of them did any business. At least not from that address.

The charity was purely a money-laundering front.

The catering company was just an excuse to bring containers in from China when the need arose.

And the English language centre was created so that no one would turn their heads as the employees for Zhou's casino came and went.

If you called to donate to the charity, they'd be happy to accept your money. Though it would go into Zhou's pocket.

If you wanted an event catered for, the call would be forwarded to an actual catering company that never thought twice about where their calls were coming from.

And if you called up to book a class to learn English, you'd be told the price and never be able to afford it – not with so many apps and online courses providing the same service for next to nothing.

So no one looked twice at the unassuming and grey building that sat above the Jade Circle. That acted as housing for the girls, as a place that those who needed to live in the city without anyone knowing could stay, as a place that drugs could be cut in peace, that money could be laundered, and that rich assholes could get secretly filmed doing things they shouldn't be with women who were not their wives.

It was many things, but mostly, it was everything that Zhou needed it to be.

And the five cameras that covered it all gave Zhou power. Power to see and hear everything in crisp and clear high-definition video and audio. They gave him the power to know who was coming and going from his casino.

It was the impenetrability of the Jade Circle that made it special. It was the ability Zhou had to see them coming and keep those who he didn't want inside out.

So to see two detectives, not only coming to the door and asking to be let in, but standing at the mouth of his alley, scaring away his customers. Turning them towards other casinos. Sending them home under a cloud of shame. Well, that made his perfectly manicured nails curl up under his knuckles, scraping on the ironwood desk in his office that had been illegally harvested from the very rainforest his fake charity was supposed to be protecting.

His veneered teeth ground together as he thought. As he sat, watching them standing in the rain – this Jamie Johansson and Paul Roper.

He'd found out who they were in the first five minutes. He'd gotten stills of their faces and forwarded them to the detective that came here every week. The one who had a wife and three kids who would be devastated to see the video that Zhou had of him lapping tequila out of the ass crack of one of his girls, his nose whiter with cocaine than a baker's hands are with flour.

Their names had come easily. The question of what they were doing here took a little longer.

And the question of how easy they would be to dissuade took the longest of all.

Roper, Zhou was told, wouldn't be a problem. The girl, though… she could be… *tenacious.* And tenacity was a trait that Zhou didn't have the time or patience for.

The question was what did they know, and did they have a case? He could turn them away – he had done with twenty other detectives over the course of his tenure as the manager of several establishments like this. But if they wouldn't leave it alone, could he afford to be under the microscope?

He saw this as *his* casino. And it was. All that happened within its walls was under his command. Every penny of profit earned was because of him, and every foot put wrong by him, his staff, his girls... That was on him, too. And while he reigned supreme here, he couldn't help but feel — while staring at Detectives Sergeants Jamie Johansson and Paul Roper – that the silk, paisley print tie around his clean-shaven throat felt more like a choke chain than anything else.

He may have been the biggest dog at the park, but there was someone holding his leash. And if they got wind that two detectives were making trouble due to an oversight on his part. Well, they'd waste no time in snapping it tight. And they weren't the sort of people known to let go until your legs stopped kicking.

He wouldn't be the first.

But he didn't intend to be one at all.

The only reason that it was taking him so long to act at all was because the progress bar on his computer seemed to be moving so slowly.

When the words 'Transfer Complete' had finally shown up, and the seventeen terabytes of HD video captured from the casino in the last eighteen months had been backed up to an external hard drive, only then had he reached for the phone.

He'd taken advice on how to scrub the hard drives of the security system at the casino. On how to obliterate everything. And he had the command window open. All it would need was the touch of a button and everything would be gone. But Zhou knew that doing that made it look like you had something to hide. And he wouldn't do that until he had a subpoena hanging in front of his face and he was well and truly backed into a corner. All he could do now was prepare for that eventuality, if it ever came.

He'd spoken to the barristers that his employers had on retainer. And they didn't seem worried.

There was nothing to tie the girl to the casino. Not really.

They didn't seem worried.

But as Zhou made the call to bring the two detectives in, and watched Jamie Johansson step through the door and down the stairs, the fine lines of her face, every pore and crease of determination painted bloody red in the deep and sharp neon lights, he felt his finger-nails bend back against the grains of the ironwood. He felt his chest tighten and his mouth run a little dry.

Men could be bought, plied, manipulated. Money, drugs, women. Power. That was what they craved. Zhou knew them. He knew men. It was his business to know them. But her? This woman? He did not see in her what he saw in men.

He did not see weakness.

He did not see an opening.

And if you could have split his skull open and looked inside his brain, at the turning cogs there, you would have seen that Zhou, for the first time in a very long time, didn't know what he was looking at.

He couldn't measure her, and that made her unpredictable. And he didn't like unpredictable.

And before he could make the conscious link, his mind turned to another question.

It wasn't how he could exploit her, how he could bend her to his will as he was so used to doing. No, it was much simpler than that, and required far less finesse. The question that asked itself of his cruel mind was simply, how could he get rid of her?

How could he get rid of a detective from the Metropolitan Police before she ever had a chance to cause a problem?

The details hadn't formed themselves in his mind. But one word had, and he knew that it was true.

Quickly.

The phone on his desk rang quietly, a muted tone that cut the dead-silence in his office.

He picked it up, the gold rings on his finger glinting in the light over his desk. 'Yes?' he answered carefully.

'They're at your door,' came the voice of the head of his security team.

'Send them in,' Zhou replied, putting the handset down and pushing himself out of his leather chair.

The screen on his desk was now locked, displaying nothing.

He cleared his throat and flattened the jacket of his tailored black suit against his lean stomach, and then buttoned it up, straightening his black-on-black paisley tie.

The security light above the door turned from red to green and the corners of Zhou's mouth pushed up into his cheeks. 'Detectives,' he said, the door opening wide in front of him. 'Welcome to the Jade Circle.'

14

Ho Zhou was five feet and seven inches tall.

In his expensive leather loafers, and in her boots, Jamie was practically looking him dead in the eye. And the man she saw staring back was no more than a waxwork.

From the second she clocked him she felt her skin hackle, her back stiffen, blood rise.

He was around fifty, she would have said, and held himself like a man who was used to power. Chest out, shoulders back, a smile that was warm, bordering on smug, cut into his face. His hair was still black, not a hint of grey in it, his skin smooth. No laugh lines, she thought. Yeah, he didn't look like a guy with much of a sense of humour.

He stepped forward smoothly, covering half the distance to the door, hand already extended, gold rings around his third and pinky finger clicking together.

Usually, they reached for Roper's hand first, but Zhou gravitated towards Jamie like a comet on a collision course with a sun.

Her hand came up reflexively and she already felt on the back foot. Whatever subtle power-play was going on here, he'd made the first move and she'd already lost ground.

He grasped her hand and squeezed firmly, no doubt testing her grip.

Roper sort of turned half on and stepped back like there was heat coming off them, thrown by the fact that Zhou had just ignored him completely, his attention solely focused on Jamie.

'It's a pleasure to meet you, Detective. My name is Ho Zhou, and I'm the manager of the Jade Circle. How can I be of help?' Zhou said in impeccable English. He had no accent. Totally neutral, and perfectly spoken. Too good, even. He wasn't native, but Jamie knew that no facet of the language would escape him. Zhou was smart. Jamie could see it in his face. The way his eyes glinted like a bird's. Seeing the situation from a mile up, missing nothing. Everything moving more slowly for him than it did for others.

Jamie remembered her father's advice when you were dealing with an unknown. That's how he'd put it. An unknown. Someone you had no information about. Someone who's capabilities were yet unassessed. Someone whose intelligence, whose strength, whose mental state was yet to be revealed. Someone who could be very dangerous, and you wouldn't even know it.

Jamie nodded, but didn't say a word, letting Zhou shake a limp hand.

Zhou was an unknown and he'd come at Jamie to size her up.

Her father had said not to give them anything. Not a fucking thing until you knew.

And she didn't.

He shook for longer than was normal and searched for her attention. She did nothing but stare at a tiny pockmark between his eyebrows, her expression vacant.

Don't look them in the eye, don't engage. Let them tell you what you need to know.

Zhou released her after a few seconds and turned cursorily to Roper, shaking his hand as well, clasping it with his left so that Roper's was sandwiched. 'Detective.'

Jamie watched his body language change, the way he dropped his shoulders, came closer to Roper than was necessary, his own hands close to his gut, his head kept lowered, eyes looking up at Roper's.

He was nearly a head shorter than Roper, and he wanted him to know it.

She saw Roper's posture straighten, his shoulders broadening automatically.

It was subconscious science. Twenty million years of evolution taking hold in the lizard brain. Roper was being presented with a lesser male, and was assuming dominance. Or at least he thought he was.

Jamie studied Zhou closely. Learning everything she could.

Zhou was doing it on purpose, providing that illusion. And Jamie had to admit he was damn good at it.

But it didn't escape her.

She was operating on a heightened plane suddenly. She was a deer at a watering hole, a twig snapping in the undergrowth pulling her attention to the forest.

Zhou was a wolf, circling slowly, hidden in the brush.

He drew back now, giving them both space to move forward into the room, his hands coming together into a sort of prayer gesture. 'My apologies for earlier,' he said. 'I was out attending to some business and have only just returned back. Matthew informed me that you wanted to see me and I asked him to bring you in as soon as he could.' Zhou's voice was soft, docile even. Intentionally so.

'Why aren't you wet?' Jamie asked, pushing the conversation in another direction. She wanted the confrontation, to see how Zhou handled it.

'I beg your pardon?' Zhou said, creasing his brow apologetically.

'If you'd just come back, then you'd have been walking in the rain.' She kept her face straight. 'Your clothes are perfectly dry.'

'I was driven.'

'And on the walk from the car?'

'I wore a coat,' he answered, striking the perfect note between direct and friendly.

'Did it cover your legs too?'

'I had an umbrella.'

'Your shoes are dry, too.'

'It's a big umbrella.'

'We didn't see you come in.'

Zhou's hands lowered, clasped in front of him. 'I used another entrance.'

'Where is it?'

Zhou's quick responses came to an end as quickly as they'd gone on. His eyes twitched, his tongue pushing against the back of his teeth.

He broke the stare first, looked down, and then chuckled to himself a little.

Jamie wasn't sure if she'd won that joust, or revealed more about herself than she'd learned about Zhou, but she liked how it felt.

If Zhou was on the fence about the risk and reward of putting a detective in his crosshairs, he wasn't any more.

'What is it I can do for you, detectives... What were your names?'

'Roper,' Roper said quickly, trying to regain the little dominance he thought he'd gotten during their handshake.

'Johansson.'

Zhou cocked his head a little. 'And your warrant card numbers to go with your names?'

Jamie tried to stay relaxed.

Roper was less suppressed. 'Is that really necessary?'

'Roper,' Jamie said before Zhou could answer. 'Why wouldn't we? We're required by law to provide those details to anyone who asks.'

Roper narrowed his eyes. 'I don't have a pen.'

'There's a pen and paper on my desk,' Zhou said, gesturing to it. 'Please.'

'Of course,' Jamie said, stepping forward. 'And I hope should we ask something of you that you'll be equally obliging.'

'I suppose that depends what you ask, doesn't it?'

She stopped writing and cast a glance in his direction. 'Nothing that will force you to incriminate yourself,' she answered airily. 'Providing you haven't committed any crimes.'

Zhou chuckled again. A low, amused laugh. 'I assume that you're here about something serious?'

'Yes,' Jamie said, standing squarely as Roper scribbled down his card number almost illegibly. Though that was the point. 'Murder,' Jamie said.

'Oh,' Zhou replied, seemingly about as far from shocked as anyone could get. He turned and walked towards the leather sofa against the red papered wall. He eased down onto it and crossed his legs, lacing his fingers around his knee. 'Go on.'

Go on? Jamie let it roll off her back, forcing the tension out of her jaw. 'We're investigating the murder of a young woman we believe to have worked here.'

'What is her name?'

'We don't know.'

'Why do you believe she worked here?'

'She has a tattoo on her wrist that matches that of the other women who… *work* here.' Jamie's teeth gritted without her meaning for them to, the word squeezing between them.

Zhou didn't miss it. 'And what tattoo would that be?' His eye twitched almost imperceptibly. But Jamie clocked it. He tried to sound absent, but it was too close to home.

She felt like it touched a nerve. And she wanted to press harder.

'A dragon, the same one painted on the front door, the same one on every rug in this place. The same one that's sitting on the wall behind you.' Jamie lifted her eyes to the golden swirl on the wall behind Zhou. It was a sculpture suspended above the sofa, a dim light spilling from behind it.

'A dragon?' He raised an eyebrow. 'One of the most common symbols in Chinese culture?' He thought it was funny. Or at least wanted to appear that way. 'Detectives, please, there must be a thousand girls in the city with a tattoo like that. Why are you wasting your time here?'

'I don't believe we are,' Roper said, standing next to Jamie now.

'And why is that?' Zhou seemed unphased.

'Because we've got a witness that says they saw her working here. One who's prepared to testify to it.'

Zhou's eyes went to Jamie.

She stood there, trying to remain expressionless. For a guy who'd been on her case for bending the rules, lying to a suspect's face about a positive ID was a pretty big jump.

Zhou studied her like a polygraph.

She didn't know if he found anything.

Roper went on. 'So if you don't mind, we'd appreciate a little cooperation.' He folded his arms impressively, the leather of his damp jacket groaning. 'I'm sure you've got lots of official paperwork that says that the girls downstairs are bar staff, waitresses, but we know what they really do here. And we're going to speak to them. We're going to get the victim's name. And we're going to interview every single person she ever had contact with – her co-workers, her clients' — Roper counted them out on his fingers — 'and the piece of shit who makes it happen.'

Zhou was a statue. 'Are you, Detective Roper? And I suppose you have a warrant that says so? Because you need one, don't you? Unless you have probable cause, of course. But I don't think you do.' Zhou took a slow breath. 'The evidence you have is circumstantial at best. An eye witness who says that a tattoo he saw on a girls' wrist in this casino is not dissimilar to that which appears on the arm of a victim?'

'An eye witness who can place the victim here, *working* in this casino.'

'He spoke to her?'

Roper paused for a second, deciding how far he could push the lie. 'No.' He was playing it safe.

'So he *saw* her then?'

'Yes.' Roper narrowed his eyes.

'And he's sure of it?'

'We're here, aren't we?'

Zhou laughed again. 'Have you ever been downstairs, detective?'

'No.'

'Then perhaps you should.' He pushed off the sofa, grinning now with perfect teeth. 'Come, let me show you.' He clapped his hands together, bowing slightly. 'It is of course my intention to assist you however I can. But I must also consider my business. And your time, most of all. I wouldn't want you to waste even a minute of it on hearsay.' He moved past them and opened the door, proffering it. 'Please,' he said. 'After you.'

Jamie and Roper glanced at each other, neither of them liking what they were seeing or hearing.

They weren't sure what they were going to be looking at downstairs, but judging by the way the smile wasn't moving from Zhou's smug face, they both figured that their circumstantial evidence was about to disintegrate altogether.

Zhou led them down the staircase that rose to his office door, and onto the flat landing that let into the casino.

There was a wide set of polished wooden double doors, stained dark to match the red velvet drapes hanging around them. From behind, a quiet throb of music rose.

The two bouncers, both Chinese, both big, both well-dressed, and both silent statues, pushed open the doors to the main room to let them through.

Beyond, the casino opened up.

Zhou stepped out onto a raised balcony, a pair of staircases leading down in either direction, wrapping around to the floor.

He stood at the bannister and looked out over it.

Right below them, Jamie could see the window that served chips and cashed patrons out.

In the middle of the floor were a pair of roulette tables back to back. At the far end were three poker tables, three blackjack tables, and three rows of slot machines.

Along the right-hand wall was a bar, the countertop lit from underneath, causing the golden beer taps to glimmer.

Along the left were booths where people sat, getting served drinks by waitresses in short, sequinned dresses that seemed to catch the glow of the chandeliers hanging over each table, showing off every curve and undulation.

The guys sitting in the booths were well-dressed businessmen mostly looking to blow off steam. Jamie recognised every one of them as the guys who'd walked past them at the mouth of the alley.

They sat sipping drinks, getting fawned over by more girls. These ones in different dresses. Reds, blacks, whites, blues. Each shorter and deeper cut than the last, showing off their young, slim bodies. The girls were all well-manicured, made up in various ways. Some with heavy makeup, others with light make up. Some with their hair up, some with their hair down. Some with short hair, others with long hair. A style for every taste, Jamie thought.

As she looked down into the gloom – because that was the only way to describe it. Gloom. The air, heavy with incense smoke, no doubt emulating what would have once been the smoky haze from the cigars of the high rollers, was impenetrable – Jamie could barely make out the luminous dials of the slot machines, flashing distantly across the room.

Each booth had a chandelier over it, but the bulbs could have been no more than twenty watts. Above each table there was a hanging light, casting a yellow glow, but the shade was spherical, directing the brilliance directly down onto the playing surface. The figures around it were no more than shadows.

And the bar, despite being lit from underneath, was no more than a white strip in the dark. The shelving behind the bottles at the back were dimly illuminated with red LED lights, but Jamie's eyes struggled to make out anything except shapes.

And with all the men dressed in suits, and all the women dressed in glittering dresses, dolled up, grinning with white teeth – each hovering perilously around twenty, each no more than five feet three or four, each a size six, each with black hair and heels so high they turned Jamie nauseous to think about walking on them – or maybe that was the incense – telling anyone apart was impossible. From this distance or any.

What went on here – gambling, sex… Drugs. Jamie clocked someone at one of the booths lean sideways and drive a key into one of their nostrils, the tip packed with what she had to assume was cocaine – needed to be anonymous to work. So the closed booths which wrapped around to obscure the interior from anyone outside, the heavily shaded lights at the table, the smoke. It made the whole place dark, and easy to hide in. Which in turn would make any eye witness testimony saying that they could positively identify anyone in this bloody mess worth basically nothing.

And that was if they even had one. Which they didn't.

Zhou turned back to Roper and Jamie and waited, smiling softly. 'Is there anything else I can do for you?'

Jamie drew in a deep breath and then let it out. 'Not unless you'd like to voluntarily give us access to all of your security tapes for the last six months?'

Roper chimed in. 'And let us interview all your... *girls*?'

Zhou chuckled with closed lips. 'Matthew will show you out.'

Jamie and Roper were suddenly aware that the head bouncer, Matt, had appeared behind them, proffering the doors that had never closed.

Roper and Jamie exchanged a look and then submitted, heading back up the stairs towards the street.

'Oh, and detectives,' Zhou said, straightening the cuffs on his suit. 'If I see you causing my customers, or my business any more distress, well... I'll let you imagine the lengths I'd be prepared to go to in recompense.'

Jamie paused on the step and looked back. 'Yes, Mr Zhou,' she said lightly. 'I'm sure that revenge comes naturally to you.' She took another few steps up. 'In fact, I think we've seen that already.'

Zhou stared up at her, his smile widening into a satisfied grin, like he had suddenly decided on something that made him happy. 'Have a pleasant evening, Detective Johansson,' he said, his voice smooth and cold. 'I'll see you soon.'

15

JAMIE WAS STARING at her computer screen, her nostrils flaring gently as she breathed.

'What's up your ass?' Roper asked tactfully, approaching from Smith's office and dropping a stapled stack of papers on Jamie's desk with a dull thwap.

'Nothing,' she growled. 'Just this damn Raymond case. The kid's still not turned up and his mother's losing her shit.' She rubbed her eyes with the heels of her hands. 'But none of his friends will speak to me, he's not been in school…' She sighed. 'He's really making her sweat this time.'

'So what's the move?'

'You know,' she said, leaning back in her chair and staring up at him with tired eyes. 'You could actually try helping out once in a while, rather than just asking me how it's going.'

He grinned at her. 'If I was wasting my time with phone calls, I'd never be able to bring you presents like this.' He pointed at the papers he'd dropped on the desk. 'But seriously, what are we going to do about the Raymond kid?'

Jamie sat forward and scanned the top page. 'I've pinged a description out to the patrols in the area, asked the uniforms to keep their eyes peeled, ask around some, you know, the usual. And if they spot anyone smoking, to stop and search, lean on them for any leads on Raymond or who that cannabis belonged to.' She turned the top page. 'But if no one else is going to give up their dealer voluntarily, all we can do is hope that the uniforms get someone to crack. I'll stay on it.'

'Good,' Roper said. 'Page four is where it gets good.'

Jamie glanced up at him, nodded, and then flipped two more pages.

She was looking at the surveillance report on the casino.

They'd gone to Smith with what they had – which wasn't much – but they'd managed to convince him to put a surveillance team out there on a twenty-four-hour watch. And now that it had come to an end, some thirty-nine hours after their meeting with Zhou, the notes had been transcribed and the footage uploaded to the quickly expanding case file.

'What am I looking at?' Jamie said, scanning up and down the page.

'There,' Roper said. 'About halfway down.' He leaned in and motioned to an entry topped with the time stamp 03.09 a.m. Jamie's eyes settled on Roper's yellowed fingernail for a moment before he pulled it away. Smoking would do that to you, she thought.

Her eyes refocused on the entry and she read it aloud.

'Three figures observed leaving via main entrance. One male, mid-forties, Caucasian. Dressed in grey suit. Two females, early-twenties, Asian. One in red dress. One in blue dress. All appear intoxicated. Approached main street, turned left, moving away. Proceeded to inter-section and met by car. License plate unknown. New model Mercedes, black.'

Jamie cocked her eyebrow and looked up at Roper. 'Not exactly a smoking gun, is it.'

He curled his lip like he knew something she didn't.

'What?'

'It means they can leave. That they do leave.'

'I'm not following.'

'The casino. The girls – the prostitutes. They can leave.'

Jamie felt like her mind had melted after a two hour stretch digging into the Raymond case.

'Why wouldn't they be able to?'

Roper looked at her. 'It's not that they wouldn't be able to – I wasn't suggesting that the casino was a prison. Though judging by that Zhou asshole, I wouldn't be surprised if—'

'Get to the point, Roper.'

'Over the course of the surveillance, only those two girls left.'

'Right.'

'From what you said your trainer said—'

'Cake.'

'Right. Cake.' It always sounded weird coming out of his mouth. 'He said that inside the casino, that players can take the girls upstairs, right?'

'Yeah.'

'Well, the casino is underneath an office building. I looked it up.'

'You mean you actually did some police work?'

'Mmm.' He made a grumbling noise. 'But for high rollers, it seems, there are exceptions.'

'I assume you're closing in on a revelation here?'

He ignored her. 'The thing is, they never came back.'

'Who didn't?'

'The girls.'

'The two who went with the guy in the grey suit?' Jamie sat up a little straighter and flicked more pages.

'Don't bother, I checked.'

Jamie looked up at him, believing it. 'So they're still out there?' Jamie tried to keep the positivity out of her voice. One of the girls was already dead for trying to run from the place, and the last thing she wanted to do was put another in harm's way. But if they could catch one out in the wild, away from the casino, they could question her without Zhou ever finding out.

Roper shrugged. 'I don't know. Maybe. Maybe not. But it got me thinking – if when the casino closes, the girls don't leave, then it means they live there.'

'A lot of brothels are like that,' Jamie said, folding her arms.

'Sure. But this is a casino, not a brothel.'

'Okay.'

'And *upstairs* is an office block.'

'Right.'

'So it's not got planning for residential.'

Jamie eased forward. 'Can we prove this?'

'Not right now. The businesses there are all up to date on their rates, they're all legal enterprises. But I don't think any of them actually do anything. They're just a front.'

'For the brothel?'

'Probably. But it's a big building. I looked it up on street-view. Got an entrance on the opposite road.' He drew a slow breath. 'If the girls did come back, I think they must have used a different entrance. Maybe that one.'

Jamie champed her lips, thinking about it. 'Zhou said he came in through a different entrance.' It could be that one. 'You want to go in there, ruffle some feathers?'

Roper turned and leaned against her desk. It shuddered a little under his weight.

She hated when he did it.

It wasn't that she was a clean freak, but she didn't like anyone's butt being pressed against the surface that she ate her lunch off.

She pushed back and got up. 'Coffee?' she asked, trying to peel his jeans off her desk. He was looking too comfortable and she didn't want it to become a habit.

'Sure.' Roper pushed off and followed her. 'And no,' he added, speeding up to keep pace. 'I don't think we should go in there. Zhou doesn't seem like the type to respond well to having his feathers ruffled, and I don't want to risk blowing this before we start.'

'Good point.' Jamie thought about Zhou. He'd all but threatened her on the way out. And any guy who was running a place like that and had a hand in the murder of an innocent girl… Well, she didn't want to know what he'd do if pushed. But she doubted it was anything good. 'So what do you suggest?'

'I don't think Smith will give us another surveillance detail. Not without anything more solid. So I think we should head around, stake out the entrance a little. If any of the girls leave, we follow them, at the very least get them to confirm that they're living there, and then we can hit Zhou with a planning violation.'

'I thought the goal here was to *not* piss the guy off?' Jamie pushed a cup under the machine and pressed the button for a skimmed latte. The machine whined and then shook as it spat coffee into the mug she wished she'd checked was clean before using it. She didn't think she could stomach the caffeine hit from the mud-thick pot in the drip filter.

Roper shrugged again. 'Got a better idea?'

Jamie exhaled and pulled the mug to her lips, blowing on the foamy surface. 'We could find the father of the baby.'

'Well, if he is one of the clients, then the girls will know more about that, surely?' Roper moved past her and reached for a mug off the rack.

'That's our best move,' Jamie agreed.

'Good. Well, it's…' He checked his watch and then pushed the button for a black coffee. The beans jumped and swirled in the hopper as the machine ground them up. 'Two-twenty now. If we head out and set up we might be able to catch a few of them before their shift starts.'

Jamie swallowed a mouthful of scalding coffee, winced, and then put the cup down. 'Then let's go.'

When Roper was right, he was right.

They were only sitting in the coffee shop for forty minutes when the first girl returned to the office block at the back of casino.

The sky was grey and slow, like the ocean after a storm.

The clouds looked bruised and beaten up and they threatened to open up again. But for now the air was clear, if not thick. Warm for the time of year. Close.

The girl was wearing a pair of jeans, high heels, and a brown coat, her hair long and curled. She looked… glamorous. That was the word that came to Jamie's mind.

The girl on the slab at the coroner's office was far from that.

It was hard to imagine whether they lived in lavish luxury inside the building or if it was more like a prison.

Jamie's eyes moved up and down the street, but she saw no one with the girl. She appeared to be alone. But then again, her chaperone wouldn't be good at his job if he was easily spotted.

Roper couldn't confirm if she was one of the two that'd gone home with the high roller the night before. And neither could Jamie.

A few minutes later, another girl came out of the door. She was wearing a dress cut above the knee and high boots with thin heels. On top she had an oversized, military-style parka, her hair tied up in a bun, eyes covered with oversized sunglasses despite the murkiness in the sky.

She closed the door behind her, turned to make sure that it was locked – it seemed to latch automatically, but Jamie couldn't recall the other girl who entered having gotten out a key. She looked like she'd walked right in. Magnetic fobs? Too high tech. Probably just a camera over the door with someone on the other end. Jamie made a mental note of it.

The girl came out of the door and strode quickly down the street.

Jamie and Roper had paid for their coffees when they ordered, so just got up and walked out, keeping to their own side of the road, about fifteen metres back so as not to get spotted.

Though they were clocked the second they'd set up on the table in the window. Firstly by the guy that Zhou had paid to watch the rear entrance since Roper and Jamie had been in the casino. Secondly by Zhou's head of security standing behind a mirror-coated window on the third floor of the office building – in *his* office. And lastly by Marco De Voge, the French-Algerian in charge of Zhou's stable.

Zhou never really cared for the word, but didn't really care enough to ever question De Voge on it. He was six-two, sinewy, and had arms like the cables on a suspension bridge, all rolled muscle fibres and veins. You'd think that a guy like that would stick out in a crowd, but he had a remarkable knack for going unseen. He prided himself on it. It was what made him so good at what he did.

De Voge didn't even glance at Zhou's paid watchman, a young kid no more than nineteen looking to make a name for himself in the operation, sitting on the front step of an apartment entrance between two shops. He had a blue puffer jacket on, a big backpack, and a cigarette in his mouth. He was staring at his phone the entire time that Jamie and Roper sat in the window, and he might as well have been painted on the door for all the attention they paid him.

He'd let Zhou's head of security know, an Eastern European guy by the name of Kosiah, who'd homed in on their location about six seconds after the text had come through. He wasn't a large man, but you'd only need to take one look at him to know exactly why Zhou had put him in charge of keeping everything running. Sure, Zhou managed it all, but every pharaoh needed someone to work the whips. And between Kosiah running the security for the whole thing from on high, De Voge ruling the girls with an iron fist, and Matt – full name Matthew Tan – making sure no one put a foot out of place on the casino floor, he didn't just have one man on the whips. He had a trio of them. And between the three, no one ever dared try anything. Each was willing to spill blood, and each was adept at doing so in their own way.

Jamie and Roper eyed the girl, making idle conversation as they racked up the distance between themselves and the casino.

De Voge was wearing a black coat with the hood up, hands in his pockets. He tailed them about ten metres back, on the same side of the street as the girl. He always followed them. It was his job. They were allowed out – but never unchaperoned. If they were, there was too much chance of them running. De Voge didn't like it when they did that. It wasn't that he minded the violence. It was the time it took to do it right that irked him.

Though they never got far.

Zhou had told De Voge to deal with the detectives if they showed up again.

Those were his words. *Deal with them.*

De Voge had no intention of killing them. Not right here in broad daylight at least. But there were a myriad of options between doing nothing and slitting someone's throat.

His long, bony fingers rolled the knife he had in his pocket over and over. It was spring-loaded and flicked out with a certain amount of pressure applied to the release catch under the heel of De Voge's hand.

He knew exactly how hard he could press it for it not to pop out in his pocket.

There was no danger of it.

The girl cut right down a street and Jamie and Roper paused, turning to watch her go.

At the far end, the street hit a T and went right, back towards the casino, as well as left. Jamie and Roper exchanged a quick glance, both coming to the conclusion that she wasn't likely to double back.

'I'll go up to the next junction and head her off,' Jamie said. 'You follow her here in case she tries to run or double back.'

'In those heels?' Roper said coquettishly.

Jamie rolled her eyes. 'Just do it. We're losing her.' She took off at a light jog, reaching the corner in record time.

Roper looked both ways and then stepped off the curb, hopping up onto the opposite one in pursuit, not seeing that De Voge had slowed his pace just enough that Roper cut across his path no more than a metre ahead of him.

It made falling into step, within lunging distance, all too easy.

And as they walked, he couldn't help but wonder how the hell a detective in the Met wasn't aware that he was right there on his shoulder, the knife still rolling over in his deft hands, its pace quickening.

16

JAMIE TURNED RIGHT, heading back towards the casino, headlong towards the girl. Or so she hoped.

There was no sign of her.

'Shit,' she muttered, picking up the pace.

Her heart thumped against her ribs.

She looked left and right, scanning the thin streams of people milling down both sides of the street. And where the hell was Roper?

Jamie stopped and took a breath, studying the shopfronts.

Two were cafes. A handful were takeaways. A couple of little shops. This was hardly one of the main drags in the city.

And a beauty salon. Texas Nails & Hair. 'Everything's Bigger In The USA!'

Jamie's eyes settled on it and she thought back to the girl who'd come in just before her. She was done up to the nines, her hair perfectly curled and quaffed. *Freshly* curled and quaffed. Maybe it was a one-in one-out deal. Fridays were, after all, probably their big money-making night. Maybe the girls were sent here every week to get their beauty-fix.

Jamie approached quickly, keen to look in the window and confirm, and then back-track to catch Roper if she came up empty.

The sounds of hairdryers hummed in the air as she got close and slowed at the glass, catching her breath. She had three layers on – a long sleeved under-layer, a charcoal zip-through hoodie, and her coat. And in the thick air, she was sweating. Or maybe it was just the feeling of unease that had laid its hand on the back of her neck and dug its fingers into her skin.

The window was steamed-up against the cool winter air, but Jamie could make out the setup inside.

Down the left were the salon chairs. There were four of them. Three were filled with bodies. One had foils in her hair, another was getting a curl, the third a cut. On the opposite side, what looked like dentist chairs were lined up with plastic bowls the bases, where the feet would go. And on the arm rests were trays with articulated lights and magnifying lenses.

Of the four chairs, two were occupied. One of the women sitting there was having a foot bath, her tray filled with bubbling, pink water. She was leaning back, her eyes closed. The other was having a manicure.

At the rear, a long bench stretched from left to right and a row of Asian women in white smocks and face masks worked on the nails of the patrons. In fact, all of the women working there seemed to be Asian. Either Chinese or South-East Asian by the structures of their faces.

Jamie's eyes documented it all and then fell on the silhouette of the woman she was looking for.

She recognised the dress and the knee-high boots.

Now that the girl had taken her coat off, Jamie could make her out a little better. She must have been around five-two or three, and lithe. Her dress wasn't tightly fitted or that revealing, but even through the window Jamie could make out a tiny waist, slim shoulders, long legs for her stature, and skin that looked like poured honey.

A quick glance over her shoulder told her Roper must have been lagging – probably stopped for a cigarette. He could see her now, no doubt, and had taken the opportunity to rest on his laurels, let Jamie do the heavy lifting as usual.

She moved towards the door with only a vague sense of what she was about to do and went inside.

The air was pungent with the smell of nail polish remover. It was like paint thinner on steroids and always turned her stomach. Her mother used to paint her nails four times a week when they lived in Sweden. She'd come home from work, open a bottle of wine, and sit in the living room, right in front of the door, TV blaring, stripping and recoating her nails. Just waiting for Jamie's father to come home so that she could pick a fight with him about where he'd been and who he'd been with.

The stench of acetone brought up a lot more for her than just her lunch. But this wasn't about her or her parents' broken marriage. This was about finding out who put a bullet in an innocent girl's back.

She shrugged off the fumes, resigned herself to breathing through her mouth, and stepped forward.

The girl was standing at the bench at the back, chatting to one of the technicians happily in their shared language. Jamie would have guessed Mandarin, but she didn't know it well enough to put a definitive label on it.

Jamie hung back, looking aimlessly around the room until they finished their conversation and the girl turned back towards her, heading for one of the manicurist's chairs.

Jamie nodded to her and stepped aside.

The girl flashed her a smile with straight white teeth and Jamie felt her cheeks flush.

She was beautiful. There was no denying that. Jamie might have put her somewhere around the twenty-four or twenty-five-year-old mark, but it was hard to tell. She wasn't wearing any makeup, but her skin was still impeccable and smooth, her eyes like almonds, the colour of raw cocoa. With make up on, she probably could have passed for eighteen. Which was what the clients no doubt wanted.

The technician that the girl had been speaking to was now right in front of Jamie.

'What do you want?' she asked, almost curtly. Jamie could see that while the other technicians and stylists had plain white smocks with black accents, the lady standing in front of her was probably double their average age and had a pair of purple strips across her shoulders. Jamie guessed that it was some sort of pseudo-military hierarchy. Stripes meant she was the owner. Or manager.

'Uh,' Jamie said, turning to look at the girl she'd followed in. 'What she's having.' Jamie hooked a thumb over her shoulder at her. She had now taken one of the free chairs at the end and picked up a magazine from the little tray next to it.

Jamie cast her eyes around the room quickly. Almost everyone in there was on their phones. Except the girl from the casino. Though Jamie guessed they weren't allowed phones. But they had the freedom to go out like this?

Before she could interrogate that thought any more, she was pulled back to the woman at the counter.

'Full works?' The she asked, surprised. 'Hair, nails, toes, *wax?*' She moved her finger up and down in front of Jamie, waggling it at everywhere hair grew and pausing at the fly of Jamie's jeans.

Jamie met her eyes, the only thing showing above her mask, and cleared her throat. 'Maybe just the nails,' she said sheepishly. 'A manicure, I guess?' she added, trying to sound like she knew what the hell she was talking about.

'Okay, you sit,' the woman replied and pointed to the empty chair next to the girl.

Jamie nodded thanks and went over to it, getting in.

The girl didn't acknowledge her.

Jamie sighed and leaned her head back against the plastic-coated headrest. She was nervous. More so for the manicure than for the questioning. She'd never had one before. 'This weather, huh?' she asked absently.

The girl just glanced over, smiled with closed lips, and then went back to the magazine.

'I've never been here before,' Jamie said again, turning to her. Her father always said that if you were trying to open a genuine line of dialogue with a witness, then being genuine was a good way to go about it. 'This place any good?'

The girl nodded, doing her best to keep reading.

'I'm not sure what to get. Do you come here a lot?'

The girl sighed, not doing much to hide it. 'Yeah.' Her accent was fairly strong, but her English seemed colloquial from the way the word rolled off her tongue.

'This is my first manicure,' Jamie said.

The girl glanced at Jamie's hands. 'I can tell.'

She tucked her fingernails into her palms. 'I'm Jamie.'

She narrowed her eyes at Jamie for a second. 'Yanmei.'

'It's good to meet you.' As Jamie finished the words, two technicians approached, carrying silver trays with tools on them. Between the chair and the way that they looked more like weapons than anything else, Jamie felt like she was about to undergo dental surgery.

Yanmei rested her arm on the rest just above the table and a technician sat down on a stool she pulled from underneath the chair, putting the tools on the tray and turning on the magnifying light.

Jamie followed suit, letting the technician who'd sat down in front of her take her hand and pull it into position. She dragged the magnifying glass into place and muttered something under her breath. Jamie didn't know the translation, but by the tone of it she was saying, *Oh shit, this is going to take a while.* Jamie's hands were constantly being jammed into gloves, they were hitting bags and pads, and they were getting chewed on. She used to bite them when she was a kid – mostly in her teens when her parents were… She shook off the thought. The acetone in the air was invading her brain. She looked down at her hand now in the latex gloves of the technician, and tried to remember when she'd started biting them again. She couldn't put a finger on it, but she had an idea. They'd been fine before the Oliver Hammond case. Before Elliot.

'Basic?' The technician asked abruptly.

'Sorry?' Jamie replied, feeling out of her depth immediately.

'French?'

'Uh…'

'Gel? What you want?'

Jamie stared at her impatient eyes and felt herself squirm in the chair. The woman in front of her was small but had a vice grip around her hand.

Jamie laughed nervously. 'Can you repeat the options?'

The technician's impatient stare turned into a bored glare.

Yanmei leaned out of her chair, the technician working on her nails not letting go, and cast a judgmental eye over Jamie's fingers. 'Mm,' she said, not impressed. 'Paraffin.' She sat back down, not second-guessing her assessment.

The technician at Jamie's chair looked at her for confirmation.

'Uh, sure,' Jamie said, forcing a smile. 'Sounds great.' She had no idea what a paraffin manicure was, but it was an avenue with Yanmei and that was what mattered most.

The technician at Jamie's side left to get the necessaries and the one at Yanmei's was handed a little steaming plastic trough by another smock-wearing salon-worker. She pushed Yanmei's fingers into the hot liquid on one side while the next technician placed the second bath on the side closest to Jamie and placed Yanmei's other hand in it.

Yanmei didn't seem phased by any of it. Well practised now, no doubt.

The two technicians then retreated from the chair and suddenly Jamie and Yanmei were alone. And by the look of the hot baths that Yanmei's fingers were taking, she wasn't going to be moving for a few minutes at least.

That meant, if Jamie was going to ask any questions without anyone else hearing, she had however long it took for her technician to prepare whatever she needed to perform the manicure, or when Yanmei's hands were sufficiently wet, or hot, or soft enough, or what-ever the hell it was they were trying to do to them. Whichever came first.

Jamie drew a deep breath and swung her legs off the side of the chair so she was facing the girl.

In the silence, the howling whine of a hairdryer across the way filled the space.

Distantly, sirens wailed.

'Yanmei,' Jamie said, allowing the assertiveness in her voice to shine through.

The girl opened her eyes and stared at Jamie questioningly, not turning her head.

'My name is Detective Sergeant Jamie Johansson and I'm with the London Metropolitan Police.'

Yanmei began to recoil, twisting towards Jamie now with a look of disgust in her eyes. Most witnesses looked scared when Jamie dropped that line, but it was definitely disgust in the girl's eyes. Revulsion even.

'I'm investigating the death of an unidentified girl that we believe worked at the Jade Circle with you.' Her eyes flicked to the technicians at the nail bar at the back. They didn't seem to care, so far. 'And Yanmei, I need your help.'

She stared at Jamie for a second, weighing up whether to say it or not, Jamie thought, and then the words that Jamie was dreading to hear came out of her mouth.

'If I speak to you, they'll kill me.'

Jamie knew that it was the truth, but as much as it pained her, she couldn't let up. She quickly rewired her brain to ignore it and ploughed on, knowing that time was short, and the stakes were about as high as they got. 'They've already killed one of you, I won't let them make it two,' Jamie said assertively.

'You're not scared of them?'

'I'm a detective in the London Metropolitan Police.'

'They don't care. It won't matter to them.'

Jamie could hear the fear in her voice, felt the skin on the back of her neck hackle. 'We can protect you.'

'You won't even be able to protect yourself.'

Jamie didn't have time for this. 'What's her name?'

Yanmei fell quiet.

'Yanmei, please,' Jamie urged. 'They killed her for running away, didn't they? Who was it, Yanmei? Who killed her?'

Yanmei's eyes roved across the window and then fell back to Jamie. She nodded, almost imperceptibly. 'I can't—'

'Who killed her? Was it Zhou?'

'I don't know. I…'

She couldn't afford to waste any time. She needed information. Anything she could get. 'What was her name?'

'Qiang.' She almost whispered it, like saying it would cause a bullet to fly through the window and punch a hole in her chest, too.

Jamie was half expecting it. 'Good,' she said, her voice choked. 'What was her second name?'

Yanmei shook her head a little again. 'I don't know.' Jamie had to read her lips as much as hear the words. Her English was fluent. But Jamie suspected it had to be to deal with the clients effectively. 'She never said… We weren't allowed to…'

Jamie watched her fingers begin to curl up in the hot baths and cast an eye across the room to see whether the technicians were coming back.

She had a second.

Behind her, the sirens grew to a piercing shriek and then an ambulance whipped past the window, drowning the inside of the salon in blue light for an instant.

Jamie's eyes never left Yanmei's. 'She was pregnant, you knew that?'

Another minute nod, this one tentative.

'Who was the father?' Jamie asked, reshuffling the order of questions in her head. She needed to prioritise.

'I— I don't know,' Yanmei answered apologetically. 'I never knew his name, he always picked Qiang – but he called her Rose – that's what it means… Meant.' Yanmei's eyes filled suddenly, her cheeks reddening. 'She was my friend,' she muttered. 'And they…'

'It's okay,' Jamie said dutifully. 'Now listen to me.'

Yanmei's eyes refocused.

'I need you to come in with me—'

She hadn't even finished speaking before Yanmei began shaking her head. 'I can't—'

'I need you to go on record about what they're doing in there.'

'I can't. I can't leave. They'll find me.'

'No they won't. We can protect you.'

'You can't. *I* can't – the others... They'll...' Her voice was cracking.

Jamie couldn't afford to lose her. 'We can...' She trailed off, not sure she could keep a promise she was about to make. Was that that how they controlled them? Kept them coming back? Threatened the life of all the others if one decided...

She shook it off. She could contemplate that later, decode this all then. 'We need to know who killed Qiang.' Jamie did her best to pronounce it right.

'I don't know who...' She trailed off, her eyes going to the window and back. 'I don't know... Qiang was there one night and then... she was gone. A few weeks later...' She began to sob fitfully. Silent, tiny convulsions. She did all she could to hide it. 'They stuck a photograph of her body on the wall... That was it.'

'Jesus,' Jamie mumbled, not able to stop herself.

The sirens continued to echo outside.

'Yanmei – please, I need something else.' She was basically pleading now. 'Who is the father? If we can positively identify Qiang, and place her at the casino, we can get Zhou. We can stop him from hurting anyone else.' She didn't know if it sounded as confident as it was meant to. She didn't think so.

Yanmei shook her head more vigorously now. 'I don't know his name – but guys don't give their real names anyway. But...' She swallowed hard, fighting back the tears. 'But he liked Qiang. A lot. She told me that he was going to take her away, you know? Was going to... I don't know.' She began to sob again.

'Yanmei,' Jamie said, more forcefully now. 'Please. I need you to hold it together. Just give me *something.*'

'I... I... He was...' She searched her memories. 'He was a solicitor, I think. A barrister, he said, maybe?'

'Good. Good. What else?' Jamie was keeping one eye on the technicians. They were watching them talk now. She had to be fast, and careful. 'Did he say what company? What did he look like? How old was he?'

She kept shaking. 'He didn't. But he said something about a big case he was working on, before Qiang…'

'What was it?'

'I don't know – she said it was something to do with taxes? A big company was avoiding paying tax or something – maybe something to do with Ireland or Jersey, or somewhere like that?'

Jesus. A big company trying to avoid paying taxes by putting their money in Jersey or Ireland? It didn't exactly narrow it down. And was he fighting for or against the company? This wasn't enough.

'What did he look like? Describe him for me.' She was all but commanding her now.

'Tall? Mid-forties, fifties? Handsome, I suppose.'

'Hair? Ethnicity?'

'White – his skin, I mean – brown hair, short. Clean-shaven.'

That was too broad. It would take months to round them all up.

'*Anything,* Yanmei. Anything distinctive. A scar, a tattoo – anything like that?'

She screwed her face up, tears running down her cheeks. 'His cufflinks.'

'What about them?'

'He always wore the same ones – I remember. They were shiny, gold – two lines crossed, like an X.'

'An "X"?'

She began to shudder. 'With a little circle in the middle – a diamond in it.'

Jamie's stomach began to sink. The technician was coming back with a steaming bowl of paraffin.

Sirens echoed and cried in the streets through the steamed up window.

She was out of time. And Yanmei wasn't giving her anything else. The girl had nothing left to give. And staying any longer would only put her in more danger.

'Thank you, Yanmei,' Jamie said quickly. 'You've really helped.'

She slid forward out of the chair and hit the floor. 'If you ever need anything, ask any police officer for help, okay?' The words were a blur coming out of her mouth. She needed to get out of there. 'Ask for Detective Jamie Johansson. They'll do the rest.' She reached out and squeezed Yanmei's arm for a second, and then slipped around the chair and headed for the door.

The technician with the paraffin called after her but she ignored it and was out on the pavement before the woman finished yelling for her to stop.

Jamie's head turned back, catching a last glimpse of Yanmei through the gap, her eyes full and fearful, wondering whether she'd just saved her life or signed her death warrant. Or whether it was still too early to tell.

She shoved a boot on top of that thought and crushed it under her heel. She couldn't think like that. She had to keep pushing. She had a lead now – she had something. A name for the girl, a description of the father, and the knowledge that the people she was up against were playing for keeps.

She looked left and right, keen to get away, and started walking in the direction Roper would have been coming from.

Where the hell was he?

Jamie's eyes focused on the scene ahead and she stopped, stumbling a little as she did.

Sirens blared all around her and a police car roared up on her shoulder and sped past, its blue lights flashing.

She could see the ambulance that had passed when she was inside propped up on the curb about fifty metres down, a string of cars zigzagged behind it, brake lights cutting through the thick city air like red slits.

The police car ground to a halt, mounting the curb with its front wheel, the suspension tossing the bumper into the air before crunching it into the pavement.

Two uniforms threw the doors open and rushed forwards past the open rear of the ambulance, shouldering through the quickly-growing crowd.

'Roper…' Jamie muttered, not sure if she said it out loud or just in her head.

Her heart seized in her chest, her blood freezing in her veins.

'Roper,' she almost shouted this time, the word lurching out between ragged breaths.

She hadn't realised, but she was already running.

17

THE RAIN HAD COME BACK in, sweeping through the city in sheets.

It rattled against the window, silver explosions against the black glass.

Outside, darkness had swallowed the earth, blotting out the distant lights on the city skyline.

The smell of disinfectant burned Jamie's nostrils as she peered out over her elbow, her head buried in her arms, watching the water run down the pane. The slow and gentle beeping of Roper's heart monitor was keeping her awake. Or maybe it was the guilt.

Jamie lifted her head up and sighed, rubbing the loose fibres from the blanket out of her eyes with the knuckles of her right hand.

She didn't know how anyone could sleep on a rubberised mattress with stiff sheets, but it probably had something to do with all the sedatives they'd given him.

And that stab-wound that Roper had sustained.

Right in the back. Just to the right of his spine.

The blade had nicked his liver and punctured his small intestine.

He'd nearly died.

Jamie ground her teeth and stared up at Roper, all shadows in the dark, eyes sunken like holes in his head, a white tube sticking out from between his lips. It was taped to his mouth, stuck two feet down his throat, rising and falling as it forced air into his lungs with a cold hiss.

The middle of the street.

Right there in the middle of the bloody street.

The son of a bitch had taken his wallet, too, his warrant card. Left his phone and his car keys.

It was one stab.

One.

One, sure-handed stab, to the hilt. The bruising around the entry wound proved that, the doctor said.

Roper had been in surgery for six hours, and lost as many pints of blood.

If the ambulance had got there any later, he would have died.

They said he still might. *He's not out of the woods yet,* the surgeon had said.

Jamie felt sick.

This was Zhou. She knew it was. But she'd already read the reports from the scene. No one had seen anything. And there were no suspects, no cameras covering the street from the junction to where Roper was shot, and there were four directions the guy could have gone in. He'd waited until Roper was at the mouth of a walkway between two shops and then struck.

He could have kept going forward, doubled back, headed down the passageway, or crossed the road.

And no one saw a fucking thing.

Smith was outraged first, ready to tear the city apart looking for whoever did it. And second, he was as upset as she'd ever heard someone get on the phone.

Smith had known Roper for a lot of years, and despite their differences, they'd been through more than most brothers had.

No one deserved what happened to Roper. They both agreed on that.

And Smith would dig into this personally, review everything they'd found so far, give Jamie the resources she needed to catch whoever did this and bring them to justice.

Justice. The word tasted bitter even in Jamie's mind.

What did that even mean any more?

For now, she had nothing but time to think about it.

Smith had put her on mandatory twenty-four hour leave, and then he would let her know his decision. Roper wouldn't be coming back to work in the near future, and this was too big for Jamie to handle alone.

But Smith realised that taking her off it wasn't the right call. It wasn't her fault this had happened, but someone was sending a message. And a pretty clear one.

And those didn't come unless you were bearing down on someone.

Zhou had put on a show of strength. Showed them what he was willing to do if backed into a corner.

Smith wasn't afraid.

But Jamie was.

Roper had always been the one watching her back.

Sure, she could look after herself, but they'd been a team. They'd always looked out for *each other.* He'd kept her safe, and she'd… not done the same.

Anger began to move in her, like melting rock. Dislodging from the sides of her ribs and dripping hot, burning into the pit of her stomach.

Jesus. She should have just focused on the Raymond kid like Roper wanted. She'd forced him into this. Into pursuing this damn case. And now look what she'd gone and done. Nearly gotten him killed.

There was a quiet knock at the door and she looked up, realising she was grinding her teeth.

A nurse stood there, looking as tired as Jamie felt, her spiky brown hair less bouncy than when she started her shift who-knows-how-long ago.

She lifted her watch. It had a pearl face and a pink band. 'It's after midnight,' she said, her voice perfectly measured. Loud enough to be unmistakably assertive, but quiet enough not to disturb the strange silence on the ward.

'Oh,' Jamie said, sitting back from Roper's bed, unhooking her clenched fingers from the blanket. The thin steel legs of the chair she'd pulled up groaned a little under her.

'Doctor will be doing rounds soon,' she said, as if it was the second invitation to leave.

'Okay,' Jamie said, pushing up onto unsteady legs.

'You can't be in here when he—'

'I said okay,' Jamie half snapped it this time and the nurse held her hands up innocently, lifted her eyebrows at the tone, and then walked away, clipboard in hand, trainers squeaking on the tiles.

Jamie sighed, blew out as much of the stink of bleach as she could from her lungs, and then walked around Roper's bed. He was out cold, and would be until morning at the very least. He was being kept sedated until he was stable enough to have the ventilator removed. And then it would be a long road to recovery.

They didn't know how long it would be before he could walk again.

The assailant had gone close to the spine and they didn't know if there'd been any nerve damage. It was too early to tell.

Jamie dragged her eyes away from him, feeling them glaze over.

She felt blindly, numbly for the bony mass of his foot and squeezed it through the covers.

She held on for as long as she could bear, and then stepped into the weak light of the corridor and headed home, smearing tears across her cheeks with her sleeve.

Jamie walked out into the cold January air and shivered, zipping up against the rain.

She'd not even thought to do it before stepping out and now she was already wet. Though it barely registered.

Jamie blinked, looking around, trying to remember where she'd parked her car. Then it occurred to her that she'd parked it in a multi-storey about ten minutes walk from the Jade Circle.

She'd ridden here in the ambulance with Roper.

Jamie grimaced, feeling her stomach twist emptily. The last thing she'd eaten or drunk was the coffee she and Roper had ordered before they'd followed Yanmei. And that was nearly nine hours ago now.

Jamie swallowed and stepped forward, digging her hands into her pockets.

She grabbed one of the taxis waiting at the rank at the curb and gave the driver her address.

He pulled wordlessly into traffic and wound through the city.

The windows misted and turned the lights outside to coloured halos.

They hypnotised her and then the brakes were squeaking the car to the stop, the clacking of the handbrake coming up telling Jamie they were there.

The driver's voice echoed tinnily in the cabin and Jamie leaned forward, pressing her phone against the contactless payment pad.

She didn't even register how much he'd said it was before she paid.

Her hands weren't really her own.

They grabbed at the door handles and then she was back in the rain, once more zipping up after the fact.

It took her a second to acclimate as the taxi whipped around in a circle and accelerated away into the darkness.

And then she was alone again on the street, the water beating heavily at her shoulders.

God she was tired.

She could barely lift her feet.

Jamie took a deep breath and then forced herself forward, leaning into the step.

The forty feet to her front door seemed like a long way.

She made it about a third of the way there when something kick-started in her brain. A part which had been dormant for millions of years. The part that seemed to have an uncanny way of detecting what couldn't be seen or heard.

She froze, all of her muscles tightening, her head snapping up.

Ahead, she could see the porch of her building, the streetlight in front of the steps throwing down a puddle of orange-yellow light.

It fell in a rough circle, the edges alight with sparks of rain as they splattered off the pavement.

Jamie looked through it with narrow eyes, feeling the droplets splatter on her forehead. She'd not pulled her hood up.

She tried to focus, closing her eyes down to slits, ignoring the cold ache behind her temples.

There was darkness behind the light. A wall of it.

Nothing moved there, and the next streetlight was too far down to make any difference, the air heavy and thick, choking their halos.

The noise of the rain was like frying bacon. A thousand rashers in a red-hot pan.

The cold of the air seared her cheeks.

Jamie's legs wouldn't move any further.

She was rooted in place, watching. Waiting.

She couldn't see anything, but she knew. In that ancient part of her brain. She knew.

'Who's there?' she called, as sternly as she could. 'Show yourself.' She rattled a breath into her lungs, ignoring the pain as the tense muscles between her ribs fought her expanding chest. 'I'm a detective with the London Met,' she called again, forcing her volume to rise above the clattering of the rain.

A figure stepped forward into the light, no more than a dark shape.

He was big, broad, and was standing right between Jamie and her apartment.

Her first thought should have been to turn and run. There was no need to engage in whatever the fuck this was. She should call it in. But what would that achieve? Nothing. Nothing would be achieved unless she took a stand. Unless she stood up to this person, and the man pulling his strings.

'You don't have to do this,' she said, her voice now rock steady, her heart settling into a low and fast rhythm.

Jamie stepped forward slowly, carefully, the part of her brain that had alerted her to the presence of this new threat now wringing every ounce of adrenaline her glands had to offer into her bloodstream.

Her eyes danced across the pavement, measuring the distance, calculating the steps.

They weighed him.

He was over six-feet, dressed in a dark coat. Not a raincoat as such, but a smart black coat, buttoned up to the neck with a high collar. His shoes were black, too. Not heavy boots, but not polished loafers. Somewhere in between. Smart but functional.

They were met by trousers. Black trousers. Suit trousers. Tailored, ironed with a crease.

The hands at the man's sides were gloved. Leather, black. They flexed as he took a step forward.

Jamie couldn't see his face. He was wearing a black beanie hat pulled down to his eyebrows and had a scarf tucked inside the collar of his coat, pulled up under his eyes.

There wasn't a scrap of skin showing except for the centimetre above and below them.

Nowhere near enough to make any sort of ID. Not legally.

But she knew. She knew exactly who she was looking at. And she was wondering if this was what Qiang had seen moments before she'd died.

'Matt,' Jamie called and the man paused for a second.

It was the head bouncer from the Jade Circle. She didn't have a doubt in her mind.

They were no more than fifteen feet apart now, separated by the pool of light dripping from the streetlamp.

'You don't have to do this,' she said, not needing to shout anymore. 'I'm taking Zhou down, but you don't have to go with him.'

They stopped, like gunfighters.

'Come in with me – give a statement, turn evidence against him. If you killed—' She cut herself off, being careful not to say Qiang's name. 'The girl – if you did it under duress, under threat for your life, then we can—'

But she didn't get to finish.

Either he didn't want to hear it, or he needed to strike before he lost his nerve, she didn't know, but he came in hard and fast, and it was all she could do to react in time.

He stepped wide to the right and Jamie went with him, anticipating a wide hook. It was how most people came in – on their strong side, twisting momentum. A haymaker out of the gate.

And it was why Cake taught her half a dozen ways to counter a blow like that from a bigger opponent.

She stepped forwards, turning to her left, squaring up to the punch so she could roll past it, get on his blindside.

But he wasn't there as she threw her hands up ready to take the strike against her forearms.

Matt feinted to his left instead and was at her right shoulder before she could move.

The shot came over the top from his off-hand and was set to take her head clean off. A hit like that to the side of the head would have floored her, concussed her, and maybe killed her.

But she was fast. That's about all she had going for her. And Cake's training wasn't lax by any stretch.

Jamie's left knee folded under her reflexively and she twisted downwards and out, away from the punch, pushing her hips under his arm, her head in the opposite direction.

His knuckles connected with the upper part of her bicep and glanced upwards, bouncing off the crown of her head instead, her ear tucked against her shoulder.

Her skull rang like a bell, her eyes screwing closed against the pain. But the blow hadn't hit her square on, and that had saved her life.

Cake had always told her to execute a defensive move and a counter simultaneously. Attacking and defending at the same time was impossible, but defending and countering could turn the tide of a fight in an instant.

Whether that echoed with her subconsciously or if it was just muscle memory at this point, she didn't know, but her heel was flying out at the same instant that Matt's fist connected with the side of her head.

She was throwing the low side-kick blindly, aiming in her mind for the knee-cap with only a rough idea of where it was.

The corner of her heel struck it at an angle, bouncing off, and threw her off balance.

Jamie stumbled, swinging in a circle on one foot between the force of the punch and the missed kick, and then dived headlong in the opposite direction in an attempt to get out of arm's reach.

She heard a grunt from behind her over the high-pitched wailing in her head, and then felt the hard surface of the pavement under her forearm as she hit the ground, scrambling to her feet as quickly as she could, now sopping wet.

Matt took two steps sideways, favouring his right leg, dragging his left behind him like it was made of wood.

She'd not caught him straight-on and definitely not broken anything, but it had hurt. She knew that much.

He raised his fists and she did the same, balling them in front of her chin in a tight guard.

Jamie didn't know if he was trained or what in, but she wasn't going to underestimate him again.

Her eyes stung in the rain, her vision threatening to blur between the water and the blow to her head.

But Matt had no intention of letting up and came forward again, more surefooted with each step.

Jamie came in to meet him, determined not to let him wind up for a second time.

She still didn't know if he was right or left-handed. He'd come in orthodox before but struck with his left. And now he was leading with his left foot, right cocked like a cannon ready to blow her off her feet.

Like always with bigger opponents, she needed to put him down fast. She could never match him punch for punch. But her best weapon was at the end of her leg.

Jamie turned in with her left shoulder, widening her guard, bating a straight jab from either hand, straight through her wrists.

She watched his eyes, waiting for it, and then moved.

Matt struck, as she'd hoped, slotting his fist right between her hands, except her nose wasn't where his fist was. Not anymore.

She ducked forward, leaving her hands high, and let Matt's hand sail past her left ear.

Jamie had all her weight on her right foot, her left planted at a ninety-degree angle ready to brace her weight.

She pushed forward, inside Matt's reach, throwing her body upwards, her head with it so Matt's forearm was stretched over her shoulder.

Her left hand moved in the opposite direction, her fist closing around Matt's wrist, pinning it against the nape of her neck as her right knee came up to chest-height outside his elbow, her full weight dragging Matt off balance, opening him up to what was going to be a high kick. Over his shoulder. Kevlar toe-cap of her boot to the temple.

It sailed steeply upwards, her leg straightening, slingshotting her foot almost vertically. Her toe arced around dangerously, flattening out on a collision course with Matt's left eye. If it landed, it would break the socket and he would go down for the count.

But he wasn't a brawler, not a thug by any means.

He knew how to fight, and the second Jamie saw his right hand flying up to protect his face, she knew she was in trouble.

Her shin thudded into his forearm as he guarded his jaw, blocking her attack, his left arm still in Jamie's grasp.

The momentum of her kick was deflected, killed mid-swing.

His right hand rolled over her leg like it wasn't even moving and she felt his left fingers dig into the depression between the muscles on the back of her neck.

She barely had one foot on the floor, and now he had hold of her.

Rubber scraped on concrete as she was dragged off her feet and spun around.

It was all she could do to fill her body with air and tense for the impact.

She felt herself being thrown against something and blacked out for a second, not knowing where she was – on the ground or upright.

An alarm screamed in her ear and she blinked twice, waiting for her eyes to stop lolling.

He'd slammed her against the side of a parked car.

She was still off the ground, still in Matt's hands, fighting for breath.

Her feet had gone numb, the impact rattling every bone in her body.

In a great throb, she felt the pain, like a surge of electricity bolting upwards through her spine.

Her diaphragm spasmed, trying desperately to force air into her body. Her left hand scrabbled behind her, trying to gain a sense of position, and hit on something bulbous.

The world came back into focus and Matt released her.

She dropped to the ground and her left leg buckled, her fingers clawing at the thing she now knew to be the wing mirror.

A yellow light blinked furiously between her fingers, the alarm still blaring somewhere a mile behind her.

Her right leg flopped to the pavement and pushed her back against the curved steel of the door.

She could feel the broken window sharp and jagged against the back of her head, pressing through her hair.

Jamie was half propped up, fighting to stay on her feet, her right arm snaking through the air in front of her as she tried to make some semblance of a guard.

But she didn't have the strength. Didn't have the breath. Didn't have the focus.

Matt squared up now and stood over her, snatching her right wrist out of the air and pulling her onto her feet.

Her legs straightened themselves underneath her like a rickety lawn chair and held. Barely.

The world lurched and she clenched her jaw just in time to weather the low hook that he fired into her gut.

Jamie spat or vomited blood – she didn't know which – and doubled forward, still held up by Matt's grip. Kept aloft by her own right arm. Dangling from his fist.

It shot from between her teeth in a thick spray and splattered on the pavement next to him in a red cloud, swirling in the beating rain.

She made a whining sound as her body forced what little air there was in her chest out through her throat, and looked up, knowing from Matt's feet alone that it wasn't over.

Jamie could feel her eyes bulging in her cheeks, her mouth thick with her own blood, and watched in slow motion as his fist hung in the air behind his shoulder.

A thin mist came off it as the drops smashed against the leather, and then it came down.

Her eyes closed and the darkness strobed inside her head, the pain coming a second later.

She was limp, her legs as good as paper now.

Matt let her go and she slumped sideways, sliding down the side of the car into a heap right there on the pavement.

Her eyes were still closed, the rain hitting her cheek carrying the blood off her lips. She was barely conscious, her head throbbing, her mouth filled with old coins.

If she'd have had the strength or anything in her stomach, she was sure she would have thrown up again.

Matt's leather shoes squeaked underneath him as he knelt down, the alarm still cutting the winter air in two above them.

But despite it, and the roar of the rain, she heard the words that came out of his mouth as clear as day.

'Drop the case,' he said, not a hint of remorse in his voice. 'Drop the case, or next time I'll kill you. And then your partner, too.'

She wanted to get up and kick his head off.

She wanted to claw his eyes out.

But she couldn't. She couldn't do anything.

Couldn't even open her eyes.

She felt them sting, her throat aching, jaw on fire, tongue cut and bloodied against her teeth.

And then Matt stood up and walked away.

His shoes squeaked for a moment, and then they were gone.

Once more, Jamie Johansson was alone.

And this time, there was no one coming to help.

18

A KNOCK at her door woke her up.

Jamie sat upright in her shower, choked on the sharp lump wedged in her throat, coughed, doubled over onto her knees, and then wretched a chunk of congealed blood the size of a peach stone between her feet.

She blinked herself clear, her head pounding, and looked at her legs. Her jeans were soaked with blood.

She lifted her hands and saw they were covered too.

Jamie could feel it dried on her cheeks, cracking as she squinted around getting her bearings.

She was in her apartment, but didn't remember getting there.

Her fingers were raw, and there was a trail of blood leading from the hallway into the bathroom, across the tiles. Handprints that were smeared by her knees and toes.

It looked like she'd managed to drag herself in there.

Jamie dared to run her tongue along her teeth. They hurt. The whole of her bottom jaw was throbbing and two of her top left molars were loose.

She could taste blood, feel that her tongue was cut. She'd bit it when she'd been hit. That explained the wad of blood in her throat.

She leaned her head back against the cool tiles and turned her face to the side, pressing her swollen cheek against them.

The knock came at the door again and she lifted her head, forcing her brain to work. She'd completely forgotten that someone had knocked, and her eyes were aching from the daylight spilling in through the doorway.

She was concussed. That much she was pretty sure of.

Jamie forced herself onto her hands and knees, staring down at her filthy clothes. She was covered in grit from the road, dirt from the pavement, her own blood, and she had glass in her hair.

Fragments fell out as she slid her feet underneath her hips and spidered her hands up the wall, holding herself in a shaky stance in the tray.

She coughed again, spat more blood into the plughole and then stepped down onto the tiled floor, jolts of pain lancing through her spine.

It felt like she'd been in a car accident.

The reality wasn't far off.

The knock came again.

'Yeah,' she tried to call, finding her voice thin and cracked.

The sink came into reach and she slumped onto it, slapping the handle of the faucet until water splashed into the porcelain bowl.

Jamie wasted no time sticking her face under the stream and sucking in great mouthfuls of water.

Her throat didn't want to cooperate, but she forced the water down her gullet, carrying pieces of blood with it.

It seeped into her dry chest and cooled her bruised ribs from the inside.

The knock came again now, harder, and longer.

Jamie grumbled, tried to speak, but couldn't. Her face was swollen and her tongue was shredded. Words weren't coming.

She splashed the cold water against her nose, swore – which came out more like an angry sound than anything coherent – and then massaged her cheeks as firmly as she could bear.

Tears formed at the corners of her eyes and cut paths through the blood that had poured out of her nose and mouth through the night.

It dissolved and dripped into the sink and in a moment of madness she pinched the bridge of her nose and ejected its contents forcefully into the bowl.

More tears came after that and she curled down onto it, screwing her face up from the pain.

She whimpered as the knocking became a hammering and didn't stop. 'Jamie!' came a deep and familiar voice.

Jamie stumbled into the hallway, pressing a soaked flannel to her face.

She hadn't looked in the mirror.

Couldn't bear to.

The sunlight stung her eyes as she moved through the beam coming in from the living room, aiming for the front door, which was now shaking in the frame.

'Jamie! Open the door! Can you hear me?'

She fell against it, her feet only half in her control, and twisted the latch.

It flew inwards and nearly knocked her off her feet.

Cake caught her before she fell, and she saw her hand in front of her, the flannel reddened already, her wrist plum-purple with welts in the shape of fingers.

Where Matt had gripped her.

'Jesus,' Cake muttered, his arms encircling her, his eyes wide with fear. 'What the hell happened?'

Jamie swallowed, looked up at him, and felt a twisting pain in the back of her throat. The tears came again, and all conscious thought left her mind. She closed her eyes and felt her forehead against his chest, tears streaming down her face.

He held her, kicking the door closed behind him, and scooped her off her feet.

A moment later he was laying her down on her sofa and moving to the kitchen.

Jamie pulled a cushion into her stomach and curled around it, bringing her knees as high as she could.

Cake returned after a few seconds with her washing up bowl filled with warm water, the flannel she'd had in her hand now in his fist, droplets of bloodied water running over his knuckles.

He reached out and took her face in his off-hand, lifting it with the skill and confidence of a trainer who'd sponged blood off a hundred bloodied faces.

Jamie looked at him through her right eye, feeling her left swelling shut.

Matt had hit her square in the cheek. An expertly placed punch that was high enough not to dislocate her jaw, but low enough not to obliterate her cheek bone or eye socket.

He'd wanted it to hurt, but he'd not wanted to break anything. Not wanted to kill her.

It was a message, and it was one that was received loud and clear.

Cake ignored her cries as he wiped the dried blood and dirt off her bloated cheek and then cleaned her lips. He wasn't gentle, but he was efficient.

It took ten minutes, and after, the bowl was dark, nearly black in Cake's shadow.

He was in training bottoms, a zipped-up hoodie, and running shoes. He was dressed ready to train.

What time was it?

Jamie's eye moved to the clock above the cooker. Just after seven twenty.

She tried to think. Shit. They'd had a training session booked that morning. With everything happening with Roper, she'd forgotten to text him. Though she probably would have gotten up and gone to train anyway, had she not crossed paths with Matt.

Her routine was her stability.

Come to think of it, where was her phone? Had he taken it off her? No, it was in her coat. But where was that? She wasn't wearing it. She was in the same long-sleeve she'd been in the night before.

She'd not taken it off before the fight, either.

It must be close – her keys were in her pocket and she'd managed to let herself back in.

She guessed she'd pulled it off sometime between getting inside and crawling into the shower tray. But she couldn't remember doing any of those things, let alone where she'd thrown it.

Her brain didn't want to work.

How had Cake known? How had he gotten in downstairs?

She tried to ask. 'How—' she started, before the pain came, killing the words on her lacerated tongue.

'You missed training,' Cake said plainly, anger more apparent in his voice than anything else. 'Then I read in the paper that a detective was stabbed yesterday in Chinatown – Paul Roper.' He met her eye and she squinted back at him. 'I tried your phone, it went straight to the answering machine.' He let out a long sigh. 'That was all the red flags I needed.' He pushed himself to his feet and planted his hands on his hips.

She'd never thought of her apartment as small, but he seemed to fill it.

He'd never been there before.

'I came straight over,' he said. 'And when I got outside, I saw the car all smashed up, the blood on the ground, and then a trail leading in through your door – it was wedged open, broken glass trapped in the jamb.'

Jamie winced, moving onto her back.

Cake was gone for a second and then came back with a glass of water, pressing it into her hands. He cupped them as she lifted it to her lips, spluttering as she poured it into her mouth and swallowed painfully.

'How did you…' She cleared her throat, speaking quietly, slurring. 'Know where I lived?'

'Believe it or not, my paperwork isn't that bad. You wrote your address on the insurance waiver.' Cake folded his arms now, not standing still.

Jamie nodded, wondering what it must have looked like outside. What *did* it look like? She thought back to the car, being slammed against it, the window cracking under her skull. She could feel the back of her head raw and tender.

'I knew it wasn't a coincidence,' Cake said, shaking his head. 'You never miss training. But you know – I thought, it's a big case, maybe you just forgot. But then when I read about your partner, and you didn't answer your phone… Jesus, Jamie. I know what these guys are like. I thought the worst.'

She tried on a smile and found it lopsided. 'Maybe *you* should be a detective. I'm going to need a new partner.' It was meant to be a joke, but it tasted sour even on her lips. She grimaced and felt sick at her own words.

'Well if I was,' Cake said, scoffing, 'this never would have happened.'

Jamie chuckled and then whimpered, her eyes closing. 'No offence, but the guy wasn't asking.'

'So it was them, then? Something to do with the case?'

Jamie nodded slightly. 'Though I couldn't ever prove it. They're smart.'

'What do you mean?'

'The guy was wearing a mask – totally covered. No way an ID will stand up in court.'

'Shit,' Cake muttered, walking backwards until he hit the breakfast bar across from the couch. He pulled out one of the wire-legged stools and put his hundred-odd kilos down on it. The metal groaned gently and threatened to bow. 'I didn't think this sort of shit happened.'

'It does when you pull the right threads.'

'Apparently.' He looked around. 'What are you going to do? Do you need me to call someone – your boss, or…?'

Jamie shook her head and it felt like it was filled with broken glass. 'No, don't.'

'Jamie…'

'Cake, please.' She coughed again and tipped more water into her mouth, pushing the cushion in her arms behind her head. 'Leave it, okay?'

'Why?'

'Because…' She winced, snorting back and swallowing more blood. 'Because if I call this in, they'll take me off it…'

'You can't be serious?'

'They will.'

'No, I mean you can't be serious that you still want to work this case?'

'Who else is going to solve it?'

'Solve it? Jamie, you're lucky to be alive.' Cake rocked onto his feet and threw his large arms in the air.

She twisted her face up. 'If they wanted to kill me, I'd be dead. It was just a warning.'

'So you think that now's the time to go barrelling back in?'

'Next time,' she said, forcing herself to sit up, trying her best to keep her lip from quivering, 'I'll be ready.'

'Jamie…' He was incredulous. 'You're lying here, beaten to hell. Your partner's in the hospital fighting for his life. I'm not trying to put you down, but don't you think you're out of your depth here?'

Jamie looked up, conscious that she was hunched over, her hands in fists in the seat cushions. She stared at Cake through her one good eye, and then let her gaze drift over his shoulder. Her eyes left his concerned face and moved to the new shape that had appeared in her kitchen.

He was bigger than Cake – his round shoulders making the coffee machine next to him look like a toy. He had grey-blonde hair, and a peacoat that weighed as much as she did as a child. Her father, even from the back, was unmistakable. He was leaning on the counter, hands spread wide, head bowed.

She watched him for a moment as he pushed up and turned around, his face that same disinterested picture it always was. *Maybe he's right,* her father said. *Maybe you are out of your depth.*

'No,' she said to both of them. 'That's what they want.'

So what are you going to do about it? her father asked. *Because it looks like you just got your ass kicked.*

'If I back down, they'll put someone else on this. And if they do,' Jamie said, her teeth gritting by themselves. The loose one began to smart. 'They'll read the case file, see what's happened, and then not follow through with it.' She exhaled hard. 'This case is thin as it is – barely anything to go on. Any detective who's more concerned about their own skin than some dead sex-worker with no name, no family, and no one looking for them – which will be all of them – will let this case die. And with it, any chance of putting Zhou, and whoever else is responsible for this, behind bars.'

Cake stared at her. Studied her. He knew she wasn't going to be argued with. She couldn't be. 'You know who did it?' he asked.

'To me?'

'To you, to Roper. To the girl.'

She swallowed, hearing the bile in her own words. 'I have a fair idea.'

'Same person?'

'Maybe. Maybe not.'

Cake took a long breath in. 'And you're really not going to let this go? There's nothing I can say?'

'Even if they take me off the case I'm still going to hunt this son of a bitch down,' Jamie spat.

'Okay,' Cake said.

'Okay?'

'Okay.' He nodded. 'Tell me what I can do to help. Because from where I'm sitting, you look like you need it.'

19

WHILE JAMIE SHOWERED, Cake took the mop and bucket in her hallway cupboard and cleaned up the mess she'd left on all four flights of stairs.

Owning a gym and training boxers, he said, had given him lots of practice mopping up blood, and he was efficient at it now.

When he came back in, his brow shining with sweat, Jamie was out of the shower and pushing one of the co-dydramols left over from her broken arm out of the pack and onto her kitchen counter.

Cake put the mop down and ran the back of his hand across his forehead.

Jamie looked up, still damp from the shower, her hair hanging down onto her shoulders in long, thick, brown tendrils, wetting the zip-through hoodie she had on.

'Any trouble?' she asked, her mouth more swollen than bloody now and her nose practically clear. It sounded like she had cotton wool stuffed in her gums.

He shook his head. 'No, I didn't see anyone, and so long as no one comes out in the next ten minutes, they shouldn't slip and break their necks, either.'

Jamie smiled for a brief moment. 'What about the car? The pavement?'

He put his hands on his hips, his eyes moving to the coffee machine. 'Nothing. Didn't seem like anyone's been out there yet – no one called the police or anything. I left the glass where it was, mopped across the pavement and kicked some of the glass a little down the road, scraped my shoes a little, made it look like the person who did it ran away.'

She pushed a tablet the size of a button between her teeth and threw some water in after it, swallowing painfully. She winced. 'Good,' she said. 'Sounds like you've got a knack for dressing crime scenes.'

He looked at her like he didn't know if that was a compliment, a joke, or if he should be offended.

Jamie hated tampering with evidence and not reporting a crime as much as the next honest detective, but there was nothing else she could do. Whoever owned the car could claim on their insurance, and maybe Jamie would pin a little stack of twenty-pound notes under the wind-screen wiper in a few weeks to say sorry. For now, all she could do was hope that if the owner called the police they'd do what they almost always did in those situations – and she knew because she'd been a uniformed officer who'd attended a hundred too many calls like it – and that was to tell them that without evidence – an eye witness, photos, videos, a confession and a culprit there at the scene – there was little that could be done, and that it was a matter for the insurance companies to deal with.

She didn't think anyone had seen her, but if they had she'd deal with it if and when.

If they hadn't, then she'd keep her head down, act like she heard and saw nothing herself, and push forward.

It sounded like Cake had done a good job, and she had to trust him.

'Help yourself,' Jamie mumbled, nodding to the coffee machine.

He was practically salivating.

Cake squeezed behind her as she popped another two tablets out of the packet and crushed them under the base of the glass. They crunched as Cake took the jug of coffee out of the machine and filled it with water. He poured it into the machine, slotted it back into place and lifted the top, reaching for the jar of grounds Jamie kept at the back of the counter. He pulled off the lid and shook enough into the filter to caffeinate a racehorse.

He closed it and pushed the button as Jamie scooped the powder into her glass, swirled it, and then downed it in one.

It stung going down and coated her mouth in chalk, but it was necessary. One to numb the pain, and two to make her brain numb enough to think that calling Smith and trying to play it off like nothing had happened was even remotely a good idea.

He'd already told her yesterday, called her at the hospital to say that she should take a personal day. But she needed to head him off, tell him that she wasn't going to go after Zhou and the Jade Circle again – not without actual proof.

She had a lead in terms of the father, and it had occurred to her that she'd come into this late, got swept up in everything, and jumped the gun.

Jamie and Roper had gone after Zhou – straight for the throat. But they didn't have a clear shot. And they'd paid the price.

She'd never even been to the crime scene. Never seen it for herself.

That was where she needed to start. And she wanted to make sure Smith knew that she didn't have an axe to grind. That she was laying low, and doing her job. The last thing she needed was to get blindsided by Zhou again.

She had to play this smart now. With Zhou, with Smith.

It was almost eight. Smith would be headed in, and if she timed it right she could catch him on his commute. That would divide his attention, hopefully give him less brainpower to think about what she was saying.

As Cake held up a coffee cup to ask if she wanted one, she dialled Smith's mobile number and put it on loud speaker. She nodded, hoping that the chugging and growling of the coffee machine would create enough interference to mask her slurred speech.

It rang four times and then Smith answered. 'Smith,' he said, sounding tired.

'It's Johansson,' Jamie said, trying to enunciate her words as best she could.

'Detective Johansson,' he said, sighing. It sounded like he was driving, his voice echoing from the loudspeaker. 'I assume this couldn't wait until I got to the office?' Smith was as upset about Roper as anyone, but Jamie had never known him to show a softer side, and he wasn't about to start now.

'No, sir,' Jamie said out of the side of her mouth. 'I, uh—'

'What's wrong with your voice, Johansson?'

She cleared her throat, ignoring the pain. 'Nothing,' she said, not sure if the slurring was from the co-dydramols or the swelling in her jaw. It sure as hell wasn't hurting as much any more and it had only been a few minutes. 'Toothache,' Jamie lied quickly. 'Wisdom teeth, I think.'

Smith was silent for a second. 'So?' he said, seemingly buying the excuse. 'What do you want? If you're calling to ask about Zhou or the Jade Circle, then I can tell you right now that you're not going anywhere near either until—'

'No, I don't want to.' Jamie didn't want to cut him off but she didn't feel like hearing a tirade, nor being on the receiving end of one.

'Then what?'

'It was my fault – I pressured Roper into going after Zhou, baited Zhou into hitting us.'

Smith said nothing. He didn't have sufficient evidence to agree or disagree but everyone knew that was the likely story.

'I want to dig into the father, head to the crime scene, see if I can't pick up a fresh trail.'

He made a *mmm* sound through closed lips. 'Amherst and Brock both attended the scene, and it was swept thoroughly by the SOCOs, too. There's nothing to be found.'

'Please, sir,' Jamie said. 'I just…'

'Why don't you take the personal day, Johansson? I'll get Michaels and Dunham up to speed on the case and—'

'With all due respect, sir, this is my case.'

'And you and Roper are my responsibility. And your welfare is my top priority.'

She was starting to think that ringing Smith was the wrong call. 'Please,' she said, not having to feign the genuine sincerity in her voice. 'Let me compile my report from home, submit it for you to review along with my recommended course of action, and then decide.'

'The case isn't going anywhere,' Smith said, not seeming to want to budge. 'Relax. Recuperate. You sound exhausted. What happened to Paul was terrible, but running yourself into the ground over it won't help anyone.'

'I don't think anything could make me relax, sir,' she said, confident that if three co-dydramols weren't going to take the edge off, a day sitting on the sofa watching videos on the internet wasn't going to help either. 'Let me put my energy into figuring this out... And then, if, after you read my report, you still think that Michaels and Dunham are a better fit, I'll...' She forced herself to say it. 'Step aside and hand it off to them without another word.'

He sighed. 'Jesus, Johansson, you'll be the death of me.'

Jamie swallowed.

'Fine. But if I find out that you've gone within a hundred miles of Zhou or the Jade Circle, it'll be your job as well as the case.'

She couldn't help herself. 'I think we're already within a hundred miles of—'

'Don't test me, Johansson.'

'Sorry, sir.'

There was more silence, and then Smith spoke again. 'How are you doing?'

'I'm...' She glanced at Cake, who smiled at her. 'I'm okay,' she said. 'Getting by.'

'Okay. Well, if you need anything,' he said awkwardly, 'call me. I'm always here.'

The words sounded stilted coming from him, but she knew it was sincere, and she appreciated it. 'Thank you, sir,' Jamie said. 'I'll have a report on your desk in the morning.'

'Look after yourself, Johansson.' He was back to his stern self. 'I can't afford another detective turning up in A&E.'

Jamie touched her fingers to her swollen jaw and puffy eye, felt her ribs and back ache fiercely as she inhaled. 'Of course, sir. You don't have to worry about me.'

'No, Johansson,' he said, letting out a long breath. 'It's you I worry about the most.'

Cake refused to leave her for the day.

'I've got nothing to do,' he said. 'And I already put a sign on the door and a status on Facebook saying the gym would be closed for the morning.'

'Facebook?' Jamie asked, arching an eyebrow and locking her apartment door behind them.

He shrugged, standing in the stairwell. 'My brother told me that all businesses should be on social media.' He proffered her the stairs first and she took the top one, her hand against the wall for support. Every step hurt. 'I don't buy into it much – doubt it'll help at this point. I don't know what will.' His big fist closed around the railing. 'But hey, doesn't hurt to try.'

Jamie glanced back at him. She knew the gym wasn't flush with new members, but she didn't think things were that bad. But maybe she wasn't paying enough attention. She knew that he was paying reduced rent and had said that he couldn't afford the place if it was raised. And hell, he was living there, too.

She'd never seen anything except instant noodle pots dotted around his office, and though he did buy good coffee, she hardly thought that was indicative of his financial state.

He had been pressuring her pretty hard before Christmas to try and go pro, or at least get in the ring for some cash.

Maybe the situation *was* worse than she thought.

And if taking a day off meant not losing enough business to make a difference, maybe it was past the point of no return.

She felt sick, suddenly, thinking about it.

It was so easy to get wrapped up in her own thoughts, her own problems. Her cases. *Important things.* Stuff that mattered, like killers and dead bodies. To ignore what the people around her were facing.

They hit the bottom step and stepped out onto the street.

The car that she'd been thrown against was gone, but the pieces of glass from the broken driver's side window were still strewn across the pavement and laying in the road.

'We'll take your car,' Jamie said, tearing her eyes away from it. 'Mine's still over in Chinatown.'

The rain had abated, finally, but the sky was roiling grey, like crumpled newspaper.

She was wearing her boots as normal, a pair of skinny jeans, the same zip-through hoodie she'd had on inside, and a leather jacket she'd bought last year but hardly worn. It was genuine leather, but she didn't wear it for work usually, and didn't go out anywhere else to wear it. As such, it sat in limbo. But with her suede coat ruined and binned after her run in with Simon Paxton on the Hammond case, and her rain jacket snagged and bloodied from last night's incident, she was quickly running out of wardrobe options.

She glanced in the window of a car to check whether pulling her hood up had obscured her face enough so that she wouldn't get stared at.

It hadn't.

Cake drove a Ford hatchback he could barely fit in with a scuffed bumper she didn't think he could afford to have fixed.

She didn't ask.

At least it wasn't full of cigarette butts and fast food wrappers like Roper's. That was a nice change.

In the car, Jamie called ahead to HQ and asked to have the key to Qiang's apartment brought down to the front desk. She'd pick it up from there.

She wanted as few people as possible to see her today.

Jamie also asked for a copy of the notes pertaining to Grigoryan's rental company to be printed and left for her along with the key.

Specifically she wanted the names and phone numbers of the guys who handled the check-ins for new tenants.

Amherst and Brock had called them all, but got hold of none of them. Then Grigoryan's walls had gone up, and his solicitors had told Amherst and Brock that they had no information that would help them and had signed statements to that effect. It had been a legal battle since. One that Amherst and Brock weren't equipped to fight.

Jamie suspected that it was because Grigoryan had broken about a dozen housing laws with his less-than-scrupulous rental agreements and methods. Though they couldn't prove he was breaking the law until they got the contracts or interviewed his employees, and they couldn't do that without beating back his solicitors.

So they'd handed it off to the Met's legal department and that was that.

Jamie didn't know where it was in the long backlog of cases they were trying to surmount, but she wanted to take another crack at Grigoryan's guys anyway. Yanmei had said that before Qiang had run away, that a regular – the father – had said he was going to take her away. And maybe he had made good on it. Maybe he was the one who put Qiang in that hell hole.

She thought back to what Effy, Grigoryan's mistress-cum-apartment-sitter had said about the place. That she'd been told about it, not that she'd found it. And Jamie checked – the building wasn't listed on any rental sites. Wasn't listed anywhere online. That's how it stayed under the radar. It was word of mouth. That's how *he* stayed under the radar. Grigoryan was smart, but it was his smarts that were leaving a breadcrumb trail for Jamie to follow.

If it was word of mouth then it meant that the father already knew about the place, or knew someone who did. So if he hadn't gone there with Qiang to check her in, then maybe his proxy had. So if Jamie could find who checked them in, get some more information on who the father might be, or who the connection was, she could track him down.

If she could do that, she could get a positive ID on Qiang, get a timeline, get statements, as much circumstantial evidence as she could, and then she could nail Zhou to the damn wall. Or at least crush the Jade Circle. Human trafficking for one, was enough of a charge to get a warrant and bring an army of detectives, SOCOs, and every other type of officer the Met had down on top of the place.

Jamie was finding justice to be a malleable word these days.

She didn't really expect any of Grigoryan's men to talk.

But she had another idea for that, too.

20

JAMIE SLIPPED IN AND OUT, leaving Cake in the car.

She gave her name to the receptionist at the front desk, and was handed a sealed A4 envelope. The woman behind the glass gave her a questioning look, but didn't ask about her bruised face or casual dress.

Jamie hoped it wouldn't be something she asked about upstairs either. She didn't know why she would, but it was just one more thing she didn't need.

She got back to the car and got in without a word. Cake cast a sideways look at her. 'Conversation between you and Roper always this scintillating?'

'You wanted to come,' Jamie said, emptying the contents of the envelope onto her lap. The key to the apartment fell out, along with printed copies of the crime scene photos and a copy of the coroner's report, both of which she'd asked for. She'd also requested copies of the information they had on Grigoryan's business deals, his associations, anything in the public domain that tied him to law firms, solicitors' offices, tax cases, and anything else that could put a link between Qiang's mystery John and Grigoryan. There was a link there somewhere – a thread that tied Grigoryan to the father, and to Qiang.

She doubted that the girls who worked at the Jade Circle would know of Grigoryan's cash-only squats, so she figured that it had to come through the father. And if he was a high roller there – or at least well-off – then she doubted he'd know about it through affiliation with any tenants.

Jamie figured that the barrister was tied to one of Grigoryan's business deals or businesses. She hadn't looped Amherst and Brock in on any of this yet, but they would see she had requisitioned the information and no doubt come calling about it. By then, she wanted something solid enough to make the intrusion on their case worthwhile.

She hoped it wouldn't be today.

She knew that conversation wasn't going to be an easy one, and she didn't feel like doing it with a busted up face.

For right now, she had ground to cover and plenty of stones to turn over.

What she really wanted to do was dig into the Jade Circle and Ho Zhou. She wondered how many people were listed there as employees, and how many she could get at. What she could line up to take Zhou out with if she couldn't pin down Qiang's killer.

She was almost certain that the girls were coming into the country illegally – but how, and who was doing it was still a mystery to her. She'd be compiling her report later, including everything she found today, everything that happened yesterday, and her recommended course of action. Which would be to put a surveillance net around the entire block. Catch everyone coming in and out of that place, then put a tail on them. Deal with them one by one.

Zhou had a lot of walls around him, and it was time she took some down. Brick by bloody brick.

Her father had always said that investigations were like chess – a series of moves and counter moves. You want the king, but he's always protected.

Clear the board first. Weaken the defences. Then strike.

She needed to do that. Think tactically now. She'd already lost some pieces. She was on the back foot, and she'd need to outthink Zhou if she was going to win this. She'd already proven that she'd lose in a battle of brute strength.

He face was proof of that.

Jamie tossed the key for the apartment into the centre console, began leafing through the documents, and motioned for Cake to pull away from the curb.

'Where are we going?' he asked.

'I'll tell you when to turn,' Jamie said, staring intensely at the page in front of her.

Cake pressed his lips into a thin line and watched the city go by through the window.

Jamie appreciated that he could read the fact that she didn't want to talk. Aside from the pain it caused, she also just wasn't in the mood.

It was a quality that Roper often lacked.

She needed to think, and the silence Cake was affording her would give her time to do that.

Jamie didn't know what would be waiting for her at the apartment, but she hoped there would be something there. Either to help point her towards the father, or in another direction.

Any direction.

At the very least, it would put her back at the starting blocks, and let her get a clean run at the case. See if she couldn't come at it from another angle.

There was a girl lying in the coroner's office counting on it.

'Pull up here.'

They parked up outside the apartment block that she and Roper had visited what seemed like months ago. In reality it was just a few days. But time felt alien to her suddenly.

'This the place?' Cake asked, looking up at the run-down building. He leaned forward onto the wheel and it disappeared under him.

Jamie stared up out of the passenger window. 'Not pretty, is it.'

Cake shrugged. 'I grew up in a block worse than this.'

Jamie wasn't sure what to say to that. 'Come on,' she said instead, opening the door and getting out, envelope with the key, photos, and contact details in hand.

It was a little after nine-forty and she wanted to make the most of the morning.

The apartment was on the second floor and she gave the apartment that she'd met Effy in just a passing glance. That whole exchange had resulted in more trouble than it was worth, and while she was sure Effy was probably out on bail now, awaiting the trial where she'd confess to possession of an unlicensed firearm and be sentenced to who knows what for it, Jamie had no intention of seeing whether she was in there or not.

She suspected not.

Grigoryan didn't sound like the forgiving type.

He'd probably never see Effy again. Just have one of his employees hand her an envelope full of cash and point at the exit.

Jamie and Cake headed for the stairwell.

The door creaked as she pushed her heel into it and stepped inside. It smelled like stale urine.

She didn't even grimace. It was a stench she'd become accustomed to. When you were a uniform, you dealt a lot with alleyways, multi-storey car parks, tunnels, and other places that people liked to relieve themselves. The odour of old piss was something that got lodged in your nose and never quite left.

Cake screwed his face up at it as Jamie took the stairs, her back throbbing distantly with each step.

The co-dydramols were still riding high in her system.

She was a little glad she hadn't driven.

At the door to the second floor, she paused and dug in her pocket, pulling out a pair of latex gloves she'd grabbed from the glovebox before she'd come in.

She slid them on now and turned to Cake, remembering that he wasn't Roper. 'Don't touch anything,' she said plainly. 'This place has already been swept for prints, but if we find something and they end up doing another pass, I don't want to have to explain why your finger-prints are in a crime scene.'

Cake nodded and pushed his hands into the pockets of his training zip-through.

The apartment door was easy to spot.

It still had a line of police tape stretched across the frame.

While Grigoryan's solicitors maintained he had nothing to do with it and the SOCOs had already been through there, it was still a crime scene and with the investigation where it was, still locked to the public and Grigoryan. She doubted he really missed the few-hundred a month it pulled in and was happy to let it sit in limbo if it meant keeping them off his back a while longer.

Jamie approached it and paused, seeing the second length of police tape dangling from one side of the frame and lying on the floor.

Cake slowed down behind her as she stepped a little wider to get a look at the door.

It was hard to tell what was old damage and what was new, but it was clear that it had been forced open recently – the wood around the lock splintered.

The door had been pulled closed, but someone had pried their way in since it was closed off.

And they didn't have a key.

So that ruled out Grigoryan. Unless he was smarter than Jamie thought.

She shook her head. No, leaping to conclusions had already got her into trouble once.

She needed to trust her eyes and her mind, not her gut.

Jamie glanced back at Cake who smiled briefly at her, though his nervousness was apparent.

She knew what to expect, but he didn't, and this was new ground for him. A bead of sweat was forming on his temple, his nostrils flaring as he drew deep breaths, trying to steady himself.

She nodded once, reassuringly, and then pushed the key into the lock, turning as she did.

It popped open strangely, like it was wedged closed rather than shut, and swung inwards.

Someone had definitely broken in there, and damaged the latch to do it.

Jamie inspected the wood. Crowbar by the looks of it.

Someone had been back here and broken in. Someone from the other side of this. Not a detective. The killer maybe? Coming back to sweep the scene? Coming back to find something they suspected the police had missed? That was curious. Why would they risk coming back to an active crime scene so soon after the crime? Did they have reason to believe something was hidden inside? Something that the SOCOs and Amherst and Brock would have missed? Or did they just want to make sure. Absolutely sure. Because the thing that was maybe there was that important… Stolen, maybe? Had Qiang taken something before she'd left? Something valuable… Incriminating, maybe?

These were all assumptions that were worth nothing unless she could find it or prove it.

Jamie glanced back at Cake again. 'Don't touch *anything,*' she said, more assertively this time.

Cake pushed his hands deeper into his pockets. 'I can wait out here if you'd prefer?' He didn't often sound nervous, but Jamie could tell he was.

'No,' Jamie said, stepping under the tape and into the room, careful of her footing. 'We don't want to draw any more attention to you being here than we need to. And having you stand in the corridor will just be suspicious.' She beckoned him in. 'Plus – who knows, you might be of some help.'

'Not unless someone needs a right cross thrown at them,' he muttered, crouching to get under the police tape.

Jamie chuckled painfully, her jaw singing. 'Doesn't look like it. But you never know, the day is young.'

They stepped into the room and Jamie pushed the door closed behind Cake. He was being good, his hands still in his pockets.

Jamie stood next to him and looked around.

The room was a studio. And a small one.

Directly across from them, facing the door, was the only window in the room. It pointed out across the street and into the disused lot across the way. It had been a building site up to some point, but now had been filled with rubble and had trees growing out of it.

It was partially obscured as the window – an old fashioned single

glazed sash window with a rotting wooden frame – had the bottom
section covered by a translucent plastic sheet. The SOCOs had taped
over the bottom pane to cover the bullet hole.

Jamie could still see it though, a thumbnail-sized hole with a
spider's web of cracks around it.

Between them and it was a deep red stain on the carpet the size of a
shipping pallet. Jamie was always surprised by the amount of blood
that came out of a human body, and how vast it always looked when it
was spread across the floor. The cleaners had done their best to sponge
most of it up, but it was never coming out of the carpet. Not truly.

Jamie looked down at it, and then back up at the window, then at
her feet. She suspected that she was in the exact spot that the killer had
been when they'd shot Qiang. She sighed, shrugged off the gnawing
unease in her gut and peeled open the envelope, dragging out the stack
of crime scene photos and the coroner's report.

Jamie stepped forward around the blood and approached the
window first.

Cake followed tentatively and she gave him the envelope with the
contact sheet in it just so he had something to occupy himself. He held
it between both hands, breathing through his teeth, which he'd pressed
together into a nervous snarl.

She flicked quickly to the photo of the window and leafed through
from there, the latex of her gloves squeaking on the glossy surface of
the pictures.

The bullet hole was a hundred and fourteen centimetres off the
floor. She knew from the tape measure being held up in the photo.

From the picture of Qiang's body and the coroner's report, she
confirmed that the entry wound was approximately one hundred and
fifteen centimetres from the ground, and the exit wound around a
centimetre lower. They could work out the trajectory of the bullet from
there, which meant they could work out the approximate height that the
gun was fired from.

Though that wasn't that useful unless they had a suspect in custody
that they could try and lean on with it.

A flat trajectory meant a few things. Seeing as the bullet had gone through the middle of her back, and travelled in a flat path, it meant that the shooter was either shorter than Qiang and shot from shoulder height, was the same height and shot with their hand below shoulder height, or they were taller, and shot from an even lower position. Anyone with any sense and experience would keep a gun concealed. And if he was taller than Qiang, he could draw from his belt and shoot without aiming down the sights. One clean shot to the middle of the back from point-blank range – yeah, you wouldn't have to be a sharp-shooter.

Jamie made a gun out of her hand and turned to Cake, throwing it up, her elbow against her ribs, arm crooked at a right angle. She looked down at it, in line with her naval.

If the shooter was taller and Qiang was five-three, which Jamie knew from the report, then that would give that slight downward angle, be the right sort of entry height.

None of it was perfect science. But it fit.

And yet, Jamie didn't like it, somehow. It didn't feel right.

Cake stuck his hands up nervously. 'Don't shoot,' he said, trying to cover the mix of nerves and nausea he looked to be feeling.

Jamie glanced up, remembering he wasn't Roper suddenly.

She cracked a little smile and closed the top page of the report.

Cake was standing to the side of the bloodstain, feet together like he was balancing on a toadstool.

Jamie looked around the room, studying it, trying to visualise.

The doorway let into the room, and then directly to the right of it, there was a cupboard-sized bathroom that fit a shower cubicle, a sink, and a toilet. It was tight enough in there that you could go to the bath-room, wash your hair, and your hands all from the doorway.

Two steps into the studio from the front door, there was a corner. Right behind it was the kitchen, which was just a counter top and some cupboards. Under the counter was a small fridge, and that was it. On top was an old one-ring hotplate and a microwave. On the far end, against the wall, was a metal sink that made most mixing bowls feel big.

Jamie let her eyes move to the left of it, onto the single bed that was wedged in the corner, just more than arm's reach from the kitchen. There wasn't even a difference in the flooring. Just thin, ratty brown carpet all the way through.

At the foot of the bed was a battered desk – though it was more like a table than a desk, with a single metal and plastic chair under it that wouldn't be out of place in a school classroom circa 1960.

Jamie sighed, now facing the window again, and pulled the chair out, sitting in it.

It groaned a little under her weight.

She leaned forward and peeled up the edge of the plastic sheet over the bottom pane, folding it back to clear her view through the glass.

She sat back and stared out of it.

From that level, she couldn't see the street itself without craning her neck – so all the rubbish that was collecting in the gutter, the graffiti that covered the buildings, the overflowing bins – she couldn't see them. What she could see were the trees poking through the building site. A little patch of green, that even in this endless grey January tumult, looked… not unpleasant.

'What are you thinking?' Cake asked.

Jamie realised she'd been completely silent for a few minutes now, and that Cake, standing practically in the spot a woman had died in, next to a dried pool of her blood, in a crime scene he had no business being in, probably wasn't feeling too comfortable.

'Sorry,' Jamie said, not looking away from the window. She took in everything she could see – beyond the trees was another building, and beyond that, the city. She could just see a few taller buildings in the distance, but for the most part, it was the trees that filled the scene. 'I'm just trying to imagine it.'

'Imagine what?' Cake asked, moving the envelope back and forth in his hands.

'Being here.' Jamie let out a long breath. The air was stale and the draft coming in through the bullet hole was a welcome reprieve. 'What it must have been like – to run from a place like the Jade Circle. To run from the people there.' Jamie turned to face him. 'People who do this,' she said, pointing to her own beaten face.

Cake swallowed. 'Oh,' he said quietly, unsure what else to say.

It unnerved Jamie seeing him so ill at ease.

She inhaled, shrugged it off and focused. 'I need you to do something for me,' she said to him. 'Usually I have Roper to help, but you'll have to do.' She glanced at him, fired him what little of a reassuring look she could make.

'Thanks,' he said, trying to return it. 'I'm flattered.'

Jamie turned back to the window. 'So let's play this out.'

'Okay.'

'It's the evening – eightish, maybe a little later.' Jamie planted herself in the chair and looked out of the window. 'Just before things pick up at the Jade Circle,' she added, trying to picture Matt or another of Zhou's cronies putting a crowbar in the doorframe.

'Right.'

'You're on the run – running for your life.'

'Mm.' Cake sort of cleared his throat and agreed at the same time.

'You haven't got a friend in the world. No money, no phone. You don't have a penny to your name. Just the clothes on your back.' Jamie distanced herself from the situation. Objectivity was key. 'There's only one person in the world that's looking out for you. The father of your child.' She laid her hands across her stomach.

She heard Cake shift from one door to the other behind her.

'And he's stashed you here until he can figure out what to do with you.' She bit her lip. 'You're alone. Scared. Lonely. You don't know what the future holds.'

'Sounds rough,' Cake said, barely whispering.

'In this place,' Jamie said, lifting her hands and looking around. 'This chair is the best spot. The bed – lumpy and filthy – the kitchen, the bathroom…' She didn't need to elaborate. Cake had eyes. 'But this chair' — she gestured to it — 'is the best seat in the house. Not a bad outlook. And with no phone, no TV, nothing but a few cheap magazines to read' — she recalled from the inventory of the room — 'you might sit here and dream of a better life.' She paused and strained it in her mind, seeing if it held up. 'In fact, it's the only thing you'd do in that position.'

Cake didn't know where she was going with it, so he said nothing.

'So it's after eight, and you're just sitting. Waiting. Watching. And then – bang.'

Cake jumped a little.

'A knock at the door.' Jamie swivelled on the chair and stared at it. 'But who knows you're here? Only one person, right? The father.'

'Right,' Cake said, trying to sound sure. Or supportive. Jamie didn't have time to think about which.

'So you get up, go to answer it – right?' She looked at him now.

He nodded. 'Right.' More definitive.

'You go to the door – still tentative, of course.' Jamie stepped over the blood. 'And you check the peephole.'

She pulled up in front of the door and held her eye close to it.

'So it was the father?' Cake asked, making a leap.

Jamie didn't answer. 'We know that the killer didn't shoot through the door.'

'Uh…' Cake wasn't sure how to respond.

'Which is sort of odd.'

'How come?'

'I mean, odd if the killer was a professional.' Jamie imagined how she'd do it. 'They shot her point-blank anyway. And that's cold blooded. And no one heard the shot – or at least didn't rush out to investigate. But the killer would have cased the place first, right?' She looked at Cake again now, wishing he was Roper.

'Yeah,' Cake replied, pressing his lips into a smile.

'If the killer wasn't the father – i.e. someone that Qiang wouldn't open the door for – then shooting through the door would have been the best option.' Jamie closed her eyes. 'You knock, you wait until you see the shadow of her feet under the door, and then bang – one shot, gut-height, right through the wood. Then, you kick the door through,' Jamie said, turning back to the room and taking a step in. She made a finger gun again and pointed it down. 'And you finish her off. Bang. Bang.'

Cake looked at her, clutching the envelope. The look on his face told Jamie that he was way out of his depth, and that given the choice again, he probably would have stayed in the car.

'So it... *was* the father?' Cake arched an eyebrow.

'A high-flying barrister who makes a living working on tax cases?' Jamie pursed her lips. 'It doesn't really fit. We don't know who he is, but why go to the trouble of putting her here, leaving her for who-knows-how-long, having her in a place where she'd *definitely* be found... Just to come back and kill her?'

Cake bit his lip like he'd said something wrong.

'No, that doesn't play either. Shit.' She sighed and rubbed her jaw. Talking was hurting. 'If he was going to kill her, he could have done it the night he put her here. Just drive her out of the city, somewhere quiet...'

'Maybe he needed time to get the gun?' Cake was trying to redeem himself.

'Why even bother? You just create a bigger trail. You could use a knife, or drown her, strangle her...' Jamie grimaced at how casually she'd reeled those off. 'Why waste the time and money and risk getting seen by coming back here and doing it in public?'

'To make a statement?'

'To who? She was a Jane Doe. No one claimed her.' Jamie remembered then what Yanmei had said, that Zhou had posted a photo of her body on the wall for the other girls to see.

Wait – a photo? So the killer snapped a photo? Or someone else did... If it was the killer, then it confirmed that it was someone working for Zhou. Jamie made a grumbling sound and kept going.

'Okay, okay,' she said, cutting her hands through the air. 'Let's just say for a second that the father didn't do it – that he's just an innocent guy caught up in all this.'

Cake nodded.

'One – who else would know, could know, and how could they know that Qiang was here? And two, if it was *anyone* other than the father, then why the hell would Qiang open the door to them?'

'How do you know she opened the door?'

Jamie inhaled, shook her head a little. 'No signs of forced entry for one.'

'So she goes to the peephole, sees that it's the fa—' He cut himself off. 'Sees that it's someone she recognises – trusts – and then what, realises that they've got a gun, turns, tries to run?'

'Run where?' Jamie asked flatly.

Cake looked down. 'Jesus, I don't know, Jamie, I'm not a detective,' he said quietly.

She rubbed her head, a headache coming on fiercely. She should probably get her concussion checked. She'd do it later when she dropped in on Roper. 'I'm sorry,' she muttered, looking up. 'I don't think she ran. The blood was pooled in one spot, not smeared. There were no splashes like she'd run, or stumbled. She was practically still.'

'Which means?'

'She opens the door, invites them in, turns her back, and...'

'Bang.' Cake nodded, understanding now.

'Goddammit,' Jamie mumbled. 'Who else would know she was here? Who else would be trusted enough for Qiang to turn her back on them?' She racked her brain and came up dry.

Cake swallowed again, licking his lips. 'I, uh...' He started.

'What is it?' Jamie asked.

'Nothing,' he said dismissively. 'It's just...'

'Yeah?'

'What if...'

'Spit it out, Cake.'

'I'm not saying you're missing the obvious here, but what about, what do they call it – something's razor?'

'Occam's Razor,' Jamie said through gritted teeth, suddenly irked by the bashfulness of it.

'Yeah, the simplest answer is often the...' He trailed off, seeing the hard look on her face, and cleared his throat. 'If – Qiang, is it? – If she wouldn't open the door to anyone other than the father, and the father didn't have it in him to kill her, but knew where she was... And the guys from the Jade Circle had the means and the motive to kill her, but they didn't know where she was...'

'I swear to God, Cake, if you don't tell me what—'

'Have you considered maybe the killer wasn't alone?'

Jamie's eyes narrowed and her brain stuttered. Occam's bloody razor.

'If the father came to the door, knocked, she looked, saw it was him, answered, and then the shooter, waiting in the wings...'

'Steps into the doorway and...'

'Bang.' Cake nodded. 'Just a thought.'

'Shit,' Jamie said, putting her hand on her head.

'What? Is it wrong?' Cake looked at her apologetically.

'No,' Jamie said, sighing. 'I'm just pissed at myself that I didn't think of it.'

21

'Here,' Jamie said, lifting the plastic cup to his lips.

Roper sipped from it and winced, coughed, gripped his stomach, and then let out a long breath, tears forming at the corner of his eyes. 'Shit that hurts,' he muttered.

It was a little after seven and Jamie was at his bedside. She'd had herself checked out already, and the doctor had told her she had a mild concussion and that she should take a few days off. She told him she would, declined a paracetamol prescription, not wanting to mix her pills, and then took another co-dydramol on her way out of the door.

She wasn't sure how many she'd taken so far today, but she thought if she stopped that the pain under the surface of her high would reach up and drag her down. And she still had to relay all this to Roper, and go home and write her reports.

'So you found nothing?' Roper asked, barely above a whisper. He said speaking loudly hurt too much. He eyed her cautiously, his pupils dilating and refocusing on her bruised face. Her cheek was a deep and angry purple colour now, her eye swollen.

She'd told him the truth, sort of. Jamie confided that Matt had been waiting for her and had ambushed her in the street, but not that he'd threatened her. Or Roper.

Rolling it over in her mind, she wasn't sure if he incriminated himself in stabbing Roper or not. She sure as hell hadn't seen him on the street outside the Jade Circle. But then again, Roper hadn't seen anything either. And he was the one who got stabbed.

The moment he'd woken up, the hospital had called Smith, who'd come down personally to conduct the interview. Roper hadn't seen a thing. One second he was following Yanmei down the street, then suddenly, he felt a hand on his shoulder. He turned around, feeling it in his jacket pocket suddenly, but there was no one there. Then came the pain, and the blood, pouring down his back.

He collapsed and the people around leapt back and then surged forward, clamouring around him.

And that was all he could really give.

Which was exactly shit from a legal standpoint.

'The apartment was clean,' Jamie said, leaning forward on the bed. She'd pulled a chair up and was resting on her elbows. The door was slightly ajar but it didn't matter, they were talking so quietly they could hardly hear each other.

The only other noise was the beeping of Roper's heart monitor.

He was stable, but still needed to be under constant observation.

The surgery had been a success, and while it would be a month before he was on his feet, and probably three before he was walking unassisted, the knife had missed everything important – at least in any meaningful way. The blade had nicked his liver, but they'd managed to suture it.

They said that it was actually a miracle that it hadn't killed him. That by putting a knife there, the assailant was almost guaranteed to hit something important. And that it was why he'd chosen that spot, they said. That Roper was the luckiest guy in the world to come out of this with no more than muscle damage and a nick to the liver.

He was still having pins and needles in his toes, but they said that would fade.

'You checked everywhere?' Roper asked, putting her under the microscope. She could tell he was sore that he wasn't able to come with her.

Two sets of eyes *were* better than one, and she hadn't told him she'd pulled Cake into it. Or that it was his revelation that had probably cracked this thing open.

'Yeah, Roper,' Jamie said, rubbing her head. 'It was as clean as a damn whistle. Every board that moved, every scrap of wallpaper that peeled back, every screw that twisted – I checked everything. We were there for nearly two hours.'

'We?' Roper raised an eyebrow.

Jamie looked away and then back, keeping her face straight. Maybe those pills were stronger than she thought. 'Me, we, you. Fuck, Roper, the whole damn Met. What does it matter?' she said quickly, covering. 'The apartment was clean. Whoever got in there between the SOCOs leaving and us coming back' — she thought running with the plurality might help her sell the misstep — 'found whatever it was they were looking for, and who knows, made our job ten times harder.'

'It was easy before?' Roper asked, forcing a weak grin.

'Shut up,' she muttered, shaking her head. 'This one's a real fucking mess.'

'Tell me about it.' Roper coughed, winced, and whimpered. His stomach was wrapped completely in bandage, his back braced to stop him from bending it.

He'd been propped up on a pillow but the bed was only crooked to the second setting, which meant he was more prostrate than upright.

'So what's the next move?' he asked, looking at her.

'I don't know,' Jamie lied. 'I've got to go home, write out my report for today, and then make a recommendation to put Zhou, the Jade Circle, and the office block on the other side under surveillance. After that, I need to liaise with Amherst and Brock on Grigoryan, and dig into his associations to see if we can't find the father. But for now, it's just a waiting game.' She gave him a smile and hoped that the lies weren't showing through her teeth.

In reality, she was doing all of those things. But she also had Cake in her corner, and if Zhou was playing dirty, then so would she. She was giving the Jade Circle a wide berth, but she very much doubted that they'd looked into her enough to ID Cake. He had a minuscule online presence, no Facebook beyond the personal account that served only to allow him to operate the business page for the gym, both of which had a picture of a boxing ring as the profile photo. His personal account was also set to private so couldn't be viewed by anyone other than friends. Of which he had two. His brother, and someone from Turkey that neither Jamie nor Cake knew. One glance told Jamie that it was a fake account. The bio that said that he was looking to give away his family fortune to anyone willing to click the suspicious-looking link included. Jamie wasn't worried that they'd have any idea who Cake was. And considering he'd already been there, there was no reason he wouldn't go back.

He'd been helpful during the apartment search, and Jamie knew he could be more help, official or not. A surveillance team would take too long to assemble and deploy, and with Zhou on the defensive, they'd probably come up with nothing and that would be even more reason for Smith to pull her off it.

But Cake on the inside? That was gold dust.

She'd stopped at an ATM on the way home, taken out two-hundred in cash and insisted that he take it to gamble with. And she also insisted that he lose it all. She didn't know why. Maybe to ease her guilt. And if he managed to win anything, he could keep that too. Put it towards some gym repairs, she said. Or maybe the overdue lease and bills, she thought.

He was under strict instructions – go in, gamble slowly, but steadily. Win, lose. Drink slowly, but steadily. Don't bet big, but don't bet the minimum. Play a normal night. Don't ask questions, don't ask about Yanmei or Qiang. Just keep an eye on things. But don't make it obvious. She couldn't afford anyone picking up on it, taking him into the alley and putting a knife between his ribs, too.

He was the one who offered – but as she kept laying out those instructions, he'd looked less and less sure.

'What's the goal?' he'd asked, almost timid by the end. 'What am I looking for?'

'I don't know,' Jamie had said, sorry that she didn't have a better answer. 'Anyone who looks like they're important. We know about

Zhou, but I doubt any of the other heavy hitters there are going to be on the official payroll. Just… Just tell me if you see anything suspicious. But for God's sake, don't get spotted.'

He nodded. 'You can count on me.'

Jamie rolled it over in her head, watching Roper watch her, his eyes narrowed, but barely in focus.

'It's getting late,' she said, sitting up. 'I'm going to head out. Can I bring you anything tomorrow?' Jamie asked, standing up.

Roper closed his eyes. 'A pack of cigarettes.'

'Ah, I think this is one of their non-smoking rooms. But I'll see what I can do about getting you switched.'

He chuckled. 'Don't make me laugh,' he said, letting it turn into a groan of pain. His face broke like a sheet of ice, and crumpled into a grimace.

'Get some rest, Roper,' she said, heading for the door.

She was halfway there when he called out. 'Jamie.'

'Yeah?' she said, turning back to him. 'What is it?'

'My ex-wife came to see me earlier.'

Jamie's heart sank a little. She didn't know if she had the energy for whatever drawn-out thing this was about to become. And then she told herself off for being such a bad friend. 'Yeah?'

'Yeah.'

'How did that go?'

'Weird. She hasn't so much as called in two years, and now…'

'Mm,' she said, leaning on the frame. 'I bet.'

'She said she'd always wished me dead – but now that it nearly happened…'

'Funny that,' Jamie said. 'My mum always said the same about my dad.'

'Well, if you see her in the hall or anything…'

'Yeah?'

'Tell her to piss off.'

Jamie raised an eyebrow.

'I thought getting stabbed was bad.' He shifted painfully on the bed, the brace giving him grief. 'But there's nothing quite like being stuck in a room with your ex-wife to make you appreciate a knife in the back.'

Jamie smiled sardonically. 'Good night, Roper. I'll see what I can do about slipping the nurse twenty quid to wheel you out for a smoke break.'

'Be safe out there, Jamie,' Roper said, looking at her, his eyes sharp for the first time. 'I don't like this one, and I don't like being trapped here. And mostly, I don't like you being out there without anyone watching your back.'

'I can look after myself.'

'Says the one with a concussion and a face that looks like an aubergine.'

'You know, Roper, I'm starting to see what your ex-wife did.'

'I'm serious, Jamie,' he said, his voice hard and cold. 'These guys aren't messing around. They'll kill you, and not think twice about it.'

'I know, Roper.'

'So don't go kicking the hornet's nest, alright?'

'Me?' Jamie asked emphatically, pressing her hands to her heart and hooking her foot around the door. 'I don't know what you're talking about.'

She pulled it open and slipped through it before he could reply again. If she had to hear another word, she might just lose her nerve and call Cake, tell him not to go in there.

But she couldn't do that. Not after all this.

They'd all but slipped through her fingers, but there was too much blood in the water already.

It was clouding everyone else's vision. But she was hoping she could use that to her advantage.

She was hoping that they'd never see her coming.

22

JAMIE'S CAR was still in Chinatown, and though she was beginning to dread the mounting overnight charges, she didn't have the energy or the clarity to get it and drive it all the way home.

She caught a cab back to her apartment, the same as the night before, and asked that the driver pull up directly outside. She flashed her warrant card to make sure he complied.

Then she asked him to wait until she was inside before pulling off. As she sat forward, her face coming into the light in the cockpit, he took one glance in the rear-view, and then nodded. 'Of course, love,' he said and smiled as warmly as a stranger can.

She thought about thanking him, then about explaining, and then just pressed the button to add a gratuity to the fare, flashed her phone against the reader, and got out.

Jamie wasted no time crossing the pavement and unlocking her door.

The taxi pulled away and drove into the darkness, its brake light flaring at the end of the road before it turned the corner and disappeared.

She stepped back, looking at the door for second. It was weighted to close on its own. Reinforced. Heavy. With a laser-cut lock and heavy deadbolt.

Cake had gotten in because he'd said there were chunks of glass trapped in the jamb. She fished a few out of her hair throughout the day, so she didn't doubt it.

But there were none there now, and as she pushed it inwards it swung smoothly, and then closed behind her with a satisfying thunk of the deadbolt.

There was no way Matt was getting through that.

Jamie sighed and turned to the stairs, her back, jaw, and stomach all aching equally. The first two were from getting the shit beaten out of her, and the last one was on account of her not eating pretty much all day. The thought of chewing anything was enough to make her stomach turn over.

She grimaced at the thought and took the first step, hauling herself upwards.

Jamie didn't drink. Not at all. But this was probably the sort of time people would knock one back. And just then she could sort of see the appeal.

She growled at herself for thinking it, shook her head at the notion, and then pushed onwards towards her apartment.

By the time she got to her door, she couldn't help but admire the job Cake had done cleaning up. There was no hint that she'd clawed her sorry, bloodied body up there. And the car had gone from outside. It was almost like it never happened, except for all the pain she felt in her entire body, of course.

The smell of bleach still hung faintly in the air, stinging her nostrils as she fumbled with her keys, tiredness grabbing at her eyelids, pulling at her shoulders.

She didn't think she'd get much of her report done – more likely she'd just jot down some notes, jam some food down her throat – though she didn't think there'd be anything in her fridge in date – and then fall into bed.

Jamie would leave her phone on loud so that the pre-arranged text from Cake letting her know that he was okay would wake her up. But

otherwise, she intended to sleep for a solid twelve to fourteen hours
and then hopefully wake up in the morning feeling a little more human.

Her hand reached out for the door, her mind focused on bed, and
froze.

Something lingered in the air.

The smell of food. Of cooking food.

Jamie glanced over her shoulder at the door opposite hers. The
apartment was owned by a professor at City College. He was an
esteemed anthropologist specialising in early humans, and had tenure.
As such, he spent most of his time overseas doing research. Jamie had
crossed paths with him before Christmas and he'd asked her to empty
his mailbox and put it inside his front door periodically. And though
she didn't know him beyond their odd encounter on the stairs, he
seemed friendly enough, if not a little conceited, and she did him that
favour.

He'd informed her that he'd be back at the beginning of February,
and would be in India until then, working on a significant find they'd
uncovered. And then he'd given her a key, said detectives in the
Metropolitan Police could be trusted, couldn't they?

She didn't know what to make of the comment, but she did know
one thing.

His apartment was, and would be, empty for another few weeks.
And that smell definitely hadn't been downstairs, either. Each floor had
its own distinct odour, perpetuated by the residents on each. And while
they were all tinged with bleach at the moment, it was only hers, the
second, and top floor, that had a layer of food-smell underpinning it.

Jamie's fingers quivered at the handle, her eyes inspecting the
frame. No signs of forced entry, nothing hinting at anything untoward.
And what did she think, that Matt had somehow gotten through two
locked doors, gone inside in what was still the early evening, and made
himself dinner? No, that was stupid.

Cake had brought it up that day, and she had to remember it now.
Occam's bloody Razor.

Her mother was the only other person who had a key – and that
was only for emergencies. And it was mostly so that if Jamie lost hers,

she could go and get a copy from her mother so at least she could gain entry to her apartment.

She really didn't like the idea of her mother dropping by unannounced like this, but it happened on rare occasions. Usually when she had something to tell Jamie, or when she wanted to nag her to find a man, grab a desk at the Met, and settle down. To save her from following the same wretched path as her father. No doubt she'd read about Roper, the same as Cake, and decided to drop by to fill her annual quota of motherliness.

The main thing that Jamie was concerned about right now was what state her apartment was in. Whether Cake had cleaned out the sink with all the blood. Whether the flannel he'd used was still soaked red and strewn about. Whether the remnants of crushed up painkillers still dusted her kitchen counter.

It was a scene that had awaited her mother on many mornings after her father had come home late back in Stockholm.

Jamie sighed, grabbed the handle, trying not to think about what her mother would say about her face, and then pushed the key into the door, and went in. The quicker she got the dressing down over with, the quicker they could get to whatever version of normal conversation existed between them.

She was inside in a second and locked the door behind her, taking a deep breath, resting her forehead against the cool wood.

It would be easier facing off against Matt again. And probably less painful, too. 'Mum?' she called, pulling herself upright and turning towards the hallway. The smell of food was more pungent now. Meat was frying by the sound of it, the hearty aroma of beef. Steak, maybe. She hoped. Her mother wasn't much of a chef – not since they left Sweden at least – but she wasn't going to complain. Despite the pain, hunger was beginning to burrow into her guts, her stomach squeezing and preparing for incoming sustenance.

Steak, fried onions, some baked potatoes. The smell of it all was making her dizzy. Giddy almost. Her mouth was salivating.

She didn't even care that it was being fried in a pan and not on her lean-grill with the detachable grease tray.

'Mum?' she called again, heading for the living room

Music was playing softly. Jamie didn't recognise what it was. Smooth, with a gentle beat. Probably something niche she'd been introduced to by one of the guys she'd met on her singles cruise.

Usually the thought of that inspired a little bit of bile – but she was too hungry and tired to sustain it.

'Mum?'

Jamie stepped into the living room, ready collapse on top of a plate of food, and froze, her muscles stiffening, her breath catching in her throat.

There was someone standing at the hob, a frying pan moving skilfully in his hands, turning a layer of perfectly fried butter and black pepper onions over and over. But it wasn't her mother.

The frame was tall, lean, but strong. The shoulders well defined under a simple white t-shirt, the head a little bowed, focused on the task at hand, the manicured hair cut in a defined line across the nape of his neck.

His left hand continued to move the onions while his right took a two-pronged fork and turned over the two steaks frying in her griddle pan.

He replaced it on the counter and reached into a little ceramic bowl she never used, took a pinch of what looked like salt and cracked black pepper mix, lifted it over the meat, and sprinkled it on without a hint of haste.

The hot metal sizzled and crackled and he put the pan of onions down on the heat, spreading his hands and placing them either side of the hob.

He rested his weight there, his shoulder blades protruding as his chest lowered, back arching away from the flames. His fingers, just centimetres from the two-pronged fork, lay still. 'Jamie,' he said, his voice soft and calm. 'Do you want to eat first, or talk?'

'Elliot,' Jamie said, her voice caught in her throat.

Elliot Day didn't turn around. He just lifted himself straight and picked up the two-pronged fork, taking the steaks out of the pan and putting them on a plate next to the hob.

Jamie was rooted in place, unable to speak or do anything. Half of her was screaming out to turn and run for the door. The other half was telling her to charge forward and make a dive for the knife block.

But the loudest voice in her head was telling her to do neither. It was saying to stand there and see what happened. To ask why the hell he was here, and what he wanted.

If he'd come to kill her, he could have done it a thousand other ways, and she'd never have even known. But there was no cloak-and-dagger about this. He was standing in her kitchen cooking dinner. And by the smell of it, doing a damn good job.

'Please,' he said gently. 'Sit.' He'd already moved the two stools that sat next to each other on the living room side of the breakfast island so that one was on either side.

'And if I refuse?' Jamie said, her voice sharp and barely above a whisper, her voice nearly lost in the slow drone of the music.

'Then you'll be wasting a prime cut of fillet beef.' He leaned down and took a plate of baked potatoes from the oven, turned for the first time, and put them on the island.

They steamed, making him look hazy.

But there was no mistaking him, even in the dim lighting he'd set. Even through one good eye. He was as he had always been, except maybe a little more tanned, his hair a little longer. But Jamie figured being an international fugitive would do that to you.

'Where's Grace?' Jamie asked, not moving. Grace Melver was his ward, his conspirator, his… Jamie didn't know what.

'She's safe,' he said, not trying to convince her.

Jamie doubted he'd say any more on the matter. And there were a thousand other questions to ask.

His eyes moved over her face, the bruises there, and narrowed fractionally, a brief flash of rage seizing his features. And then it was gone. But he couldn't hide it from her. He couldn't hide anything from her anymore.

Elliot's mouth curled into a what could pass for a warm smile to anyone who didn't know who he really was – *what* he really was.

Jamie forced herself to remember that as he turned back to the counter, took the two-pronged fork again, pulled two plates out of the plate-warmer at the bottom of her oven, and then placed one piece of seared meat on each. 'Onions?' he asked, spooning some onto his, and pausing at the pan for Jamie's.

'What are you doing here?' she asked, daring to take a step forward.

'Cooking you dinner.' He placed the last of the onions onto her steak and picked up both plates, turning to face her. He had a tea-towel draped over his shoulder like this was perfectly normal. 'It looks like you could use it.'

Jamie set her jaw. 'Don't fuck with me, Elliot,' she said, stepping forward again.

He put the plates in front of the stools and sat on the one on the far side of the island.

Resting his elbows on the surface, he gestured to the chair opposite. 'I'm not, Jamie,' he replied, his voice even and calm. 'I'm here to help you. But please, first, sit. Eat.' He let himself smile again.

It made her shiver.

'Come on,' he said, pulling the tea-towel from his shoulder and laying it across his lap. He picked up the knife and fork he'd laid out and deftly carved a piece of meat off his steak. 'It's getting cold.'

23

'IT'S NOT POISON,' he said, chewing his steak, eyes fixed on Jamie.

She thought it was about ninety-percent the food that made her sit down, and ten-percent morbid curiosity.

Jamie scowled and picked up the knife and fork, watching as Elliot reached over and skewered a potato with his own, lifting it to his plate.

She calculated that he was out of lunging distance. Which meant that neither could attack the other. Though despite the anger that clouded the air like smoke, there was no aura of impending violence. Both knew that if that was coming, it would have already surged in a bloody wave and one of them would be lying on the floor in a pool of their own juices.

So what was it then?

As Jamie looked at him, lifting the tender meat to her bruised lips, she had to force herself to remember what he had done. What had led them here.

Of course, neither would breathe a word of this. And while Jamie wanted him out of her apartment, there was a hole inside her that Elliot filled. Not one of love, or longing. Nothing so mundane. It was one that had been torn and cauterised, never to heal.

He had burrowed into her life, gained her trust, lied to her, made her a part of his narrative, and then excised himself with perfect, surgical precision. Like an appendix that had removed itself. Not necessary to function, but missing all the same.

A little space inside her that was all scar tissue, that twinged in the night, reminding her of the hurt.

And she felt like taking her fork and jamming it into the flesh above her right hip to remind herself of that.

'How is it?' Elliot asked, smiling.

'It's good.' She didn't see any point in lying. 'Are you going to start, or should I?'

'What happened to your face?' he asked, taking another bite of steak. He rested on his elbows, studying her cheek.

'I got punched.'

'Looks painful.'

'You should see the other guy.'

'I have.' Elliot said, giving her a wider smile, the corners of his mouth curling into his cheeks.

Jamie wasn't sure whether to ask what that even meant.

She figured there was little left to lose at this point. And if he hadn't already drugged her in order to harvest her organs and sell them, then that probably wasn't his modus operandi. At least not tonight. 'You didn't kill him, did you?'

Elliot stood up without answering and went to the cupboard. 'Water?' he asked, reaching without hesitation for the cupboard that she kept the glasses in.

She watched him, not sure if he'd acquainted himself with the layout of her kitchen before she arrived, or whether this wasn't the first time he'd been in there. He knew where she lived – he'd picked her up. But had he been inside before? While she was out? Or asleep. That was a terrifying thought. Of him walking silently around her apartment in the dark hours of the night. Picking the lock and slipping in without her knowing whenever he pleased.

'How did you get in here?'

'Does it really matter?' He put a glass down in front of her and took his seat again.

'In the grand scheme of things, I suppose not.'

'So how have you been?'

'Better.'

'I'm sorry.'

'About what exactly?' Jamie asked, the scorn rising in her voice. 'About lying to me? About kidnapping, harvesting, and then trafficking the organs of innocent people – who *trusted* you?'

'I think *innocent* is a relative term.'

'You would.'

He chuckled a little. 'I missed this.'

Jamie shuddered. 'Did you kill Matt?'

'I'm sorry,' he began. 'That I sent you into this half-cocked.' Elliot sighed. 'The others. Cunningham, Bowman. Those were simple cases.'

Jamie set her knife and fork down, her stomach fighting her mind.

'But this one. This girl… I should have waited.'

'Why didn't you?'

'Grace.'

Jamie's jaw flexed. 'What about her?'

'She… *insisted* that I pass it along.'

'Insisted? You don't strike me as the type of man easily swayed.'

He turned his head and looked into her living room. 'I'm not a robot, Jamie.'

She said nothing.

'I do feel. Just perhaps not in the same way you do.'

'If you make a comparison to lions and sheep I'm going to leap over the table.' She felt her hand move towards the knife.

'Lions, sheep. Black, white. Innocent, guilty. If only life were that simple.' He met her eyes again now, seemingly unphased by the serrated steak knife she was clutching in her fist.

'It is for the most part.'

'I feel responsible for what happened to your partner, Detective Roper. For what has happened to you.'

Jamie stiffened at his name. It was like a violation in itself, hearing it come from his mouth.

'And I've come to rectify that.'

She didn't feel in control of this conversation in the slightest.

They trained her to do exactly that. To control the ebb and flow of an exchange. To lead a suspect to confession. To twist them up, trip them, make them talk. And yet the steak between her back teeth felt more like a noose around her throat, and Elliot had the other end firmly in his grasp. He would tell her exactly what he wanted to, and nothing more. 'How did you know about her?' Jamie asked, making one last attempt.

'There's a code, you know,' he said measuredly.

'Jesus Christ,' Jamie muttered.

'A balance.'

She wondered what the odds of her hitting him somewhere vital with the knife were if she hurled it across the island.

'This city is a living organism, and each part must perform its function.'

'You want to get to the fucking point?' Jamie snarled, pushing the meal away. She didn't have to force herself to remember the rage anymore.

'There are many criminal elements, all of which feed at the same trough – the single commodity that makes it all possible. That keeps it all alive.'

'Money.'

'People, Jamie.'

She narrowed her eyes.

'People. People demand that which they cannot get legally, and those with the means, the hunger, the morality to supply it, do. People want drugs, drug dealers supply them, People want weapons, gun dealers supply them. People want women, property—'

'Organs?'

His eye twitched almost imperceptibly. 'There are people to supply them.'

'What a quaint story.'

'Each need met' — he moved his hand in little bounds across the surface of the island — 'by its respective supplier. All of whom have carved out a niche for themselves, a structure preserved by mutual respect.'

'A regular fucking utopia,' Jamie grunted.

'And when something, or someone, upsets the balance, the problem needs to be dealt with.' He met her stare. 'Do you understand what I'm saying?'

'No.' Jamie shook her head. 'And I don't really care.'

'Zhou and the people he works for are becoming a problem for the city.'

Jamie arched an eyebrow.

'They're becoming too bold, too powerful. And they needed to be handled.'

'Handled?' Jamie watched him. 'So is that what I'm doing, *handling* them?'

'Currently, no.'

Jamie seethed.

'That wasn't meant offensively.'

'And yet…' Jamie grinned sarcastically at him.

'But with my help…' He opened his hands. 'It can be done.'

'That still doesn't explain anything. Cunningham, Bowman, Qiang…' Jamie folded her arms. 'How did you know about them? And why pass them to me? If this structure is in such fine balance, why not deal with them yourself? No honour among thieves?'

'And who's job would that be?' Elliot sat back now, putting his knife and fork on his plate. 'A man walking into a mosque to commit an act of racial hatred only serves to raise tensions in the city, making trade more difficult for everyone.'

'Oh, I don't know, there must be enforcers? Flunkies you have to deal with stuff like this. Preserve your precious status quo.'

'We do,' Elliot said plainly. 'They're called the Met.'

Jamie's teeth nearly split she was clenching them so hard. 'And what about Bowman? What higher purpose did getting him off the street serve?'

'Paedophiles are the scum of the earth,' Elliot said, the acid in his voice stripping the flesh from Jamie's ears. 'He made a point of bragging to the wrong person about what he was going to do – and that got back to the right person.'

'You?'

'Eventually.'

'And you thought you'd sick me on him? Your own personal attack dog?' Jamie scoffed, shaking her head. If she hated being complicit before, she felt sick to her stomach over it now.

'I afforded you the opportunity to arrest him before he caused any more harm.'

'How thoughtful.'

'He would have been dealt with at some point – but how many he would have hurt before he was put back inside, or crossed the wrong person, I don't know.'

'So what, you've got a network of spies' — Jamie raised her hands and twiddled her fingers in the air — 'with their ears to the ground, feeding you all this information. Is that it?'

'Call it an exchange of favours.'

She scoffed again. 'To keep your fingers in all the right pies?'

He looked at her minutely. Inspecting her. 'To help you.'

'To help me?' She couldn't help but laugh. 'Yeah, I feel pretty fucking helped right now.' She gestured to her face.

He leaned forward now, the vein in his temple throbbing gently. 'I received a hell of a lot more information than I passed on.'

'Good for you.'

'The names I passed on were mutually beneficial.'

'Whatever you say.' She shook her head.

'You got Bowman off the streets, didn't you?'

'That's not the point.'

'Saved that girl's life?'

'That's *not* the point.'

'You chose to act on that information.'

'That's not the fucking point!'

'What does it matter where it came from? She's safe, he's behind bars. Isn't that more important?'

She could feel her cheeks burning, her throat tightening. 'That's not the way justice works!'

'It seems like it's working so far.'

Her mouth quivered, her jaw quivering with anger. 'And Zhou? What about that? The Jane Doe? Your noble sensibilities walked me right into that fucking buzz saw, didn't they.'

'That was my mistake.'

She nodded. 'You fucking bet it was.'

'I should have waited. Waited for more information before putting you onto it. There are lots of people who want to see Zhou and the people he works for taken down a few pegs – but they didn't really give a shit how many girls got bought, sold, murdered before that happened.'

'And you did?'

He drew a slow breath. 'Grace did.'

'Grace.' Jamie almost spat the name. 'You say that name like you give two shits about her.'

'I do.'

'Bullshit.'

'If I didn't, I wouldn't have taken her with me.'

'The only reason you did was because she could have testified against you.'

'If that was my main concern I would have slit her throat the second that I knew I was leaving, and been done with it.'

Jamie swallowed and kept her eyes locked on his. 'And you're going to tell me now that she pleaded with you? To help find Qiang's killers? To bring them to whatever twisted form of justice you feel you're enacting here with this white-knight act of yours?'

'That's exactly what I'm saying. And I gave in. And because of that, you're sitting here beaten half to hell, and your partner is lying in a hospital bed. And for that, I'm sorry.'

Jamie lowered her head and shook it, laughing to herself. 'You expect me to believe this crap? Why on earth would Grace give two shits about this girl, huh? After what she's been through?'

'It's because of what she's been through.' Elliot inhaled and leaned forward again. 'Grace was pregnant, Jamie.'

She studied his face for any hint of falsehood and found none. 'Oliver's?' Her voice was sharp, like razor blades. 'That why you gave in? Guilt?' She scoffed again. 'Killed the father of her child to cut him up for spare parts, and now you're seeking redemption.'

'Paxton's.'

Jamie's stomach turned over. 'Paxton's?'

'Paxton was the father.'

'You're lying.'

'Why would I?'

'Is Grace still…?'

'No.' He answered evenly, without emotion.

'She lost the child?'

'We took care of it.'

'Jesus,' Jamie said. 'Was that her choice or yours?'

'Hers. It was… a difficult decision for her. But for the best.'

'You convinced her of that, I'm sure.'

'Once the reality of the situation set in, she came to the conclusion on her own.'

'The reality of the situation? What was that, raising a child while fleeing from Interpol as an international fugitive?'

'Raising a child with little access to regular high-quality healthcare, while living with her condition.'

'Her condition?' Jamie narrowed her eyes.

'HIV, Jamie,' Elliot said, a hint of remorse in his voice. 'Paxton used her – before I knew her, and after, too. Kept her addicted to heroin, prostituted her, sold her. That's why she wanted to go with me. To get away from it. From the city. From that life.'

Jamie's throat had all but closed up. She was looking for a tell in his face that he was lying. She looked for it desperately. 'And Oliver Hammond? What was he in all this? Grace and him were getting clean together. They were getting out.' Jamie slapped the table. 'And you killed him. Does she even know?' She was sickened by the sight of him.

Elliot looked down for a second, staring at his steak, resting in a shallow pool of blood. 'Jamie, Grace *brought* Oliver to me.'

She stiffened on the stool.

'She chose him. She chose them all.'

Her throat tied itself in a knot, her guts braiding like a rope. 'Bullshit.'

He let out a long breath. 'Grace is… special. She's a special girl who was dealt a very bad hand. But now, at least, she's free. She's clean. She's—'

'If you say *happy* I'm going to fucking kill you.'

He chuckled a little bit. 'Would that be justice, Jamie?'

'Fuck justice.'

'Fuck justice.' He said the words slowly. 'You should frame that and put it on the wall above your desk.'

She swallowed hard. 'If you're intending to kill me, then I'd prefer you just get it over with.' The co-dydramols had well and truly worn off now and it felt like she had a hatchet buried in her skull. 'I'm bored, and I'd like to go to bed now that you've read me a story.'

'I'm not going to hurt you, Jamie. As I said, I only want to help. And that's why I came back.' He stood up, holding his hands out wide. 'Believe me, I didn't want to. But you're going up against people who don't think twice about killing police officers. You backed Zhou into a corner, and he bit you. Smith will no doubt want to take you off the case when he gets wind of what happened.'

'He won't ever find out.'

He ignored her and pressed on. 'And Zhou has enough connections in the Met to make it all go away if it lands on anyone else's desk. So if you want this done, you're going to have to do it yourself, Jamie.'

'Nothing's changed, then.'

He chuckled in mild amusement. 'Zhou's attack dog, the one who did this to you,' he said, pointing gently to her face. 'He won't be a problem anymore.'

'Did you kill him?'

'But the others – the one who went after your partner? He's still out there, and he's dangerous.'

'Who is he?'

Elliot stood up. 'You want his name?'

Jamie weighed it up. Did she want his help? More than she wanted to see this done right? Was that even possible any more? 'Who is he?' she asked before she could decide.

'Marco De Voge.'

'Marco De Voge.'

'He looks after the girls for Zhou.'

'Did he kill Qiang?'

'That I don't know.'

Jamie pushed her hair off her forehead, feeling a sheen of sweat cling to the back of her neck. 'Anything else?' she asked derisively.

'Leos Kosiah.'

'Who's that?'

'The head of Zhou's security team for the Jade Circle.'

'Wouldn't it just be easier to kill all of them yourself?' Jamie looked up at him haughtily.

'And deprive you of all the fun?' He took his plate and put it on the counter next to the sink. 'No, it's better for everyone if you finish this.'

'I don't need your help.'

'So turn down the promotion when Smith offers it to you. It makes no difference to me.' He met her eyes again. 'I'm not here to scrub my conscience clean.'

'Fooled me.'

He took one step towards her and she sat back, flinching. Elliot paused, amused, and gestured to her plate. 'Want me to take it?'

'I'll do it myself.'

'Okay, Jamie.' He sighed, turned, and headed around the island and into the living room, giving her a wide berth. He took his jacket from the back of the sofa. 'And one more thing. Does *Princess Of The Sun* mean anything to you?' He asked casually, pulling it on.

The name stirred something in the back of her mind. 'Princess Of The Sun? Sun Princess?' she said, her mouth and mind working at the same rate. It was written on top of one of the magazines pulled from the apartment that Qiang was staying in. 'What does it mean?'

'What do you think it means?'

'Nothing. They checked it out – there was nothing of interest. No results that meant anything.'

'Sounds like whoever translated it doesn't know much about Chinese syntax.'

'And you do?' The scorn came naturally.

'Apparently more than whoever the Met is subcontracting their translation services to.'

'What are you getting at?'

'Monday morning – about three a.m.'

She was on her feet now, too. As soon as her heels hit the floor her lizard brain kicked in, keeping her back, her hackles rising.

Elliot, standing there, not especially tall, or especially strong, was still dangerous. It came off him like heat. An unassuming killer. An unseen blade.

'What the hell's that supposed to mean?' Jamie snapped.

He zipped up his jacket and glanced at the window. 'Looks like the rain's coming in again.'

'Elliot – don't fuck with me.'

'It was good to see you, Jamie. Be careful out there,' he said, pulling his hood up. Without another word, he reached into his pocket and pulled out a small black device. 'If you need me.' He tossed it into the air and her eyes went to it, her hands leaping upwards to grab it.

Plastic hit her fingers and snapped closed. She brought it down, unfurling them. In her palm was a disposable phone.

Her mind stuttered for a second and she looked up, faced only with her empty living room.

The front door closed softly in the hallway and Jamie was alone, surrounded by the smell of high quality meat, expertly cut by an expert hand.

She looked down at the phone again, shivered, and closed her fingers around it.

Every ounce of her wanted to turn and launch it into the wall, shatter it into a million pieces.

But she didn't.

Instead, she pushed it into her jeans pocket so she could feel it against her hip, and then picked up her plate, taking it to the sink.

She put the water on and cranked it until it was scalding, and then started washing up, deeply desiring to scrub away every trace that he'd been there.

Her mind spun as she did, processing all the information.

She caught up slowly, each item of data collating neatly and then filing itself away in the appropriate folder of her brain, and then arrived at the present, the sharp corner of the cheap phone digging into her leg.

Jamie turned the water off and put her hands on either side of the sink, sudsy and burning red.

She took two deep breaths, closed her eyes, and then rushed to the bathroom, collapsing onto her knees and emptying her stomach into the toilet.

Jamie slumped sideways against the wall and rested her arm on the rim of the bowl.

She leant her head forward until it was pressed to the back of her hand and stayed like that, listening as tears pattered softly on the tiles under her.

She didn't sob, or make a single sound. She just sat there, legs folded under her like a cheap lawn chair, waiting for the door to open and for Elliot to come back in.

But he never did.

He never came to finish her off.

And that was what hurt the most.

24

SMITH LOOKED up as Jamie walked in without knocking, the immediate look of indignation on his face at being interrupted replaced just as quickly with surprise.

His eyebrows raised towards his scalp, his forehead rippling into thin, olive-coloured rolls. 'Jesus, Johansson,' he said quietly, tactful of the fact that the desks outside his office door were within earshot. 'What the hell happened?'

No one was watching, but then again it was still twenty-to-nine and Jamie had bolted straight from the elevator to his door, a navy-coloured beanie pulled down low on her head, her hooded sweatshirt fully zipped with the hood up, and a coating of makeup doing what it could to cover the bruising on her face. She'd woken up early and jumped on YouTube to try and find a tutorial on how best to disguise it. She found an alarming number of videos for-and-by women on how to cover facial bruising with makeup. Most of them were ambiguous as to the potential causes of the bruising, but the woman who was leading the tutorial had a pretty nasty welt on the side of her face that definitely didn't come from a doorframe.

Jamie, as she found herself doing a lot recently, filed it away in the back of her mind as an issue to delve into when she had some time to herself. But when that would be, she didn't know.

Despite having loathed receiving it at the time – or perhaps she just hated the spirit in which it was given – Jamie was glad that she had that make-up kit from her Mother in the bottom of her wardrobe. The sentiment may have been misplaced – because no daughter wants to hear, 'You'll never find a guy who's interested in you when you look more manly than he does,' on her birthday – but the quality of the kit itself was quite high. As such, Jamie had felt she did a reasonable job, considering her lack of experience, in covering up the bruise. At least until she saw Smith's face.

She was just glad the swelling had gone down and she could speak and swallow without tears coming to her eyes.

'Nothing – sparring accident. Bobbed when I should have weaved. Can we talk?' Jamie asked, closing the door and sitting down.

Smith watched her intensely as she sat down, well aware that she trained in martial arts, but still not sure whether he was going to buy it or not. 'You can talk. I'll reserve judgement until you're finished,' he said matter-of-factly.

Jamie sat, ignoring the derision there. Though she sort of understood. No other detective spent as much time in here as her, or caused him as much trouble. She was starting to think maybe she should have just stuck with the Raymond case – which reminded her that she needed to follow up with the uniforms to see whether they'd turned anything up.

She exhaled, cleared her head, and met Smith's wide eyes. His stare was unflinching, waiting for her to start.

'The Jade Circle,' she said.

He sat back in his chair and put his hand to his face, pushing in at his eyeballs with his thumb and forefinger. 'Are you about to tell me that the mess on your face is because of them? Or that you have the suicidal intention of asking me if you can go back there?'

She wasn't quite sure whether he meant that going back there was suicide, or that it was suicidal just to ask. She suspected both.

'This,' she said, pointing to her face. 'Doesn't matter. There's bigger things at stake than my face.'

He leaned forward now. 'It matters to me, Johansson – because if one of my detectives is getting beaten up because of their case, or they're engaging in illegal bare-knuckle boxing matches to satiate their death wish, then I need to know. And react accordingly.'

'I don't have a death wish,' Jamie said, trying to keep her voice even.

'Really? Because the last few months tell me otherwise.' He clasped his hands together on his desk. 'I know you're trying your best, but it's coming off as reckless, and despite achieving what you have – the results, on paper at least...' He kept shifting in his chair. 'Don't justify letting you run around without any sort of... restraint.'

'Sir, if you'd just let me explain,' Jamie said, realising she was picking at a hangnail on her finger with little regard for how much damage she was doing.

She clasped her hands instead and carried on, pulling the stack of papers she'd brought with her off her lap and putting them down in front of him.

'What is this?'

'This is enough to put Zhou and everyone else with their fingers in the Jade Circle and the human trafficking operation they're running out of there behind bars for a very long time.' She held back a smile of triumph.

He looked at the papers, and then back at her. 'Is it, Johansson? Is this really enough to go in there with a hundred officers and put them all in handcuffs and have a judge drop a gavel on each and every one without a hope in hell they could walk? Iron clad evidence? Hand in the cookie jar?'

'Well, no, but—'

'When was the last time you slept, Jamie?' he asked, his voice soft, more concerned than condescending, but just as painful to hear.

'I sleep fine,' Jamie said defensively. 'I've been up since four, but that's not the point,' she added, realising that despite the makeup, the bags under her eyes still looked pretty dark. And she'd definitely not been getting her prescribed vegetable and fluid intake. Not the state-recommended amount, or her usual standard, which was higher again. She knew she looked like shit, but that didn't matter to her, and with what was in the report that she'd spent four hours typing out, it shouldn't have mattered to Smith either.

'I want you to take a few days off, Jamie,' he said, putting his hand flat on the papers. 'I'll read this in the meanwhile, we can keep an eye on Roper's recovery, and look to formulate more of a long-term plan.' His words were slow, enunciated, like he was speaking to a child.

'With all due respect, sir—'

'Saying that, Johansson,' he said, cutting in. 'Doesn't give you the right to say whatever you damn well please.'

Jamie was getting tired of coming in here and getting her legs cut out from under her. 'I know, sir,' she said diligently. 'But can we just discuss this? Trust me – if you think I look like crap, I'd love for you to be able to feel how I'm feeling. But if I'm still here – with my partner laid-up in intensive care, all beat to hell, running on little to no sleep, then don't you think what I've got to say is worth hearing? Or do you think that little of me as a detective?' It was the only play she had. If he said no, then she'd go home and take those days off. Begrudgingly. But she would. And if she did, then their best chance to nail Zhou would pass them right by. Their advantage would disappear, and they'd be back to square one with shit-all to go on and months before they got another shot at him.

Smith sighed and took his hand off the report. 'I never knew your father, Johansson, but from what I've read of his career, I think you're probably a lot like him.'

'Hopefully not too much,' Jamie replied, trying not to overthink it. Smith had an uncanny way of saying things that were both compliments and seriously offensive at the same time.

'In all the ways that count, I'm sure.'

'Much to my mother's dismay.'

He gave a short, polite smile and then tapped a finger on the papers. 'Do you want to give me the short-and-sweet on this? Lay it out for me, Johansson, don't waste my time, don't bullshit me. And don't lie. I want to know what you know. No more games.'

Jamie nodded, and then immediately lied. 'Of course.' She'd been welding the story together in her mind since Cake had called her at four to tell her he was home without issue, and that he'd found out a fair amount.

He didn't know who was running the girls or get any names, but he spoke to some regulars, and apparently, the girls changed regularly. Every six months there was a new selection – which should be any day now by the guy's own reckoning – minus some long-standing members of the line-ups. Favourites, he'd called them. What happened to the girls who left, the regular didn't know. Jamie didn't suspect anything good. The options were either sold, killed, or set free – and she doubted it was the last one.

The girls were generally 'without charge' for anyone who hit the thousand-pound cap. If you bought over a thousand worth of chips, you had free *service* all night, courtesy of whichever girl you chose, and then, providing you lost it all, you'd get use of one of their private rooms for a 'consolation' prize. And if you won anything, the number of girls who would descend on you were proportionate. Cake said that as the money started flowing, and these were his words – *the dresses got shorter and the drinks stronger. After that, it was drugs, and a whole lot of over-the-trousers rubbing, if you know what I mean.*

She knew what he meant.

The house would always recoup the money somehow.

But Cake hadn't seen anyone on the floor who looked like he was in charge of them. No sign of whoever this De Voge was. Of course, at that time, Jamie didn't know who he was either. But now she did.

Still, the information he provided was more than valuable. New girls meant that there was a supply chain going on. And with the information Jamie had gotten from Elliot – which had turned out to be just what the case needed – which Jamie hated, but couldn't deny – formulating a plan of attack was simple.

'Marco De Voge,' Jamie said.

'Marco De-Vojay?' Smith repeated.

'De Voge, yeah.'

'Who is that?'

'Well he's not whoever is living in cell C-12 in Mogilev Prison.'

'Am I supposed to know what that means?'

'Marco De Voge is supposed to be serving a minimum of fifteen years in Mogilev Prison in Belarus for Human Trafficking. Arrested, tried, and convicted four years ago. Check out the top page.' Jamie pointed to the report in Smith's hands. 'Except he's not.'

'Okay, I'll bite,' Smith said, looking down at the second page, at the mean and grainy face staring back at him.

'Three years ago, a gas-explosion at the Mogilev Prison caused a fire to break out in C-wing. All of the prisoners were evacuated and held temporarily in the prison grounds. During the holding, a fight broke out, two of the guards were overpowered, their weapons taken from them. One was shot and killed, the other put in hospital. Now the other guards at the prison reported hearing two distinct explosions about thirty minutes apart. In the confusion following the second – which coincides with the timeframe of the revolt – several inmates escaped with the help of an unknown person or persons.'

'And this De Voge one was one of them?'

Jamie nodded. 'The official statement from Mogilev Prison said that all of the escaped inmates were later recaptured and mentioned nothing about the second explosion, which from the photos I found from a local Mogilev newspaper, appeared to damage the outer fence.'

'But you don't think he was recaptured?' Smith was keeping a straight face, so far unimpressed.

Jamie shook her head. 'No, I don't think so. De Voge has been involved in trafficking for the last two decades. I think he was too valuable to be left behind bars.'

'And I suppose you're getting to the part where you believe him to be somehow involved in your case?'

'Turn the page.'

'What am I looking at?' Smith asked, staring at an even more grainy, black and white still from a security camera.

'Marco De Voge.'

He studied it a little more closely. 'Not exactly definitive proof of his escape, is it? This will hardly stand up in court,' Smith said. 'And you know that anything outside of the Greater London area isn't our jurisdiction, let alone an escaped convict in Belarus.'

'Except that's not Belarus. It's Chinatown. Take a look at the time stamp.'

'Jesus. This is Saturday.'

'That was taken less than two minutes before Roper was stabbed.'

Smith looked up, his expression grave suddenly.

'Less than a hundred metres from where Roper was stabbed.'

'You're saying De Voge stabbed Roper?'

Jamie nodded. 'I am.'

Smith narrowed his eyes. 'How did you find out about this? About De Voge? Is he even on our radar?'

Jamie bit her lip. This is when the lying started. 'I have an informant – someone who frequents the Jade Circle.'

Smith said nothing, but his eyes closed down to slits. 'Who?'

'I'd rather keep his identity a secret. To protect him.'

'Jesus, Jamie – you know we can't do shit with hearsay.' Smith leaned back again, swinging on his chair. 'So this is the story you're peddling – your informant gave you his name, and then you looked him up? Found his record? And then on a hunch scrubbed through hours of security footage requisitioned from where? And when did you have time to do all this?' He looked accusatively at her.

'That's exactly what I did,' Jamie said flatly. 'Like I said, I've been up since four and you can check with reception downstairs, I've been here since half-past six.' Jamie drew a breath. 'Roper and I were set up outside the Jade Circle for hours, and left to follow Yanmei, one of the girls from the Circle.'

'You never told me that.'

'It's all in the report.'

'Mm.' He made a disapproving noise.

'We never clocked De Voge, but he must follow the girls back and forth to the salon. Which was where I met with Yanmei. Now, Roper and I split up to head her off. And Roper said that De Voge came up behind him.

'The route we took could have only been about five-hundred metres. From the time that Roper was on his own, De Voge must have closed in on him.'

'Sure,' Smith said, not agreeing or disagreeing.

'I checked the route, and Roper passed a Job Centre. And being a state-run enterprise, their CCTV footage is readily available to us without a warrant.'

The corner of Smith's mouth twitched almost imperceptibly.

'So I sent them an email at seven this morning, asking for a copy of the two minutes of footage leading up to the attack. They sent a copy of it forty minutes ago. Turn the page.'

Smith tried not to look impressed as he came forward and flipped the page again, seeing a photo of Roper striding in the rain, looking grizzled, smoking a cigarette. It was black and white and a little blurry, but there was no mistaking him. But it wasn't Roper that Smith was looking at. Jamie had drawn a red circle around the figure no more than fifteen behind him.

On each subsequent page the time stamp moved forward a second until De Voge was as clearly in focus as he was going to be.

Smith looked up and drew a deep breath. 'Circumstantial at best. The photo quality is shit, and the Belarus government are never going to admit that De Voge isn't still in custody – and I'm not convinced that he isn't, either. There must be a thousand people in the city who would trip facial rec for this guy.'

'I thought it might not be enough.' She made a circular motion with her finger for him to flip the page.

On the next one was a definition photo of a girl wrapped up in a scarf, hugging a large cup of coffee, smiling at the camera. 'Who the hell is this?' Smith looked up at her, one eyebrow arched.

'Melanie Jones. But that's not important,' Jamie said, waving it off. 'This photo is from the coffee shop Roper and I were set up in. It was taken a month and a half ago.'

'Right?'

'This is on Melanie's Facebook page, but because she checked into the coffee shop and tagged them in her photo, it shows up in their album.'

Smith held his hand up. 'Spare me the crash course on social media use in cases – I get enough of that from cyber. Just skip to the part which is important.'

'Look over her left shoulder. Through the window. The building opposite. What do you see?'

Smith looked back down at the image, which, thank God, had been taken on a smartphone equipped with a great camera. Social media made their lives a lot easier when it came to getting photo evidence of things these days. There was barely a square inch of the city that wasn't being snapped, uploaded, and tagged.

'See him?' Jamie asked.

'The guy leaning against the wall smoking?'

'It's De Voge.'

'It could be.' He had to play devil's advocate.

'Okay, keep turning.'

Smith did so, picking up page after page. Photos from a dozen different Facebook profiles. All in and around the coffee shop. All of them displaying Marco De Voge outside the building opposite, in various situations, in various qualities. Sometimes alone. Sometimes talking to one of the girls from the Jade Circle. And in the final photo, talking to another guy – one dressed in a long black pea coat with leather gloves, a flat nose, cheek-bones that wouldn't have been out of place on the corners of a clothes line, and a fuzz of black hair cut into a close shave.

Smith stared right past the man who was balancing a cappuccino on his head and squinted at it.

'Who's that?'

'I thought you'd never ask.'

He looked up and pursed his lips.

'Leos Kosiah.'

'Should that name mean anything to me?'

'No, probably not. And I only knew about it about five minutes before I came in here,' Jamie lied. 'Turn the—'

'I got it,' Smith said, flipping the page.

There, in the background of the photo – this one of a chihuahua lapping out of a decaf-frappuccino, much to the amusement of the woman holding it – was Kosiah, stepping through the door of the coffee shop, in perfect focus.

'The coffee shop runs a promotion – if you take a photo with one of their cups in it and tag them, you get half off your next coffee. Lucky for us.'

'It will be if you're about to tell me what good this is to the case, and why I still shouldn't send you home for a few days.'

She cleared her throat. 'I took that photo and ran it through our facial-rec database. Nothing came of it. So then I reached out to Interpol, taking a punt based on his facial structure, and got in touch with their European headquarters, who referred me to their Russian branch. They took the photo on and ran a search on their own database.'

'And came up with…'

'Leos Kosiah.'

'Okay, so who is he?'

'Ex-military turned private contractor, turned private security consultant. And you want to know the best part?'

'Enlighten me.'

'Why don't you take a guess where he's from.'

Smith stared at her. 'Guess?'

'Belarus.'

He sat over a little, resting on his elbow, rubbing his chin. 'Could just be a coincidence.'

'Sure, it could.' Jamie shrugged. 'But how's this for coincidental – he was working in Minsk, his company was doing well. Founded in two-thousand-and-eleven, it was on the up. And then suddenly, in March twenty-seventeen – the eighth – poof. He closes down out of nowhere. Liquidates completely. Buys out of his lease in cash, and disappears.'

'Change of personal circumstance. Family bereavement. There could be a hundred reasons that someone—'

'The fire at the prison happened on March eleventh.'

Smith bit his lip.

'Kosiah liquidates his company in Belarus, De Voge gets broken out of prison a hundred miles away three days later, and then they show up in London together? You want to talk about coincidence, this is the coincidence of the fucking century.' Jamie laughed and folded her arms.

'Watch it, Johansson.'

'You have to admit, this is pretty damning.'

'I'm not disagreeing. But unless you can show me proof of either De Voge putting a knife between Roper's ribs, or of this Kosiah character doing something illegal, any solicitor will wipe a courtroom with us. Not to mention filing a claim for wrongful arrest. Hell, this isn't even circumstantial – because you're showing me photos of some people that we could at *best* argue are here illegally. But if they're half as well connected as you're intimating – which is pretty well bloody connected – then getting something like that to stick will be damn-near impossible.'

'Then it's a good thing I'm not suggesting we nail them for Roper or for being in the UK without a valid immigration license.'

'If you tell me to turn the page, I'm going to suspend you.'

Jamie cleared her throat. 'In your own time.'

He turned it, seeing another photo now. One of a beaten up old ship, painted pale blue, streaked with rust. It looked like a small cargo vessel and had Chinese characters painted on the bow.

'And what's this? The ship they used to get into the UK?'

'That's the *Princess of the Sun*,' Jamie said, leaning forward and resting on her elbows. 'And it's the ship they use to bring in their new shipments of girls.'

'*Princess of the Sun* – why does that sound familiar?'

'It's what the victim wrote on the top of one of the magazines recovered from the crime scene – sort of.'

'And we're only finding out about this now?' Smith asked, the anger in his voice immediately apparent.

'Well, the translation we got from it was "Sun Princess", which turned up no results. At least nothing of note. Simple syntax oversight.' Jamie shrugged and played it off as casually as she could.

'Jesus Christ,' Smith said, letting the page fall closed. 'Was it before or after you took over from Brock and Amherst that we missed this?'

'Does it really matter?' Jamie asked diplomatically.

'Yes.'

'Before.'

He set his jaw, pinching at his chin with his hand. 'Go on.' He rocked on the chair, giving Jamie his full attention now.

'My informant said that his information indicated that new girls were brought into the Jade Circle every six months or so, and that the arrival of new girls was imminent.'

Smith was silent now, hanging on her every word.

'I checked out the *Princess of the Sun*. It sails out of Xiamen in China. Mostly it runs from there to the Philippines, Taiwan, Japan, nowhere really far. But every six months, it makes a straight trip from Xiamen to Felixstowe. It always arrives by night, and always on a Monday morning.'

'What do the shipping manifests say it's carrying?'

'Livestock.'

He clicked his teeth together. 'Who orders it?'

'A Chinese catering company registered here in London who cater for specific, large scale events. They buy in large volumes of produce with a special license usually issued to high-end restaurants, hotels, that sort of thing, which gives them the ability to procure items that aren't FSA approved.'

He inhaled slowly, processing. 'Is there more?'

Jamie grinned. 'Oh yeah, there's more.'

He sat up straighter now. Focused on her.

'The catering company who order this food – their director is some nobody. A twenty-nine-year-old guy living in London who relocated from China with his parents when he was seventeen. He's been arrested a couple of times for petty theft, breaking and entering. Served a suspended sentence a few years back. Now he lives in a privately owned apartment not far from Chinatown. Quite the comeback story.'

'So he's what, a scapegoat?'

'Just someone to take the fall if it all goes sideways. On paper, the Xinxian Food Company is a legit business. But dig deeper, knowing what we know…'

Smith nodded, still holding onto his poker face.

'And just to top it all off, the registered business address?'

Smith was already reading the page that Jamie had downloaded from the Companies House website and placed in the file. 'This is the building right behind the Jade Circle.' Smith looked up quickly.

'Yep. It's the one that Roper and I staked out.'

'You know what this means, don't you?' Smith let himself smile for the first time since they'd started. 'We've got them.'

Jamie nodded, knocking on the table with her fist. 'This is the part where you tell me good job.'

Smith shook his head, letting the report fall closed in front of him. 'Let's not get ahead of ourselves.'

25

By four o'clock that afternoon, just eleven hours before the *Princess of the Sun* was due to arrive at Felixstowe carrying who-knew-how-many women, Smith had already assembled a small task force and had amassed enough information and intelligence to get the go-ahead for a full-scale insurgency with armed response.

Smith had cleared his schedule and set to work. Jamie wasn't experienced enough to head up something like this, but he wasn't about to take her off it – that might have just put her over the edge.

He'd drafted in a tightly-knit core of officers that included a senior advisor who worked in Trafficking, the head of Interpol Relations, along with an Interpol agent who was coming in via video-chat to advise on both Kosiah and De Voge, both of whom were on their radar. From their own circle, Smith had called both Brock and Amherst in on this to get a rundown of the information they'd dug up on Grigoryan, and to see whether he did have a hand in this after all. Jamie was on her own, and Smith wanted two more detectives waiting in the wings for support.

In terms of firepower, Smith had requested Nasir Hassan and his team again – the guys who ran point on the Donnie Bats takedown.

Though the closest Hassan had got to any action on that day was taking
a kick to the groin from Jamie.

She was standing at the back of the briefing room, leaning against
the wall when he walked in, his shoulders nearly bumping the frame of
the door.

Hassan clocked Jamie instantly, his tactical-trained eyes sweeping
the room on auto. 'Johansson,' he said, pausing. 'Good to see you back
on your feet. How's the arm?' His eyes settled on her face for a second,
but he said nothing, smiling instead with white teeth.

'It's healing,' she said. 'Still aches every now and then. How's the
groin?'

'It's okay.' He laughed a little. 'The wife's glad – she was nagging
me to get a vasectomy anyway.'

'Did you a favour then,' Jamie replied, unable to stop herself from
smiling back. She was feeling good despite the dull throbbing in her
cheek.

'Sort of. The wife's happy,' he said with a sigh. 'The girlfriend, not
so much.' He gave her a wink and headed off towards Smith, who was
standing like a half-fallen-down scarecrow, leaning on the lectern at the
front of the room.

Jamie watched Hassan take a seat in the first row, the six officers in
his squad forming up around him. They were all laughing and joking
with one another, like a herd of bison, all shoulders and necks, their
long-sleeve tops pulled tight around their muscular frames.

She wondered how they did it – how they armed up and went into the
situations they did, pulled the triggers, did what they did, and then could
come in laughing and joking, shrugging it all off like it was nothing.

Her father's voice answered the question in her head and she
pictured the revolver he carried on his ribs, big, dull, silver, and well-
used.

Practice, Jamie. It's just practice.

Brock and Amherst were the last to arrive.

Brock walked in, glanced at Jamie, gave a quick nod, noticed her
face, and then smirked a little.

Jamie narrowed her eyes, unsure what to make of the reaction, and then Amherst came between them, his big body filling the space.

He looked over at Jamie and sighed, folding his arms. Despite it being perfectly warm in the room, he was wearing a big parka. 'Johansson,' he said gruffly. 'Caught a break, did we?'

There was a hint of derision in his voice. This was his case, after all. Or at least it was until he got taken off it.

He didn't seem like the kind of guy to carry a grudge. But then again, Jamie didn't know him all that well.

She smiled. 'Something like that.'

'Nngg,' he hummed, then followed Brock and slouched down on one of the back seats.

Smith gave Jamie a quick thumbs up and she closed the door and circled up to the front of the room.

It would be her first time there. And though Smith wouldn't be asking her to say much, he said it was important that she get her first time over with.

It was a passing comment, but it suggested he thought she might be up there again at some point. Which was a good thing. Probably meant that he wasn't going to shove her on desk duty forever after all.

'Okay,' Smith began, not wasting any time. 'This is a bit of a rush, but we're not dictating the timeframe, and if we miss this window, we're stuck for another six months. Tonight is the best shot we've got, and I feel confident that this is the team to do it.'

He looked around the room, flashed everyone a stern smile, and then carried on. He had a laptop on the lectern in front of him, and hit enter on it, starting the slideshow and kicking the projector into motion.

Behind him, two photos popped up. The one on the left was Kosiah's face – square, with angled cheek bones and a grim snarl. He was wearing military fatigues and the muzzle of a rifle was poking into frame next to his left shoulder. This was a snap from his time in the military.

On the right was De Voge. This was the mugshot Jamie had found from when he was arrested in Belarus. He was glaring at the camera like he was willing it to burst into flames.

'Leos Kosiah,' Smith said, gesturing over his shoulder with a pen. 'And Marco De Voge.'

He let it sink in.

'Both are involved with the Jade Circle and the trafficking operation moving through there. De Voge has a history of trafficking, possession with intent, kidnapping, possession of a deadly weapon, assault with the intent to do serious harm, assault with the intent to kill, indecent assault… You get the idea.'

'Sounds like a charmer,' Hassan said coolly. His men grunted their amusement behind him and one clapped him on the shoulder.

Jamie looked at them. Boys club. Though it wasn't a bad thing. They needed to be close-knit to do what they did. Their lives depended on it. And looking at them, Jamie suspected any one of them would have taken a bullet for Hassan in a heartbeat, and he would have done the same for them.

'Yeah,' Smith replied. 'He is. And Kosiah isn't far behind. Joined the military at sixteen, served for seventeen years. Medal for Bravery, medal for Distinction In Military Service, medal for Distinction in Protecting The State Border. Nineteen confirmed kills. Dishonourably discharged at thirty-three for getting into a fight in a bar while on leave.' He paused and looked around. 'He killed someone. Charged with involuntary manslaughter – served three years in prison, was released, and then started a private security company by the grace of an unknown benefactor. Worked both government and private contracts, and then in early twenty-seventeen, he liquidates his company, sells his assets, and disappears. At the same time, Marco De Voge is broken out of prison a hundred miles away.'

Smith clicked to the next slide, the picture of De Voge and Kosiah speaking outside the Jade Circle's back entrance.

'This was taken six weeks ago.' He let it sit in the air. 'In Chinatown.'

The guys from Interpol and Trafficking were silent, but taking notes fastidiously, and the tripod set up in the corner that was

streaming the meeting to the Interpol officer at their headquarters in
Lyon, France sat silently, the person on the other end no doubt doing
the same.

'And this,' Smith continued, clicking again. 'Was taken about two
minutes before Detective Sergeant Paul Roper was stabbed.' Smith
turned to look at the screen. 'That's Roper in the foreground, and
behind him, De Voge.'

He drew a breath and turned again to face everyone.

'These are the people we're dealing with. Killers. Trained killers.
Career criminals. And it's important that we don't underestimate them.
By our intelligence, De Voge is in charge of looking after the girls who
work in the Jade Circle, and Kosiah works as an enforcer, as security,
or as whatever else whoever they're working for needs them to be.'
Smith leaned forward on the lectern. 'They're both attack dogs, and
that's all you need to know. Now, the mission is simple. A ship is due
to arrive at Felixstowe tonight at around two a.m. Intelligence points to
there being imprisoned young women on-board, ready to be trafficked
into the possession of De Voge and Kosiah. Security footage from the
last few drops shows that they arrive together—' Smith clicked again
and a still image from a security camera showing Kosiah and De Voge
rolling through the security gates at Felixstowe in a G-Class Mercedes
four-by-four filled the screen. 'We expect them to be there together
tonight, as well. When they leave, they're tailed by a lorry with a
container on the trailer. We think the girls are inside.' Smith looked
stern for a moment. 'Now, due to the time constraints on this, we don't
have as much intelligence as we'd usually have in order to move
forward with an operation like this. But there are an unknown number
of women in one of the containers on that ship who are about to be sold
into sex slavery, and we've got a chance to stop that from happening.
And I need your help to do it.'

Everyone nodded.

'The objective is simple. We arrive early, watch from a distance.
Wait for the ship to arrive, confirm that De Voge and Kosiah are on the
scene, then we blockade the exit and close in. We apprehend both De
Voge and Kosiah, take them into custody, then hand them over to

Interpol as quickly as we can. They'll be extradited to Lyon to face interrogation there. If we can do it cleanly, their employers won't know what's happened, and with some luck, we can flip them.'

Everyone nodded again.

'We'll have eyes on the exchange the whole time, and I want to make sure that we don't jump the gun on this one. If we're going to nail them dead-to-rights, then we need to let it happen. I want that container unloaded from the ship, I want to have video of them inspecting the girls. I want to have video of the money changing hands. I want the deal to be *done*. And then we move in.' Smith looked at everyone in turn. 'Hassan,' he said, looking at the captain. 'You have the plans for the dock and the layout of the ship. Over to you.'

Hassan stood up, shook Smith's hand, and then took the lectern, holding the edges like he was about to tear it off the stage. 'Okay, so the *Princess Of The Sun* is a small merchant trade ship. It has the capacity for twenty-four containers, and from the manifest, it looks like it's going to be full. The crew is numbered at six men. Who they are, we don't know. Whether they know what's going on, we don't know. Training, unknown. Whether they're armed... Not a clue. We're going in blind here. But it's nothing we can't handle.'

His men all nodded along, focused solely on him.

'I'm told that Detective Sergeant Johansson will be making the arrests, so our mission is to subdue both De Voge and Kosiah. Do not shoot to kill unless absolutely necessary.' He stopped for a second as if to let that process. He clicked the laptop and the scene changed behind him, a blueprint of the dock appearing. There were circles drawn on it, numbered A through G. 'A coordinated strike will happen on my go ahead. Johansson and I will be here, at position B, ready to move in when the scene is secure, providing ground support, and ready to intercept if Kosiah or De Voge make a break for the main exit, marked C.' He didn't even need to look at the screen. He had it memorised already. His men's lives hinged on it. 'Colwill and Brooks – you'll be stationed on overwatch at position F. On my signal, you're to disable their vehicle, as well as the transport that will be with them.'

Two of the men nodded, and then fist-bumped.

'The ship will dock at position A, and the exchange will happen either on-board, or on the loading platform. Either way, we'll be well-equipped to handle it. Charlier and Lucas, Mick and Simms, you will be waiting here, in positions D and E, ready to move in on the target in two pairs. Take the primary targets first.'

That meant Kosiah and De Voge.

'And then, once Johansson has made the arrests, we sweep the ship, take everyone else in, one by one. Got it?'

'Like clockwork,' one of the guys in his squad said.

'Good. After that, we call in the cavalry from position F.'

G was off to the corner of the map, and would be where the patrol cars would be stationed, ready to lock down the port after the operation was a success.

Jamie had to admit, it sounded simple, and neither Hassan nor his men seemed phased by it.

She wasn't so sure.

De Voge and Kosiah were nasty pieces of work, and she didn't think they'd go down easy.

And definitely not without a fight.

26

FELIXSTOWE PORT WAS one of the top fifty busiest ports in the world, and handled more than four million containers each year, coming in from some three-thousand-odd ships.

That meant that nearly a hundred ships a day, every day, docked, and unloaded over a thousand containers.

Jamie checked the figures twice on two separate sites.

She couldn't believe they were correct, but they were.

Each ship, upon docking, was supposed to be inspected by a port official, and have each of its containers logged and scanned in before being unloaded.

Though with so many people, so many containers, and so many ships to get through, Jamie was hardly surprised to find out that by greasing the right person's palm they could easily make the delay between docking and inspection long enough to unload a container and drive it out of there.

Jamie pulled up to the rear of the hospital that Roper was at before eight that night. She'd finally gone to collect her car, and was calling in before meeting Hassan at HQ at nine. From there they'd make the two-hour drive out to Felixstowe and tuck themselves up somewhere out of sight, ready to await the arrival of Kosiah and De Voge.

Smith had a surveillance team on the casino – both exits. Long-range of course. As well as a follow-team posted up on the A12, ready to tail them to the port.

Their intel showed De Voge coming and going from the casino, but he'd been inside since around five, and they'd positively identified Kosiah, too. He'd been spotted doing the rounds and checking up on the bouncers at the alley-entrance. Preliminary reports indicated that the head bouncer, a Matthew Tan, hadn't shown up for work in the last two days.

Though Jamie didn't know anything about that, she said.

She sighed and leaned back on the same chair she'd sat in the last two times she'd visited, and stared up at Roper, his stubble now more like bristles than sandpaper. Jamie was surprised to see so much grey in there. But then again, lying there, he looked older to her than he ever had before.

'Wish I was going with you,' Roper said, spooning jelly into his mouth. He didn't seem that broken up about it.

'Me too.' Jamie nodded, folding her arms. 'They're your arrests as much as mine. And I bet you want nothing more than to put that scumbag in cuffs.'

'I trust you to kneel on his back on my behalf,' Roper said, sticking his tongue into the pot to get the last dregs out.

Jamie looked away, not enjoying seeing it slither around the clear plastic. 'I will, don't worry.'

'What's on your mind?' he asked, tossing it on the table hovering above his bed. 'You should be happy. Ebullient, even.'

'Ebullient?' She raised an eyebrow.

He shrugged. 'I've been reading a lot. There's not exactly much to do in here.'

She smiled at that. 'I'm glad. Seems like you're doing better, at least.'

'I am, I guess. Though it's hard to tell when you can't get out of bed.'

'It'll take time,' she said tactfully. 'You've got to give your body a chance to heal.'

He snorted. 'You sound like the doctors.'

'That's because they're as smart as I am,' Jamie said, smirking, trying to drive the conversation any direction except towards that one question she was dreading – *what aren't you telling me?* Lots, Roper. I'm not telling you lots.

'If you weren't so good at police work, I'd tell you to give it up and go study medicine.' He shifted uncomfortably, wincing. 'Be a lot safer for you.'

'What do you mean?'

'You think I can't see those bruises on your face?' He narrowed his eyes at her. 'Make-up or not, a fresh dose of morphine in my IV or not, Jamie, I can tell when a woman's trying to hide a black eye. I've been a detective for twenty years. Know how many domestics I've worked in that time?'

'Alright, alright,' she said quietly, letting her face turn back towards the light now. She had been making a conscious effort to sit at an angle that shaded the left side.

'So are you going to tell me what happened or are you going to lie to me?' Roper asked lightly, reaching for a cup of water. He'd not long had dinner. Or they'd not cleared it away and it'd been there for a few hours. Fish and chips, supposedly, but it looked more like someone had baked the sole of a shoe.

Roper hadn't eaten most of it.

'I never lie to you,' Jamie lied. She'd felt compelled to say it and then immediately regretted it. Roper was far from a dull blade. 'I got jumped.'

'Jumped? By who?'

Her shoulders immediately began to rise into a shrug, but then she stopped herself. 'Matt, the head bouncer at the Jade Circle.'

'You went back there?' he said, sitting upright, then hissing in pain and slumping back.

She shook her head. 'No, he caught me on the way home. Outside my apartment.'

'Jesus. How did he know where— never mind. Are you okay? What happened?'

She let out a long breath, playing it over in her head. 'Yeah, I'm okay,' she said, forcing a quick smile. 'He approached me quickly, caught me by surprise, threw me against a car, smacked me. Right hook.' She raised her fist to her face and made a clicking noise with her tongue. 'Told me to back off or he'd come back.'

She didn't know why she'd lied then. About him catching her by surprise. Maybe to make herself feel better about going into the exchange half-cocked. Wounded pride as much as a wounded face, maybe.

'And then he just walked off?'

'Pretty much.'

'Did you arrest him? Tell Smith?'

She shook her head. 'No, the fucker had a mask on. He was smart. Zhou sent him to deliver a message. First you, then me. Trying to clear the field.'

Roper laughed painfully. 'Joke's on him I guess. After tonight, he'll be missing his two lapdogs. That should shit him up a bit.' Roper smiled grimly. 'Frankly I hope they put up a fight and Hassan and his guys put the two of them down.'

Jamie stayed quiet. Openly encouraging that sort of thing was a great way to get suspended. Shooting anyone was, and should always be, a last resort.

She checked her watch. 'Yeah, well, I've got to go. Hassan will be waiting for me. But I just wanted to call in and check up on you.'

'You don't have to come every day, Jamie,' Roper said.

She smiled and stood up, clapping him on the cylindrical lump under the cover that she suspected was his shin. 'If I don't, who will?'

He looked sad then, and Jamie realised the joke was too true to be funny. 'Be careful out there,' he said. 'It sounds like they've got it all sewn up… But still. Zhou's a mean son of a bitch, and has the brains to be dangerous. And we already know what De Voge is capable of.'

Jamie nodded. 'I will.'

'I'm being serious, Jamie. These guys are killers. And they won't hesitate.'

Jamie threw her hands up into a gun shape, held it next to her chin, and grinned at him. 'Neither will I.'

'Okay,' he said. 'I'll see you tomorrow, yeah?'

'Yeah, you will.'

She turned and walked out, her hands falling to her sides.

They didn't uncurl though, and as she pushed through the door to the stairwell, the gravity of the whole situation really began to sink in.

This was bigger than she'd thought it was going to get. And collaring De Voge and Kosiah would mean big things for her. Heck, stepping up like she had in the last few months – a serial killer and now a trafficking ring? She hated to admit being out of her depth, but she was on her tiptoes already and the water was lapping at her nose.

She took the floors quickly, her face aching as she screwed it up, clenching her jaw against the nerves.

God she wished Roper was going with her.

She trusted Hassan with her life – she pretty much had to.

But still, she wanted Roper there.

That Brock and Amherst would be waiting in the wings was only a minor reassurance. They'd be coming in with the uniforms afterwards, assisting on the sweep of the scene.

But neither was her partner, and neither was Roper.

She was on her own, any way she spun it.

And she didn't think she liked it. Not one bit.

27

JAMIE'S FINGERS were slick on the wheel as she pulled into the car park under HQ, the wiper blades on her car bucketing water off the windshield as quickly as they could.

Hassan was already parked up and waiting. Smith had set them up with one of the plain-clothes Traffic cars for the operation. Though they didn't anticipate any sort of pursuit, putting them in a car that was equipped for the task was only natural. And with Hassan being a qualified traffic officer – he'd worked as one for six years before transitioning into armed response – it seemed like a solid tactical choice.

Jamie swung into a space in front of the midnight-blue BMW, a stout 5-Series whose engine was more than five times the size of the one in her car – a nought-point-six litre eco-hybrid. The beast under the bonnet of the BMW kicked out some serious power. But then again, it had to haul the thing along at the speed it did. A three-litre turbo diesel that would outrun everything that wasn't made in Italy and didn't have a farm animal on the badge.

Hassan looked up from his phone and gave her a wave of acknowledgement as she moved around the front of the car, the engine already chugging away.

She pulled on the handle and found it locked.

Hassan was still engrossed in his phone. He looked up when she knocked on the glass and twiddled his fingers in front of the central system looking for the button. He found it after a second, hidden among the screens and switches that had been installed, and pressed it.

The bolts moved and Jamie got in, sinking into the pre-warmed leather seat.

She hadn't realised how cold she'd been until she was inside the cabin. Even just going from the hospital to her car was enough to make her damp, and the water seemed to have burrowed deeply into her jacket, chilling her to the bone.

Hassan dropped his phone between his muscular thighs and looked up at her, grinning widely. The thick bristles of his short beard stuck out at all angles like an upturned cactus, and his greased hair clung to his head like he'd just waded out of the sea in an aftershave commercial, though Jamie guessed that was the point.

He was wearing a black t-shirt that said 'Armed Response' across the front, and a pair of what looked like armed response tactical trousers. An ultra-tough and stretchy polyamide and elastane blend with pockets the perfect size to carry extra magazines that fit in the SIG Sauer SIG516 automatic carbine rifle. It took 5.56mm NATO rounds. Thirty to a magazine.

Jamie always liked specs. Facts. Factoids. Though 'factoid' originally never meant something true, but actually the opposite. But the meaning had changed. That was a factoid in itself now.

She had good recall. Found it easy to remember things. Numbers especially. She could recite the long card number off all three of her bank cards, as well as her driver's license number, her national insurance number, and also the number plate of the car she was sitting in, even though she'd just glanced at it as she pulled into the car park.

But she guessed that was what made her effective at her job. Maybe if she ever got tired of it she could be an accountant. But that would be too boring—

She cut off the train of thought and shook her head once to dislodge it from her brain.

Jesus, what was wrong with her? Her mind was racing. Rambling. To itself.

'Nervous?' Hassan asked, still grinning, still looking at her.

How long had they been sitting in silence? How long had she been staring at the pocket of his trousers?

Jamie cleared her throat. 'Yeah, I guess you could say that.'

He nodded. 'Understandable. Not your first active op?' he said casually, pressing the screen of one of the centre console terminals, bringing it to life. He already knew the answer. She'd worked the Donnie Bats case – he was there – as well as a few others. But this was the first where she was on her own. Or at least running point.

'No,' Jamie said. 'But I usually have Roper with me.'

He chuckled softly, bringing the sat-nav online. 'Roper'd be about as useful as a wet noodle in a live engagement.'

'I meant more for moral support,' Jamie said, her mouth finding a smile.

'Look,' Hassan said, leaning on the wheel and turning to her. His broad shoulders nearly blocked the entire window. The leather groaned under his bulk. 'If I didn't think you were the right person to be here, you wouldn't be.'

Jamie furrowed her brow, not sure what to say.

'Smith asked me point-blank if I thought you were up to this. Offered me Amherst instead.'

'Oh.'

'But I remember the way you took down Bats. The way you faced down Bats, and then kicked me square in the knackers, too.' He laughed a little and she joined him, the nerves dispelling with every passing moment. 'You can do this, Johansson. Trust me.' He slotted the car into drive and let off the handbrake.

They immediately started moving.

'And plus, I looked up the results of your firearm proficiency test.' He cast her a sideways glance. 'You knocked spots off Amherst. And that makes me feel a lot better about you sitting there than him. That and that he's not much of a conversationalist.'

Jamie looked away, unable to restrain a grin. Her father had taught her to shoot when she was ten. Her mother never knew that. She would have lost her mind if she found out. That made her feel happy in a strange sort of way. She really should call her mother.

Whether Hassan was being straight with her or not, he had a reassuring way about him, a calming presence. An essential trait for the captain of an armed response team, she thought.

'Does that, uh, mean,' she started, not wanting to sound eager, 'that I, uh, get a gun?'

The corner of his mouth pushed up into his cheek as they pulled out onto the street, the rain falling in heavy bullets. 'Do you want one?'

They talked about 'normal' things on the drive.

Hassan's family – his wife, his children, how they coped with him doing what he did. He seemed to have no idea who her father was, or maybe he didn't care. Both worked equally as well for Jamie. He asked where she was from – which he said 'explained her weird accent'. She didn't really consider herself to have one. Her father's English had been impeccable – her mother had never bothered to learn Swedish. And she'd been taught both from the time she'd started speaking. Leaving Sweden at sixteen and moving to London had eliminated what remained of the Scandinavian in her voice. And now she just sounded… neutral, she thought. Though Hassan begged to differ. Then again, he did sound a little like an actor trying to play a London gangster on a seventies TV show, so she wasn't that surprised.

He'd grown up in the city, come from practically nothing, faced adversity, lived through difficult times. But he'd still give his life for the city that always tried to rid itself of him. Those were his words, and Jamie respected the hell out of him for it.

Jamie wasn't sure what she expected, but as they arrived at Felixstowe, the whole place was drowned in floodlights, the rain coming through in great bands, silver in the harsh brilliance.

Trucks queued to get in and out in long lines, inspectors in high visibility jackets with torches and clipboards checked and inventoried them, and ships moved in the background like huge spiked beasts.

Their shadows swam against the bludgeoned sky as they moved, silent in the din that rose out of the port.

Some were leaving, others were arriving.

But one thing was for certain – the port was far from deserted.

Cranes swung over docked ships and dragged containers onto the concrete. A low beeping echoed over the wire-hemmed compound and the clanging of containers meeting on stacks cut through it all.

For some reason Jamie expected everything to be shutdown. For this small goods ship to come slinking in under the cover of darkness to deliver its illicit cargo. But nothing could have been further from the truth.

Hassan drove up the employees' lane towards the gate at just before eleven. They'd be the first ones there – with Hassan's team close behind. No one else would arrive until after the trail car following De Voge and Kosiah had entered the port. They couldn't risk anyone seeing them and derailing the operation. Inside the port it would just be the eight of them. Hassan's six officers, Hassan himself, and Jamie. A skeleton crew by all accounts.

But once Kosiah and De Voge were through the gates, the cavalry would station themselves just outside. Smith had promised them at least six patrol cars, ten uniformed officers, and a backup team of Armed Response officers on standby to be deployed if there was more resistance than expected.

As they queued towards the security gate, the rain still beating against the car, Hassan didn't seem phased at all. He was singing along with the song coming through the radio, drumming on the wheel with his thumb.

They were coming in from the far side of the port – what would be the 'back entrance' for Kosiah and De Voge. The *Princess Of The Sun* would be docking at slip seventeen-C, which put it at the other end of the port, some two kilometres away, where all the smaller ships were set to unload.

Smith and Hassan really weren't taking any chances. Hassan had even put on a jacket to cover his armed response t-shirt.

The car in front was waved through and the barrier settled in front of them.

Hassan pulled up to the security hut and wound down the window, letting all the heat flood out.

Jamie shivered.

'Alright, mate,' Hassan said brightly. 'Lovely night for it.'

The smell of the salt and diesel stung Jamie's nostrils, the noise from the port suddenly defeating without the layer of glass to mute it.

The guy in the hut leaned out, looking over the top of his glasses, his white hair waving in the wind. Jamie hadn't checked the forecast, but it felt like a storm was bearing down on them.

'And who are you supposed to be?' he asked with a thick west-country accent. His high-visibility vest glowed in the glare of the huge floodlights that surrounded the place.

Hassan flashed his warrant card, holding it up over the sill of the window. 'Surprise inspection,' he said casually.

'Nobody told me nothing,' the gate attendant said, scratching his chin.

'Wouldn't be much of a surprise if they did, would it?'

'I suppose.' He stuck his bottom lip out now. 'But I can't let no one in without the right papers, coppers or not.'

Hassan nodded. 'Of course.' He turned to Jamie, pointing to the glovebox. 'Would you?'

Jamie reached out and opened it, pulling out a folded sheet of paper. She handed it over and Hassan passed it along.

The attendant swung back into his booth and squinted at it, tapping into his computer with painful slowness.

Hassan glanced at Jamie, half-smiling with a sort of *what're you gonna do?* look.

'Okay,' the attendant said eventually. 'Looks like you got the run of the place.'

'Thanks,' Hassan said, taking the paper back.

Jamie looked at it and saw that it was a court order to allow them access to the port for an active operation.

'Just don't cause too much trouble. And don't get lost,' the attendant asked. 'I don't want nobody calling me, dragging me out in this weather cause the pair of you ended up somewhere you shouldn't be.'

Hassan smiled politely. 'We'll do our best.' And then he wound up the window.

The attendant closed his own window with a thud and raised the barrier.

Hassan pushed forward and followed the painted road, weaving through the endless stacks of containers with quiet confidence.

His demeanour had changed suddenly, the happy, friendly man she'd spent two hours with gone, and in his place a statue carved from stone.

The second the gate closed behind them it was like a switch had flipped.

He breathed slowly, evenly, taking them across the port.

Towards whatever lay ahead.

28

W ATER RAN off the containers in thick streams, slapping at the tarmac, sending spray across the ground.

The rain was unrelenting.

Hassan pulled into a car park to the side of a row of stacks and chose a spot in the middle, obscured from all sides by the cars around the edges.

It was bordered by white concrete bollards, a chain strung between them in lazy curves. It swung heavily in the wind.

The sign next to the entrance – a gap in the chain – had said 'Employees Only'. Jamie guessed crane operators and the drivers in charge of ferrying the containers around. There were huge forklifts, flatbed trucks, and pick-ups all moving around, orange light flashing silently on their roofs, yellow stripes slashed across their bodies.

Articulated lorries sidled by and containers zipped into the air on thick cables, swinging to and fro as they were positioned, loaded, and unloaded in an endless cycle.

'Come on,' Hassan said, speaking for the first time in about ten minutes. They'd been in silence since the gate. 'Let's do a walk-around.'

'In this weather?' Jamie asked, suddenly realising she hadn't brought her coat. She hadn't brought anything in fact – just herself and a bag of nerves apparently.

'You need to know the layout of the place,' Hassan said plainly.

She felt like that was a shot at her. He'd never walked around there before, but he was insinuating that she needed it more than he did. Though she didn't doubt it in reality. He had the lives of his six men resting on how well he could plan and bend the next few hours to his will. Jamie had looked the place up on Google Maps on her phone.

'Here,' he added, reaching behind the seat and pulling out a jacket. 'Take this.' He dumped a black coat on her lap. She turned it out and saw a GoreTex label inside. It looked to be a women's medium – probably a little large for her. But she wasn't complaining. He must have requisitioned it along with the rest of the gear for the operation. She was thankful for that but annoyed at herself that he'd planned for her incompetence, and that she'd needed him to.

He unzipped the fleece jacket he'd pulled on and donned his own coat – pretty much the same as Jamie's, except about five sizes larger.

By the time she'd taken her leather jacket off he was already out of the car.

She doubted that he'd wait, and she was right.

Jamie was just glad she had her walking boots on as she sloshed through the surface-water after him, dragging the zipper up to her chin and shoving her plait down inside the collar at the same time.

Hassan was moving with powerful strides, hands jammed in his pocket, shoulders hunched against the rain.

She kept time with him, practically jogging to keep up.

He was heading straight for the slips – concrete jetties.

Their ship would be coming in some time after midnight. They still had a while yet, but she didn't think Hassan would spend any of that time playing on his phone.

Hassan paused in front of slip 17C, standing against the wind like an Easter Island head. He looked out over the black water, surging and sloshing, windblown against the sea walls.

A container ship let out a low, long drone, pushing back from one of the cargo slips further up the port.

Hassan didn't even turn his head as it sidled into deeper water and then began to trundle past, the waves coming off its prow ten metres high.

Jamie swayed in the storm and screwed her eyes up against the oily spray. 'What do you think?' She asked, feeling like he was doing some sort of mental run-through of the whole thing.

He turned slowly, looking around in all directions. His eyes swept the long, empty stretch of concrete in front of the slips, the markings denoting where the various machines should go. And then he kept going, up to the crane positioned at the end.

In the floor, huge steel runners spanned the length of the section, and a massive four-legged crane, painted cobalt blue, squatted on them. At the top of it, a metal box sat, its windows pointing out to sea, a catwalk running around it and out along the arm which hung over the water. At the end of it a huge flat claw twisted in the wind, lowering down towards the ship that was docked under it.

Jamie and Hassan watched as the crane lowered and positioned itself over a container, latching on and then hefting it over the side and onto land.

Hassan checked his watch and made a disapproving sound. 'We've shifted the arrival schedule,' he said, his voice not raised but carrying through the wind. 'Another ship should be coming in any time now, and then the rest have been pushed until morning. We should have an open window.' He dropped his hand. 'So long as these idiots get their shit together.' He nodded towards the crane.

Jamie looked up at it, watching as the operator guided the container down onto the concrete. 'What about the guy running it?'

'The operators have a screen,' Hassan said, not missing a beat. 'It gives them the container codes and order that they need to unload them in.' He cracked his neck, rolling his head side to side. 'Chances are that the guys unloading the containers for De Voge and Kosiah never know what's in them. And with all twenty-four set to be unloaded from the *Princess*, the whole thing is perfectly normal.' He shrugged. 'But we're still not taking chances. We had the regular operator picked up and detained for questioning an hour ago. They'll pull a replacement in for him, just in case, and not know the difference.' He turned and started pacing away. 'The whole thing's need to know. Come on.'

Jamie turned and followed him, glad that the rain was at her back now, though her jeans were soaked already.

Hassan walked directly away from the slip and nodded at a two-story building set across an open space that looked like offices.

The road markings on the ground showed the stretch of tarmac they were on as a main through-way for vehicles.

Hassan paused and Jamie stopped alongside him. 'Targets will move in through here and overwatch will set up there – position F – second floor window – and maintain a clear line of sight to the pick-up.' He glanced towards the building ahead of them. 'Charlie and Lucas will wait in the site office, ready to move in on my mark.' He glanced left then, towards another smaller building and a set of bright-yellow railing set up in a wide rectangle. 'And Mick and Simms will hold there, at the weigh-station. When we have confirmation that the deal has been made and that the transports have been neutralised, they move in from both sides to intercept.' He kept walking and Jamie looked from the site office to the weigh station and back.

'And what about us?'

'When the targets are in position, we'll take up a secondary over-watch position in the car park, provide covering fire if need be, and then move to intercept.'

Jamie nodded. Hassan was talking about it like it had already happened. In his mind Jamie thought it had. Planned and rolled over and over, tested for water-tightness. And now, it just had to fall into place.

'You happy with the layout?' Hassan asked, looking at her intensely.

'Yep,' Jamie said quickly.

'You sure? Because once we head back, that's it. We won't get another opportunity to do this before everything kicks off.' He narrowed his eyes slightly, the hood pinned to the side of his face by the wind.

Jamie smiled for a second and laughed nervously. 'Maybe run through it once more for me?'

By the time they got back to the car, Jamie was soaked.

She wanted nothing more than to slide into the front seat and blast the heaters, try and restore some warmth to her skin.

Hassan went to the boot instead and popped it open, pulling one of the two duffle bags in there forward.

Jamie huddled closer to him, to get under the meagre cover of the boot lid, and to use him as an umbrella. He was big enough.

Hassan unzipped the bag and pulled it open, the light from the boot lid casting a pale glow over the contents – two kevlar vests, a pair of radios and ear pieces, a pair of thigh holsters and utility belts, as well as a case with the words 'Surveillance Equipment' embossed on the front.

He reached forward and pushed the two back seats down flat in front of him and then shoved the first bag onto them so it would be reachable from the front.

A second later he had the second bag in front of him. It thudded as he dropped it, settling unevenly. Jamie already knew what was in this one.

He opened it, turning the thing side on, and then lifted out two hard plastic cases the size of a good hardback. Pistol cases. He placed them on the floor of the boot and then turned to the dark canvas packages sitting at the bottom of the bag. He lifted the first, weighed it in his hands, and then put it back, taking the second instead.

He placed it on top of the bag and Jamie watched in silence as he undid the fastening strap and lifted the top flap, exposing a SIG Sauer SIG516 automatic rifle.

It gleamed black, ridged and sharp in the darkness.

Hassan looked over both shoulders, and satisfied that he wasn't being watched, lifted it up, holding it flat so that the side was facing the sky. He pulled back on the bolt a few times, listening to the well-oiled click, and then let it snap back into place. When he was satisfied that it was functional, he put it back down, folded the flap back over and then laid it on the flattened back seats next to the first duffle.

He went for the other rifle now and lifted that one too, unfurling it in the same clinical manner. Inside was a rifle. Not a carbine like the SIG516, but a longer, sleeker semi-automatic affair with a magnified sight.

'SIG Sauer MCX,' Jamie said, nodding. 'Are we expecting that much resistance?' It was a powerful, precise rifle designed for mid-range engagement. And it packed a hell of a punch. She'd carried a bruise on her shoulder for weeks after firing one during her firearms tests.

'You know your weapons,' Hassan said, almost passively. He pulled back on the bolt a few times and then lifted it to his shoulder, aiming into the car. He pressed his cheek to the body and looked down the sight. After a moment he lowered it and dropped it back into the carry bag, happy that it was going to shoot straight. 'And hopefully no. But I'd rather have them and not need them, than need them and not have them.' He closed the boot with a dull thud. 'Come on, you're getting soaked.'

She laughed, moving to the other side of the car, wondering if she'd ever be warm or dry again. 'Yeah, *getting* soaked. Right.'

29

Jamie and Hassan sat in the cockpit with the radio on barely above a whisper.

The storm was roiling above them, shaking the car every now and then just to let them know it still had more to give.

Hassan's team all arrived before midnight and got into position. Now, it was almost time.

Smith had arranged with the port's brass to have a reduced security presence and to remove all non-essential personnel from circulation in the section of the port they were operating in. But no one knew anything. There could be no risk of the operation getting out. Everything had to be air-tight.

Hassan's team had even come in wearing plain clothes, high visibility vests, and hard hats so there was no way to tell them apart from the port workers.

Jamie and he slowly dried off while everything fell into place.

Hassan watched on the monitor between them, a laptop perched on a specially designed structure attached to the centre console. He had the screen split – half with a birds-eye view of the port. It was a still, but had all the notes and positions he'd added on there. The second was a live speech-rec record of the operation. It was a program looped into their comms channel and every time someone spoke, their words popped up in a long-running conversation.

Hassan pulled his radio mouthpiece up to his chin, the coiled wire stretching to the dash, lengthening out in the darkness. The tinted windows dulled the glare of the floodlights, reducing everything inside to pale outlines.

Jamie watched Hassan's chest rise slowly in the gloom. 'Follow car,' he said, speaking softly. 'What is your position?' He looked at his watch as he spoke – a heavy piece of machinery with green, glowing letters giving him the time, as well as lots of other readings that he probably equally needed and didn't. Heart rate, oxygen saturation, GPS coordinates of his current position, elevation. It also tracked exercise, sleep, and linked to an app on his phone that recommended changes to his eating, sleeping, and exercise habits based on his biometric data.

It was overkill by a large margin, but Jamie didn't think she'd ever wanted a piece of tech so much in her life. It made her Fitbit feel like one of those solar calculators that would die if you put your thumb over the cell.

Hassan's words wrote themselves on screen and the line crackled in response, the cursor flashing gently as it waited to transcribe.

'This is follow car,' a voice came back. 'Holding steady at two hundred metres. Target Yankee, no change. No deviations to route. We're approximately seventeen minutes out.'

'Good.' Hassan nodded to himself. 'Intel-one – do we have a lock on the *Princess*?'

'Target Zulu is currently on approach. Should be docking in about ten to twelve minutes.'

Hassan glanced at Jamie, then at her hands. They were in fists on her thighs. She uncurled them.

'Good,' Hassan said again. 'Intel-two – what is the status of the port? Any chatter?'

'Negative,' came a stiff reply. 'All quiet. We're good to go.'

Hassan exhaled. 'Overwatch, sit-rep.'

'All good on our end, chief,' came a speedy reply. That was Colwill or Brooks. Jamie didn't know which.

'Strike Team Alpha?'

'In position. Ready on your go.' That was Charlie or Lucas. Jamie didn't know if they were their first names, nicknames, or surnames. She didn't think it really mattered just then.

She was distinctly aware of her heartbeat. And that was weird. It was like she had a stethoscope pressed to her own chest, fed right into her ears.

'Strike Team Bravo?'

'Affirmative. We're here and ready to dance.' That was Mick or Simms.

'Okay. Stay cool – Follow Car, keep us updated. Intel-one, let us know when the ship is on approach. Overwatch, I want numbers, all the info you can get. Copy?'

'Got it.'

'Confirmed.'

'On it.'

Hassan put the radio down and laid his head back. 'You nervous, Johansson?' He asked, closed his eyes.

'No,' Jamie lied.

'Humph,' he said, smirking. 'That makes one of us.'

30

'TARGET ZULU IS IN THE AO,' came the clinical voice of Intel-One, an intelligence officer in the back of one of the vans parked on the outskirts of the port. He was jacked into the shipping routes and live updates system.

Hassan picked up the radio. 'Confirmed. Follow Car, update.'

'Coming into Felixstowe town now, approaching handover.'

'Patrol One?' Hassan asked into the ether.

'Confirmed, we have eyes on Target Yankee. Follow Car, you're relieved,' came the reply from one of the plain-clothes units positioned on the access road to the port.

Jamie's throat had tightened into a knot. Everyone sounded so calm.

'Overwatch,' Hassan said. 'What's the status on Zulu? Do you have eyes on the target?'

'Negative,' came the reply. 'Visual confirmation is compromised. The storm is too rough. There are no bodies on deck. I repeat, no personnel sighted.'

Hassan's finger let off the button. 'Shit,' he muttered before pressing it again. 'Strike Team Bravo – do you have clear line of sight to the gate? I want you locked on Yankee as soon as they're inside the port.'

'Affirmative. We have eyes on.'

Hassan breathed a little sigh of relief and nodded to himself. 'Good. Overwatch, keep us updated. Intel-two, are we clear?'

'We're okay for go. No port employees on-site, area is clear.'

Hassan put the handset on the hangar and looked at his watch. Two minutes past two. Right on time.

Without looking at Jamie he reached between his knees and pulled out his kevlar vest, pushing it down over his head and wiggling into it behind the wheel. Despite the seat being all the way back there was still little room for him to manoeuvre.

Jamie followed suit, her chest clamping down like she'd been kicked by a horse, her heart doing double-time now.

'Breathe, Johansson,' Hassan ordered, pulling the articulated shoulder pads straight along the top of his arms and strapping them in place. These were full tactical vests that offered maximum coverage. They even came with little collars that reached up the neck and over-lapping, shell-like panels on the abdomen and chest that allowed for greater freedom of movement.

Jamie followed the order and forced her chest to fill, pushing the Velcro flap hard against its counterpart and securing it with a pair of plastic buckles. The vest felt lighter than the ones she'd worn before, but she trusted it to stop a bullet. She didn't really have much choice.

Hassan levered himself up and turned, pulling the two pistol cases from the back into the cockpit and putting them on the dashboard. Then he went back for the duffle with the ammo in it and pulled a blue and white box into the cockpit and placed it on the centre console.

He glanced at Jamie, nodded at her rather than to her, commanding her to be alright rather than asking if she was.

She nodded back diligently. She'd wanted to be here, and if she wasn't she'd be annoyed about that. So she forced herself to calm, to breathe, to steady. But it wasn't as easy as she'd hoped. She could feel the holster pressing against her leg uncomfortably all of a sudden. She'd put hers on under instruction from Hassan before they'd gotten back in the car. And for the last two hours she' hadn't even thought about it. But now, it was itchy, sharp, and she wanted it off.

Hassan pulled one of the cases onto his lap and opened it, a gleaming Glock 17 sunk into the foam there.

He lifted it free, snapped back the mechanism and released it with a metallic clack, and then picked up the magazine, inspecting it quickly in the half-light. 'You know how to load one of these?' He asked quickly, efficiently.

She nodded again, realised he wasn't looking at her and then spoke. 'Y—' she started, her voice catching. She cleared her throat. 'Yes.'

'Good. Then do it.'

'Right,' she said awkwardly, her hand flying out towards the case, knocking it into the glass of the windscreen rather than grabbing it. She dragged it down onto her lap and got it open on the second try. The clasp was stiff and her fingers were shaking.

'Are you good?' Hassan asked with the sort of *don't give me a bullshit platitude answer* tone that made Jamie freeze.

'Yeah,' she answered, exhaling slowly. 'Just nervous.'

'That's natural,' Hassan said, thumbing rounds into the magazine with practised ease. 'But I need you sharp. I need to know you're not going to freeze up out there, not going to be a liability.'

'I'm not.'

'You sure?'

Jamie looked at him, her eyes hard now, like shards of flint in the darkness. 'I'm sure.'

'Alright then.' Hassan seemed satisfied. 'Two magazines.'

'Okay,' she answered, taking a handful of shells and forcing the first one into place. With each successive bullet, the spring fought back a little harder. Click. Click. Click. Seventeen rounds. Seventeen shots. Thirty-four in total across both magazines.

And she dreaded firing a single one.

Hassan slotted the first magazine into the grip of the pistol, and then banged it in with the heel of his hand.

A second later it was in his holster and he was refilling a second magazine. 'A word of advice?' Hassan asked, not looking up.

'Sure,' she answered, trying to keep her voice from cracking.

He paused, looking at her now. 'You're a good shot. Trust that. If it comes to it. Out,' he said, his pistol suddenly in his hand. 'Up.' The magazine was on his lap, his left hand against his right in an instant. 'Sight.' The gun lurched forward until it was hanging in the air between them, muzzle twelve inches in front of her nose. 'And shoot.' His finger whitened against the stock as he pressed it into the metal, not against the trigger, but rehearsing a swift and concerted pull. 'When it comes to that moment, all you need to know is that your shot is saving your life, or someone else's. Anything else that enters your mind is a problem. You got that?'

'Up, sight, shoot,' Jamie parroted, tasting the bag of ready salted crisps she'd forced down an hour ago burn the back of her throat. 'Got it.'

'Good,' he said, pushing his pistol back into his holster and nodding out the windscreen at the silhouette of a small cargo ship fighting its way towards slip seventeen-C. 'Because they're here.'

31

THE RAIN SWIRLED through the port, painting murky halos around the floodlights.

'Overwatch,' Hassan said, lifting the radio to his mouth. 'Tell me the crane operator is on lock?'

'Affirmative. Searched and detained. He's not going anywhere.'

'Good. Keep me updated on crew numbers.'

'We will.'

The *Princess of the Sun* sidled up to the slip and slowed, rocking back and forth on the waves. They clapped against the concrete, the noise echoing through the port. White crests rose and fell beyond the edge, punching at the wild sky before disappearing into the water.

The ship hauled itself sideways towards the jetty and bumped against the rubber floats.

Even in the shelter of the port the water was being whipped into a frenzy.

Hassan handed Jamie a pair of compact binoculars and she pulled them up to her eyes, seeing that he already had a set against his own, the radio hovering next to his mouth. He pressed the eyepieces into his face until his skin rolled around the edges, forming tight folds. 'I see...' he started, his lips moving soundlessly as he counted. 'Two on deck – wait, three on deck.'

Jamie watched through her own binoculars as two crew members, wearing black raincoats that touched their rubber boots, hauled a rickety gangplank from next to the guard rail and threw it down onto the jetty.

A third was trying to lasso one of the moorings on the slip.

'I count three on the bridge,' Overwatch said.

'Intel one – confirm?'

'Manifest states six crew members.'

Hassan nodded to himself. 'Overwatch – do we see any weapons?'

There was silence.

'Overwatch?' Hassan asked again.

'Negative – we don't see anything.'

Hassan drew a tentative breath. 'Patrol One?'

'Target Yankee entering the port as we speak.'

Jamie's binoculars drifted left from the jostling deck of the ship to the blur that was flying into the port. She refocused, wondering whether it was a pay-off, falsified documents, or just straight-up threat of death that had gotten them through the gate. Either way, that was something the port could investigate after everything was said and done.

The G-Class became crisp in the binoculars as Jamie rolled the focus dial with her finger, its xenon headlights slicing through the rain.

The droplets fell like stones, bouncing off the surface-water spread across the black tarmac.

The reflections of the floodlights danced as the G-Class skated over them, skimming towards the ship.

The lines had gone deadly quiet.

'Overwatch,' Hassan muttered. 'Keep eyes on target. Alpha Team, Bravo Team – stay frosty. I want you ready to move on a dime.'

No one answered but Jamie took that as confirmation.

The G-Class decelerated violently, and swung in short of the gangplank, its brake lights flaring.

Hassan smacked his lips. 'I see both targets. Overwatch, can you confirm?'

'Both targets confirmed – Kosiah and De Voge on-site. Positive ID on both.'

'Any other hostiles?'

'Negative. Just the two of them.'

Hassan breathed a quiet sigh of relief. 'Stay eyes-up, I want the vehicle neutralised on my go.'

'On your mark.'

'We wait until the exchange has happened. Nobody move. Hold until my go.'

'Affirmative.' All three teams answered in unison.

The passenger side door opened on the G-Class and De Voge exited, stepping into the rain, his muscled frame like scaffolding under his clothes, pulled tight in the wind. He wasted no time moving towards the gangplank, stepping onto it without even looking at the crew members who were holding it steady for him.

Overwatch came over the radio again. 'I have De Voge boarding the ship – and what looks like the captain moving off the bridge to greet him.'

'Hold,' Hassan commanded, his voice cold and even. 'We wait for the exchange to take place.'

De Voge got about five paces onto the deck before the captain reached him. They shook hands formally, and the captain gave a slight bow, clutching his hat to his head to stop it from blowing off. De Voge put his hands on his hips and they exchanged terse words before the captain gestured towards the bridge and he and De Voge moved quickly down the length of the ship past the multi-coloured containers. They were stacked slightly forward, an empty space of around fifteen metres sitting between them and the raised bridge. Jamie counted twenty – five stacks of four – on deck and remembered twenty-four total had been on the manifest, which meant that there was a lower hold – probably accessed via an opening hatch in that gap – where the other four were. It made sense they'd keep the girls below. Out of sight, no risk of them throwing themselves overboard.

She gritted her teeth at the thought as the captain opened a solid steel door below the windows of the bridge and proffered it to De Voge.

He lifted his foot and ducked at the same time, the black space swallowing him up. The captain went in behind him and the door shut tightly in the distance.

'De Voge and the captain are below,' Overwatch said. 'What are your orders?'

'Hold,' Hassan said again. 'We wait for De Voge to come out, then we make the call.'

Jamie had the question on her mind that everyone was thinking. How would they know whether the exchange had happened? De Voge and Kosiah would leave before the container was unloaded, probably, and then a truck would appear to take the container out of the port – because there didn't seem to be one there already, waiting – there was no clear end here.

And she doubted De Voge and Kosiah would wait around to supervise the operation. Hassan would have to make a call and she could see that in his face, the slight downturn of his lips, the quickened pulse in his temple.

Jamie's heart had all but stopped in her chest, her throat tight, like someone had their fist around it.

Overwatch's voice rang in the cabin. 'We have movement,' it said, tentative almost.

'Where?' Hassan demanded.

'Kosiah – the car. Looks like he's getting out.'

Jamie and Hassan both lowered their binoculars to the G-Class.

Overwatch were right, Kosiah had opened the door and stepped into the rain. He was wearing a long black coat without a hood, his close shaven head like a floating white orb in the storm. He had a phone pressed to his ear.

His eyes swept around in a full three-sixty and then he walked towards the back of the car.

'What's he doing?' Hassan asked, maybe rhetorically, maybe to Overwatch.

No one answered either way.

Kosiah paused at the rear of the car and then turned his eyes towards the crane. Towards Overwatch.

'Overwatch,' Hassan asked quickly. 'Status? Are you made?'

'I… I don't know. I don't think so,' they replied, the voice over the airwaves strained.

Kosiah pushed his phone back into his coat pocket and reached for the handle of the boot.

'Hold,' Hassan said, his voice thin suddenly.

'Should we re-target Kosiah?' Overwatch asked, the nerves in their voice like jangling keys.

Hassan licked his lips, staring as hard as he could into the binoculars, waiting for something, anything to happen. Anything to answer the question for him.

Kosiah had the boot up now, back to Jamie and Hassan.

'Captain?' came Overwatch's voice. 'Should we – Jesus! Shit—'

Before they could even finish, gunfire filled the air, the strobing muzzle flash of an assault rifle painting everything white for a moment.

Jamie's eyes couldn't even relay what she was seeing to her brain before Kosiah had the rifle against his shoulder, firing at the crane.

Sparks danced off the metal arm as Kosiah peppered it with bullets, bright bare metal marks suddenly littering the rusted paint.

Two tiny black figures scrambled to their feet on the catwalk and ran for cover, ducking inside.

'Overwatch? Overwatch!?' Hassan yelled. 'Damnit!' He threw down the binoculars. 'All teams, all teams move in. We're made. We take the ship – neutralise all targets. I repeat, engage!' He kicked the driver's door open and got out, the whole car rocking.

Jamie watched as Kosiah turned now towards the office building and fired tight, controlled bursts towards the upper windows, then towards the weigh station doing the same, pinning the teams down.

And then she watched as he finally turned towards the car park – looking over the nose of his rifle at them – and pulled the trigger.

She threw herself forward instinctively as the muzzle flashed in front of her. He was at least a hundred metres away, but the bullets still sprayed across the roofs of the cars, bouncing skywards and shattering side windows.

Hassan swore loudly and sank low, moving for the back door. It opened as Kosiah pressed himself against the back of the G-Class, pulling another magazine from an ammo crate in the boot and smacking it into the underside of the rifle – what looked like a military-grade AK-47M. He turned again and fired at the crane, then the office building, then them, then the weigh station.

Jamie heard a round glance off the top of the windscreen just above her head, a crack launching itself down the glass.

'Johansson!' Hassan roared through the open back door. 'Get out of the car!'

Jamie nodded, her face between her knees, and forced herself to move, her heart hammering against her teeth.

She lifted her head a few inches and looked backwards over her thigh at Hassan's face between the seats. He was crouched next to the open rear driver's-side door, pulling the MCX onto his lap and the duffle bag full of ammunition onto the ground in front of him.

Jamie twisted out of the car and onto her hands and knees, the bullets zipping through overhead, turning the heavy droplets of water into a thin mist as they tore through them.

She bear-crawled around the back of the car, the tarmac digging into her palms, the frigid surface water soaking her sleeves under the open cuffs of her jacket.

Hassan was slotting a magazine into the body of the MCX when she got there, simultaneously pushing spares into the pouches on the front of his ballistic vest.

'What the hell happened?' Jamie asked, yelling over the echoing sound of gunfire

It seemed that Hassan's men were finally shooting back.

Hassan growled and then dipped into the first duffle he'd pushed onto the back seats, grabbing the two ear-pieces and radios. 'We're made. The operation is blown.'

'How?' Jamie asked quickly, trying to keep the franticness out of her voice.

'How the fuck should I know?' he grunted. 'Someone tipped Kosiah off by the looks of it. A port worker? Maybe they've got eyes of their own. Maybe they've got someone on the inside.' He shook his head, moving fast, but not with the sort of haste that suggested someone was shooting a gun at him. Jamie supposed you developed that sort of steely reserve over time.

Hassan attached the earpieces to the radios and affixed one onto his chest, the second onto Jamie's, the steel belt-clasp hooking into a tough fabric strap inside her left shoulder. Without looking he pushed the earpiece through a routing loop next to the collar and then tucked the bud into his ear, nodding at Jamie to do the same.

His fingers worked the radios in tandem – her's and his – flicking them on and tuning them in on autopilot as he raised his head and checked through the glass.

'Someone on the inside?' Jamie repeated, hearing voices in her ear suddenly as the transmissions started coming through.

Hassan ignored her, already dealing with the situation. 'Overwatch, Strike Teams – report. Status?'

Overwatch came through, panting. 'We're pinned down. Two on deck – armed with automatic weapons – shit – goddamnit.' The tinny sound of ricocheting bullets rang through the line and in the distance, Jamie watched as sparks danced off the body of the crane, two of the crew on the *Princess* now firing up at them, too.

There was a bright flash on the catwalk of the crane, then a second later a resounding bang as the report from the marksman's rifle challenged the storm.

On deck, one of the shooters was blown backwards, spinning to the ground. His screams cut through the din and then washed away on the wind.

Overwatch were shooting back.

'Strike Team Alpha, moving to engage,' came another voice.

'Strike Team Brave, pinned down. We can't move closer until we have covering fire.'

'Copy,' Hassan said. 'Laying down covering fire. Overwatch, give me sit-rep on the Princess. I want to know what's happening as it happens. We can't lose the ship.' He exhaled and pulled the bolt back on the MCX, feeding a round into the chamber. 'Intel One – scramble backup – I want the standby team here five minutes ago.'

'That's a no go, Captain,' a voice replied quickly. 'The standby team were forced to respond to a suspected armed robbery. They're currently en route.'

'God fucking damnit! Who called that in?'

'Anonymous caller,' they said, the tension in their voice like a bag of nails in Jamie's ear.

Hassan glanced at her. Someone on the inside. An anonymous tip that pulls away the standby armed response team minutes before Kosiah and De Voge arrive, and then Kosiah being tipped off? What else could it be.

'What about Patrol One? Uniforms on standby outside the port?'

'That's a negative, Captain,' Intel One said. 'Threat to life is too high. You're recommended to pull back until we can scramble air support.'

'How long will that be?'

'Approximately thirty minutes – maybe more in this storm.'

'Captain—' Overwatch's voice cut through. 'Target Zulu is attempting to push back.'

Bullets clattered into the windshield of the 5-Series, punching icy holes through it. They flew through the open doors and over Jamie and Hassan's head and buried themselves in the side of a Transit parked adjacent.

'Say again?' Hassan called, holding his fist against his other ear.

'They're going for the mooring – trying to push back from the slip.' Overwatch was breathing hard. 'The fucking ship's leaving!'

Another boom rang out as the marksman's rifle barked in the distance, a loud twang singing in the night as the round hit the mooring just in front of the crewman's hand and leapt off into the darkness.

The crewman recoiled, dived for cover, and hid behind the gang-plank, firing blindly up at the crane.

Jamie's eyes roved across the open space ahead of them, looking for a route, for any sort of safe way across the tarmac. If the ship left, then it left with De Voge on it, and the cargo they were due to deliver.

And while they could probably ditch the ship somewhere down the coast and escape to shore, they'd not leave the girls alive to talk about it. Which meant that unless they got on-board before they pushed back from the slip, those girls were as good as dead. Either De Voge would put a bullet in each of them, or maybe he'd just sink the whole fucking thing and drown them in their steel coffin.

Jamie ground her teeth, feeling fire in her guts, eating up the cold dread that had settled there.

'Johansson!' Hassan yelled, right in her ear.

She looked around and saw he was pointing at the SIG516 lying on the back seat. 'We have to move.'

Her fingers closed around the grip of the assault rifle as Hassan's closed around the top of her arm.

Jamie barely had time to get her feet under her before she was dragged into the open, chasing Hassan across the car park, behind the first row of cars, the only barrier between them and Kosiah.

Hassan came to a stop behind a beaten-up old Toyota pickup and pressed himself against the rust-speckled tailgate, rain running off his shining black hair in streams. He raised himself until he could see over it and then scanned the area. Kosiah was crouched against the side of the G-Class, shielded from the crane by the broad side of the vehicle, and partially shielded from Strike Team Bravo, who by the looks of it had made a break from the weigh station and were now pinned down behind a security booth halfway to Kosiah.

He had the AK against his shoulder, firing controlled bursts towards the office building.

A window exploded and fragments of glass rained down onto the tarmac outside it.

He couldn't be accurate at that distance. He was just trying to buy enough time for the ship to get clear.

Hassan dropped back down, exhaled and then pulled the MCX

against his shoulder. It was a clean one hundred metres to Kosiah, and making any shot in this weather wouldn't be easy.

'I'm going to fire on him – and when I do,' he said to Jamie, steadying his breathing, 'you need to move in.'

She swallowed, unable to protest, her fingers wet and slick against the rifle. Instead, she nodded.

'Strike Teams, I'm giving you a window. I'll draw his fire. Ready? One, two—'

He didn't even get to three before he shoved Jamie out from behind the Toyota and stood up, stepping into the open.

She was running by the time the first shot rang out being her.

The rifle was heavy in her arms, her breath tight in her chest.

She felt like she was running through tar.

The first round from Hassan's MCX hit the rear window a few inches from Kosiah's head and bounced off with a dull thud. Bullet-proof glass. He ducked reflexively, getting to a knee and returning fire.

Hassan strafed steadily, walking in the opposite direction that Jamie was running, firing a shot every few seconds.

Kosiah rolled, the next round punching a dent into the rear driver's door, and fired a slicing arc back. The bullets raked across the fronts of the cars in the car park and alarms began to howl at each other, lights flashing as they were set into frenzy.

Jamie kept running, watching as Hassan pulled Kosiah's fire towards him like a magnet, his focus absolute, his movements unflinching as Kosiah crushed his finger against the trigger, his muzzle flashing continuously.

Jamie could see Strike Team Alpha move from behind the security booth and run across the tarmac, aiming for a fire utility vehicle parked inside a yellow crosshatched box and the cover it offered.

Bullets came raining down off the deck as those on-board the *Princess* scrambled to defend the ship.

Kosiah dropped to his back and rolled sideways towards the front wheel.

Strike Team Bravo were clear of the office block now, firing at Kosiah as they ran forward, converging on him in a pincer movement.

Jamie kept running.

A stack of containers that ran parallel to the water would give her cover – but she'd have to cross the path of Strike Team Bravo. Her eyes went right, then left, and she stumbled to a halt, out in the open, completely exposed.

Her heart seized in her chest as she looked from Kosiah to the ship and back.

In the distance, a flash from the crane blinded her and one of the black shapes on the deck of the *Princess* staggered backwards, arms flailing, and pitched over the side, crunching into the corner of the jetty before plunging into the boiling water between the ship and the slip.

Jamie's stomach sank suddenly and she looked down at the rifle. She was cradling it awkwardly. It felt alien in her hands, looked odd to her, like a think she'd never seen.

'Johansson!' Hassan's voice split her ear drums. 'What the hell are you doing?'

She looked up and around, her knees twitching like she wanted to run, but her feet stayed planted.

Her eyes scanned the line of cars she'd run from and caught sight of Hassan's face between two of them. Even from this distance she could see the shock and surprise in it.

'Shoot!' he roared at her.

She blinked once, her mind not even working, her heart like a hummingbird in her ears, and then her hands tightened into fists, feeling the ridges of metal beneath them, recognising the shape suddenly.

Up. Point. Shoot.

The muzzle came up on its own, the hard rubber of the stock finding the soft patch of flesh just inside her shoulder.

Her right hand left the grip for an instant, her knuckle hooking over the bolt, and snapped it back.

It rebounded forward and then her finger was against the smooth metal of the trigger. She exhaled once, homing in on the G-Class, on Kosiah's body, crouched against the front grille, and pulled until the pad of her finger touched the stock.

It kicked back into her body and vibrated violently. She held onto it, forcing the nose to stay down, fighting the recoil. She couldn't even hear it.

The mechanism on the side danced wildly in the corner of her vision slingshotting forward and backwards as round after round was pushed into the chamber and then ignited.

She was walking now too, firing continuously at the G-Class.

Kosiah scrambled, suddenly aware of this new onslaught, and made for the ship, ditching his spent rifle in the process.

It clattered to the floor and Jamie cut over the top of it with a line of fire, chasing him down with nothing but instinct guiding her.

Kosiah was running hard, his coat flapping madly behind him

He made it almost halfway before he was blown off his feet.

Jamie froze and released the trigger, not sure if she'd done that or not.

But it wasn't her – Kosiah left the ground and went sideways, his heels sweeping up into the rain-filled air, sending streams of water in snail shells before landing heavily on his side and folding into a hump of tangled coat.

The death-call of the high-calibre marksman's rifle rose around her and she realised it was Overwatch.

She looked in the direction of the crane, not able to make anything out in the rain as it sheeted down across the port.

Bravo Team were in front of her then, still advancing on the ship, keeping the guy cowering behind the gangplank pinned there. She could see the barrel of a gun waving skywards as the guy pushed it over the guard-rail and pulled the trigger.

It whirled bullets into the sky.

Jamie jolted suddenly as something moved her from behind.

She felt Hassan's bulk pushing her, his left hand against her shoulder, shoving her forward. 'Move!' He commanded, and she did.

They made up ground, heading straight for the ship.

'Cover us,' Hassan yelled into the ether and both Alpha and Bravo Team circled towards the G-Class, firing on the deck.

Overwatch's voice came through the airways. 'Three on deck, one at the gangplank.' The sniper rifle bit again. 'Two on deck,' Overwatch said, correcting themselves.

Hassan stepped past Jamie, now no more than thirty metres from the gang-plank, and swept her behind him with his arm, pulling the rifle back to his shoulder.

He slowed to a walk and lined up the sights.

His first round hit the gangplank and the crew-man shrank behind it further. The next two hit the support struts of the guard rail.

Hassan closed in. Fifteen metres, still moving faster than Jamie thought anyone had the right to while firing with that sort of accuracy.

She stayed on his shoulder. The SIG516 pointed downwards in her hands.

The fourth bullet pinged off the metal edging on the gangplank an inch above the crewman's scalp and the guy made a decision.

He stood, twisted, and tried to raise his own rifle to fire back – the only thing he could do.

Before he'd even swung a one-eighty, Hassan stopped in his tracks and put two rounds into the guy's centre-mass.

He convulsed, took a step backwards, and then fell over the mooring he'd given his life to try and untie.

The guy draped over it and then rolled onto the ground and lay still.

Hassan glanced back to make sure Jamie was still there, and then stepped onto the gangplank as his team kept the rest of the crew busy.

Jamie could see his shoulders rising and falling quickly with his breaths as he climbed up onto the rocking deck.

Images of the crewman still swam in front of her eyes. The convulsions, the quickness of it all. Like a fleeting dream that leaves only the worst snapshot when you wake up, playing on repeat.

Hassan paused, and lowered himself, ejecting the nearly spent mag of the MCX and slotting another in from his vest. 'You good?' he asked her, not looking back.

Jamie nodded, finding her voice. 'I'm good,' she croaked.

'You're doing fine,' he called, cheek against the stock.

It helped to hear that.

'Ready?' he asked.

She wasn't. But he still pushed forward anyway.

And she followed.

32

THE GANGPLANK WAS POSITIONED towards the front of the ship.

The captain had swung around and backed the ship in, putting the bridge and the two crew members left alive on deck between Hassan and Jamie and the strike teams.

The two remaining crewmen were at the stern of the ship, taking shelter behind the steel-panelled barrier that stopped people and things from sliding overboard, exchanging fire with Hassan's team.

Every ten seconds or so, a loud, thundering report would pierce the air and sparks would explode off the top of the rail or the deck, Over-watch doing their best to pick them off and having a tough time of it. Between the wind and the rocking of the ship it was like trying to shoot the eye out of a needle that someone had thrown into the air.

They advanced quickly, Hassan completely focused, Jamie right on his six.

'Cover me,' Hassan growled over his shoulder.

Jamie did, letting him stride ahead, covering their flanks as they passed the containers. There were only supposed to be six on-board, but then again they weren't supposed to be smuggling a dozen women, either, so Jamie didn't think too much of whoever conducted the ship inspection.

She brought her rifle up, forcing herself to breathe, squinting in the rain. She'd not pulled her hood up and her hair was soaked, heavy, and cold against her scalp. It was making her brain ache.

Though this was no time to take her finger off the trigger.

She suppressed it, turning, and strafed backwards, covering every corner she could, distinctly aware of Hassan's bulk behind her, moving like a stalking panther.

'Closing in on the two targets on deck. Cease fire on my mark,' his voice whispered in her ear through the radio.

Jamie felt Hassan's hand touch her elbow and she turned to see him motioning her to move up alongside him.

She did so, turning and stepping quickly until they were advancing together.

'Now,' he said.

The fire from his team stopped in unison. Immediately.

The two crewmen, now just twenty metres away, backs to Hassan and Jamie, froze, and then stole a glance over the rail.

'You take the right,' Hassan whispered out of the corner of his mouth, the words cold against the stock of his rifle.

Jamie nearly stumbled at the words.

'Ready?' He asked, not waiting for a confirmation. 'On you.'

She was staring down the sights of her SIG516, right at the right-hand crewman. He was half-crouched, wearing tattered jeans cut off to the mid-shin, broken-down old trainers, a coat that would have been new when Jamie was in school. He was only mid-twenties. Young. A kid swept up in all this. And Hassan wanted her just to open fire on him?

'Johansson,' Hassan hissed, slowing his pace, not daring to take his weapon off the other. 'Now. Do it!'

Her finger quivered on the trigger, her eyes aching against the rain, her heart pounding in her throat.

The metal felt immovable under her finger. Stiff and sharp to the touch, like pushing her finger down onto a knife-edge.

She couldn't do it. Couldn't shoot someone in the back.

Hassan wasn't waiting anymore.

She felt his weight hit her in the shoulder as he stepped sideways shoving her out of the way.

Jamie staggered sideways, letting go of the rifle with her off-hand, struggling to stay upright on the slick deck.

Hassan stopped, exhaled, tightened his arms around the weapon and then squeezed off two well-placed shots.

The first struck the left-hand crewman between the shoulders and he collapsed forwards onto his knees and curled into a ball, head on the floor, arms folded limply under him.

Hassan moved the barrel fractionally right, putting the second bullet into the second crewman a tenth of a second later.

It struck him in the arm and he twisted, falling backwards against the rail, legs splayed in front of him, face contorted in fear, eyes wide.

He screamed, trying to pull the rusted assault rifle up in front of him – some ancient Type 81 that looked like it had been dredged from the bottom of the sea – but never even got it halfway before Hassan charged forward and put two more into centre-mass.

The crewman convulsed, dropping the rifle, and then fell still, his chin lolling against his chest.

Hassan lowered the rifle and exhaled, watching for confirmation.

They were both dead. Jamie had no doubt of it.

And then Hassan was on her, storming back, his face carved in stone, the rain beating against it as he closed the gap.

His hand shot out and snatched the barrel of the SIG516 out of the air, holding it to the side. 'What the hell was that?' he demanded.

'I—' Jamie started, not able to find the words, her voice dying in her throat.

'If you're here, if you've got a weapon in your hands, you do as I say.' He pulled it from her grasp. 'If I say shoot, you shoot, if I say cover me, you cover me. If that means putting a bullet in someone to stop them from killing me or you, then you bloody do it.'

She shrank in front of him, the taste of raw metal in the back of her throat.

'If you can't, then you're no fucking good to me.' He threw the rifle down, seething, and then touched the radio on his chest. 'Deck is clear,' he said into the ether. 'Moving below to secure package.' He let off the button and bored into Jamie with his eyes. 'Follow me. Stay down. Don't move unless I tell you to. Don't say a fucking word.' He turned and headed for the hatch that the captain and De Voge had entered through, pausing to add something. 'And whatever you, don't get yourself shot. We get in there, we save these girls. If De Voge stands in the way, I'm putting him down. Got it?'

Jamie grit her teeth and nodded. 'Got it,' she said in a small voice.

'Good. Now let's go. Stay on my ass.' He was already moving before he finished, making up good ground towards the hatch.

She knew he didn't want her with him, suddenly, but didn't have a choice. The longer De Voge was below the longer he had to kill the girls, to get away. They had to get down there, and they had to do it now. And Hassan knew that he was on his own. That she wasn't going to shoot before she was shot. Wasn't going to be what he needed her to be.

She'd failed him. Twice she'd frozen now. Once in the open with Kosiah, and now on deck. Had she even been trying to hit Kosiah? Or had she just been shooting? Did she have it in her? Her father's face flashed in front of her, something he said long ago ringing in her ears, his heavy, rough knuckles smoothing the skin on her face. *You're a lot more like your mum than you are me. And that's a good thing...*

She prised the image out of her head and caught up with Hassan, watching as his hands closed around the handle of the hatch and twisted.

It creaked open, clanging against the steel of the hull.

Jamie looked up as they passed into the ship beneath the bridge, the shape of it rising into the sky above her.

She couldn't help but think it looked like a tombstone.

And then she was under it and inside, heading down a steel staircase, her heels clanging on the rungs.

Hassan had taken her rifle, but the Glock was still sitting in her thigh holster.

Maybe Hassan figured that if she looked unarmed, De Voge or the captain would be less likely to shoot her.

She hoped it wouldn't come to that.

They followed the stairs as it doubled back on itself and let down to a dimly lit corridor, a pair of lazy flies swimming in circles around a dirty-looking ceiling light.

The whole place pitched left and right, the noise of the storm outside muted and distant.

Every few seconds the ship lurched a little, knocking against the rubber stoppers on the slip, and then righted itself as the waves ebbed.

Hassan blinked and wiped off his face with his hand, moving cautiously.

The corridor stretched out ahead, under the length of the ship. About fifteen feet ahead, a door led off left, and then another led right about fifteen feet after that.

Hassan looked back and lifted his left hand to his mouth, keeping the rifle pinned to his shoulder with his other, fixed around the grip. His finger pushed into his lips as he made the universal *shut the hell up* sign.

Jamie nodded in confirmation and then moved forward with him.

His fist rose and clenched next to his head as they reached the doorway on the left, the sinister silence in the hull deafening them both.

Between the creaking, the moaning of the water, and the noise of the wind whistling through the rust holes, they were crawling through something alive, deeper into the jaws of a monster that was ready to clamp down on them.

And they weren't the only ones in here.

Somewhere, De Voge was lurking.

Jamie shivered and let her fists curl at her sides.

Hassan twisted and stepped into the space, aiming into the darkness.

Jamie's heart skipped a beat, but then Hassan went inside, swept what looked like a small and badly equipped galley, and came back out. Clear.

Jamie exhaled and followed him back into the corridor.

Hassan was moving steadily now, coming up on the next door.

In the distance, Jamie could see a closed hatch. By the size of the ship, it had to lead into the lower hold. That's where the girls would be.

She was shuddering now, soaked through to the bone, her skin tight and goose-pimpled under her clothes.

Jamie flexed her fingers, willing blood into them, willing them not to snatch the Glock out of her holster.

Hassan neared the second doorway and slowed, glancing back to make sure Jamie was still with him. He motioned her against the wall and drew a slow breath.

She inspected the lines of his face in the darkness, wondering if it was residual water or sweat on his brow.

He was stern, tough, probably one of the toughest people Jamie had ever met – and she'd had a long history of knowing guys you wouldn't fuck with.

But down here, in the dark, on someone else's home turf, all bets were off.

She felt sick that she didn't have her rifle, that she couldn't be trusted to help him.

The Glock stayed firmly in its holster and she pressed herself against the wall.

He exhaled now and closed his eyes for a second collecting himself.

And then he was moving, steady and poised, the bowed and moist walls of the ship pressing in on them from all sides.

Jamie's heart beat against her ribs.

Hassan paused for a moment at the frame and brought the rifle vertical, edging as close as he could without giving himself away.

He stepped from behind it and sailed across the opening, the muzzle dropping back to firing position, before taking cover on the other side.

Jamie could see the whites of his eyes in the dirty glow of the bulbs overhead.

He took another breath and then moved into the space again, satisfied he wasn't going to get blown off his feet.

Jamie stayed where she was as Hassan moved in to what she

guessed were the staff quarters. The stench of stale sweat coming out
of there a giveaway.

She strained her ears, listening to the almost inaudible tapping of
his feet as he moved in. And then they were gone, stolen by the noise
of the ship.

Swallowed up.

Would there be gunshots? Would they be hiding there? Would he
get a bullet through the back of the head? A knife between the ribs like
Roper did? De Voge was on their tail the whole time, inches from them
and they'd never even known it.

He was a ghost. As good as invisible. And he was cruel. He could
have put his knife in Hassan's neck already and she'd not even know it.
Hassan could be bleeding out as she thought that – and De Voge could
be coming for her.

A dark shape appeared in front of her and she jolted, almost ripping
the Glock from her thigh on reflex. Though it would have been too
slow anyway. The knife would have been in her gut before she even
got her fingers around it.

Hassan's fingers squeezed her forearm. He could see the fear in her
eyes.

What was worse was that she could see the fear in his.

He let go and touched the radio, whispering. 'Galley clear, bunks
clear. Moving on lower hold. Move in on our position.'

Hassan nodded at her and then turned back to the dim corridor.

They had to keep moving. Time was running out, and De Voge
only had one place left to hide.

They'd not heard any shots – he hadn't shot the girls, yet. But
maybe he preferred the personal touch.

Jamie's insides turned over and she fell into step behind Hassan,
forcing her stomach not to expel what little was in it.

He was moving faster now, keen not to get caught in the corridor. It
was a stretch of open space. There was no cover, nowhere to go. If the
hatch ahead opened while they were standing there, they'd be dead.

Jamie's mind recalled something she'd read, or seen. The words
'kill-box' etched themselves into her brain. Somewhere you'd lure a

target where they had no escape. Where you had absolute tactical advantage. Where you could kill them.

If that hatch opens, we're dead.

It was all that Jamie could think about.

And then it happened.

Hassan froze, the sound of the creaking hinge slicing through the air towards them.

He lurched forward and down, cramming himself against the wall, and the corridor opened up in front of Jamie.

The hatch in front of them swung wide and a middle-aged Chinese man stood there in a dirty white t-shirt and work boots, a single-barrel pump-action shotgun in his hands.

Jamie threw herself down on the ground, muzzle flash filling the ship and painting everything white.

Flame leapt out of the barrel and buckshot rattled off the walls.

Jamie heard a scream, felt her hands cupping the back of her head instinctively, her nose hitting the rough metal floor and push between the grating, a sear pain across the fingers of her right hand and over her knuckles, three more gunshots, a wail, a gargling noise, and then a heavy thud.

She looked up, rolling to her side, putting her hands on the ground in front of her. She could see shapes swimming in her vision like strobe lights, ghosts of the muzzle flash burned onto her retinas. Her ears were ringing.

She looked down, smelling burning metal and copper. The back of her hand was raw, bloodied. The buckshot had sliced across her fingers and over her knuckles – two grains by the look of it. Glancing blows – she got under most of it – but barely.

She screwed up her face, her hearing coming back, and squinted at the smoke-filled doorway, at the guy who had to be the captain, slumped down against the door, one hand jammed behind the handle, holding him up at an odd angle.

He had three red roses on his white shirt, the shotgun spilled from his grip and lying just inside the corridor.

Hassan had shot him.

Hassan!

Jamie's mind focused and she scrambled to her feet, pulling the Glock from its holster and training it on the doorway ahead.

The captain may have lost his nerve and opened it a few seconds too soon, but De Voge was still in there, and they weren't getting caught out twice.

Jamie ignored the blinding pain in her hand, kept the pistol raised, and moved towards Hassan, who was crumpled against the left-hand wall, the rifle across his lap.

He was hissing like a cat, his right hand pressed to his left shoulder, his left clamped around his right hip.

He had taken the brunt of the shot and it had torn his vest apart.

The outer layer was shredded, the kevlar plating inside shining through, dented and scored.

It didn't look like it had been breached.

The vest had stopped the shot.

But the outer edges of the spray had caught him in the shoulder and hip.

It was too damn dark to see how badly he was hit, but by the blood coming through Hassan's fingers, it wasn't good.

'Jesus,' she muttered, glancing up at the door ahead and then back at him.

There was fear in his eyes.

'Come on,' Jamie said, her mind already made up, her voice strained. 'We've got to get you out of here.'

She reached for his vest with her left hand, the gun waving widely in her right. His hand grabbed hers out of the air, staining it red.

'No, don't,' he protested. 'Stop.' He gritted his teeth, breathing hard, flecks of saliva flying from his lips. 'I'm okay.'

'You don't look okay!' Blood was oozing out of his shoulder now, the glinting black buckshot still lodged in his dark skin.

'You try and drag me out of here and we're both going to die,' he muttered, pulling her in close. 'You get behind me, cover the door, and we wait for backup—'

Before he could finish, a blood curdling scream pierced the din in the ship.

High pitched. Female. From beyond the door.

It sustained for a few seconds and then died.

A scream of fear.

A scream of pain.

Jamie's stomach twisted and she looked at the Glock in her right hand, the swaying stopping suddenly.

She held it firmly, an anger rising in her.

Her jaw quivered, her teeth locking together.

De Voge.

'Johansson,' Hassan said flatly, as you would to a dog that's sizing up another. Before it bolts. 'Don't.'

'I…' Jamie started, not able to finish the words. She was already rising to her feet.

'Don't do it! Johansson!' He was increasing in volume.

She was walking now, moving towards the door, Glock firmly in her grip. Roper's face appeared in her mind. Then Qiang's. There was blood on De Voge's hands. He'd hurt enough people.

Hassan growled, grunted, and then rolled over, dragging his limp leg behind him as he tried to get to his knees. 'He'll kill you!'

She paused at the threshold and looked back. 'If I don't,' she said, her voice even in her ears. 'He'll kill them.' She swallowed what little fear was left in her. 'And I'm not about to let that happen.'

33

Blood dripped slowly from her knuckles as she stepped over the prostrate body of the captain and into the cargo bay.

Her breath was slow, her heart beating hard in her ears.

She could hear her muscles flexing between the thuds.

Boom.

Boom.

Boom.

The floor rocked and levelled under her feet, her boots fighting for grip on the wet floor.

Every time it pitched, a thin layer of water shifted and ran one way, and then back.

Overhead, the seam in the bay doors cut a line forward. Water poured down in ragged streams, clapping down onto the tops of the containers that sat in the middle of the room.

Lights ran the length of the walls on either side, but the hold was dark.

Dark enough to hide in.

The containers were laid out side by side, their broadsides to Jamie, a gap of just a few feet between each of them.

She exhaled, checked the empty, dank space behind the door and then stepped forward towards the first, unsure whether to go left or right.

A droplet of water ran down her temple and Jamie didn't know if it had come out of her hair, or if it was just the cold sweat of dread pushing its way through her skin.

She swallowed hard, her mouth dry, and pushed forward, trying to remember all the training she'd had for this sort of thing.

And then she realised that she hadn't had any.

Her firearms and tactics class hadn't covered hunting a murderous sex slaver in the bowels of a rusted out Chinese merchant ship.

It hadn't covered anything fucking close.

Her father's bulk swam over her, his 'balance of good and evil' speech reciting itself in her head.

She tried to get it out, but it had its hooks in deep.

Good. Evil, his voice said, slurring, piss-drunk, sitting at their kitchen table, revolver next to the vodka bottle. *Who fucking cares...*

Jamie crept up on the right-hand-side of the containers and shuffled towards the first corner, holding her breath.

We do what we think is right.

She licked her lips and leaned out, ducking back in straight away.

She didn't get her head blown off.

That was a good start.

It's all we can do.

She exhaled and stepped into the darkness, levelling the pistol at the empty space ahead.

The first container was closed, padlocked.

Jamie forced her feet to move and continued forward, coming up on the first corridor between them.

No badge, no gun can make you do what's right, what's just... Those are constructs. Crutches that they make for themselves to help them sleep at night...

Jamie paused and tweaked her ears, the darkness crushing down on her.

The waves crashed against the sides of the ship, right through the wall just inches from her elbow.

She couldn't hear anything. Not a damn thing except the storm…

Shit. That's why De Voge had made the girl scream. To draw her in here.

And she'd fallen for it.

Jamie swung the pistol around the corner, her finger twitching on the trigger.

Empty.

They need that. They need to know, her father said, *that what they're doing is okay. That when they hurt someone, shoot someone, kill someone, that it's okay. That it's right. That it's just.* He looked up at her, eyes watery, blue, pale, shining in the darkness of their four a.m. kitchen. *But not us.*

Her diaphragm didn't want to move, didn't want to draw air into her lungs.

She made it. She had to stay oxygenated. Had to stay sharp.

She wiped the water from her eyes with the back of her sleeve, her knuckles now throbbing around the gun, and kept moving.

Next container.

Come on, Jamie. Hold it together. One step at a time.

Her breath was tiny and sharp.

We know that it's a balance – that it's us and them – that it's a necessary evil. That it's about having the guts, in here – he pounded his chest with a big, calloused hand *– to recognise it, to be it. To be that evil, and to know it, and to still do what we do.*

Her footsteps echoed in her head, her heart pumping wildly, her scalp tightening around her skull painfully. It was like someone had poured acid in her throat.

Second container. Blue. Rusty. Padlocked.

Her eyes fought the gloom. The last container was at an angle, its end pointing away towards the front of the ship.

To know that evil knows evil, sees evil, gravitates towards it. And to know that it's on you to do something about it. To do it for those who don't have it in them to do it for themselves. It's why we do this – why we immerse ourselves in their world. In the killing, the blood. It's how we know them, it's how we think like them, how we catch them. It's how we come face to face with them, and it doesn't change us. Because we're already like them…

She suppressed the image of De Voge waiting behind the corner and moved into the gap between the second and third container, looking for centre mass.

Empty.

She lowered the gun an inch and straightened her back.

Come on. Keep moving. You're hunting *him*, remember?

The badge, the gun – some need it to feel… important. To feel right, and just… Us? We need it to feel justified. It's their reason – our excuse. Good and evil, Jamie…

Container three. Locked. Keep going.

There's no such fucking thing.

She paused at the corner, exhaled, and then followed the nose of the Glock around it, covering every filthy inch of the space between the last two containers.

Nothing.

Fuck.

'It's all evil. We're all evil,' she muttered to herself, finishing her father's speech.

We just want to make ours feel right… Right to us. That's all that right ever is. It's what you think is right. What you feel is right. What your fucking fucked up version of just, or justice, or law is. And when it boils down to it – it's you or them. Always. That's always what it comes to, Jamie… They won't lose sleep over killing you. And the sooner you stop losing sleep over them, you won't be scared anymore. You won't be scared to do what you need to do to be good at this… thing… this 'job'… He laughed loudly, sadly, in her ears, eyes glimmering. *This thing that steals your life and everything you ever were. And for what? I'll tell you what. What they never will. What no one will admit to. It's so we can exercise that part of us that wants to be evil. And the sooner you accept that, the better you'll be. Stop caring, Jamie. It'll only get you killed. Be what you are – be what I am. You can't change it… Or at least I couldn't.* Her mother stormed in then, wrestled the revolver that was suddenly in his hand from him.

Jamie had pressed her hands to her ears. Cried. Ran. She didn't remember where. It was a distant blur in the depths of her mind.

She grit her teeth now, in the belly of the beast, face to face with evil, her hands tight on the grip of the Glock 17 as she got to the corner of the final container, hearing now the faint and scared whimpers of girls creeping through the rusted metal.

Well, Dad, here we are. This is it. Let's see what evil really looks like. Jamie grit her teeth, the smell of urine and sweat curling out of the container, and stepped from behind it.

The space beyond was dark and dank, the mouth of the container facing towards the front corner of the hold.

The dim lights on the walls did little to illuminate what was down there with no edges to hold onto.

Jamie's breath echoed in her ears, the sights of the gun scanning every inch of the blackness, and seeing nothing.

For a second, she wondered if De Voge had slipped out somehow. If there, beyond the reach of the light there was another hatch, another exit. A hole that he'd scurried out of. That he'd already made a break for it.

She set her teeth and took a damp breath. Thinking like that would get her killed.

A whimper over her shoulder brought her back to the room and she turned to the container, its end pointing right at her, its doors closed but not latched, not locked. No chain. No padlock.

Jamie swallowed and stepped towards it, holding the pistol in her right hand, her heart rattling in her chest. Her fingers stretched out, bloodied from the streams running off the knuckles of her other hand, and touched the cold steel of the container.

She swallowed, feeling it heavy, and dragged the handle up with a dull clunk.

Another collective whimper echoed through the steel, a chorus of whispers coming with it. Fear in every one of them.

She could feel her lips dry, her eyes burning in the dusty air as she pulled the door towards herself.

It swung outwards with some difficulty as the ship pitched, and then moved on its own as it rocked back, swinging wide out of her grasp.

Her left hand leapt back to her pistol and she brought it upwards, not knowing what she'd find.

The stench of human waste invaded her nose and she did her best not to gag, throwing the crease of her elbow to her mouth and coughing into it. She could already taste the air ripe with it.

By the looks of it the buckets that had been keeping it all together had upended themselves in the storm.

Everything was sloshing back and forth on the floor.

Jamie coughed, trying to spit it out, and then squinted inside, forcing her eyes to adjust to the deeper darkness.

She counted eleven. Twelve. One stood up at the back.

Their eyes shone in the gloom, catching the faintest glimmer of brilliance from the dull and dirty lights.

They were knotted up, crouched, sitting, standing at the back, all huddled together in filthy, cheap dresses that looked more like vegetable sacks than anything else.

The women, all dirty and malnourished, clinging to their humanity, began to whisper.

Jamie didn't understand it, but she could tell the confusion in their voice by the tone. The fear. The anxiety. For all they knew, this was the person who was buying them. Who'd throw them into slavery. Who'd sell them night after night.

'Shh, shh,' she urged them, forcing herself to step forward into the smell.

The girls clamoured, cowered backwards, pressing themselves into the back wall of their steel box.

'It's okay,' Jamie said, as softly as she could. Not daring to rise above a whisper. 'You're okay.'

Their hands came up, shielding themselves. Their voices rose, begging. Begging not to be hurt, to be taken wherever she was going to take them.

'Look, look,' Jamie said, fumbling to her pocket with her off hand, pulling out her warrant card.

They whimpered again – one let out a muted cry. Another sobbed.

'I'm a police officer, see,' she said, holding it up and open. 'Police, okay? Police. I'm here to—'

Jamie didn't know what it was. The girls maybe – the flitting of an eye from hers over her shoulder. A tiny change in the light in her peripheral vision, a shadow in the darkness. Maybe just a shift in the space. A pressure change. The warmth of a breath. Something as tiny as feeling something occupying the empty space in your blind spot. In that ancient, primal part of your brain that sets your skin alight. All the things you could never define. The intangible. The all-but-silent slither of a blade moving through the air.

Jamie's fingers left her warrant card.

It began to fall, tumbling through the air.

Jamie twisted on her heels and jumped backwards, skidding on the filth-covered floor of the container, her boots carving a path through the liquid.

The long thrust fell short, the tip of the blade just slicing the fabric on Jamie's coat – right where her naval had been.

De Voge's eyes were wide in the darkness.

The warrant card hit the ground with a dull slap and Jamie's off-hand thudded into the grip.

She didn't think.

The trigger rebounded off the body twice.

Two dull reports rang out, the container filled with light.

De Voge moved backwards in the strobe, captured in the snapshots, framed in the mouth of the container.

The air was hot with fire and the smell of burning metal.

The blade hit the ground and bounced away and then De Voge landed flat on his back with a heavy bang.

Jamie came forward, her fists like clamps around the pistol, and moved over him, the muzzle trained on his chest.

In the dim light he was even uglier than she thought.

This is what it looks like.

She grimaced and scanned his body for the entry wounds. There was no blood.

His jacket was open, the sweater underneath bearing two holes the size of coins. But no blood.

Jamie lifted her foot and brought it down on his chest.

It hit something solid and De Voge convulsed a little, coughed heavily and then groaned, his head lolling to the side.

'I hope that hurt,' she growled, taking her foot off the bullet-proof vest. She left a boot print in human excrement and hoped Interpol would keep him in that sweater for days.

De Voge was winded. Two shots into the solar-plexus, dead-centre-mass, from arm's length, would knock the wind out of anyone. But he wouldn't stay down for long.

Her left hand came up to her own chest, touched the button on the radio there and paused.

She narrowed her eyes, staring at the shape of her father standing just the other side of De Voge. He was looking at her curiously, and then he lowered himself, his heavy pea coat falling either side of his tree-trunk knees.

He sighed under the strain and looked down into De Voge's half shuttered eyes.

He fought for tiny breaths, staring at the ceiling.

You could do it, you know, her father said, his voice quiet, but clear as a bell in her ears.

'Do what?' she muttered, still fingering the button on the radio. If she called Hassan's team, they'd come running.

They'd be here soon anyway.

Be done with this piece of shit. Her father flicked a limp hand at De Voge's prostrate form.

Jamie's jaw flexed, her grip tightening on the pistol. She drew a rancid breath. 'No.'

Think of Roper. Lying in a hospital. Of Qiang. She never got that chance. She died alone because of him. Left to bleed out. He looked up, his expression grave. *And you.*

'What about me?' She swallowed.

Another few centimetres and you'd be the one lying here. He tried to put a knife in you too, Jamie.

She said nothing.

You could do it, right now. No one would blame you. He smiled. *No one would know.*

She glanced over her shoulder at the girls in the container, still whimpering, still crying.

You think they'd say a word? You saved their lives. If you could ask them, they'd tell you to kill him. To put a bullet right here.' He reached down, his finger hovering just between De Voge's eyes.

'I'd know,' Jamie whispered. The pistol clicked faintly in her hand as it shook, a thin wisp of smoke still drifting from the muzzle.

He chuckled softly. *It'll happen. You'll do it eventually – kill someone. And they probably won't be as bad as this guy. Won't have done as much.* He shrugged. *This one would be clean. Quick. Would make a real difference. You hand him over to Interpol, he'll go for a plea deal. A rat like this will roll on every shitbag he knows and in a month he'll be back out on the streets.*

Jamie closed her eyes, tried to suppress the raw anger welling up in her.

But you can stop that. Right now. You have the chance. You can scrub a little bit of evil from the earth.

She opened them and found herself standing over De Voge, the pistol levelled at his head.

He killed the girl. Tried to kill Roper. Tried to kill you. Her father stood now, towering over her. *Look at where you are, Jamie. Look at what he was here to do.*

'I know.' Jamie's voice was small and foreign to her. Someone else's in the darkness.

You don't have much time. Hassan's men will be here in a few seconds. One shot, Jamie. That's all it takes. You're the only one here. You can do it, you can say he came at you, got up, tried to go for you with the knife again… No one would dispute it. They wouldn't look at you twice. He paused, lowered his head to her. *You can get away with it, Jamie.*

She froze. Roper. Qiang. Her. She glanced over her shoulder. The girls. All the ones that came before them, and the ones that would come after.

De Voge was groaning in front of her, trying to roll onto his side now.

The gun shivered in the air and she kicked him onto his back again.

He flattened out, his arm flopping to the ground, his dark eyes fluttering open.

De Voge stared up at her over the barrel of her pistol and fell still.

Her father was gone now.

It was just her and him and her finger on the trigger.

Evil against evil.

Jamie exhaled, steadied her grip.

Now or never.

The girls whimpered behind her and she thought of Roper.

What would he do? Would he want revenge? Would he kill De Voge?

Would he want her to?

The button felt smooth under her finger, her left hand still hovering at her chest, on the radio.

Her father would do it. She knew that much.

Without a second's thought.

Roper wouldn't.

One against one.

Elliot would. And he'd like it.

She felt sick, her finger pressing against the spring in the mechanism.

A tiny amount of force. That's all it would take.

She exhaled.

She pressed.

'This is DS Jamie Johansson,' she said into the ether, lowering the pistol to her side. 'I have Marco De Voge in custody. Send backup immediately.'

Under her, De Voge cracked a little smirk and laughed hoarsely. 'I knew you didn't have it in you.'

Jamie took a deep breath, and looked up. Her knee lifted into the air and then she slammed her boot down onto his chest again. De Voge's legs jumped up and then fell limp as he fought for breath, his eyes rolling into the back of his head.

'Shut up,' she muttered, holstering her pistol. Jamie didn't know if she broke a rib, but she hoped so. 'And by the way, you're under arrest.'

She brushed the hair back off her forehead and then dug her toe under his shoulder, kicking him onto his front.

She took a little pleasure in folding his arms behind his back, pressing her knee into his spine just like she promised Roper.

Jamie pulled a heavy zip-tie from a pocket on the front of her vest, threaded it around his wrists and yanked it tight.

De Voge groaned and she stood up, listening as the steps of Hassan's men grew behind her.

She swallowed hard, still feeling the phantom of the pistol in her hand, wondering what would have happened if she had pulled the trigger.

Jamie felt tired all of a sudden, beaten and bruised, and then thought that it didn't matter.

She made her choice, and she would have to live with it.

Only time would tell if it was the right one or not.

The worst thing was, that she didn't really know.

34

THE JADE CIRCLE had a distinctly stale smell at eight in the morning.

They'd closed an hour earlier, and once they were sure that the last of the patrons had left and the bouncers were off shift, they moved in.

Their warrants allowed them to search the entire place, seize anything they wanted, take Zhou and all of his staff into custody on trafficking and slavery charges, and accessory to.

Though Jamie knew that Zhou wasn't there.

He hadn't been seen since Sunday evening, when Kosiah and De Voge had made their trip to Felixstowe.

The phone that Kosiah had gotten the tip-off on had been a prepaid disposable thing, and the call had been bounced all over the place before going to it. Their computer forensics guys said that the call originated in Tajikistan. Though Jamie knew that was bullshit. Hassan had hit the nail on the head first time.

It had come from inside. There were only a handful of people who knew about the operation, and when shit had gone sideways, the backup armed response team had already been en route to another bogus call, and Brock and Amherst had been tipped on a lead for another case last minute and never made it to the port.

Smith himself hadn't been there either.

Jamie didn't peg Amherst and Brock as the dirty type. And she'd bet it wasn't Smith. He was above reproach as far as she was concerned. And there was no way that he was going to side with De Voge after what he did to Roper. But then again, there were at least ten uniformed officers who knew about it by the time it went down, half a dozen traffic officers, half a dozen intelligence officers, an aerial surveillance team, the armed response team... They didn't know the details, most of them, but knowing it was at Felixstowe would be enough for anyone with half a brain cell to put two and two together.

It only made sense that Zhou had someone on the inside, it's why he wasn't here now. They just needed to know who.

An officer by the name of Harris came out of the front door of the Jade Circle in a high -visibility vest. It glowed in the dim morning light.

The air was light and cold and the sky overhead was grey and moving fast, but the rain had finally abated. The storm that had rolled in on Sunday evening had been one of the biggest of the last few years. Storm Regina. Who the hell named them Jamie didn't know.

'Detective Johansson,' he said, nodding, trying not to look at the fading bruise on Jamie's face.

It was Tuesday morning. A full day and some change after they'd taken De Voge down and rescued the girls.

'What is it?' Jamie asked, her arms folded tightly across her chest, a look of grim determination on her face.

'There's no sign of Zhou,' he said, sounding disappointed.

'Not surprised,' Jamie said, shaking her head.

'You want us to keep sweeping?'

She nodded. 'I want this place turned inside out.'

'Okay, I'll keep you updated.' He turned and went back inside.

Jamie was running the operation. Smith had given her the responsibility. Told her she'd earned it. And then he said the nicest thing he'd ever said to her. In his backhanded way. 'I'm trusting you not to fuck it up.'

A few seconds later, another officer appeared. She pushed back the door and a string of girls walked out in a line. They were all still dressed from the night before. Tight, short dresses. Sequins. Lace. Made up heavily, their cheeks blushed and glittered, their lips red and pouting. Immaculate skin. Slim, young, nubile. Enough to drive any man with two beers in him wild.

She counted them in her head as they walked past, being led to whatever semblance of freedom was ahead for them. They'd all be taken into custody for a few days, questioned in regards to what went on at the Jade Circle, and then they'd be allowed to travel home. To wherever that was for them.

The girls all looked scared walking out, unsure. Like they'd been caught rather than saved.

Jamie folded her arms, looking at them all. When she got to fourteen she stopped counting. One of them caught her eye.

'Yanmei,' she said out loud, stepping forward and reaching out. She touched one of the girls on the arm – the same one she had spoken to in the nail salon. She was in stiletto heels and a blue dress that started high and finished low, hugging every tiny curve of her body. Her hair was coloured with shades of auburn and she jolted when Jamie said her name.

It took her a second to recognise her and then she stepped from the procession and forced a quick smile, glancing at the line of girls.

'Yanmei – I don't know if you remember me. I'm—'

'The detective,' she said, nodding. 'From the salon.'

'That's right. How are you?' Jamie asked, instantly regretting asking, realising what the last twelve hours had probably entailed for her.

'You know,' she said, leaving it at that, with a little shrug added on the end. She took her left elbow in her right hand and scratched at it with her long red nails. Up close, Jamie could see the lines at the corners of her eyes. The bags under them that the makeup couldn't quite hide. This life had taken its toll.

'Look,' Jamie said, not sure what she'd intended to say when she stopped her. 'I just wanted to thank you – for what you told me. It really... it really helped.'

'Did you...' She trailed off and cleared her throat, sort of squinting a little, her voice tight. 'Did you find the father?'

'No,' Jamie said. 'Not yet. But we're still looking. We've got some leads, got the search narrowed down a lot, thanks to you.'

She nodded, softening a little with relief. 'That's good. And what about her killer?' she asked, biting her bottom lip.

'We have De Voge in custody,' Jamie said. 'Whether he confesses to it or not, he'll be going away for a long time.'

She sighed audibly with relief this time. 'That's good. She was a close friend.' Yanmei smiled now, widely, and Jamie felt warmth inside her. It was enough of a reminder that she was standing on the right side of the evil and evil battle.

'I'll do right by her,' Jamie promised. 'Don't worry.'

The girls had all left the building now and had been ushered into a minibus with blacked out windows that was parked on the street at the entrance to the alley.

'That's good,' Yanmei said, looking at the bus. 'I think I have to...'

'Of course,' Jamie said, touching her arm awkwardly. 'Good luck.'

Yanmei gave a little wave and then walked off towards the bus, striding on heels the width of razors with utter confidence. They made Jamie's ankles twitch just looking at them.

De Voge was already in France at the Interpol HQ. It was officially their investigation now, an international trafficking operation beyond the reach of the Met. And while it was unlikely they'd even question him about Qiang, let alone try to nail him for her murder, it was enough that he was going down for something. You can't win them all.

Jamie exhaled, blowing out the stench of rotten rubbish, and checked her phone. Nothing. Smith had given her free rein over the clear up, but was holding back anything new that came in. He'd even told her to take a few days off, regenerate, and then come back in on Wednesday.

She'd slept almost all of yesterday. She didn't get home until gone ten in the morning when all was said and done, and then she'd woken up at three, cranky and disoriented, eaten everything in her fridge –

which wasn't much – and then had gone back to bed. She'd slept fitfully until four this morning, and then went for a run.

She did twenty-two kilometres despite the ache in her back, and felt a lot better for it.

An email from Smith told her what was happening and where to be this morning. But she still felt out-of-it. Tired. Like she was jet-lagged.

Another day off would help. But it was hardly like she didn't have lots to do. She hadn't dropped in on Roper and she felt like he should hear all about the operation from her before anyone else.

She just hoped that this wouldn't take too long.

'No one told me running a clean-up would be so boring,' Jamie said, leaning back on the plastic-covered chair next to Roper's bed.

He'd been off cigarettes for going on five days now and had probably been fed more fruits and vegetables in that time than he'd consumed in the last year on his own. As such, he was looking healthy – despite the stab-wound in his back, of course.

His cheeks had more colour and his skin didn't look so much like an old leather book anymore.

He said that the attack had put years on him, but Jamie disagreed. She just hoped he would take his rehab seriously. Though she doubted he'd come jogging with her any time soon.

'I could have,' Roper said airily, lifting the page on the file he was looking at. 'If you'd bothered to ask.' He glanced up at her, smirking.

The light was fading from the sky despite it only being just after three in the afternoon.

Jamie scoffed. 'It's been a day.' She shook her head. 'I haven't been here for one day – and that's because I was up all night the night before, you know, saving the world. And then I was sleeping.'

'Excuses, excuses,' he said with a sigh. 'And don't you think "saving the world" is a little strong?'

Jamie shrugged, scanning down the information on her own file. In reality it was one that she'd split down the middle. 'Someone's gotta do it, right?' She'd given half to Roper to look through, to keep him feeling useful.

He laughed. 'If you say so. And speaking of saving the world. Did the Raymond kid ever turn up?'

Jamie sighed. 'Yep. He was brought in a few days ago. Arrested for possession with intent. Was carrying twice what his mother had flushed. Probably trying to make back the cash he owed.'

'With interest.' Roper drew in a slow breath, focusing on the page in front of him. 'What'd his mother say?'

'I doubt she was happy. And it was probably my fault.'

'Probably,' Roper said. 'I'm just glad it all worked out in the end.'

'You could say that,' Jamie said, turning the page. She was trying not to think about it.

'Hey, he could have turned up dead. Wouldn't be the first one.'

Jamie thought about that. And hated immediately that if he had done, she would have cared more. It would have been a *real* case then. It all seemed trivial to her when it was going on. Paling in comparison to everything else that was happening. But it would affect his whole life now. Every decision he made, every loan, every job he applied for. Could she have done more? Or was this always where things were going to end up? Why did the dead deserve more justice?

Because they can't get it for themselves.

Roper dragged her back to the moment at hand. 'What about this one?' He held up a photo from his file and a middle-aged guy with a smarmy grin looked out at her.

'Richard Brunner. Tax Specialist.' Jamie stuck her bottom lip out, reading the name and title under his photo. It was a little grainy – a screengrab from the company website – but it was clear enough for him to fit.

She'd taken the list of Grigoryan's associates that she'd had since she searched Qiang's apartment, and had the go ahead from Smith to draft in a junior detective to do the legwork. She always hated getting handed jobs like this from more senior detectives when she was just starting out, and had even promised herself she'd never shit on anyone below her.

Jamie didn't want to think about all the promises she'd made to herself and then broken over the years.

She'd had the junior detective cross-check all of the law firms and solicitors that Grigoryan had worked with, as well as their affiliates and their prior cases, against the description that Yanmei had given. Between thirty-five and sixty, Caucasian, dark hair. That was about all she was prepared to go on as gospel. She couldn't be sure that Yanmei's description was accurate. And she wouldn't be surprised if the guy was lying about his station. It was a long shot as it was. It wouldn't be surprising if the guy had lied completely about what he did. But Jamie had to take a swing. Whether the case was sewn up or not, she needed to at least make an effort to tell the father that Qiang was gone. As was his child. He had a right to know that much.

'Add him to the pile,' Jamie said.

Roper pulled the sheet from the file and laid the picture of Brunner, along with his address and contact information, on a slowly growing pile on the tray-table next to Roper's bed.

There were nearly a hundred names and faces that could have been the father. And so far they'd found three that were likely matches if he had been telling the truth about what he did. Brunner worked for a big firm. And the difference between barristers and solicitors was like apples and apples. One sounded fancier, and probably played better with women.

Jamie glanced over at the photo again. Smarmy looking guy. Short brown hair, like Yanmei said. He was probably late forties. Right in the band she'd described. Clean-shaven. He worked in tax law. That fit. And all the faces here worked for or with firms who'd consulted on or directly worked big tax cases in the last eighteen months.

She picked it up and held it in front of her.

'You think that's the guy?' Roper asked, letting the page in front of him leaf down.

Jamie bit her lip. 'I don't know. He's as good a fit as any.' She sighed and put him back on the pile. 'Let's keep looking. What are you, about halfway through?'

'A third,' Roper said, sizing up his pile.

Jamie grumbled. 'This is worse than the clean up.'

'At least the company's better.'

She laughed. 'Debatable.'

It was nearing ten that evening when Jamie pulled up outside Richard Brunner's townhouse.

It wasn't in the best part of the city, but it would still run you a couple of million to buy one. And the Mercedes coupe parked in front, with all of the chrome extras added, told her he both had the money, and the need to be noticed, to be the sort of guy who'd throw around big money at a casino and get off on being fawned over by beautiful women.

There'd been six names on their list of likely suspects by the end of the pile. All of them as good candidates as the last. But the other five hadn't felt right. Two of them seemed genuinely nice when she met them, settled down with families, and were more than obliging. She'd not called ahead with any of them. She'd just turned up at their front doors with her warrant card – now that she'd cleaned all the urine off it – held up. They'd invited her in, offered tea, and helped with the investigation however they could. Except neither of them could. They weren't the father, and had been more than forthcoming with their information. They'd even offered to hand over their credit card records to ease things. Both seemed genuinely appalled by the whole situation.

Two had been less helpful, but still didn't quite fit. One wasn't into women – his husband attested to that. And the other said that the women he paid for never came free with anything, and if he was going to throw his money away at a casino, it wouldn't be some rat-infested basement in China Town. That was verbatim.

The fifth had been a strange one. Coy at first, then suspicious. He didn't want to answer the questions, but when Jamie threatened to pull him into the station, he admitted to having been to the Jade Circle with a co-worker. But just the once, and he didn't know the name of the girl he slept with. And please don't tell his wife. He'd been forced to go.

He worked for a different firm then, he said. And the guy he went with loved it there. Went all the time. Raved about it.

His name was Richard Brunner.

Jamie kept the smile off her face, and told the guy to stay reachable.

He begged her to call him at work and not come back there again.

She hadn't decided yet if she wanted to ruin that marriage, whether he was a bit of an arsehole or not.

But she guessed that was a civil matter rather than a legal one. Being a cheater wasn't illegal. It would have made her own father a top-drawer hypocrite if it was. And a hell of a criminal.

She left there with Brunner in her sights, and now here she was.

The Mercedes was black and had the size of the engine on the back. Six-point-three litres. Vroom. The bigger the engine the smaller the...

She cleared her throat and straightened her jacket, already on the top step in front of his door.

Jamie knocked firmly and then stepped back.

Half a minute later the light in the hallway came on, throwing a rectangle of yellow into the dark air.

The door opened and Richard Brunner stood before Jamie.

He was five-eight, a little overweight, with blotchy cheeks. His hair was short and brown, and even now he was wearing a white work-shirt, his tie loosened around his neck. He had a pair of thin spectacles halfway down his nose and a gold pen in his hand. 'Yes?' he asked, almost accusatory.

Jamie was wearing a leather jacket and walking boots, and she did have a bruise spread down the left side of her face.

'Detective Sergeant Jamie Johansson,' Jamie said, lifting her warrant card. 'Richard Brunner?' she asked, already knowing he was.

'Yes. What is this about?' He was defensive already, trying to keep his eyes from twitching.

'I'm conducting an investigation into the murder of an unidentified young woman, and I was hoping you might be able to answer a few ques—'

'I'm sorry,' he said. 'I think you've got the wrong person. Now please, I'm very busy.' He tried to close the door and Jamie's hand hit the wood with a loud slap, her foot moving into place as a stopper, right on the threshold.

She knew better than to go past it, especially into the house of a solicitor, without permission.

'Excuse me,' he said loudly, lifting his other hand to the door to try and force it. 'Remove your foot, or I'll—'

'Two crossed lines,' Jamie said, restraining a smile. She couldn't believe she hadn't thought of it before.

'What?' Brunner asked, a little confused – taken aback maybe. Perhaps scared.

'Your cufflinks,' Jamie said, pointing at them.

His left hand had come up to the edge of the door, his thick fingers curled there, an expensive gold watch poking out of his shirt sleeve. The cuff was folded back. Held in place by a gold cufflink. A pair of golf clubs with a diamond ball in the middle. Two crossed lines. In the shape of an X. Exactly like Yanmei said.

'What about them?' Brunner asked. Definitely scared.

'They're an exact match for a description we got from a material witness,' Jamie said plainly. There would be no bullshitting him. Whether he was the father or not, he was a barrister and Jamie had to tread carefully.

Brunner fell quiet and Jamie felt the pressure release against her foot.

She continued. 'One of the girls at the Jade Circle gave us a description that matches you exactly. Right down to your cufflinks. And a former co-worker attested to your love of the place.'

His mouth opened but no sound came out. His chin lowered, making a little fold of skin bunch above his collar.

'Mister Brunner – I would very much appreciate it if you would let me in so that we can talk.' She paused and let his mind work. 'If not, that's perfectly fine. But we raided the Jade Circle this morning, seized everything in there, and I've been told by both my senior officer and the judge who granted us the warrant to do that, that they're ready to grant me an arrest warrant the moment that I find the father.'

He looked up now, the colour draining from his face as she said it.

That was enough for Jamie to know that Brunner knew exactly who and what she was talking about. 'So you decide, Richard,' Jamie said, taking her hand off the door. 'You want to do this quietly, or do you want me to come back with a few officers, flashing lights, the works – and drag you into the street in handcuffs for obstruction of justice?'

His knuckles whitened on the door as he gripped it, not sure whether to slam it in Jamie's face or not.

'Richie?' A female voice echoed down the stairs behind him. 'Who's there?'

He swallowed. 'It's nothing, dear – just a… just a client,' he called back, trying to sound calm. Jamie didn't know if he sold it.

'At this time?' His wife called back. 'Can't you tell them to—'

'No, no,' he interrupted. 'I can't. It's an important case and I'm…' He trailed off and pulled the door wide. 'It won't take long.' He beckoned Jamie in. 'Tuck the kids in for me… I'll be up in a little while.'

Jamie stepped past him and into the hallway. The floor was polished checkerboard tiles. Probably more expensive per square metre than her monthly rent.

She didn't have the heart to tell Richie that she still probably had chunks of human faeces lodged between the treads of her boots.

Richard Brunner led her past the stairs and down another set to his office. It was wood-panelled and regal, outfitted with leather chester-field sofas, a solid oak desk, and antique bookcases filled with expensive-looking leather-bound law textbooks and other expensive ornaments. Framed photos of him with clients. Other photos of himself doing various things. In one he was holding up a large marlin on a boat somewhere wearing shorts that showed off thin white legs. He was grinning widely. In another he was on a jet ski. Then in another he was at a party somewhere in a tuxedo with a woman Jamie guessed probably wasn't his wife considering the age gap and the fact that she was dressed more like a Victoria's Secret model than anything else. She had lingerie on, heels, and then a large, feathered gown and intricate head-dress that made her look like a peacock.

In the background, lots of other well-dressed men and scantily clad models were visible.

In every photo, it was Brunner.

He cared a lot about appearances.

Jamie could use that.

'Please,' he said, gesturing to the chesterfield.

She sat and he went to an antique sideboard and lifted a panel, exposing decanters full of amber liquid.

He poured a serious measure into one of the glasses and looked over his shoulder. 'Drink?' he asked.

'No thanks,' Jamie said.

'You mind if I do?' He laughed nervously, bringing the glass to his lips.

'Depends what kind of conversation you want to have.'

The glass froze at his lips.

'I'm about ninety-nine percent sure you didn't kill Qiang,' she said airily. 'But I can't make my mind up as to whether or not you had anything to do with it. You don't strike me as the violent type. But then again I doubt you strike your wife as the type to get a twenty-year-old Chinese prostitute pregnant either.' She shrugged. 'And she probably knows you a lot better than I do.'

He swallowed and then slugged the contents of the glass, refilling it before he came back and sat on the chesterfield opposite, putting it down hard on the table.

Some of the amber liquid spilled onto the polished wood.

'Look,' he said, leaning forward, his elbows pressing into the tops of his knees. 'I didn't kill her okay? And I don't know who did.'

'But you admit that you knew her, and that you knew you were the father?'

He looked at Jamie for a second, weighing up whether or not he was implicating himself in anything.

'Off the record – informal chat,' Jamie said, holding a hand up.

'Yes,' he said, nearly whispering. 'I do.' His face had already flushed, a thin sweat forming on his brow.

'Okay, that's a start.' Jamie kept her face straight, but inside she was fist-pumping the air. Everything was coming together. Finally. 'And you put her at Grigoryan's? At the apartment where she was killed?'

'Yes,' he answered slowly.

'How did you know about it?'

'Our firm was brought on to review Mister Grigoryan's tax vulnerabilities. A few years ago I did a tour of the premises he owned to do a risk assessment.'

'The prognosis?'

'Not good,' he said, laughing a little and taking another mouthful.

'So that's how you knew about the building.' She nodded to herself, filing it away.

'Yeah. It was... I couldn't think of where else to put her that was...' He trailed off and then loosened his collar a little more.

'And you called Grigoryan, told him you'd slide him some extra cash if he asked no questions? If he just had one of his guys move her in, no contract, no references...'

He didn't answer, but she took his silence as confirmation.

'How did you find out?'

'That she was pregnant?'

'If you like.'

'She turned up at my door. Just like you did.' There was scorn in that one.

'Not quite like me, though. I'm not carrying your child.'

'Keep your voice down,' he urged her, eyes wide.

'If you want to trade snide remarks, Richard, I think I've probably got a little more ammunition here than you do.'

He made an indignant humming sound. 'She turned up here one evening – middle of the week. I didn't know what the hell to do. She was crying, terrified – I didn't know what the hell else to do! I couldn't let her in.'

Jamie thought on it. 'You gave her your address?'

'What? No! Of course not.'

'Then how did she know where you lived?'

'I don't know.'

Jamie nodded slowly, processing. 'And you didn't know she was pregnant before that?'

'No.'

'You realise that for someone who's supposed to be trying to convince me you didn't kill her in order to stop your wife from finding out you cheated on her with, and then impregnated, a sex worker, you're not doing a very good job of it.'

'Jesus Christ,' Richard muttered to himself. He ran one hand through his gelled hair and lifted the glass to his mouth with the other, draining it in one.

'She ran away from the Jade Circle, carrying your child.' Jamie paused for a second. 'Now I've spent the last week tracking and hunting down the pieces of shit who ran that place – and I know what they're capable of. One of them tried to kill my partner, and very nearly succeeded. Then he tried to put a knife in me, too. Came about this close.' She lifted her index finger and thumb and held them a centimetre apart. 'You probably know him. De Voge?'

Brunner paled.

'Thought you might.' Jamie flashed him a wry smile. 'And I have it on good authority that they make examples of girls who run away. That they put a picture of Qiang's body on the wall of the girls' room above the Jade Circle, as a message.'

'My God.' He eyed the decanter, licking his lips.

'So if she made a break for it and came here, then I have to figure that there were two things which led to that – firstly, she knew exactly where you lived. And secondly, she was under the impression that you were going to save her life. And no offence, but by looking at you, I don't think you'd be the sort to defend a woman's honour in mortal combat.'

He scowled at her and pressed his hands together. 'I may,' he started, looking down, 'have said some things – while drunk, you know?'

'What things?'

'That I… loved her. And that she was… special.'

'Cocaine will do that to you.'

He clenched his jaw and tried not to meet her eye. He said nothing.

'What else did you say?'

He sighed and shook his head. 'That I would…' He fought with himself to repeat the words. 'That I would take her away from it. Save her…'

Jamie nodded again. 'Whatever it takes to make her do the dirty stuff, I suppose,' she said, trying her best to keep the derision out of her voice.

'I meant it,' he said quickly. Defensively. 'I did love her.'

'Of course you did.'

'I did!' He almost yelled it, then cleared his throat and calmed down. 'But she was… her, and I'm…' He gestured around. 'And my wife… and kids. I couldn't ever follow through on any of it – and she knew that.'

'Did she? Because it seems to me like she got killed precisely because she didn't know that.'

He inhaled for a long time, choosing his words. 'When she turned up here, and told me she was pregnant – and that she was almost four months along.' He shook his head. 'Jesus, it was… I don't even know.'

'She risked her life to keep your child. She really believed that you'd save her.' Jamie didn't try to keep the coldness out of her voice that time.

'I know,' he said, more to himself than her. She could hear his throat tight. The sadness in it.

'So how did she find you, huh?'

'I don't know.'

'You're a smart guy, Richard. Think. How did she know where you lived? How *could* she?'

He looked up and met her eye. His were full of shame. 'Last year, there was… a party.'

'Okay.'

'My wife, the kids… They were visiting family we have in the

States. I was supposed to go, but something cropped up with work – a case – and I couldn't. They were gone for two weeks.'

Jamie stayed silent as Richard wrestled with the truth.

'Some co-workers and I were here, working on it, and we wanted to blow off some steam…' He weighed his hands in the air.

'So you went out?'

He nodded.

'To the Jade Circle?'

He nodded.

Jamie thought back to the surveillance team. One of the girls had gone home with one of the high rollers. She put it together. 'So you and your buddies dropped a bunch of money, closed out the casino, brought the girls back for a little afterparty?'

He buried his head in his hands and sobbed twice. 'Jesus Christ.'

'And Qiang was one of them?'

He dropped his hands suddenly. 'No, she wasn't there then – she came to the Circle a few months later.'

'But the girls that were here could have told her where you lived?'

'I suppose,' he said. 'But most of them are gone, now. Moved on.'

Moved on? Was that what the patrons called it when the girls got sold to whoever would pay for damaged goods. She held back her disgust.

'But not all of them?' Jamie asked.

'No – well, just one, I think.'

'Do you know her name?'

'Yanmei,' he said quickly.

'Yanmei?' Jamie heard the surprise in her own voice. 'Are you sure?'

'Oh, I'm sure,' he said, turning his head to the side a little.

Jamie thought that indicated that they were very well acquainted. 'You knew her well?'

'Yeah, I guess.'

She took a punt. 'She was your favourite before Qiang?'

He nodded. 'But when you say it like that it makes it sound bad.'

'I'm sorry, was she the prostitute that you had sex with most regularly before Qiang's arrival?'

He glared at her now.

Shit. Yanmei had given such a vague description of him, she'd made it sound like she didn't know him. But she did. She knew his name, his address, everything about him. Maybe she just didn't want to complicate things for herself, get dragged into it. Maybe she still held a candle for Richard – wanted to protect him?

A cold sense of dread crept up her spine. She had to start putting pressure on him. To get the truth.

'This is the story that's starting to form, here. Qiang shows up at your door, afraid for her life. You, terrified your wife will find out, stash her at Grigoryan's.'

He watched her, still as a statue.

'She's there for a few weeks while you sort things out – that's what you tell her, right? While you rack your brain trying to figure out what the hell to do.'

He kept watching her.

'Only she starts to get anxious. Worried. She wants out. She wants her happily ever after.'

He swallowed, clutching his glass in both hands.

'And you're running out of options. What if your wife finds out? What if your perfect life goes away? Imagine the fallout. The scandal. It would cost you *everything.*'

His jaw twitched, his skin squeezing beads of sweat out onto his forehead.

'So you start to think differently. How can you *fix* this.'

He eyed her cautiously.

'For good. Because she's not going away on her own, and there are people out there who, if they find out you're helping her, are probably going to want to send a message to all the other guys who think they can steal from the Circle.'

He said nothing, his thumb sliding over the rim of the glass nervously.

'So you speak to Grigoryan, or to Zhou – a regular like you must know the management, especially if they let you take their girls home.'

He looked away.

'Or hell, maybe you just have De Voge on speed dial for whenever you need a little—'

'No.'

'No?'

'He… he scares the shit out of me.'

'He scares the shit out of everyone,' Jamie said. 'It's what he's there for. But either way, you called someone, made one phone call – and tipped them off. Knowing what would happen.'

'I didn't.'

'I think you thought it would solve all your problems. They come in, and then your Qiang problem is taken care of. She's no danger to you any more. And for being such a good boy, you get welcomed back to the Circle with open arms.'

'No.'

'Except it wasn't that simple, was it? They wanted to make an example of you – to you – to make sure you didn't do it again.'

'That's not what happened.'

'They made you go there, didn't they?'

'No!' He was flushing now.

'That's why Qiang opened the door. Because you were standing on the other side of it.'

'No.' He shook his head fervently.

'She opened the door, and invited you in – her saviour, her lover. And then you stepped aside and let De Voge shoot her in the back.'

'No!' He was on his feet now. He turned and slingshotted the glass into the wall.

It exploded into a thousand fragments and they rained down on an antique cabinet with a bronze statue of lady justice on it.

Jamie stared up at him, measuring him. Angry, yes, but not capable of much. She could be up and throwing her heel into his temple before he could even cock his fist.

But she wouldn't need to. He didn't have violence in him, and was already deflating like a week-old birthday balloon.

As cut and dry as it would have been, the voice in her head was telling her he didn't do it.

And if anything, he was borderline distraught that someone had. Maybe he did love her after all. In his own way.

'Sit down, Richard,' Jamie said calmly.

He swallowed and straightened his tie, glancing at the closed door over Jamie's shoulder.

There were no feet rushing down the stairs.

No one had heard.

Perks of a four-story townhouse, she guessed. All the smashing glasses and prostitutes you could handle, and your wife could be sleeping soundly upstairs, none the wiser.

Richard sat, straightening his shirt. Sweat stains were already appearing under his arms.

'That's not what happened,' he said evenly, running his hands through his hair. 'I wasn't there when it happened.'

'No?'

'No.' He narrowed his eyes at her. 'I was away the whole weekend. For work. In Sheffield.'

'Anyone who can corroborate that?'

'The three people I was at the hotel with? My wife? The hotel staff? How many do you want?'

Jamie resisted the urge to quip about his wife's testimony about his whereabouts being worth shit considering all the crap he did behind her back without her knowing. 'Okay, Richard. If that's not what happened. Tell me what did.'

'You're the bloody detective, you tell me!' He scoffed, got up, and went to get another drink.

'That's what I'm trying to figure out,' Jamie mused. 'Because something's not adding up here. Yanmei gives me an intentionally vague description of you to protect you, knowing full-well exactly who you are and where you live?'

'Yeah? So?' He drained another glass before he put down the decanter.

'Why do you think that is? Did she think you did it?'

'How should I know?'

'It just strikes me as odd that she'd do that considering how close her and Qiang were.'

He laughed, his back to Jamie, round shoulders moving up and down.

'What's funny?'

'They weren't friends,' Richard said, filling a tumbler half full and coming back to the sofa. 'Or at least, she wasn't Qiang's friend. Not that Qiang knew that, mind.'

Jamie pursed her lips. 'What do you mean?'

'Hell, maybe it was Yanmei who killed her.' He shrugged and took the top off his drink. 'She'd have as much reason as any.'

Jamie leaned forward now, her focus tightening. 'What do you mean?'

Richard seemed to relax a bit, the alcohol numbing him to the gravity of the situation. 'I suppose that's why they kept her around, though. The others moved on, but she stayed.'

'Who? Yanmei?'

He nodded. 'Yeah. A few years now. As long as I've been going there.'

'Why? What's so special about her?'

'I don't know if special is the word. Scary maybe?' He laughed to himself again.

'Richard – you need to start making sense, or I'm going to pull you in for questioning and throw you in a cell until you sober up.'

He read the seriousness in her voice and put the glass down. 'I used to go to Yanmei, before Qiang. I got to know her a bit.'

'Okay.'

'There was always something about her. This kind of... power. It was sexy.'

'Okay.' Jamie blinked, trying to ignore the salacity in his voice.

'But then I started to notice things, you know?'

'I will if you tell me.'

'Her and De Voge, they were… closer than the other girls.'

'So what, she was his favourite? His, what do they call it, a bottom girl?' Jamie asked, calling on her very limited knowledge of the industry.

'More than that,' Brunner said, making a weird face that pulled the corners of his mouth towards his ears. 'She kept the girls in line, yeah – but they never knew it.'

'I don't understand.'

'That was what made her so good. The girls were terrified of De Voge, but it was Yanmei who kept everything running, from the inside.' He couldn't resist another sip, despite Jamie's eyes boring into him. 'But the art of it was, that none of the other girls knew. They'd come in fresh, young, and Yanmei would make friends with them. Get close. She'd convince them she was one of them, and that she was just like them. But she wasn't. She was as cold, as cruel as De Voge.'

Jamie's chest felt heavy, her heart quickening. 'And that's why you switched to Qiang?'

He smirked a little. 'No, once I saw it, I stopped seeing Yanmei – and that was before Qiang even got there. She was… I don't know… But that power that I saw before, I realised what it was then. And after that…'

'So you think Yanmei could have…'

He shrugged. 'Who knows. But it was her job to keep everything running smoothly. To keep the girls working. To keep them happy. If they thought that running was a viable option, then that would reflect badly on Yanmei.' He took another drink. 'I think, in your game, that's what they call motive, isn't it, detective?'

Jamie pressed her lips into a tight line.

'De Voge, Zhou – they're smart. Smart enough not to go after Qiang themselves. And if they did, I don't think it would have happened as you said. I'm not saying it was Yanmei, but there's a cruelty in her that's hard to see. One that scares the shit out of me.' He finished his glass and looked down into it. He was moving between scared and distraught with every breath. He looked like he was about to burst into tears.

'Thank you,' Jamie said quietly, her fist tightly balled on top of her knee. Yanmei had played her like a violin. She'd even point-blankly asked her whether Jamie had found Brunner. Just that morning, knowing full well that she knew exactly who he was.

It all made so much sense now. Qiang opening the door, turning her back on the shooter. On Yanmei, who she thought was her friend. Surprised to see her, sure, but never considering for a second that she'd have the ability or the cruelty to put a bullet between her shoulders. And yet, the more Jamie thought about it, the more everything fell into place. The low angle of fire – Yanmei was the right height. The slight hesitation… Qiang had been a few steps into the room. She hadn't killed her right away. Maybe she wasn't as versed in murder as the guys she worked for, but she got it done. Under duress or not, whether she wanted to or not, whether she liked it or not… Yanmei pulled the trigger. And Jamie had fallen for her act without question. She even gave her the details on a silver platter. The photo of Qiang being hung in the girls' room. Yanmei took it. Right after she killed her.

But it still didn't mean Brunner wasn't guilty of something – other than being a complete arsehole, of course. 'There are still things that don't fit,' Jamie said, choosing her words carefully.

He looked up at her, eyes glazed.

'How did Yanmei find her? How did they track her down?'

'You think it was me,' he said, staring up at the pictures that chronicled the success of his career. 'Well I didn't, okay?'

'You're going to have to do better than that.'

'Do you know why I left her there for so long?'

'Tell me.'

He chuckled sadly. 'You'd think, working with so many *criminals,* I'd know more of them. But I don't, and that's exactly what got Qiang killed.'

Jamie swallowed, bracing herself for a confession.

'Jonathan Grigoryan is one of the worst, slimiest, slipperiest pieces of shit I've ever had the displeasure of representing.'

Jamie let him speak.

'There's no one he doesn't know, and nothing he won't do to put a favour in the bank.' Brunner sighed, running his nail along the rim of his glass. 'I was at a loss for anyone else to turn to. So I called him – told him the situation.'

Jamie wasn't about to interrupt. They'd already circled through this line of questioning once, but Brunner wasn't elaborating then. A few drinks later, and it was leaking out of him. And informal conversation or not – admissible in court or not – knowing the truth was enough to get started. And it looked like Brunner wanted to clear his conscience.

'Told him that I needed to get rid of her.'

Jamie tensed a little.

'No, not like that,' Brunner said, reading Jamie's expression. 'I would never... kill...' He grimaced at his own words. 'I wanted her away from here. Away from me. My family. But I would never...' He rattled off a slow exhale, his hands shaking. 'I asked Grigoryan if he could arrange a passport for her. If he knew someone who could get her out of the country... Back to China. I was going to pay – I said that I'd pay whatever it took. I wanted her to go home, and I was going to send her money, you know? To look after the...' He cleared his throat and then roughly wiped a tear from his cheek. 'I can prove it. I set up the account and everything.'

'I'll need to see proof of that,' Jamie added quietly, cautious of throwing him off his story.

He nodded. 'And Grigoryan said that he could arrange it – that it would take some time. But that she could stay there while he sorted it out for me. But that it was going to cost me...'

'More than money,' Jamie said, finishing his sentence.

'It always does with Grigoryan.'

'But he never came through?'

Brunner shook his head. 'No, he didn't. And I was calling and calling him.' His eyes widened, cleared for an instant. 'Believe me, I wanted to get it done as soon as I could.'

'I can believe that.'

'But he wasn't taking my calls. Wouldn't answer them. And Qiang was getting worried. Saying that it wasn't safe. That she didn't believe me…' His voice began to shake. 'I told her it was going to be okay. I told her that she was going to be okay.' He pinched the bridge of his nose and sobbed into his palm, cradling the glass on his stomach.

Jamie steeled herself and looked away, the image of Qiang's pale and lifeless body lying on the coroner's slab still burned into her mind, the smell of industrial disinfectant as powerful in her nose now as it was then.

'So you think Grigoryan went behind your back to Zhou?' Jamie's own voice was tight now. She coughed once, and then cleared it. The lump wouldn't budge.

'I don't know,' Brunner mumbled. 'But all I know is that Grigoryan was happy to do it, to hide her, to take my money, and then…'

'He wasn't.'

'And a week later…'

'She was dead.' Jamie said the words and everything came together. Grigoryan's walls had gone up instantly around this. He made sure he was untouchable. Because he *was* guilty. If Zhou was hunting Qiang, and Grigoryan knew that, banking a favour from a guy like Zhou was going to be worth a hell of a lot more than one from a sorry cheater who could fudge some tax write-offs at best.

Jamie wondered how much Qiang's life had been worth to Grigoryan. What he'd gotten out of selling her.

She took a deep breath and pushed up out of the sofa. 'Thank you, Richard,' she said again.

He was still sobbing, and despite all the wrong he'd done, Jamie couldn't help but feel sorry for him.

Or maybe pity was more accurate.

She didn't know if she could decide or if she was prepared to even spend the time needed to make the choice. She didn't think so.

'I'll see myself out,' Jamie said. She went to the door and paused, one hand on the knob. 'Brunner?'

He stopped snivelling for a second and looked up.

'Did you really love her?'

He nodded. 'I did.'

Jamie processed. 'Then answer one more question for me?'

His cheeks were puffy and red, his eyes wet.

'Why did you go to the apartment after she was killed? Why did you break in?'

He swallowed hard, his lip quivering.

'I know it was you,' Jamie said. 'Just tell me why.'

'I… I needed to see.' He sniffed back his running nose. 'For myself.'

She looked down, and then nodded once, letting herself out. 'I'll be in touch, Mr Brunner. Don't leave the country.'

And then she closed his office door behind her, moved through the hallway in a blur and was back out in the cold January air before she knew it, facing the night, and all the darkness that came with it.

35

Jamie stepped out of the stairwell the next morning and froze.

Everyone on her floor at HQ was staring at her.

All of them were grinning, standing at their desks.

'There she is,' came a booming voice. 'Detective Sergeant Jamie Johansson.'

She homed in on the broad shape of a man, shoulder bandaged, leg in a splinted cast. He was leaning on two crutches, his greased back black hair shining in the halogens.

He took his hands off the grips and clapped them awkwardly together, grinning as he did.

The rest of the floor began to join in, clapping for her.

She smiled awkwardly, feeling her cheeks flush.

Jamie spotted Smith standing outside his office door, hands in his pockets. He gave her a slight nod, but didn't clap or smile.

She guessed he was allowing this, rather than encouraging it.

Hassan hobbled forward. 'De Voge rolled,' he said, beaming at her. 'Which means Interpol's investigation just went global. And it's all thanks to you, and as DCI Smith described it – your absolute inability to let anything go!'

Some laughed.

Jamie smiled nervously.

Hassan was close to her now, his voice dropping from a loud announcement to normal speech. Everyone around them was already going back to their own work.

Hassan held his hand out for Jamie to shake, and she took it.

He squeezed firmly. 'How are you doing?' he asked.

She nodded. 'Yeah, I'm okay. What about you?'

'I've had worse,' he said cheerfully. 'Gets me some time off for recuperation – so the wife is happy at least.'

Jamie smirked. 'And what about the girlfriend?'

'With all this to enjoy?' he said, gesturing to himself. 'How could she not be.'

She laughed a little herself, glad to have this version of Hassan back. 'Sure, whatever you say.'

'You did well,' Hassan added. 'It was a tough one – nothing went as it should have. But you held your nerve.'

'Did I?' Jamie asked seriously. 'I don't feel like I did.'

He touched her upper arm now. 'I've seen guys with years of ops experience under their belt buckle worse than that. You ought to give yourself more credit.' He smiled at her reassuringly and it made her feel better. 'And in the end, you put De Voge down, we got him in custody and talking, and I even hear that you tracked down another murderer in the meanwhile.'

'Well, technically it was the same murderer as before – just not De Voge. At least not for this one.'

He chuckled a little. 'Smith was right. You are tenacious.'

'Is that the word he used?' Jamie glanced over at him. He was still standing outside his office, hands firmly rooted in his pockets.

'No,' Hassan said, laughing. 'But my mother told me to never swear in front of a lady.' He let go of her arm, moved sideways a step to steady himself, and then started moving past her. 'I'll see you around Johansson. Hopefully we'll get to work together again.'

'Hope so.'

'Look after yourself.'

'You too.'

He winked at her, and then stepped into the elevator. 'Always do.'

The doors closed, and then he was gone.

Jamie took a slow breath and turned back to the room. Everyone was working again and no one looked up as she passed. She doubted anyone had been that enthused about celebrating to begin with, but Hassan was probably pretty hard to say no to. Still, she appreciated the gesture. This had been one hell of a rollercoaster.

And judging by the look on Smith's face, it wasn't over yet.

He took one hand out of his pocket and beckoned her over, looking stern.

She went quickly.

'Close the door behind you,' he said, sitting behind the desk.

She did.

'Sit,' he said.

She did.

'How are you?' he asked formally.

'Fine. What's this about, sir?'

'Good work tracking down Brunner. We still have Yanmei in custody, which is great news. Extraditing from China is no easy task.'

'Thank you, sir. I'd like to begin the interrogation as quickly as—'

'No, that won't be necessary.'

'With all due respect, sir, this is my case. She's my suspect, and Brunner is my key witness.' Jamie tried to keep her tone even, but she was getting sick and tired of Smith yanking her leash.

He leaned forward on his elbows, interlacing his fingers until his fists were in a tight knot. 'It won't be necessary, Detective Johansson, because she's being handed over to Interpol as part of their trafficking case. If she's as integral to their operation as your preliminary report suggests, then Interpol will use her to leverage more information out of De Voge.'

'But, sir. We have her for murder – and with Brunner's testimony, I can—'

'It's already done, Johansson. She was put on a train at six o'clock this morning. She's gone, and there's nothing we can do about it.'

Jamie's nostrils flared as she did her best to keep her anger in check.

'I know it's not ideal. But their case is far wider reaching than ours. So you'll just have to be fine with knowing that you found out who did it. It's not a victory – maybe not like you hoped. But it's a win for us. A win for Interpol. And more importantly. It's justice.'

'Justice,' she muttered to herself, shaking her head. 'Whatever that means.'

Smith ignored it. 'If their investigation falls through, I'll be sure to do everything I can to get her back, alright? But for now, I need your attention elsewhere.'

Jamie narrowed her eyes a little at him.

'Here,' Smith said, picking up a folder from his desk and dropping it in front of her.

'What's this?' Jamie asked, opening it.

'Your next case.'

She lifted the cover and her blood ran cold.

The photograph on top of the pile inside showed a young Chinese guy lying on his back on the bank of a river. He was wearing a black suit, black shirt, black tie, a black coat lying rumpled around him. The hair on the sides of his scalp was cut short, the top ruffled and soaked, a few stray leaves sticking out of it. There was a tattoo of a snake's head coming up behind his right ear.

His milky eyes stared lifelessly into the sky.

Jamie swallowed. It was Matt, the head bouncer from the Jade Circle.

The same one who'd beaten the shit out of her outside her apartment.

The same one that Elliot had promised to take care of.

'You know who that is?' Smith asked grimly.

She nodded.

'You know what it is?'

'Sir?'

'It's a love letter, Johansson. Addressed to you.'

'I don't understand,' she lied.

He nodded at the file and she moved through the photographs, her stomach twisting with every one.

Every image added to the story.

It wasn't just a riverbank. It was the bank of the Lea. It was exactly where Oliver Hammond's body had been found.

The next shot showed Matt's body, his shirt open.

A long incision ran down his torso. It looked fresh. And it hadn't been stitched up. But the cut was clean and straight. Done with an expert hand.

The skin was depressed and sagging inwards at the line of the ribs, like it had nothing to rest on.

'Lungs, Liver, Kidneys,' Smith said. 'Pancreas... Everything of value. Removed.'

'Jesus,' Jamie muttered, forcing herself to keep moving through the photos.

'Everything that can be taken out, and sold. Except his heart.'

Jamie looked up now, felt Smith's eyes burning into her.

'He left that for you.'

She couldn't even speak. It was like Elliot had his own hands around her throat.

'Has he made contact with you?'

She shook her head.

'Are you sure?'

She nodded, thinking about the disposable mobile phone sitting in her wardrobe. Right under the map filled with his postcards. 'No, he hasn't.'

Smith took it in, drew a slow breath, and then sat back. 'Well, whether he's made direct contact or not. He wants you to know that he's close by. That he knows what you're working on.'

She closed her eyes, wondering if this was it. If it was all going to come out.

'I'm going to have forensics go over your apartment, check your computer and phone for any malicious software, for anything that indicates that he's watching. Because this,' Smith said, pointing to the file. 'Is the work of someone who's got more than an unhealthy obsession.'

He looked grave. 'This is someone who wants to help you. Someone who wanted to weaken Zhou for you. Someone who wanted to do something for you.'

She could see his eyes going over the fading bruise on her face. He wasn't going to say it, but he knew the excuse she'd given about it had been bullshit.

'So what do you say?' he asked.

'About what, sir?' she said, her voice small in her throat.

'About the case. Are you up to it? Are you up to catching this piece of shit? Putting him away, once and for all?'

She nodded. 'Yes, sir.'

'Are you sure?'

She met his eyes now, feeling a sense of stony determination seize her. 'I've never been more sure in my life.' She drew a slow breath and closed the file. 'Don't worry, sir. I'll find him. And that's a promise.'

AUTHOR'S NOTE

Fresh Meat was a strange book to write. I struggled with it for a long time. Not so much the writing, but with whether to write it at all, and how to write it.

It wasn't going to be the second book in the series, and didn't materialise as such until after the first was written and the actual second book was planned. It was because of the nature of the plot, and what Jamie would have to do — I just wasn't sure that she was ready for it.

But then, I think I realised that the very fact that she wasn't ready for it is what was going to make it the book that it turned out to be. Jamie's emotions, her deep-seated desire to do the right thing — they drive her in this book to push for a case that she's neither mentally, nor professionally equipped to handle.

Jamie feels an overwhelming amount of guilt for the events of book one, believes herself responsible for Elliot's escape, and it is this that drives her to pursue this case. It's not that the crime is heinous (even though it is), but rather that it is heinous, and the person who committed it is going to get away.

Jamie's stubbornness is what keeps her going when she should back down. When the right thing to do is loosen her grip on the reins. But it is that quality that defines her, and makes her a great detective.

And as we move into the third story, she is becoming stronger, more level-headed. Her father's guiding voice is becoming more a devil in her ear. She is becoming increasingly disenchanted with the world, more cynical. She is growing closer to the people she is trying to catch. And she knows that.

This is something I've really enjoyed exploring, and will continue to explore. I love the idea of taking Jamie on a journey of growth. Of allowing her to transition into someone else. Not necessarily better, or worse, but different.

A lot of authors begin their journey with their protagonists at this point. Post-transformation. But for me, the way that it happens is what interested me. It is why I chose Jamie at thirty-four, not in her mid or late forties. It's why she's a DS not a DI or DCI. And I hope that by the time she is, that we'll be eight or ten books deep in this series, and she will be such a rich and real character, one who has covered more ground that most heroes ever could, that each new case she takes, each new villain she faces, will feel well-earned. Those big-ticket serial killers, those cases that are so nasty that she gets called in as the only detective who could possibly solve them.

Fresh Meat is pivotal in this journey. It introduces an element of impending danger. It shows how Jamie's stubbornness gets her into more trouble than she knows, and how it paints a target on her back. Elliot's reappearance here signals to Jamie that her past never quite leaves her behind. But what she sees and what's really going on are two different things. Her point of view is the one that we experience, but isn't necessarily the truth.

Elliot never does anything without a good reason, and what he reveals to Jamie isn't always the whole story.

Having these layers — the case, Jamie's personal life, her work life, Elliot... all pressing down on her — this, for me, is what creates a deep character. And whether I manage to do it, or whether it just comes off as completely convoluted, well, that's up to you. But I like to try. And I'll keep doing it in book three, and beyond.

Because in these books, like in life, little is what it seems at first glance, and few people tell the truth. And as Jamie becomes a better detective, she'll get better at seeing that. And she'll second-guess herself less.

I have big plans for Jamie, and if you're here, reading this, then hopefully you're happy to come along for the ride. Book three is on course to release in the next few months, and sees Jamie deal with a twisted killer who targets classical musicians, and then dismembers them... And book four sees Jamie asked to assist on a case that will force her to confront her past, and everything in it... I really can't wait to show them to you. If you liked Bare Skin and Fresh Meat, you won't be disappointed.

Just before I go, however, I want to ask one thing. These books have been polarising in opinion it seems. Readers either really like what I've tried to do, or they find it tiresome. I'm not sure why people dislike a book so much but still read it all the way through, just to leave a bad review. But it seems that they do. Of course, that's their choice, and I'm thankful for all the feedback I get! Goodness knows authors scream out for it. But while the comments themselves are something I can take on board and carry forward, the ratings really affect the way that other readers perceive the books. Which is a shame, because I want nothing more than to share something enjoyable with my readers.

It's difficult to ask, and I hate to do it, but if you did enjoy these two books, it would mean more than you know if you might be able to leave a review for Bare Skin. Just a few words, even. Just to let other readers know that the first book is worth reading, and what to expect if they take a chance.

Competition is fierce out here, and I want nothing more than to be able to keep writing these novels. And sadly, reviews hold more power than most people realise.

Anyway, whether you do or don't, know that I'm thankful that you're here. That you've read these books, and that you've given your time to them.

I'm always around, always reading and responding to emails and messages, so if you'd like to get in touch, you certainly can do. I'd love to hear from you!

Stay safe out there. These are weird times, but we'll get through them.

Hopefully, we can talk soon. Even if it's just like this again.

Morgan

Leave a review for Bare Skin, Book 1 in the DS Jamie Johansson Series

IDLE HANDS

Book 3 in the DS Jamie Johansson Prequel Trilogy

Three months have passed since the showdown on the *Princess of the Sun* and things are beginning to get back to normal for Jamie and Roper.

But then, a call comes in.

A young woman has been brutally murdered in a pedestrian tunnel.

Stabbed.

Her hands cut off.

The trail is hot with blood and leads Jamie back to a preeminent classical music college in the city. The victim was a prodigy who disappeared half a year before. But the details surrounding her past are murky, and no one is talking.

What drove her to run away? To leave everything she ever knew behind so suddenly?

As Jamie lines up witnesses, the killer lines up his next victims.

But it seems they're hunting the same people, and it's up to Jamie to get to them first.

She needs to crack this case before the bodies start piling up. But to do so, she'll have to get inside the mind of a killer, embrace the darkness that she's been trying so hard to keep out.

This is a case that will test Jamie in every way. One that will push her to her limits. One that will force her to answer the questions that she has been trying to avoid her whole life…

How much like her father is she really?

And once she crosses that line… Will she be able to go back?

———

Idle Hands, the twisting third instalment in the DS Jamie Johansson Series is out now!

Printed in Great Britain
by Amazon

83266768R00202